PENGUIN CLASSICS

THE DEATH OF IVAN ILYICH/ THE COSSACKS/HAPPY EVER AFTER

COUNT LEO NIKOLAYEVICH TOLSTOY was born in 1828 at Yasnaya Polyana in the Tula province, and educated privately. He studied Oriental languages and law at the University of Kazan, then led a life of pleasure until 1851 when he joined an artillery regiment in the Caucasus. He took part in the Crimean War and after the defence of Sevastopol he wrote *The Sevastopol Stories*, which established his reputation. After a period in St Petersburg and abroad, where he studied educational methods for use in his school for peasant children in Yasnaya, he married Sophie Andreyevna Behrs in 1862. The next fifteen years was a period of great happiness; they had thirteen children, and Tolstoy managed his vast estates in the Volga Steppes, continued his educational projects, cared for his peasants and wrote *War and Peace* (1865–68) and *Anna Karenin* (1874–76). *A Confession* (1879–82) marked an outward change in his life and works; he became an extreme rationalist, and in a series of pamphlets after 1880 he expressed theories such as rejection of the state and church, indictment of the demands of the flesh, and denunciation of private property. His teaching earned him numerous followers in Russia and abroad, but also much opposition, and in 1901 he was excommunicated by the Russian holy synod. He died in 1910 in the course of a dramatic flight from home, at the small railway station of Astapovo.

ROSEMARY EDMONDS was born in London and studied English, Russian, French, Italian and Old Church Slavonic at universities in England, France and Italy. During the war she was translator to General de Gaulle at Fighting France Headquarters in London and, after the liberation, in Paris. She went on to study Russian Orthodox Spirituality, and translated Archimandrite Sophrony's *The Undistorted Image* (since published in two volumes as *The Monk of Mount Athos* and *The Wisdom from Mount Athos*), *His Life Is Mine*, *We Shall See Him As He Is*, *Saint Silovan the Athonite* and other works. She also researched and translated Old Church Slavonic texts. Among the many translations she made for Penguin Classics are Tolstoy's *War and Peace*, *Anna Karenin*, *Resurrection*,

The Death of Ivan Ilyich/The Cossacks/Happy Ever After and *Childhood, Boyhood, Youth*; Pushkin's *The Queen of Spades and Other Stories*; and Turgenev's *Fathers and Sons*. She also translated works by Gogol and Leskov.

Rosemary Edmonds died in 1998, aged 92.

LEO TOLSTOY

THE DEATH OF IVAN ILYICH

THE COSSACKS

HAPPY EVER AFTER

TRANSLATED
WITH AN INTRODUCTION
BY
ROSEMARY EDMONDS

PENGUIN BOOKS

PENGUIN BOOKS

Published by the Penguin Group
Penguin Books Ltd, 80 Strand, London WC2R 0RL, England
Penguin Putnam Inc., 375 Hudson Street, New York, New York 10014, USA
Penguin Books Australia Ltd, 250 Camberwell Road, Camberwell, Victoria 3124, Australia
Penguin Books Canada Ltd, 10 Alcorn Avenue, Toronto, Ontario, Canada M4V 3B2
Penguin Books India (P) Ltd, 11 Community Centre, Panchsheel Park, New Delhi – 110 017, India
Penguin Books (NZ) Ltd, Cnr Rosedale and Airborne Roads, Albany, Auckland, New Zealand
Penguin Books (South Africa) (Pty) Ltd, 24 Sturdee Avenue, Rosebank 2196, South Africa

Penguin Books Ltd, Registered Offices: 80 Strand, London WC2R 0RL, England

www.penguin.com

This translation first published 1960
23

Printed in England by Clays Ltd, St Ives plc
Set in Linotype Pilgrim

CONTENTS

INTRODUCTION

'I AM unendurably vile in my craving for depravity,' Tolstoy confessed to himself at the age of twenty-seven. 'Actual depravity would be better.' He had long been dissatisfied with the life he was leading; but was it not too late for the remedy of marriage? 'People have given up thinking of me as a marrying man. And I've given up the idea myself this many a day,' declares his prototype in *Happy Ever After*.* But through the autumn and winter of 1856 Tolstoy did his best to fall in love with a girl who lived on a neighbouring estate – although his first visit of inspection was not too auspicious: 'It is unfortunate that she is spineless and lacks animation – like vermicelli – though she is kind. And she has a smile which is painfully submissive. Came home and sent for the soldier's wife' (a peasant woman with whom Tolstoy had illicit relations), he wrote in his diary, which over the next four months registers the progress of the affair. Valeria is 'impossibly futile' and he is not at all in love. One day she is 'charming', the next 'downright stupid'. Eventually Tolstoy suddenly departed to Moscow to give the situation a chance to clarify. From Moscow he wrote 'I already love in you your beauty, but I am only just beginning to love in you that which is eternal and ever precious – your heart, your soul ...' But the letter ends on an infuriating admonitory note: 'Please go out for a *walk* every day, no matter the weather. This is an excellent thing, as any doctor will tell you; and wear stays and put on your stockings yourself, and generally make various such-like improvements in yourself. Do not despair of becoming perfect.'

From Moscow Tolstoy went to Petersburg and then, via

* I dare to hope that Tolstoy himself, who undoubtedly meant his title to have an ironic flavour, might have approved of *Happy Ever After* in place of the more usual and misleading rendering, *Family Happiness*.

a self-portrait. And in *The Death of Ivan Ilyich* Tolstoy's understanding of Ivan Ilyich's moral life is so acute that he does not have to contrive. He has only to describe, for the reader's pulse to beat in unison.

He touched mine eyes with fingers light
As sleep that cometh in the night,
And like a frightened eagle's eyes
*They opened wide with prophecies.**

Tolstoy was a prophet.

R.E.

* From Maurice Baring's translation of *The Prophet* by Pushkin.

HAPPY EVER AFTER

'Family Happiness'

A NOVEL

PART ONE

I

We were in mourning for my mother, who had died in the autumn, and I spent all that winter alone in the country with Katya and Sonya.

Katya was an old friend of the family, our governess who had brought us all up and whom I had known and loved ever since I could remember. Sonya was my younger sister. We spent a dull, melancholy winter in our old house at Pokrovskoe. The weather was cold and windy so that the snow-drifts swept up higher than the windows, which were nearly always frozen over and dark with frost, and we hardly went out of doors the whole winter. Our visitors were few and those that came brought no increase of gaiety or happiness to the household. They all wore sad faces and spoke in low tones, as though afraid of waking someone; they never laughed, but would sigh and often – when they looked at me, and especially at little Sonya in her black dress – shed tears. Death still seemed to cling to the house: the grief and horror of death were in the air. Mamma's room was shut up, and whenever I passed it on my way to bed I felt terrified and something pulled at me to peep into that cold empty room.

I was then seventeen; and in the very year of her death mamma had intended moving to town to bring me out. The loss of my mother was a great grief to me; but I must confess that this grief was partly caused by the feeling that here was I, young and pretty (so everybody told me), wasting a second winter in the solitude of the country. Before the winter ended this sense of depression and loneliness and sheer boredom increased to such an extent that I refused to leave my room or open the piano or take up a book. When Katya urged me to find some occupation I answered, 'I don't feel like it; I can't,' while in my heart I asked: 'What is the use? What is the use of doing anything when the best years of my life are being wasted like this? What is the use' And to that *What is the use?* the only answer was tears.

They told me I was growing thin and losing my looks but even this did not rouse me. What did it matter? To whom did it matter? It seemed to me that my whole life was destined to be spent in that lonely backwater, in that helpless dreariness, from which by myself I had neither the strength nor even the will to escape. Towards the close of the winter Katya became anxious about me and made up her mind to take me abroad whatever happened. But to do this we needed money, and we scarcely knew how my mother's death had left us. Daily we expected our guardian who was to come and settle our affairs.

In March he arrived.

'Thank goodness!' Katya said to me one day when I was wandering aimlessly about like a shadow, with nothing to do, no thought, no wish in my mind. 'Sergei Mihailych has arrived. He sent to inquire after us and would like to come to dinner. You must pull yourself together, my little Masha,' she went on, 'or what will he think of you? He was always so fond of you all.'

Sergei Mihailovich was a near neighbour of ours and although much younger than my father had been a friend of his. Apart from the fact that his arrival was likely to affect our plans and make it possible to get away from the country, since my childhood I had loved and respected him; and so when Katya told me to pull myself together she knew very well it would mortify me more to appear in an unfavourable light to him than to any other of our friends. Besides, although like everyone in the house, from Katya and his god-daughter Sonya down to the humblest stableboy, I loved him from habit, for me he had a special interest because of something mamma had once said in my presence. She had said that he was the sort of husband she would like for me. At the time the idea had seemed to me extraordinary and positively disagreeable: the hero of my dreams was quite different. My hero was slight, lean, pale and melancholy, whereas Sergei Mihailovich was no longer in his first youth, was tall and thickset and, it seemed to me, always cheerful. But in spite of that, mamma's words stuck in my imagination, and even six years before, when I was only eleven and he used to say *tu* to me, and play with me and call me his little violet I sometimes wondered, not without alarm, 'What *shall* I do if he suddenly wants to marry me?'

Sergei Mihailovich arrived before dinner, for which Katya made a cream tart and a special spinach sauce. From the window I watched him drive up to the house in a little sledge, but as soon as he turned the corner I hurried to the drawing-room, meaning to pretend that I was not waiting for him at all. But when I heard the stamping of feet in the hall, his ringing voice and Katya's step, I could not restrain myself and went out to meet him. He was talking loudly, holding Katya's hand and smiling. Catching sight of me, he stopped short and gazed for some little while without any greeting. I felt awkward, and was conscious of blushing.

'Ah, is it really you?' he said in his unhesitating direct manner, holding out his hands and coming towards me. 'Can such a change be possible? How you have grown up! Where's the violet now? It's a rose in full bloom you've turned into!'

He took my hand in his own large one and squeezed it so warmly, so heartily, that it almost hurt. I expected that he would kiss my hand, and was ready to incline towards him, but he only pressed it again and looked straight into my eyes with his frank, merry glance.

It was six years since I had seen him. He was much changed: he looked older and swarthier, and had grown side-whiskers which were very unbecoming; but he had the same simple way with him, the same strong-featured, open, honest face, the same shrewd, bright eyes and friendly, almost boyish smile.

In five minutes he had ceased to be a guest and to all of us had become one of the family, even to the servants whose obvious eagerness to serve him showed their delight at his arrival.

His behaviour was quite unlike that of the neighbours who had called after mamma's death and thought it necessary to sit in silence and shed tears while they were with us. He, on the contrary, was talkative and cheerful, and did not mention mamma at all, so that at first his apparent indifference struck me as strange, and even unseemly on the part of such a close friend. But afterwards I understood that it was not indifference but sincerity, and felt grateful for it. In the evening Katya sat down in her old place in the drawing-room and poured out tea, as she had done in mamma's time. Sonya and I sat near her; old Grigori found a pipe of papa's and brought it to Sergei Mihailovich, who fell to pacing up and down the room just as in the old days.

'What a lot of terrible changes this house has lived through, when one thinks of it!' he said, stopping short.

'Yes,' said Katya with a sigh, and then she put the lid on the samovar and looked at him, on the verge of tears.

'You remember your father, don't you?' he said, turning to me.

'Only very slightly,' I replied.

'What a help he would have been to you now,' he went on in a low voice, looking at me thoughtfully just above my eyes. 'I was very fond of your father,' he added still more quietly, and it seemed to me that his eyes glistened brighter than usual.

'And now God has taken her too!' exclaimed Katya, and immediately she laid her napkin on the teapot, brought out her handkerchief and began to cry.

'Yes, this house has seen terrible changes,' he repeated, turning away. 'Sonya, show me your toys,' he added after a moment or two, and went off to the parlour. When he had gone I looked at Katya with eyes full of tears.

'What a fine friend he is!' she said.

And indeed I somehow felt warmed and comforted by the sympathy of this good man who was not a member of the family.

In the parlour we could hear squeals from Sonya and Sergei Mihailovich romping about with her. I sent tea into him and heard him sit down to the piano and start striking the keys with Sonya's little hands.

'Marya Alexandrovna!' he called. 'Come here and play something.'

I liked his easy, friendly manner with me, and the tone of command. I got up and went to him.

'Here, play this,' he said, opening the Beethoven album at the *adagio* of the Moonlight Sonata. 'Let me hear how you play,' he added, taking his glass of tea away into a corner of the room.

I felt for some reason that I could neither refuse him nor make excuses and say that I played badly; I sat down obediently at the piano and began to play to the best of my ability, although I was afraid of his criticism, knowing that he understood and loved music. The *adagio* was in harmony with the reminiscent mood evoked by our conversation at tea, and I think I played it quite well. But the *scherzo* he would not let me play. 'No,' he said, coming up to me, 'that you don't play well. Let it be. But the first movement wasn't bad. You're musical, I think.' This moderate praise delighted me so much that I positively blushed. It was so novel and agreeable that he, a friend and contemporary of my father, should no longer treat me as a child but speak to me seriously, as one grown-up to another. Katya went upstairs to put Sonya to bed, and the two of us were left alone in the parlour.

He talked to me about my father, how they had become friends and of the good times they had had together while I was still in the schoolroom and playing with toys; and his stories made me see my father for the first time as a simple, lovable person, whom I had never known till then. He asked me too about my tastes, what I read and what I planned to do, and gave me advice. The high-spirited friend, full of jokes, who used to tease me and make me toys had disappeared: here was someone serious, open-hearted and affectionate, for whom I felt an instinctive respect and liking. Talking to him, I was happy and at ease, although I was conscious of a certain involuntary tension. I weighed every word I spoke: I was so anxious to deserve on my own account the affection he already bestowed on me merely because of my father.

When she had put Sonya to bed Katya joined us and complained to him about my listlessness, which I had not mentioned.

'So the most important thing of all she never told me!' and he smiled and shook his head at me reproachfully.

'What was there to tell?' I said. 'It's very boring, and besides it will pass.' (I actually felt now not only that my depression would go but that it had already gone and indeed had never existed.)

'It's a bad thing not to be able to stand solitude,' he said. 'Are you really a grown-up young lady?'

'Of course I am,' I replied, laughing.

'Well, it's a poor sort of young lady who's only alive when people are admiring her but as soon as she's alone lets herself go and takes no interest in anything: all for show and nothing for its own sake.'

'A fine opinion of me you've got,' I riposted, for the sake of saying something.

'No,' he continued after a brief pause, 'it's not for nothing you're so like your father. There's *something* in you ...' and his kind, attentive way of looking at me flattered me and covered me with happy confusion.

It was only now I noticed that although his face at first gave one the impression of being gay his eyes had a special way of looking at one, direct to begin with and then more and more intent and rather sad.

'You ought not to be bored, and you cannot be,' he said. 'You have your music, which you appreciate, your books, study; your whole life lies before you, and now or never is the time to prepare for it and save yourself regrets later on. Another year and it will be too late.'

He talked to me like a father or an uncle, and I felt him all the time making an effort to keep on my level. Though I was hurt that he should consider me his inferior, I was pleased he thought it necessary to adapt himself just for me.

For the rest of the evening he talked about business with Katya.

'Well, good-bye, my dear friends,' he said, getting up; and coming towards me he took my hand.

'When shall we see you again?' asked Katya.

'In the spring,' he answered, still holding my hand. 'Now I am going to Danilovko' (this was another property of ours). 'I'll look into things there and make what arrangements I can. After that I go to Moscow on business of my own, and then in the summer we shall see something of each other.'

'Must you really be away so long?' I asked, feeling terribly sad. And indeed I had already begun hoping to see him every day, and I felt suddenly so miserable, and afraid that my depression would return. My face and the tone of my voice must have betrayed this.

'Try and work at your books more, and don't mope,' he said in a way which seemed to me too cold and detached. 'And in the spring I shall put you through an examination,' he added, letting go my hand and not looking at me.

In the hall where we stood seeing him off he made haste to put on his fur coat, and again his eyes looked past me. 'He needn't bother himself!' I thought. 'Does he really think I'm so anxious for him to look at me? He is a nice man, a very nice man . . . but that's all.'

That evening, however, Katya and I sat up very late, talking, not of him, but of plans for the summer, and where we should spend the winter. The dreadful question 'What's the good of it all?' did not occur to me. Now it all seemed quite plain and simple that the aim of life was to be happy, and I could see a great deal of happiness ahead. It was as if our gloomy old Pokrovskoe house were suddenly flooded with life and light.

2

In due course spring arrived. My former depression was gone, and had given place to the unrest which spring brings with it, the dreams, the vague hopes and longings. Although I no longer spent my time as I had done at the beginning of the winter, but now gave lessons to Sonya, and played the piano and read, I would often go into the park and wander on my own for hours along its avenues, or sit on a bench and give myself up to heaven knows what thoughts and wishings and hopes. Sometimes, too, I would sit up all night by my bedroom window, especially if there was a moon; or just in my night-clothes steal out into the garden without Katya knowing, and run through the dew as far as the pond, and once I went all the way to the open fields, and another night I walked right round the garden all by myself.

Looking back, I find it hard to remember and understand the dreams which then filled my imagination. Even when I *can* recall them, I can hardly believe that I could have had such dreams – they were so strange and so far removed from reality.

At the end of May Sergei Mihailovich returned from his travels, as he had promised.

The first time he came to see us was in the evening and we were not expecting him at all. We were sitting on the veranda, about to have tea. The garden was all green and the nightingales had settled themselves for the month of June in the leafy shrubs. The tips of the bushy lilac trees had a sprinkling of white and purple, where the flowers were ready to open. The foliage of the birch avenue was translucent in the light of the setting sun. It was cool and shady on the veranda. There must have been a heavy evening dew on the grass. From away beyond the garden came the last sounds of the day – the herd being driven home. Nikon, the half-witted boy, crossed in front of the veranda, going along the little path with his water-cart, the cool stream of water from the sprinkler making dark circles on the freshly-dug earth round the dahlias and the sticks that held them up. On the veranda the polished samovar shone and hissed on the white table-cloth before us, and there were cracknel biscuits, cream and cakes. Katya with her plump hands was busily rinsing out the cups. I was too hungry after bathing to wait for the tea to be made, and was eating bread heaped with thick fresh cream. I had on a wide-sleeved linen blouse, and my wet hair was tied up in a kerchief. Katya was the first to catch sight of him from the window.

'Ah, Sergei Mihailych!' she cried. 'Why, we were just talking about you!'

I jumped up, meaning to go away and change my dress, but he caught me just as I was at the door.

'Come, no need to stand on ceremony in the country,' he said, looking at the kerchief round my head and smiling. 'You don't mind Grigori seeing you like that, and I'm really only another Grigori to you.' But it seemed to me even as he was speaking that he was looking at me in a way that Grigori could never have done, and I felt embarrassed.

'I won't be a minute,' I said, as I left him.

'But what's wrong with you as you are?' he called after me. 'You look exactly like a peasant-girl.'

'How strangely he gazed at me,' I thought, as I hurriedly changed upstairs. 'But anyway, thank goodness he's come: things will be jollier now!' A brief inspection in the glass and I ran gaily down on to the veranda, not concealing my haste and arriving out of breath. He was sitting at the table, telling Katya about our affairs. Glancing up at me, he smiled and went on talking. From what he said it appeared that our finances were in excellent shape: now we need only spend the summer in the country and then we could either go to Petersburg for Sonya's education, or else abroad.

'If only you could come abroad with us,' said Katya. 'We shall be quite lost by ourselves.'

'Ah, I should like to go round the world with you!' he said, half jestingly.

'Well, do then,' I said. 'Let's go round the world.'

He smiled and shook his head.

'What about my mother? And my business? Anyway, that's beside the point. I want to know what you have been doing all this time. Not moping again, I hope?'

When he heard that I had been busy during his absence, and not bored, which Katya confirmed, he was full of praise, and in word and look caressed me as though I were a child and he had a right to do so. Somehow I felt bound to tell him very frankly and in detail all the good things I had done and make a clean breast of everything he might disapprove of, as though I were at confession. It was such a lovely evening that after the tea-things had been taken away we stayed out on the veranda; and I was too absorbed by what we were saying to notice that gradually all human sounds had ceased. All round us the scent of flowers grew stronger, heavy dew drenched the grass, a nightingale trilled in a nearby lilac bush and then, hearing our voices, hushed her song. The starry sky seemed to drop down over our heads.

I only became aware that it was getting dark when a bat suddenly flew noiselessly under the awning of the veranda and began to flutter round my white shawl. I shrank back against the wall and opened my mouth to scream but the bat darted out under the awning as silently and swiftly as it had come, to disappear in the dusk of the garden.

'How fond I am of this place of yours,' he said suddenly. 'I could spend my whole life sitting here on the veranda.'

'Why not?' said Katya. 'Just you go on sitting.'

'That's all very well,' he said, 'but life won't just stay still.'

'Why don't you get married?' said Katya. 'You would make a fine husband.'

'Because I like sitting quiet perhaps?' And he laughed. 'No, Katerina Karlovna, too late for you or me to marry. People have long given up thinking of me as a marrying man. And I've given up the idea myself this many a day; and I can assure you I have been perfectly happy ever since.'

It seemed to me that he said this with a sort of unnatural emphasis, hoping that we would disagree.

'What nonsense! Thirty-six and to have done with life!' said Katya.

'I should think I have done with life,' he went on, 'when all I want is to sit quiet. But something else is needed for marriage. Just ask her,' he added, nodding at me. 'It's for young people of her age to think of marrying, while you and I look on and rejoice in their happiness.'

There was an undertone of sadness and constraint in his voice which did not escape me. He was silent for a moment or two; neither Katya nor I spoke.

'Just imagine,' he continued, turning in his chair. 'Supposing I were all of a sudden by some unfortunate chance to marry a girl of seventeen like Mash – like Marya Alexandrovna here. That's an excellent illustration, I am very glad it came into my mind ... there couldn't be a better instance.'

I laughed, and could not see any reason at all why he should be so glad, or what it was that had come into his mind ...

'Now, tell me the truth, honestly, with your hand on your heart,' he said, addressing me jocularly. 'Wouldn't you consider it a misfortune to tie yourself to an old man who has lived his life and only wants to sit quiet, whereas you have goodness knows what wishes and desires fermenting in your heart?'

I felt uncomfortable, and was silent, not knowing what to answer.

'Remember, I'm not making you a proposal, you know,' he said, laughing. 'But tell me truly, am I really the kind of husband you dream about when you wander alone along the avenue in the park at twilight? You would be wretched, wouldn't you?'

'Not wretched . . .' I began.

'But not happy though,' he finished for me.

'No, but perhaps I may be mistaken . . .'

But again he broke in.

'There, you see, she's absolutely right and I am grateful for her frankness, and very glad we have had this conversation. And what's more, it would be the greatest calamity for me too,' he added.

'What a queer fellow you are, you've not changed a bit!' said Katya, and she went indoors from the veranda to see about supper.

We were both silent after Katya had gone, and around us all was still save for the nightingale trilling now, not as she had done earlier, hesitantly and in fits and starts, but flooding the garden with her serene, unhurried song of night, with another down below in the hollow answering her for the first time that evening. The bird nearest to us stopped and seemed to listen for a moment before pouring out again still more shrilly her piercing long-drawn cadences. There was a regal calm in the birds' notes as they rang out in the night, in a world which belonged to them and not to man. The gardener walked past on his way to his pallet in the greenhouse, the tread of his heavy boots growing fainter and fainter down the path. At the foot of the hill someone whistled twice sharply, and then again all was still. A leaf stirred almost with a sigh, the veranda awning flapped gently, and a sweet fragrance hovering in the air wafted into the veranda, filling it. After what had been said the silence made me feel awkward, but what to say now I did not know. I looked at him. In the dusk his shining eyes looked back into mine.

'It's fine to be alive in the world!' he pronounced.

I sighed, I don't know why.

'Well?'

'It's fine to be alive!' I echoed.

And again we were silent, and again I felt ill at ease. I kept thinking that I had hurt his feelings by agreeing that he was old, and I wanted to console him but did not know how.

'Well, I must say good-bye,' he said, rising. 'My mother expects me for supper. I've hardly seen her all day.'

'But I wanted to play you a new sonata,' I protested.

'Some other time.' He spoke coldly, it seemed to me. 'Good-bye.'

I felt more than ever certain that I had wounded him, and I was sorry. Katya and I went as far as the porch to see him off, and stood for a while in the open, looking at the road where he had vanished from sight. When the sound of his horse's hoofs had died away I walked round the house to the veranda and again sat gazing into the garden; and in the dewy mist full of the sounds of night for a long time still I saw and heard all that I longed to see and hear.

He came a second and a third time, and the constraint which had arisen because of that strange conversation completely disappeared, never to return. All through the summer he rode over to see us two or three times a week; and I grew so accustomed to his company that if ever he failed to visit us for long I felt lonely by myself and was angry with him, thinking he behaved badly in deserting me. He treated me like a boy whose companionship he liked, asked me questions, drew me out into the frankest of discussions, gave me advice and encouragement, and sometimes scolded me or pulled me up. But in spite of his constant effort to play down to me I was conscious that behind the part of him which I could understand there remained a whole other world into which he considered my inclusion unnecessary, and this did more than anything to foster my respect and attract me to him. I knew from Katya and the neighbours that besides caring for his old mother with whom he lived, and managing our affairs as well as his own estate, he had a great deal to do with local government matters, which were a source of much worry. But what his attitude was to all this, what were his convictions, plans and hopes, I could never find out. As soon as I brought the conversation round to his affairs he would wrinkle his brows in a way peculiar to himself, as much as to say, 'Don't, please. Why bother yourself about that?' and change the subject. At first this hurt but later on I got so used to having our talk confined to what concerned me that I came to regard it as quite natural.

Another thing that used to rile me but which I afterwards enjoyed was his complete indifference and, almost, disdain for my appearance. Never, either by word or look, was there a hint that he thought me pretty: on the contrary, he would make a wry face and laugh when people complimented me on my looks in front of him. He took a positive pleasure in picking out my defects and teasing me about them. The fashionable clothes in which Katya liked to dress me up and the way she did my hair for festive occasions only provoked his mockery, mortifying the kind-hearted Katya and at first disconcerting me. Katya, having made up her mind that he admired me, was quite unable to understand his not liking to see the woman he admired shown off to the best advantage. But I quickly came to see what was behind it. He wanted to be sure that I was devoid of vanity. And so soon as I realized this, I actually was quite free from any trace of affectation in the clothes I wore, or the way I did my hair, or how I moved; but a very obvious form of affectation took its place – an affectation of simplicity, at a time when I could not yet be really simple. I knew that he loved me; but whether as a child or as a woman I had not then asked myself; I prized his love and, feeling that he considered me better than all the other young women in the world, I could not help wishing him to continue in the illusion. And involuntarily I deceived him. But in deceiving him I became a better person myself. I felt how much better and more worthy it was for me to show him the finer side of my nature than any of my physical attractions. My hair, my hands, my face, my ways – whether good or bad, it seemed to me he had appraised them all at a glance and knew them so well that I could add nothing to them except the wish to deceive him. But my inner self he did not know, because he loved it and because it was in the very midst of growth and development; and there I could – and did – deceive him. And how easy my relations with him became once I understood this clearly! My groundless confusion and awkwardness of movement completely disappeared. I felt that from whatever angle he saw me, whether sitting or standing, with my hair up or down, all of me was known to him and, I fancied, satisfied him. If, contrary to his practice, he had suddenly told me, as other people did, that I was beautiful, I believe

I should have been anything but pleased. But, on the other hand, how happy and light-hearted I would feel when, after something I had said, he would gaze at me intently and say in a voice charged with emotion which he would try to hide with a humorous note:

'Yes, oh yes, there *is* something about you. You're a fine girl, that I must admit.'

What was it gained me such rewards, which filled me with pride and joy? I would perhaps simply remark how my heart warmed to see old Grigori's love for his little grand-daughter; or I would be moved to tears by some poem or story I read; or it might be because I preferred Mozart to Schulhoff. And, when I came to think of it, I was amazed at my extraordinary instinct for guessing what was good and what one should like, when at the time I certainly had not the slightest notion of what was good and worthy of liking. Most of my former tastes and habits did not please him; and it was enough for him to show me by the lifting of an eyebrow or a glance that he did not approve what I was trying to say; he had only to put on his very faintly scornful, woe-begone expression for me instantly to feel that I no longer cared for what until then I had held dear. Sometimes it happened that he had hardly begun to give me some piece of advice before it seemed to me that I already knew what he was going to say. When he looked into my eyes and asked a question his very look would draw out of me the answer he wanted. All my ideas at that time, all my feelings were not really mine: they were his ideas and feelings which had suddenly become mine, being assimilated into my life and illuminating it. Quite unconsciously I was beginning to look at everything with different eyes – at Katya and the servants and Sonya and myself and my pursuits. Books which I had read merely for the sake of killing time were suddenly transformed into one of my chief pleasures in life, just because he brought the books and we read and discussed them together. Before, the lessons I gave to Sonya had been a burdensome task which I forced myself to go through with from a sense of duty; he came to one of the lessons – and immediately it was a joy to me to watch Sonya's progress. To learn a whole piece of music by heart had seemed an impossibility; but now when I knew that he would hear and perhaps praise it I would practise the same passage forty times over, until poor Katya stuffed her ears with cotton-wool – while I was still ready to go on. The same old sonatas I somehow played quite differently now, and they sounded entirely different and vastly better. Even Katya, whom I loved and knew as well as I knew myself – even she was transformed in my eyes. Only now did I understand for the first time that she was under no obligation to be the mother, friend and slave to us that she was. I realized now all the self-sacrifice and devotion of this affectionate creature, appreciated all that I owed to her, and learned to love her more than ever. It was he, too, who taught me to take an entirely new view of the people who worked for us, our serfs and servants and maids. It sounds an absurd confession to make – but I had lived among these people for seventeen years and yet knew less about them than about strangers whom I had never seen: it had never once occurred to me that they had their affections, longings and sorrows just as I had. Our garden, our woods and fields, familiar for so long, suddenly acquired a new beauty in my eyes. He was right when he said that there is only one certain happiness in life – to live for others. At the time this idea of his had seemed strange, I did not understand it; but by degrees, without any conscious reasoning, it had become a conviction with me. He opened up a whole world of delight in the present, without altering anything in my daily life and adding nothing to it – except himself to every impression of mind or heart. All that had surrounded me from childhood without saying anything to me suddenly came to life. It needed only his presence for everything to begin to speak and press for admittance to my heart, filling it with happiness.

Often during that summer I would go upstairs to my room and lie on my bed, and instead of the old melancholy of spring, the longings and hopes for the future, a passionate happiness in the present would envelop me. Unable to sleep, I would get up and sit on Katya's bed and tell her how utterly happy I was, which, when I look back on it now, I can see was quite unnecessary: she had the evidence of her own eyes. But she always told me that she, too, wished for nothing and was very happy, and she kissed me. I believed her – it seemed so right and inevitable that everyone should be happy. But Katya could also think of sleep, and sometimes even pretend to be angry, and drive me off her bed and fall asleep, while I lay awake for hours going over in my mind all the reasons that made me so happy. Some nights I would get out of bed and say my prayers again, praying in my own words and thanking God for all the happiness He had given me.

And all was quiet in the room: the only sounds were Katya's even breathing as she slept and the ticking of the clock by her bedside, while I twisted and turned and whispered words of prayer or made the sign of the cross over myself and kissed the cross round my neck. The doors were shut and the windows shuttered; perhaps a fly or a mosquito hung buzzing and quivering in the air. And I felt that I never wanted to leave that room, I did not want dawn to come, I did not want the atmosphere that enfolded me to be dissolved. I felt that my dreams and thoughts and prayers were living things, living there in the darkness with me, hovering about my bed and standing over me. And every thought I had was his thought, and every feeling his feeling. I did not know then that this was love – I thought that it was something that often happened, a feeling to be enjoyed and taken for granted.

3

ONE day at harvest-time I went into the garden after dinner with Katya and Sonya to our favourite seat in the shade of the lime-trees overlooking the ravine, with forest and field stretching away into the distance. It was three days since Sergei Mihailovich had been to see us, and we were expecting him that day, all the more so because our bailiff had said that he had promised to come to the harvest-field. Round about two o'clock we saw him riding towards the rye-field. With a smile and a glance at me Katya ordered peaches and cherries, of which he was very fond, leaned back on the bench and soon slipped into a doze. I broke off a crooked flat branch of lime which made my hand wet with its sappy leaves and bark, and fanned Katya with it while I went on with my book, stopping every moment or so to glance at the path through the field by which he must come. Sonya was making a summer-house for her dolls at the foot of the old lime-tree. The day was hot and steamy, there was no wind. Dark clouds were gathering and growing blacker, and ever since the morning a storm had been brewing. I felt restless, as I always did before thunder. But after midday the clouds began to lighten at the edges, and the sun sailed out into a clear sky; only in one quarter of the heavens was there a faint rumbling, and a single heavy cloud louring over the horizon and merging with the dust from the fields was rent from time to time by pale zigzags of lightning darting down to earth. It was clear that for today the storm would pass, with us at all events. Along the road, parts of which were visible beyond the garden, an endless procession of carts creaked forward, piled high with sheaves, while those that were empty rattled quickly past them on their way back, shaking the legs of the occupants and making their shirts flap. The thick dust neither blew away nor settled but hung in the air beyond the fence, and we could see it through the transparent foliage of the trees in the garden. From a little farther off, in the yard where the threshing was done, the same sound of voices and the same creaking of wheels; and the same golden sheaves that had slowly made their way past the fence were now flying aloft, until the stacks grew before my eyes into oval houses with sharp pointed tops, with the figures of peasants swarming about them. In the dusty field in front more carts were moving and more yellow sheaves were to be seen; and from far away came the noise of carts and of talking and singing again. At one end of the field the expanse of stubble gradually spread, leaving strips of ridge-land overgrown with wormwood. Lower down to the right, dotted about the unsightly, untidy mown field, I could see the brightly-coloured dresses of the women as they bent down and swung their arms to bind the sheaves; and order was gradually restored to the untidy field, as the pretty sheaves were ranged at close intervals. It seemed as if summer suddenly turned to autumn before my eyes. The dust and the sultry heat were everywhere, except in our favourite nook in the garden; and from all sides, in the dust and heat of the burning sun, rose the clamour of the labouring peasants as they walked and moved about.

But Katya snored away peacefully on our shady bench beneath her white cambric handkerchief, the cherries shone so juicily and black on the plate, our dresses looked so fresh and clean, the water in the pitcher sparkled rainbow-bright in the sun, and I felt so happy. 'How can I help it?' I thought. 'Am I to blame for being happy? But how can I share my happiness? How and to whom can I give up my whole self with all my happiness?'

The sun had already set behind the tops of the trees in the birch avenue, the dust was settling in the fields, the distant horizon showed clearer and more luminous in the slanting rays; the clouds had quite dispersed; I could see the thatched roofs of three new corn-stacks at the threshing-floor behind the trees, with the peasants climbing down from them; carts bumped along, obviously making their last journey; peasant-women with rakes over their shoulders and binding-twine stuck in their sashes were strolling homewards, singing lustily; but still Sergei Mihailovich did not come, although I had seen him ride down the hill long ago. Suddenly he appeared in the avenue, coming from the direction from which I was least expecting him (he had skirted the ravine). He walked quickly towards me, with his hat off and his face radiant. Seeing Katya asleep, he bit his lip, shut his eyes and advanced on tiptoe: I saw at once that he was in that special mood of inexplicable high spirits which I adored in him and which we called 'wild delight'. He was just like a schoolboy playing truant; his whole being, from top to toe, breathed content, happiness and boyish exuberance.

'Well, hullo my young violet, how are you? All right?' he said in a whisper, coming up to me and taking my hand. Then, in answer to my question, 'Oh, I'm in great form. I feel like a boy of thirteen today – I want to play at horses and climb trees.'

'Is it "wild delight"?' I asked, looking into his laughing eyes and feeling that this 'wild delight' was infecting me also.

'Yes,' he answered, winking one eye and suppressing a smile. 'Only why keep hitting Katerina Karlovna on the nose?'

I had not noticed as I looked at him and went on waving

the branch that I had twitched the handkerchief off Katya and was brushing her face with the leaves. I laughed.

'And she'll tell us she wasn't asleep,' I whispered, as though to avoid waking Katya; but that was not my real reason – it was simply that I enjoyed talking to him in a whisper.

He moved his lips, mimicking me and pretending that I had spoken too softly for him to catch a word. Seeing the dish of cherries, he made as if to steal it, and carried it off to Sonya under the lime-tree, where he sat down on her dolls. Sonya was cross at first but he soon got round her by devising a game to see which of them could eat the most cherries.

'Would you like me to send for some more?' I said. 'Or shall we go and pick some ourselves?'

He picked up the plate, put the dolls on it and the three of us started for the walled garden where the cherry-trees were. Sonya ran behind us, laughing and tugging at his coat to make him surrender the dolls. He gave them back and then turned earnestly to me.

'You really are a violet,' he said, still speaking softly although now there was no fear of waking anyone. 'As soon as I came near you, out of all that dust and heat and toil, I smelt violets at once. Not the scented violet but that first little purply violet, you know, that smells of melting snow and spring grass.'

'Well, and is everything all right in the fields?' I asked, to cover up the blissful confusion which his words had caused me.

'First rate! The peasants everywhere are such a first-rate lot. The more one knows them, the better one likes them.'

'Yes,' I said, 'today, before you came, I was watching them from the garden, and suddenly I felt so ashamed that they should be working while I sat so comfortably that . . .'

'Don't talk like that, my dear,' he interrupted me, with sudden seriousness yet gently looking into my eyes. 'Work is a holy thing. God forbid that you should talk glibly about it.'

'But I was only saying it to *you*.'

'Yes, I know. Well, how about those cherries?'

The walled-in garden was shut up, and none of the gardeners was about (he had sent them all to help with the harvest).

Sonya ran off to fetch the key, but without waiting for her to come back he climbed up a corner of the wall, raised the net and jumped down on the other side.

'Like some?' I heard his voice from over the wall. 'Pass me the dish.'

'No,' I said. 'I want to pick for myself. I'll go for the key. Sonya won't find it.'

But at the same time I felt that I must see what he was doing there and how he looked and moved when he supposed that no one saw him. Yes, the truth of the matter was that just then I did not want to lose sight of him for a single minute. Running on tiptoe through the nettles to the other side of the enclosure where the wall was lower, I stood on an empty barrel so that the top of the wall was on a level with my waist, and leaned over into the orchard. I scanned the garden and its ancient gnarled trees with their broad jagged leaves and the ripe black cherries weighing down below them; then poking my head under the net I caught sight of Sergei Mihailovich from under the knotted bough of an old cherry-tree. Undoubtedly he thought that I had gone away and that no one could see him. With his hat off and his eyes shut he was sitting in the fork of an old cherry-tree carefully rolling a lump of resin into a ball. Suddenly he shrugged his shoulders, opened his eyes and muttering something smiled. Both words and smile were so unlike him that I began to be ashamed of myself for my spying. It seemed to me that he had said: 'Masha!' – 'It's not possible!' I thought. 'Dear, dear Masha!' he said again still more gently and affectionately. This time I heard the words quite distinctly. My heart throbbed so violently and such a passionate – and I felt illicit – joy took hold of me that I clutched at the wall with both hands, fearing to fall and betray myself. Hearing the movement I made, he looked up in alarm, and suddenly lowering his eyes flushed crimson like a child. He tried to say something but could not, and his face flamed more hotly still. However, he smiled as he looked at me. I smiled too. Then his whole face beamed with happiness. He was no longer the fond old uncle who spoiled or lectured me: here was my equal, a man who loved and was in awe of me as I loved and was in awe of him. We gazed at one another without speaking. But suddenly he frowned: the smile and the light in his eyes vanished and he resumed his cold paternal tone, as though we were doing something wrong, and he had come to his senses and advised me to come to mine.

'You had better get down, or you'll hurt yourself,' he said. 'And do put your hair straight – just imagine what a sight you are!'

'Why does he pretend? What makes him want to hurt my feelings?' I asked myself indignantly. And at the same instant I felt an irresistible urge to disconcert him again and test my power over him.

'No, I want to pick the cherries myself,' I said, and catching hold of the nearest branch I swung my feet up on to the wall. Then, before he had time to assist me, I jumped down on the other side.

'What silly things you do do!' he exclaimed, flushing again and trying to cloak his confusion with an air of annoyance. 'Why, you might have hurt yourself. And how are you going to get out of here?'

He was even more confused now than before but this time his confusion frightened rather than pleased me. It infected me, too; I blushed and avoiding his eye and not knowing what to say I began picking cherries though I had nothing to put them in. I reproached myself, I felt remorseful and afraid, and it seemed to me that by my behaviour I had for ever forfeited his good opinion. We were both silent and embarrassed. Sonya running up with the key rescued us from our painful situation. For some time after this we said nothing to each other but addressed our remarks to Sonya. When we returned to Katya, who assured us that she had never been asleep but had heard everything we said, I regained my composure and he tried to drop back into his fatherly, patronising manner but did not quite succeed and I was not taken in by it. A conversation which we had had some days before suddenly recalled itself most vividly to my mind.

Katya had been saying how much easier it was for a man to be in love and declare his love than it was for a woman.

'A man can say that he is in love, but a woman can't,' she argued.

'But it seems to me a man has no business to confess and cannot confess that he is in love,' he rejoined.

'Why not?' I asked.

'Because it can never be true. What sort of a discovery is it that a man is in love? Anyone would think that the moment he pronounces the word something goes pop! and there he is, in love, with something extraordinary bound to happen, with signs and portents and all the cannons firing at once. In my opinion,' he went on, 'people who solemnly bring out the words "I love you" are either deceiving themselves or, which is even worse, deceiving others.'

'Then how is a woman to find out that a man is in love with her, unless he tells her?' asked Katya.

'That I don't know,' he answered. 'Every man has his own way of telling things. If the feeling exists, it will out somehow. When I read novels I always picture to myself the intense look on the face of Lieutenant Strelsky, or Alfred, when he says "I love you, Eleanora," expecting something wonderful to happen; and nothing happens to either of them – their eyes, their noses and everything else are exactly the same as before.'

Even at the time I felt certain this banter contained something serious relating to me, but Katya could not tolerate such disrespectful treatment of the heroes of romance.

'Always contrary, you are,' she said. 'Now, tell me honestly, do you mean to say you have never told a woman you loved her?'

'Never, and never gone down on one knee,' he answered, laughing. 'And I never will.'

'Yes, he has no need to tell me he loves me,' I thought now, recalling every syllable of that conversation. 'He loves me, I know he does, and all his efforts to appear indifferent will not alter my conviction.'

All that evening he had little to say to me, but in his every word to Katya, to Sonya, and in every gesture and glance of his I saw love and had no doubt of it. I only pitied him and was sorry that he should still find it necessary to hide his feelings and affect indifference when it was all so clear and it would have been so simple and easy to be quite impossibly happy.

But my jumping down to him in the orchard weighed on me like a crime. I kept thinking that I had lost his respect in consequence, and that he was angry with me.

After tea I went to the piano and he followed.

'Play something; it's a long while since I've heard you,' he said, catching me up in the drawing-room.

'I was just going to ... Sergei Mihailych,' I said, suddenly looking him straight in the face, 'you are not angry with me, are you?'

'What for?' he asked.

'For not listening to you this afternoon,' I said, blushing.

He understood what I meant, shook his head and smiled wryly, implying that I deserved a scolding but he could not find it in his heart to give me one.

'So it's all right, and we are friends again?' I said, sitting down at the piano.

'Of course we are!' he exclaimed.

In the big, lofty ball-room there were only the two candles on the piano, the rest of the room remaining in half-darkness. The clear summer night gleamed through the open windows. Everything was quiet except for the occasional squeak of Katya's footsteps in the unlighted parlour; and his horse, tethered beneath the window, snorting and stamping its hoof on the burdocks growing there. He was sitting behind me so that I could not see him; but everywhere – in the half-light that filled the room, in the music, in my own soul – I was conscious of his presence. His every look, his every movement, though I did not see them, found an echo in my heart. I played Mozart's sonata-fantasia which he had brought me and which I had studied with him and for him. I was not thinking at all of what I was playing but I believe I played well, and I thought he was pleased. I sensed his delight, and, though I never looked at him, was aware of his eyes fastened on me from behind. Quite involuntarily, and still moving my fingers mechanically over the keyboard, I looked round. His head was silhouetted against the clear background of the night. He was sitting with his head propped on his hands, staring intently at me with shining eyes. I smiled, seeing the look on his face, and stopped playing. He smiled too and nodded reproachfully at the music, for me to go on. When I finished playing, the moon which had become brighter was riding high in the heavens; and the faint illumination of the candles was added to by a new silvery light coming in through the windows and falling on the floor. Katya called out that it was really too bad how I had stopped at the best part of the piece and was playing so badly; but he declared that on the contrary I had never played so well; and he began to walk up and down through the rooms – through the ballroom to the unlighted parlour and back again into the ballroom, and each time he looked at me and smiled. And I smiled too, and even felt like laughing for no reason at all: I was so happy at something that had happened that very day, at that very moment. Katya and I were standing by the piano and each time he disappeared through the door I hugged her and began kissing my favourite spot, the soft part of her neck under the chin, and each time he came back I put on a solemn face and with difficulty kept myself from laughing.

'What is the matter with her today?' Katya asked him.

But he did not answer and only looked at me and gave a little laugh: he knew what had happened to me.

'Just look what a night!' he said from the dressing-room, stopping in front of the balcony window which opened on to the garden.

We went over to him, and it really was a night such as I have never seen since. The full moon hung in the sky above the house, behind us, so that it was out of sight, and half the shadow thrown by the roof and pillars and by the veranda awning lay slanting and foreshortened on the gravel path and the strip of grass beyond. All the garden was bathed in silvery dew and the radiance of the moon. The wide path between the flower-beds, across which, on one side, lay the slanting shadows of the dahlias and their supports, stretched away, all bright and cool, its uneven gravel glinting, to vanish in the misty distance. The greenhouse roof gleamed through the trees, and from the dell rose a shadowy vapour. Every branch and twig of the lilac bushes, already beginning to lose their leaves, showed clear and distinct, and each dew-drenched flower was outlined. Light and shade were so interwoven in the avenues that they looked like transparent houses, swaying and quivering, instead of paths and trees. To the right, in the shadow of the house, all was black, indistinguishable and weird. By contrast with the surrounding darkness the fantastically spread crown of the poplar tree rose all the brighter, towering into the dazzling light and for some queer reason staying close to the house instead of flying far away into the retreating dark-blue of the sky.

'Let's go out for a walk,' I said.

Katya agreed but said I must put on goloshes.

'Oh no, I don't need them, Katya,' I said. 'Sergei Mihailych will give me his arm.'

As though that would prevent me from getting my feet wet! But at the time this seemed perfectly natural to the three of us and not at all odd. Though he never used to offer me his arm I now took it of my own accord, and he saw nothing strange in it. The three of us went down from the veranda together. The whole world, the sky, the garden, the air were different from those I knew.

When I looked down the avenue as we walked along I had the impression that in a moment we should be brought to a stop, that the world of the possible would end, that all this must be crystallized for ever in its beauty. But we still moved forward, and the magic wall kept dividing to let us pass beyond; and there, too, we found our old familiar garden with trees and paths and withered leaves. And we really were walking along paths, stepping into rings of light and shade, the dry leaves did rustle underfoot and a cool twig brushed my face. And this was really he, walking gently and evenly at my side, and carefully supporting my arm; and it really was Katya walking beside us with squeaking boots. And that must be the moon in the sky, shining down upon us through the motionless branches . . .

But at each step the magic wall closed behind and ahead of us, and I found it as hard as ever to believe we could go any further – I ceased to believe in the reality of it all.

'Oh, there's a frog!' cried Katya.

'Who said that, and why?' I wondered. But then I recalled that it was Katya, and that she was afraid of frogs, and I looked at the ground. A little frog gave a jump and stopped dead still in front of me, and I could see its tiny shadow on the shining clay of the path.

'You aren't afraid, are you?'

I looked round at him. One lime-tree was missing and there was a gap in the avenue at the spot we were passing – so I could see his face clearly. It was so handsome and happy ...

He had said: 'You aren't afraid?' but the words I heard him say were: 'I love you, darling girl!' – 'I love you, I love you!' his eyes repeated, and his arm; and the light and the shadow and the air all echoed it.

We made the circuit of the whole garden. Katya went with us, taking short steps and getting out of breath from her exertion. She said it was time to go in, and I felt sorry, so sorry for her. 'Poor thing, why doesn't she feel the way we do?' I thought. 'Why isn't everyone young and happy, like this night and like him and me?'

We returned to the house but it was a long while before he left, though the cocks were crowing and everyone else was asleep, and his horse stamped its hoof on the burdocks and whinnied more and more often under the window. Katya did not remind us that it was late, and we sat up talking of the most trivial things and not thinking of the hour until it was gone two. The cocks were crowing for the third time, and dawn was breaking when he rode away. He said good-bye as usual, without adding anything out of the ordinary; but I knew that from that day he was mine, and that I should not lose him now. As soon as I had confessed to myself that I loved him I told Katya all about it. She rejoiced with me, and was touched that I had told her, but she – the poor thing! – was able to go to bed and sleep, whereas for me, for a long, long time I wandered about the veranda and then, recalling every word, every gesture, went into the garden and down the same avenues we had walked together. I did not sleep at all that night and for the first time in my life saw sunrise and early dawn. And never again since have I seen such a night and such a morning ... 'Only why doesn't he tell me straight out that he loves me?' I thought. 'Why does he think up all sorts of difficulties, and call himself old, when it is all so simple and wonderful? What makes him waste precious time which maybe will never return? Just let him say "I love you", and say it in so many words – "I love you"; let him take my hand in his, bend over it and say "I love you". Let him blush and lower his eyes before me, and then I'd tell him everything. No, not tell him but throw my arms round him and press close to him and weep! ... But suppose I am mistaken and he does not love me?' I thought suddenly.

I was frightened at my own feelings – heaven knows to what length they might lead me. I remembered his embarrassment and mine when I jumped down to him in the orchard, and my heart grew very heavy. Tears streamed down my cheeks and I began to pray. And a strange idea came to me, reassuring me and bringing hope: I resolved to begin fasting that very day and prepare myself for Communion on my birthday, and on that day to become his betrothed.

By what means, in what way, how this could happen, I knew not, but from that moment I believed and felt sure that it would be so. It was broad daylight and people were getting up when I went back to my room.

4

IT was the time of preparation for the Feast of the Assumption, so no one in the house was surprised by my intention to fast.

All that week he never once came to see us; and far from wondering or being alarmed or vexed at his absence I was glad of it and did not expect him until my birthday. Every morning that week I got up early and while the horses were being harnessed I walked alone about the garden, going over in my mind my sins of the previous day, and considering what I must do today in order to be satisfied with it and not once fall into sin. Then it would seem to me so easy to be without sin – I only had to make a little effort, it seemed. When the horses were brought round I got into the trap with Katya or one of the maids and we drove the two miles to the church. Going into the church I always remembered the prayer for all those entering therein in fear of God and tried to get into just that frame of mind as I mounted the two grass-grown steps to the porch. At that hour there were not more than a dozen worshippers – household servants or peasants preparing for Communion. With strenuous humility I responded to their bows and – this seemed to me a meritorious action – went myself to the table at the back to get candles from the old churchwarden, an ex-soldier, and place them before the ikons. Through the Holy Gates of the ikonostasis I could see the altar-cloth which had been embroidered by mamma, and above the ikonostasis were the two angels with stars who had seemed to me so huge when I was little, and the dove with the golden halo which had fascinated me long ago. Behind the choir was the battered font where I had stood godmother to so many of the servants' children and had myself been christened. The old priest would come in wearing a chasuble made from my father's funeral pall and begin to read the service in the same tone in which I had heard services taken ever since I could remember – in our own home, at Sonya's christening, at the requiem for my father, at my mother's funeral. The same quavering voice of the chanter rose in the choir, and the same old woman whom I could remember at every service crouched by the wall, her weeping eyes fixed on an ikon in the choir, pressed her clasped fingers to her faded kerchief, while she mumbled something with her toothless gums. No longer did all this merely arouse my interest, nor was it associations alone that made it dear to me: now all this was lofty and sacred in my eyes, and full of deep significance. I listened to every word of the prayers that were read, trying to be at one with them, and where I failed to understand I would ask God to enlighten me, or made up prayers of my own in place of those I did not quite hear. When the prayers of repentance were read I recalled my past life, and that childish innocent past seemed to me so black in comparison with the present limpid state of my soul that I would weep and be appalled at myself; but at the same time I felt that all would be forgiven, and that if my sins had been even more heinous my repentance would have been correspondingly sweeter. At the end of the service when the priest said: 'The blessing of the Lord be with you' an immediate sensation of physical well-being seemed to come over me. It was as if some sort of light and warmth suddenly filled my heart. The service over, the priest came up to me and inquired if and when he should come to us to say Vespers; and I thanked him, touched that he should wish to do this, as I thought, for my sake, and said that I would walk or drive over to church myself.

'Is that not too much trouble?' he asked.

And I did not know what to answer for fear of falling into the sin of pride.

After the Liturgy, if Katya was not with me, I always sent the carriage home and walked back alone, bowing low with humility to all who passed, and trying to find an opportunity to help or give counsel or sacrifice myself for someone, assist in lifting an overturned cart, dandle a baby, or step into the mud to make way for others. One evening I heard the bailiff report to Katya that Simeon, one of our serfs, had come to beg some planks for his daughter's coffin, and a rouble to pay for the wake, and that he had given them to him. 'Are they as poor as that?' I asked. 'Very poor, miss, not a pinch of salt in the house,' the bailiff answered.

My heart ached when I heard this, and at the same time I was almost glad. Pretending to Katya that I was going for a walk, I ran upstairs, got out all my money (it was very little but it was all I had), made the sign of the cross and started off alone through the veranda and across the garden to Simeon's hut in the village. It was at the very end of the village and no one saw me as I went up to the window, placed the money on the sill and tapped on the pane. Simeon came out, the door creaking on its hinges, and called after me. Shivering and cold with panic I hurried home like a guilty creature. Katya asked where I had been and what was the matter with me, but I did not even understand what she was saying and did not answer. Everything suddenly seemed so pretty and insignificant, I locked myself in my room and walked up and down alone for a long time, unable to do anything, unable to think, unable to analyse my feelings. I pictured the joy of all the family, the blessing they would bestow on the one who had put the money there, and felt sorry I had not handed them the sum myself. I thought of what Sergei Mihailovich would say if he were to find out about it, and at the same time was glad that no one would ever find out. I was so happy, and everybody, myself too, seemed so full of wickedness, and yet I felt so kindly disposed to myself and all the world that the thought of death came to me like a dream of bliss. I smiled and prayed and cried, and was swept by a passion of love for every creature on earth, myself included, at that moment. Between services I would read the Gospel, and more and more comprehensible it became to me, and more and more stirring and simple the story of that Divine Life, and more awful and impenetrable the depths of feeling and thought I found in its teaching. But, on the other hand, how clear and straightforward everything seemed when I laid down the book, once more to consider and ponder life around me. It seemed so difficult to be bad, and so simple to love everyone and be loved myself. Everybody was so kind and gentle to me: even Sonya, to whom I continued to give lessons, was quite different, doing her best to understand, and please and not vex me. Everyone treated me as I treated them. Thinking over my enemies, of whom I must ask forgiveness before making my confession, I could only remember one – one of our neighbours, a girl whom I had made fun of in front of guests a year ago, and who had ceased to visit us. I wrote to her, acknowledging my fault and begging her forgiveness. She replied with a letter in which *she* asked my forgiveness, and forgave me. I cried for joy, reading into the simple lines such deep and touching feeling. My old nurse burst into tears when I asked forgiveness of her. 'Why are they all so good to me? What have I done to deserve their love?' I asked myself. And then I could not help thinking of Sergei Mihailovich, and for a long while I thought about him. I could not help it, and never even considered it as a sin. But now I thought of him in an entirely different way from the night when I first realized that I loved him. Now he was part of me and I unconsciously linked him with my every thought of the future. The sense of inferiority of which I had always been aware in his presence completely disappeared in my imagination. I felt myself his equal now, and from the heights of my present spiritual condition I could understand him completely. What had hitherto seemed strange in him was now quite clear to me. It was only now I could see what he meant when he said that happiness was only to be found in living for others, and now I agreed with him absolutely. I believed that together we should be infinitely and serenely happy. I looked forward, not to foreign travel or society of glitter, but to something entirely different – a quiet family life in the country with constant self-sacrifice, constant love for one another and constant recognition in all things of a kind and beneficent Providence.

I took the Sacrament, as I had intended, on my birthday. There was such complete happiness in my heart as I came home from church that day that I was afraid of life, afraid of any sensation – any feeling that might break in on that happiness. But we had hardly got out of the trap at the porch before a familiar vehicle rattled over the bridge and I caught sight of Sergei Mihailovich. He wished me many happy returns of the day, and we went into the parlour together. Never since I had known him had I been so much at my ease and so self-possessed with him as on that morning. I felt that there was a whole new world in me beyond his comprehension and out of his reach. I was not conscious of the slightest embarrassment with him. He must have understood the reason for this, for he showed a peculiar tender gentleness and reverent consideration in his manner towards me. I wanted to go to the piano, but he locked it and put the key in his pocket.

'Don't break the spell that holds you,' he said. 'You have the sweetest of all music in your soul just now.'

I was grateful for his thoughtfulness, and at the same time not altogether pleased at his understanding too easily and clearly what ought to have been hidden in my soul. At dinner he said that he had come to wish me many happy returns of the day and also to say good-bye, as he was going to Moscow the next day. He looked at Katya as he spoke, but then stole a fleeting glance at me and I saw that he was afraid of detecting signs of agitation on my face. But I was neither surprised nor upset: I did not even ask if he would be away for long. I had known that he would say this, and I knew that he would not go. How I knew, I cannot explain to this moment; but on that memorable day it seemed to me that I knew everything: whatever had been and whatever would be. It was like a blissful dream when all that happens seems to have happened already and to be quite familiar, and it will all happen over again, and one knows that it will happen.

He had intended to leave immediately after dinner, but Katya, tired after the service, had gone to lie down, and he was obliged to wait until she finished her nap to say good-bye to her. The sun was shining into the ball-room, and we went out to the veranda. As soon as we sat down I began, quite calmly, the conversation that was destined to decide the fortune of my love. I began to speak neither too soon nor too late, but the very moment we were seated, before a word had been spoken, before our talk had taken any tone or character that might have hindered what I wanted to say. I cannot understand how I came by such composure, such determination and preciseness of expression. It was as if something independent of my will was speaking through my lips. He sat opposite me, his elbow resting on the balustrade; and drawing a branch of lilac to him, he began stripping it of its leaves. When I started to speak, he let go the branch and leaned his head on his hand. It could have been the attitude of a man feeling completely tranquil or extremely agitated.

'Why are you going away?' I asked, pausing significantly and looking him straight in the face.

He did not answer at once.

'Business!' he said, dropping his eyes.

I saw how difficult he found it to lie to me, and in answer to a question put to him so frankly.

'Listen,' I said, 'you know what today means to me, how important it is for many reasons. If I ask you questions, it is not for the sake of showing an interest in your affairs (you know that I am used to having you here and am fond of you). I ask because I *must* know the answer. Why are you going?'

'It is not at all easy for me to tell you the true reason,' he said. 'This past week I have thought a great deal about you and about myself, and I have decided that I must go away. You know why, and if you care for me you won't ask.' He passed a hand over his forehead and covered his eyes. 'This is painful for me ... And easy for you to understand.'

My heart began to beat violently.

'I cannot understand,' I said. 'I *cannot*! *You* must tell me. For God's sake, for the sake of today, tell me. I can hear anything quietly,' I said.

He shifted his position, glanced at me and again pulled the lilac branch towards him.

'Very well,' he said, after a brief silence and in a voice that tried in vain to sound steady. 'Although it's silly, and impossible to put into words, although it's painful even, I will try and explain to you,' he added, frowning as if in pain.

'Well?' I said.

'Imagine that there was a certain Monsieur A., shall we say, and that he was old and finished; and a Mademoiselle B., young and happy, and having seen nothing as yet of life or of the world. Family circumstances of various kinds brought them together, and he grew to love her as a daughter, and had no fear of loving her in any other way.'

He paused, but I did not interrupt him.

'But he forgot that B. was so young that life for her was still a game,' he went on with sudden swiftness and determination, and not looking at me, 'and that he might easily fall in love with her in a different way, and that would seem amusing to her. And he made a mistake, and was suddenly aware of another feeling, as heavy as remorse, creeping into his heart, and he was afraid. He was afraid that their old friendly relations would be destroyed, and he made up his mind to go away before that could happen.' And so saying, as it were carelessly he again passed his hand over his eyes and hid them.

'But why was he afraid of loving her differently?' I asked very low, controlling my emotion and even my voice; but to him I must have sounded quizzical. He answered as if he were hurt.

'You are young,' he said. 'I am not. You want a gay time, but I must have something else. Have your gay time, only not with me, or I shall take you seriously, and that would make me unhappy and you sorry and ashamed. That's what A. said,' he added. 'However, this is all nonsense; but you understand why I am going. And now don't let us talk about it any more – please!'

'Yes, yes, we must talk about it!' I said, and the tears in my throat made my voice tremble. 'Did he love her, or not?'

He did not answer.

'And if he did not love her, why did he treat her as a child and pretend to her?' I asked.

'Yes, A. behaved badly,' he interrupted me quickly, 'but all that came to an end, and they parted . . . friends.'

'But that's dreadful! Is there really no other ending?' I uttered faintly, and was terrified at my question.

'Yes, there is,' he said, uncovering an agitated face and looking straight at me. 'There are two different endings. Only for God's sake, listen to me quietly and don't interrupt. Some say,' he began, standing up and twisting his face into a smile, 'some say that A. lost his head, fell madly in love with B. and told her so . . . But she only laughed. She took it as a joke, whereas for him it was a matter of life and death.'

I shivered and tried to stop him – stop him and say that he must not presume to speak for me; but he restrained me, laying his hand on mine.

'Wait,' he said, and his voice shook. 'The other story is that she took pity on him, fancying, poor child, in her ignorance of the world, that she really could love him, and so she consented to be his wife. And he was crazy enough to believe her – believe that life could begin over again for him; but in time she realized that she had misled him and he had misled her . . . But let us drop the subject for ever,' he concluded, obviously unable to go on, and he began to pace up and down in front of me in silence.

He had asked for the subject to be dropped but I saw that his whole soul was hanging on my answer. I tried to speak but couldn't: my heart ached. I glanced at him – he was pale and his lower lip was trembling. I felt sorry for him. With a sudden effort I broke the bonds of silence that held me fast, and began to speak in a quiet, intimate voice which every moment I feared would break.

'There is a third ending to the story,' I said, and stopped, but he did not speak. 'In the third ending he did not love her, but hurt her, hurt and hurt her, and thought he was right. He went away, and was actually proud of himself. The trifling is on your side, not on mine: I have loved you from the first – loved you,' I repeated, and at the word 'loved' my quiet, friendly voice changed to a wild cry which frightened me myself.

He stood before me, his lip quivering more and more violently, while two tears rolled down his pale cheeks.

'It's a shame,' I almost screamed, feeling the angry unshed tears choking me. 'Why do you do it?' I articulated, and got up to leave him.

But he did not let me go. His head lay on my knees, his lips were kissing my trembling hands, and his tears wetting them. 'Oh God, if only I had known!' he whispered.

'Why do you do it? Why?' I was still repeating, but in my heart there was happiness, happiness which had now come back after so nearly departing for ever.

Five minutes later Sonya was running upstairs to Katya and proclaiming all over the house that Masha was going to marry Sergei Mihailovich.

5

THERE was no reason for delaying our wedding, and neither he nor I wished to do so. Katya, it is true, thought we ought to go to Moscow to buy and order things for the trousseau, and his mother urged that before getting married he should provide himself with a new carriage and some new furniture, and have the house done up; but we both insisted – successfully – that all this could be seen to later if it were really so necessary, and that we would have the wedding a fortnight after my birthday, quietly, without a trousseau, without guests, without ushers or a reception or champagne and all the other conventional paraphernalia of weddings. He told me how disappointed his mother was that there was to be no band, no mountains of luggage, no redecoration of the house from ground floor to attic – all so unlike her own wedding, which had cost thirty thousand roubles; and he recounted the solemn and secret confabulations which she held in the store-room with their housekeeper Mariushka, rummaging through chests and discussing carpets, curtains and salvers essential to our happiness. At our house Katya was busy in the same way with my old nurse, Kuzminishna, and it did not do to treat the matter lightly in her presence. She was firmly convinced that when Sergei Mihailovich and I discussed our future together we simply talked the sentimental nonsense natural to people in our state; but that, in fact, our future happiness depended entirely on the correct cutting out and careful stitching of chemises and the hemming of tablecloths and dinner-napkins. Between Pokrovskoe and Nikolskoe mysterious communications passed several times a day concerning the progress of preparations in each house and though outwardly Katya and Sergei Mihailovich's mother seemed to be on the most affectionate terms, there was a feeling in the air of hostile, albeit highly subtle diplomacy. Tatiana Semeonovna, his mother, whom I now got to know better, was a dour, punctilious housewife, a lady of the old school. Her son loved her not merely out of duty, because she was his mother: he thought her the best, cleverest, kindest and most affectionate woman in the world. She was always good to us and to me especially, and was pleased that her son was getting married; but when I visited her after my betrothal I felt that she wished me to understand that as a match for her son I might have been better, and that it would be well for me to keep that in mind. And I quite saw her point and agreed with her.

During that fortnight we met each other every day. He used to come to dinner and would stay on till midnight. But though he said – and I knew he was speaking the truth – that he could not live without me, he never spent a whole day with me but tried to continue with his ordinary occupations. Outwardly, our relations remained unchanged right up to the day of our wedding: we still said *vous* to each other, not *tu*, and he did not even kiss my hand; and far from seeking opportunities of being alone with me, he seemed positively to avoid them. It was as though he feared to give way too much to the excess of tenderness he felt. I don't know which of us had changed but I now felt on an equal footing with him, found no trace in him of that effort after simplicity which had displeased me before; and often with delight I saw before me, not a grown man inspiring respect and awe, but a sweet and wildly happy child. 'How mistaken I was about him!' I often thought. 'He's just another human being like myself, no more.' I seemed to see him now as he really was, and I felt that I knew him through and through. And how simple was all that I learned of him, and how congenial! Even his plans for our life together in the future coincided with mine, only he expressed them better and more clearly.

The weather was bad just then, and we spent the greater part of our time indoors. Our best and most intimate talks took place in the corner between the piano and the window. The dark window reflected the light of the candles, and now and again raindrops would spatter on to the shining pane and roll down. Outside, the rain beat on the roof and splashed into a puddle under the water-pipe, and the damp air came in at the window. And, by contrast, our corner seemed all the brighter, warmer and cosier.

'Do you know, there is something I've wanted to say to you for a long time,' he began one evening when we were sitting up late together in our corner. 'I was thinking about it while you were playing.'

'Don't tell me, I know all about it,' I said.

'All right, I won't.'

'No, tell me, what is it?' I asked.

'Well, you remember when I told you that story about A. and B.?'

'I should think I do! That silly story! It's a good thing it ended as it did!'

'Yes, I came very near ruining my own happiness. You saved me. But the point is, I was lying to you then, and it's on my conscience, and I want to make a clean breast of it all now.'

'Oh please not!'

'Don't be afraid,' he said, smiling. 'I only want to justify myself. When I began, I was trying to be reasonable.'

'What for? It's always a mistake,' I said.

'Yes, my reasoning was at fault. After all my disillusionments, my mistakes in life, I told myself firmly when I came to the country this year that love was out of the question so far as I was concerned, and that all I had to do was to grow old decently. So for a long while I failed to recognize what my feeling for you was, and where it might lead me. I hoped, and yet I didn't hope: sometimes I thought you were flirting with me; at others I felt sure of you but could not decide what to do. But after that evening, you remember, when we walked in the garden at night, I was afraid: my happiness seemed too great to be true. Think what would have happened to me had I allowed myself to hope and found that it was in vain! But of course I was only concerned about myself because I'm disgustingly selfish.'

He paused, looking at me.

'Still, you know, what I said then was not altogether nonsense. It was both right and proper for me to be afraid. I take so much from you and can give so little. You are a child still, a bud that has yet to open; you love for the first time, whereas I ...'

'Yes, do tell me the truth ...' I began, but suddenly I was afraid of his answer. 'No, never mind,' I added.

'Have I ever been in love before, eh?' he said, instantly guessing my thoughts. 'That I can tell you. No, I haven't. There has never been anything approaching this feeling ...' But suddenly it seemed as if some bitter recollections flashed into his mind. 'No,' he said sadly, 'in this, too, I need your compassion, in order to have the right to love you. So hadn't I good reason to think twice before saying that I loved you? What is there I can give you? Love, it is true.'

'And is that so little?' I asked, looking into his eyes.

'Yes, my dear, it is little to give *you*,' he went on. 'You have beauty and youth. Often now I cannot sleep at night for happiness: I lie awake and think of our future life together. I have lived through a great deal, and I think I have found what is needed for happiness: a quiet, secluded life here in the depths of the country, with the possibility of doing good to people to whom it is easy to do good which they are not accustomed to receiving; then work – work which one hopes may be of some use; then leisure, nature, books, music, love for a kindred spirit – such is my idea of happiness, and I dreamed of none higher. And now, to crown it all, I get you, a family perhaps, and all that the heart of man could desire.'

'It should be enough,' I said.

'Enough for me whose youth is over, but not for you,' he pursued. 'You have not seen anything of life yet. You may want to seek for happiness elsewhere, and perhaps find it in something different. At present you believe that this is happiness because you love me.'

'No, all I have ever wished or cared for is a peaceful life at home,' I told him. 'And you have simply expressed what I have thought.'

He smiled.

'It only seems so to you, my dear. But a life like that is not enough for you. You have beauty and youth,' he repeated musingly.

But I was annoyed that he did not believe me and as it were reproached me for my beauty and youth.

'Why is it you love me then?' I asked angrily. 'For my youth or for myself?'

'I don't know, but I love you,' he answered, looking at me with his intent, magnetic gaze.

I made no reply, and involuntarily looked into his eyes. Suddenly a strange thing happened to me: first I ceased to see what was around me; then his face disappeared, until only his eyes seemed to be shining immediately in front of mine; next I felt that the eyes were inside me, everything became blurred, I could see nothing and was forced to shut my eyes in order to tear myself free from the sensation of rapture and awe which that gaze of his was producing in me . . .

The day before our wedding, in the late afternoon, the weather cleared. The summer rains gave way to the first cool, bright autumnal evening. Everything was wet, cool and shining, and the garden for the first time revealed the spaciousness, the fiery tints, the bareness of autumn. The sky stretched chill and pale. I went to bed happy in the knowledge that tomorrow, our wedding-day, would be fine. Next morning I awoke with the sun, and the thought that this very day . . . filled me with fear and wonder. I went out into the garden. The sun had only just risen and filtered in patches through the thin, yellowing foliage of the lime-trees in the avenue. The path was strewn with rustling leaves. Clusters of berries hung red and wrinkled on the branches of the rowan-tree among a sprinkling of frost-bitten crumpled leaves. The dahlias had withered and turned black. The first rime silvered the pale green of the grass and the trampled burdocks round the house. In the clear cold sky there was not, and could not be, a single cloud.

'Can it really be today?' I asked myself, incredulous of my

own happiness. 'Shall I really wake up tomorrow not here but in that unfamiliar Nikolskoe house with the pillars? Is it possible that I shall never again wait for his coming and go to meet him, and spend all night talking to Katya about him? No longer sit with him at the piano in the ball-room here? No longer see him off and tremble for his safety in the dark night?' But I remembered how he had said yesterday that he was coming for the last time, and that Katya had made me try on my wedding-dress, saying 'For tomorrow', and for a moment I believed in it all, and then began to doubt again. 'Can it be that after today I shall be living there with a mother-in-law, without Nadezha or old Grigori or Katya? Shall I go to bed without kissing my old nurse and hearing her say, "Good-night, dearie" as she always did when she made the sign of the cross over me? Will I really no longer give Sonya lessons and play with her and knock on the wall to her in the morning, and hear her ringing laughter? Must I today be changed into another person, a stranger to myself, and is a new life, the realization of my hopes and longings, opening before me? And will that new life last for ever?' I waited impatiently for him to come: I felt depressed alone with these thoughts. He rode over early, and once with him I was able to believe that I should really be his wife that very day, and the prospect lost its terrors for me.

Before dinner we walked to our church and had a memorial service for my father.

'If only he were alive now!' I thought as we were returning home, and silently I clung to the arm of the man who had been the dearest friend of him of whom I was thinking. During the service, while I knelt with my forehead pressed to the cold stone of the chapel floor, I saw my father so vividly in my imagination and believed so completely that he understood me and approved of my choice, that I felt his spirit hovering over us and blessing me. And memories and hopes and happiness and sorrow all melted together into one sweet solemn feeling in harmony with the still, keen air, the silence, the bareness of the fields, and the pale sky, shedding over the landscape bright but feeble sunshine that vainly tried to burn my cheek. I fancied that the man at my side understood and shared my feeling. He walked slowly and in silence, and his face, to which I peeped up from time to time, was serious with the same mixture of sadness and joy that was in my heart and the nature that surrounded us.

Suddenly he turned to me, and I saw that he was going to speak. 'Supposing he begins about something else, and not what is in my mind?' I thought. But he began speaking of my father, though not saying his name.

'Once he said to me jokingly: "You should marry my Masha!"'

'How happy he would be now,' I answered, squeezing more tightly the hand that was holding mine.

'Yes, you were still a child,' he went on, looking into my eyes. 'I used to kiss those eyes then, and loved them because they were like his: I never dreamed they would be so dear to me for their own sake. I used to call you Masha in those days.'

'Do say *tu* to me, I said.

'I was just going to,' he answered. 'It's only now that I feel that you are entirely mine.' And his serene, happy eyes that held me captive rested on me.

We walked slowly on along the vague field-path over the trampled, beaten stubble, our footsteps and voices the only sounds. In the distance a peasant was noiselessly at work with a wooden plough, cutting an ever widening black strip through the brownish stubble which stretched far away to a leafless wood across the ravine. A drove of horses scattered below the hill seemed quite close. On the other side and ahead of us, as far as the garden and our house which rose behind it, lay a field of winter corn, showing black where the sun had thawed the frost and marked with occasional patches of green. A sun without warmth shone over everything, and everywhere lay long gossamer spider-webs, which floated in the air about us and spread on the frost-withered stubble, and got into our hair and eyes and clothes. When we spoke the sound of our voices hung in the motionless air above us as if we two were alone in the whole wide world – alone under that azure dome in which the mild sunshine played and flashed and quivered.

I too wanted to say *tu* to him but I felt too shy.

'Why are you walking so fast?' I said, using the *tu* very quickly and almost in a whisper, and blushed in spite of myself.

He slackened his pace, and the look he gave me was even more affectionate, gay and happy.

When we reached home we found his mother already there with some guests whom we had been obliged to invite, and I was not alone with him again until we came out of the church and sat in the carriage to drive to Nikolskoe.

The church was nearly empty: I just caught a glimpse of his mother standing erect on a mat by the choir, Katya in a cap with lilac ribbons, the tears rolling down her cheeks, and two or three of our indoor servants staring at me excitedly. I did not look at him, but felt his presence there beside me. I listened carefully to the words of the service and repeated them, but they found no echo in my soul. I could not pray, and gazed blankly at the ikons, the candles, the embroidered cross on the back of the priest's chasuble, the ikonostasis and the window, and took in nothing. I felt only that something extraordinary was being performed over me. When at the end the priest turned towards us with the cross in his hand, congratulated us and said that he had christened me and now, by the grace of God, had lived to marry me; when Katya and his mother kissed us, and Grigori's voice was heard calling for the carriage, I was puzzled and alarmed that it was all over already without anything exceptional happening within me commensurate with the sacrament that had been performed over me. He and I exchanged kisses, but the kiss seemed strange and alien to our feelings. 'Is this all?' I thought. We came out into the porch, the carriage wheels echoed hollowly under the vaulted roof, the air blew fresh in our faces, he put on his hat and helped me into the carriage. Through the carriage window I glimpsed a frosty moon with a halo round it. He sat down beside me and shut the door after him. I felt a sudden stab of dismay. His self-assurance seemed to me an affront. Katya's voice called out to me to put something on my head, the wheels rumbled on the stone and we turned into the soft road and were off. Huddling in a corner, I looked out at the distant shining fields and the road flying past in the cold glitter of the moon. And, though I did not look at him, I felt his presence beside me. 'What, is this all that the moment of which I expected so much has to give me?' I thought, and it still seemed somehow humiliating and offensive to be sitting there alone so close to him. I turned, intending to speak; but the words would not come – it was as though my love had vanished, to be replaced by a feeling of mortification and dismay.

'Till this minute I couldn't believe it was possible,' he said in a low voice in answer to my look.

'Yes, but I'm afraid somehow,' I said.

'Afraid of me, my darling?' he answered, taking my hand and bending over it.

My hand lay lifeless in his, and my heart was so cold that it hurt.

'Yes,' I whispered.

But at that moment my heart began to beat faster, my hand trembled and pressed his. I began to feel hot, my eyes sought his in the half-darkness, and all at once I knew that I was not afraid of him, that my fear was love – a new kind of love, tenderer and stronger than the old love. I felt that I was wholly his, and that I was happy in his power over me.

PART TWO

I

DAYS, weeks, two months of seclusion in the country slipped by – imperceptibly, it seemed at the time; and yet the feelings, emotions and bliss of those two months would have sufficed to fill a whole lifetime. Our plans for the ordering of our life in the country turned out quite differently from what we had expected. But the reality was all we had ever dreamed of. There was none of the unremitting toil, the doing of one's duty, the self-sacrifice and living for others, which I had pictured to myself before our marriage: there was, on the contrary, an entirely absorbing and selfish affection for one another, a desire to be loved, unreasoning, constant gaiety and oblivion of all else in the world. He did, it is true, sometimes go off and work in his study or drive to town on business, or walk round attending to the estate; but I could see what an effort it was to tear himself away from me. And he himself would confess afterwards that everything in the world that did not concern me seemed to him so trifling that he could not understand how he could be interested in it. It was just the same with me. If I read, or played the piano, or spent time with his mother or teaching in the village school, I did so only because each of these pursuits was connected with him and would gain his approval; but as soon as anything I was doing had no connection with him I would lose interest in it, and it seemed ludicrous to think that anything existed in the universe apart from him. Possibly it was wrong and selfish of me to feel like that, but it made me happy and lifted me high above all the world. In my eyes he was the only being on earth, and I considered him the best and most perfect person in the world; and so I could not live for anything else but him, and to try to be what he thought I was: the first and most excellent woman in the world, endowed with every possible virtue. And I strove to be just such a woman in the eyes of the first and finest of men.

One day he came into my room as I was saying my prayers. I glanced round at him and continued praying. He sat down at the table so as not to disturb me, and opened a book. But I fancied he was watching me, and I looked round. He smiled, I laughed outright and could not go on.

'And you – have you said your prayers?' I asked.

'Yes. But don't you stop, I'll go away.'

'You do say your prayers, don't you?'

He would have gone from the room without answering but I stopped him.

'Dearest, for my sake, please repeat the prayers with me.' He came and stood beside me, his arms dropping awkwardly, his expression serious, and began to read falteringly. Now and then he turned to me, seeking signs of approval and encouragement in my face.

When he had finished I laughed and hugged him.

'Oh you! Oh you! I feel as though I were ten years old again,' he said, blushing and kissing my hands.

Our house was one of those old-style country houses where several generations used to pass their lives together under the one roof, respecting and loving one another. It was all steeped in good sound family traditions which as soon as I entered it seemed to become mine too. The arrangement and management of the household were conducted by my mother-in-law, Tatiana Semeonovna, on old-fashioned lines. It could not be said that everything was elegant and beautiful, but from the servants down to the furniture and food there was plenty of everything, and a general neatness, solidity and order which inspired respect. In the drawing-room the furniture was arranged with symmetrical precision, family portraits hung on the walls and the floor was spread with home-made carpets and mats. In the morning-room there was an old grand piano, chiffoniers of two distinct periods, sofas and little tables inlaid with brass. My sitting-room, arranged by Tatiana Semeonovna with especial care, contained the best furniture in the house, of many styles and periods, and including an old pier-glass, which I was almost too shy to look into at first but which in time became an old friend. Tatiana Semeonovna's voice was never heard but everything in the house went like clockwork. There were far too many servants (who wore soft boots with no heels – Tatiana Semeonovna disliked nothing more than squeaking soles and clattering heels) but they all seemed proud of their place and stood in awe of their old mistress, held my husband and me in protective affection and seemed to take a particular pleasure in doing their work. Regularly every Saturday all the floors in the house were scrubbed and the carpets beaten; on the first of the month a service was held and the house sprinkled with holy water, and always on Tatiana Semeonovna's name-day and on her son's (and on mine too, for the first time, that autumn) a banquet was given for the whole neighbourhood. And all this had gone on, without break or change, ever since Tatiana Semeonovna could remember. My husband did not interfere with the running of the house: he confined himself to managing the farm and the labourers, and a great deal of work this gave him. Even in winter he got up so early that I often woke to find him gone. He generally returned for early morning tea, which we had by ourselves; and it was then, after all the worry and difficulty with his work, that he would almost always be in that state of high spirits which we called 'wild delight'. Often I made him tell me what he had been doing in the morning, and he gave such absurd accounts that we both laughed till we cried. Sometimes I insisted on having a serious report and he would restrain a smile and tell me. I would look at his eyes, at his lips as they moved, and not take a word in: the sight of him and the sound of his voice was happiness enough.

'Well, what have I been saying? Repeat it now,' he would demand sometimes. But I could not repeat a syllable. It seemed so absurd that *he* should talk to *me* about any other subject than ourselves. As if it mattered what happened in the world outside! It was not until a much later date that I began to some extent to understand and take an interest in his work. Tatiana Semeonovna never appeared before dinner: she breakfasted alone and said good-morning to us by deputy. In our private little world of extravagant happiness a voice from the staid decorous region in which she dwelt was quite startling, so that often I could not contain myself and would only giggle in reply to the maid who stood before me with folded arms and announced sedately: 'The mistress bade me inquire how you slept after your walk yesterday; and I am to tell you that she had a pain in her side all night, and that some silly dog barked in the village and kept her awake. And I am to inquire how you liked the bread this morning and to tell you it was not Tarass who baked today but Nikolasha who was trying his hand for the first time; and didn't do at all badly, the mistress says, especially the cracknel biscuits but he overbaked the rusks.' Till dinner-time we were very little together. He wrote or went out again while I played the piano or read; but at four o'clock we all met in the drawing-room before dinner. Tatiana Semeonovna would sail out of her room and certain poor and pious maiden ladies, of whom there were always two or three living in the house, also made their appearance. Every day without fail my husband would offer his arm to his mother, to take her in to dinner as he had always done, but she insisted that he should give me the other arm, so that every day without fail we stuck in the doorway and got in each other's way. At dinner, too, it was his mother who presided, and the conversation proceeded with dignified sobriety and not a little solemnity. The few simple words that my husband and I exchanged made an agreeable contrast to the formality of those ceremonious meals. Occasionally mother and son would argue together and tease one another. I particularly enjoyed those scenes, and their squabbles, because they were the best proof of the tender and enduring love which united them. After dinner *maman* settled herself in a large armchair in the drawing-room, and ground her snuff or slit the leaves of some newly-purchased book, while we read aloud or went off to the piano in the morning-room. We read a great deal together at this time but music was our favourite and supreme enjoyment, each time touching fresh chords in our hearts and as it were revealing us to each other anew. When I played his favourite pieces he sat on a sofa some way off where I could scarcely see him, and from a sort of shamefaced embarrassment at his emotion would try to conceal the effect the music had upon him; but often when he was not expecting it I got up from the piano, went over to him and tried to detect on his face the telltale signs of agitation – the unnatural brightness and moisture in his eyes, which he vainly tried to hide from me. *Maman* often wanted to take a peep at us in the morning-room but no doubt she was afraid of disturbing us, and so she would pass through with a pseudo-serious air of indifference, pretending not to see; but I knew she had no real reason for going to her room and returning so quickly. In the evenings I poured out tea in the large drawing-room and once more the whole household would gather round the table. This duty of solemnly presiding before the sacred shrine of the samovar and the distribution of glasses and cups for a long time filled me with trepidation. I felt that I was not yet fitted for such an honour, that I was too young and frivolous to turn the tap of such a big samovar, to put a glass on Nikita's salver and say, 'For Piotr Ivanovich' or 'For Marya Minichna', inquiring 'Is it sweet enough?', and leave pieces of sugar for Nurse and other old retainers.

'Splendid, splendid!' my husband would frequently declare, 'Quite grown-up!' which only increased my nervousness.

After tea *maman* would play patience or listen to Marya Minichna fortune-telling with the cards. Then she would kiss us both and make the sign of the cross over us, and we would retire to our own rooms. But we generally sat up together till after midnight, and this was the best and nicest time of the day. He would tell me stories of his past life, we would make plans, philosophize sometimes, and we always tried to speak as quietly as possible so that we should not be heard upstairs and reported to *maman*, who was insistent that we should go to bed early. Sometimes, feeling hungry, we would steal off to the pantry, get ourselves a cold supper through the good offices of Nikita, and eat it in my boudoir by the light of a single candle. We lived like strangers in that big old house, where the uncompromising spirit of the past and of Tatiana Semeonovna reigned supreme. Not only she, but the indoor servants, the old housemaids, the furniture, the pictures – all inspired me with respect and a certain awe, and made me feel that he and I were a little out of place there and must always be very careful and cautious in our doings. Thinking back over it now I can see much – the cramping, inflexible routine and the multitude of idle, inquisitive servants – that was unsatisfactory and troublesome, but at the time the very constraint added zest to our love. Neither he nor, of course, I ever showed the slightest discontent about anything – on the contrary, he positively shut his eyes to what was amiss. My mother-in-law's footman, Dmitri Sidorov, was a great pipe-smoker, and regularly every day when we were in the morning-room after dinner he would go to my husband's study and take tobacco from the jar; and Sergei Mihailovich's hilarious dismay was a sight to behold as he tiptoed towards me, and with a wink and a warning finger indicated Dmitri Sidorov, who had no idea that he was seen. And then when Dmitri Sidorov had gone without noticing us, delighted that it had all passed off successfully, he would declare (as he did at every opportunity) that I was a darling, and kiss me. Sometimes his easy-going ways, his forgiving disposition and apparent indifference irritated me, and I took it for weakness on his part, never realizing that I was the same myself. 'Just like a child who dares not show his will,' I thought.

'My dear, my dear!' he replied once when I told him that his weakness astonished me. 'How can a man as happy as I am be displeased about anything? Better give way myself than override others: I reached that conclusion long ago. There's no situation which makes happiness impossible – but our life is such bliss! I simply cannot get cross; nothing seems *bad* to me now, but only pathetic or amusing. The main thing to remember is – *le mieux est l'ennemi du bien*. Will you believe it, when I hear a ring at the door, or receive a letter, or even wake up in the morning, I'm frightened – frightened because life must go on, frightened that something will change, whereas nothing could be better than the present.'

I believed him but I did not understand. I was happy, but I took it for granted, as the invariable experience of people in our state, and I was sure that elsewhere there existed other forms of happiness, different perhaps, but not greater.

Thus two months went by and winter came with its cold and snow; and, in spite of his company, I began to feel lonely, feel that life was repeating itself, and that neither of us had anything new to give, and that we seemed to be turning forever in our old tracks. He now spent more time away than he had before, attending to business, and again it seemed to me that he had a sort of private world of his own to which I was not to be admitted. His everlasting placidity was an irritation. I loved him as much as ever, and was as happy as ever in his love; but my love, instead of growing, had come to a standstill, and a new sensation of restlessness gradually invaded my spirit. Loving was not enough for me after the happiness I had known in falling in love. I longed for activity, instead of an even flow of existence. I wanted excitement and danger and the chance to renounce self for the sake of my love. I was conscious of a superabundance of energy which found no outlet in our quiet life. I had bouts of depression, which I tried to hide, as something to be ashamed of, and transports of violent affection and gaiety which alarmed him. He noticed my state of mind before I did, and proposed a visit to Petersburg; but I begged him to give this idea up, not to change our mode of life, not to spoil our happiness. And I really was happy, but it tormented me that this happiness cost me no effort, no sacrifice, while my capacity for effort and sacrifice consumed me. I loved him and saw that I was all in all to him; but I wanted everyone to see our love and put obstacles in its way, so that I could love him in spite of everything. My mind, and even my senses, were occupied, but there was another feeling – the feeling of youth and a craving for activity – which found no scope in our quiet life. Why had he told me that we could move to town whenever I wanted to? If he had not said that, I might have realized that the feeling which oppressed me was pernicious nonsense, for which I was to blame; that the very sacrifice I sought lay right in front of me – in the suppression of that feeling. The idea that escape from my depression could be found merely by moving to town haunted me, yet at the same time it seemed a shame and a pity for selfish motives to drag him away from all he cared for. So time went by, the snow piled higher and higher round the house, and there we remained together, always and for ever alone and just the same in each other's eyes; while somewhere far away amidst glitter and noise multitudes of people thrilled, suffered and rejoiced, without one thought of us and our existence which was ebbing away. Worst of all, I felt that every day that passed riveted another link to the chain of habit which was binding our life into a fixed shape, that our emotions, ceasing to be spontaneous, were being subordinated to the even, passionless flow of time. In the morning we were bright and cheerful, at dinner polite, in the evening affectionate. 'It's all very well ...' I thought, 'it's all very well to do good and lead upright lives, as he says, but we'll have plenty of time for that later, and there are other things for which the time is now or never.' I wanted, not what I had got, but a life of challenge; I wanted feeling to guide us in life, and not life to be the guide of feeling. If only I could go with him to the edge of a precipice and say, 'One more step, and I shall be over; one more movement and I die!', and then, pale with fear, he would catch me in his strong arms and hold me over the edge till my blood froze, and carry me off whither he pleased.

My state of mind affected my health, and I began to suffer from nerves. One morning it was worse than usual, and he came back from the estate-office out of sorts, which was rare with him. I noticed at once and asked what had happened. But he would not tell me and said it was of no consequence. I found out afterwards that the district police inspector was summoning our peasants and, because he disliked my husband, making illegal demands and using threats to them. My husband, unable as yet to brook this and regard it as merely 'pathetic or amusing', was angry, and therefore unwilling to discuss it with me. But I fancied he did not want to talk because he thought me a child who could not understand his preoccupations. I turned away, saying nothing, and told the servants to ask Marya Minichna, who was staying in the house, to join us at breakfast. After we had drunk our tea – and I hurried through the meal more quickly than usual – I took her to the morning-room and began a loud conversation about some nonsense in which I had absolutely no interest. He walked up and down the room, glancing at us every now and then. Those glances of his for some reason made me want to talk all the more, and even to laugh: everything I said, and everything Marya Minichna said, seemed funny. Without a word to me he went off to his study and shut the door behind him. As soon as he was out of our hearing all my high spirits immediately vanished – to the surprise of Marya Minichna, who asked what was the matter. I did not answer, and sat down on the sofa, feeling ready to cry. 'What's he worrying himself about?' I thought. 'Some trifle which he thinks important; but if he just tried to tell me about it, I'd soon show him it was all rubbish. But no, he must needs suppose I shouldn't understand, must needs humiliate me by his lofty composure and always be in the right against me. But I am just as right as he is when I'm bored and dreary, when I long for an active life, instead of stagnating here and feeling time passing me by,' I reflected. 'I want to advance, and for something new to happen every day, every hour, while he wants to stand still and keep me standing still beside him. And how easy it would be for him! He would not have to take me to town – he need only be like me, not force himself to go against his nature and hold himself back, but live simply. That's the advice he gives me, but he is not a bit simple himself. So there! That's what the trouble is!'

I felt the tears rising to choke me, and that I was angry with him. My anger frightened me, and I went to him. He was sitting in his study, writing. Hearing my step, he glanced round for an instant, calmly and indifferently, and continued to write. The look vexed me: instead of going up to him I stood beside his writing table, opened a book and began turning over the pages. He broke off again and looked at me.

'Masha, are you out of spirits?' he asked.

I replied with a cold glance, as much as to say: 'What makes you ask? Why the politeness?' He shook his head, with a sweet, affectionate smile; but for the first time I had no answering smile for him.

'What happened today?' I asked. 'Why didn't you tell me?'

'Nothing much, just a little unpleasantness!' he said. 'I can tell you now though. Two of our peasants set out for town ...'

But I did not let him finish.

'Why wouldn't you tell me when I asked you at breakfast?'

'I should have said something foolish: I was angry then.'

'But it was just then that I wanted you to tell me.'

'What for?'

'Why do you suppose I can never help you in anything?'

'Not help me?' he said, throwing down his pen. 'Why, I believe that without you I couldn't live. You not only help me in everything I do – everything – you do it yourself! However could you get such an idea!' he exclaimed with a laugh. 'You are my life. All's well with the world simply because you are here, because I need you ...'

'Yes, I know all that: I'm a delightful child who must be humoured and kept quiet,' I said in a tone which made him look up in surprise as if he were seeing something for the first time. 'I don't want quiet – there's enough of that and to spare with you,' I added.

'Well, you see, it was like this,' he interrupted quickly, evidently afraid to let me say all that was on my mind. 'When I tell you the facts I should like to hear your opinion.'

'I don't want to know now,' I answered. I did want to hear the story, but I was finding it very pleasant to disturb his equanimity. 'I don't care to play at life,' I said, 'I want to live, just as you do.'

A look of pain and increasing attention came into his face, which always reflected every emotion so swiftly and so vividly.

'I want to live with you on equal terms, to ...' but I could not go on – his face showed such deep distress. He was silent for a little.

'But in what way are you not on equal terms with me?' he asked. 'Is it because I, and not you, have to bother with the inspector and with peasants who drink too much ....?'

'No, it's not only that,' I said.

'For God's sake try to understand me, my dear!' he cried. 'I know that worry is always very bad for one – I have learned that from experience. I love you, and so I cannot help wanting to save you from worry. My whole life is made up of my love for you – so you should let me go on in my own way.'

'You are always in the right!' I said, not looking at him.

It annoyed me that he should be all serene and calm again, whereas I was full of vexation and a feeling akin to remorse.

'Masha, what is the matter?' he asked. 'The point is not which of us is in the right – not a bit of it – but rather, what grievance have you against me? Don't answer at once, take time to think, and tell me all that's on your mind. You are vexed with me, and no doubt you have good reason, but do let me understand what I have done wrong.'

But how could I put my feelings into words? The fact that he understood me so quickly, that once again I was a child to him, that I could not do anything that he would not understand and anticipate, exasperated me more than ever.

'I haven't anything against you,' I said. 'It's simply that I'm bored, and don't want to be bored. But you say that must be the way of things, and, as always, you are right.'

I glanced at him as I spoke. I had gained my object: his serenity had disappeared, and I read alarm and pain in his face.

'Masha,' he began in a low, troubled voice, 'what we are doing now is no trifling matter. Our future is at stake. I beg of you not to reply but to listen. Why do you want to make me suffer?'

But I interrupted him.

'Oh, I know you will turn out to be right. It's better not to say anything: of course you are right,' I said coldly, as though not I but some evil spirit were speaking with my voice.

'If you only knew what you are doing,' he cried, and his voice shook.

I burst into tears, and felt better. He sat beside me and said nothing. I felt sorry for him and ashamed of myself, and vexed at what I had done. I did not look at him. I felt that there could only be severity or perplexity in his eyes at that moment. I glanced round: he was looking at me with gentle affection, seeming to plead for forgiveness. I caught his hand and said:

'Forgive me! I don't know myself what I was saying.'

'But I do; and you spoke the truth.'

'What do you mean?' I asked.

'That we must go to Petersburg,' he said. 'There is nothing for us to do here just now.'

'As you please,' I said.

He put his arms round me and kissed me.

'Forgive me,' he said. 'It is all my fault.'

That evening I played to him for a long time, while he walked about the room, murmuring something. He had a habit of doing this, and whenever I asked him what he was muttering he would always think for a moment and then tell me exactly what it was. Generally it was lines of verse, terrible nonsense sometimes, but nonsense from which I could gauge his mood.

'What are you repeating to yourself now?' I asked.

He stood still, considered a moment, and with a smile quoted two lines from Lermontov –

'... And in his madness prays for tempests,
Dreaming in tempests to find peace!'

'No, he's more than human: he knows everything,' I thought. 'How can one help loving him?'

I got up, took his arm and we began to walk up and down, trying to keep in step.

'Well?' he asked, smiling and looking at me.

'All right,' I replied in a whisper, and then a sudden fit of merriment seized us both: our eyes laughed, we took longer and longer strides and rose higher and higher on tiptoe. And like this, to the profound dissatisfaction of the butler and the amazement of my mother-in-law, who was playing patience in the parlour, we pranced through the house until we reached the dining-room, and there we stopped, looked at one another and burst out laughing.

A fortnight later, in time for Christmas, we were in Petersburg.

2

OUR journey to Petersburg, a week in Moscow, visits to his relations and mine, settling down in our new quarters, the travelling, the new places and new faces – all this passed before me like a dream. It was all so varied, festive and novel, and all so warmly and brightly illuminated by his presence and his love, that our quiet existence in the country seemed to me something very remote and insignificant. I had expected to find people in society proud and cold, but to my great surprise everyone greeted me with such genuine kindness and pleasure (not only relatives but strangers too) that I might have been the one object of their thoughts, and my arrival the one thing necessary to complete their happiness. I was also surprised to discover that my husband had many acquaintances in what appeared to be the very best circles – acquaintances he had never mentioned to me; and often I found it odd and disagreeable to hear him severely criticizing some of the people whom I had thought so nice. I could not understand why he was so short with them, and why he tried to avoid those whom I would have supposed it flattering to know. Surely the more nice acquaintances one had, the better, and everyone was nice.

'Now this is the situation,' he explained to me before we left the country. 'Here I am a little Croesus, but in town we shall be people of very modest means, and so we must not stay on after Easter, or go into society, or else we shall find ourselves in difficulties; and besides, I shouldn't care to for your sake.'

'What do we want with society?' I asked. 'We'll just go to a few theatres, see our relations, attend the opera, hear some good music, and be ready to come home well before Easter.'

But these plans were forgotten the moment we arrived in Petersburg. I found myself all of a sudden in such a new and delightful world, the centre of so many delights and with so many new interests opening up before me, that I immediately, though unconsciously, turned my back on the past and all my former ideas. 'That after all was nothing – mere playing at life: this now is the real thing. And there's the future too!' I thought. The restlessness and the fits of depression which had troubled me at home suddenly had entirely vanished, as if by magic. My love for my husband grew calmer, and I ceased to wonder if he loved me less. And indeed I could not doubt his love: my every thought was instantly understood, every feeling shared and every wish gratified by him. His placidity, if it still existed, no longer irritated me. Moreover, I began to realize that he not only loved but was proud of me. Often after we had paid a call, or made some new acquaintance, or given an evening party at which I, inwardly quaking with fear lest I disgraced myself, performed the duties of hostess, he would say: 'Ah, bravo, good girl! Capital! You needn't be nervous: that was a real success!' And I would be enormously pleased. Soon after our arrival he wrote to his mother, and called me to add a postscript to the letter; but he did not want to let me see what he had written, which, of course, led me to insist, and I read: 'You would not recognize Masha. I hardly do myself. Where can she have acquired that charming, graceful self-confidence and *poise* – I could even say, social tact and sweetness? And she does everything with such simplicity, charm and innate courtesy. Everybody is in raptures over her, and even I can't admire her enough, and should be more in love with her than ever, if that were possible.'

'Ah, so that's what I am like!' I thought. And in my joy and pride I felt that I loved him more than ever. My success with all our new acquaintances was a complete surprise to me. I was continually being told on all sides how this uncle had taken an especial fancy to me, and that aunt was raving about me. One admirer declared that there was not another woman like me in Petersburg, and I was assured by a lady that I had only to desire it to become the most sought-after woman in society. In particular there was a cousin of my husband's, a Princess D., middle-aged and very much at home in the social sphere, who loved me at first sight and paid me the most flattering compliments which turned my head. The first time she invited me to go to a ball and spoke to my husband about it, he turned and with a sly hint of a smile asked, Did I want to go? I nodded assent and felt myself blushing.

'She confesses to what she wants as if it were a crime,' he said, laughing good-humouredly.

'Because you said that we mustn't go into society, and that you didn't care for it,' I answered, smiling and looking at him with imploring eyes.

'If you want to very much, then let's go,' he said.

'Really, we'd better not.'

'Do you want to? Very badly?' he asked again.

I did not answer.

'Society in itself is no great harm,' he went on, 'but unsatisfied social aspirations are a bad and ugly business. We must certainly accept, and go,' he finished resolutely.

'To tell you the truth,' I said, 'I never longed for anything in the world so much as this ball.'

We did go, and I enjoyed myself beyond all expectations. At the ball it seemed to me more than ever that I was the centre round which everything revolved, that it was only for my sake that the great ball-room was lighted up, and the band was playing and this admiring crowd of people had assembled. It seemed to me that everyone, from the hairdresser and the lady's maid to my partners and the old gentlemen promenading the ball-room, either declared or gave me to understand that they were in love with me. I gathered from my cousin that the general verdict at the ball was that I was quite unlike other women – that there was something special about me, a kind of rural simplicity and charm. I was so elated by my success that I frankly told my husband I should like to go to two or three more balls during the season, 'so as to have my fill of them' I added insincerely.

He readily agreed; and at first accompanied me with obvious willingness, enjoying my triumph. He seemed to have quite forgotten all he had said before, or, at least, to have changed his mind about it.

Presently the time came when he had evidently had enough and was tired of the life we were leading. But I was too busy to think about that, and if I did sometimes notice his intent, serious gaze fixed inquiringly on me I refused to understand its meaning. I was so blinded by the spontaneous affection which I apparently inspired from all around me, so dazed by the unfamiliar atmosphere of luxury and enjoyment; it was so agreeable to find myself in this new world not merely his equal but his superior (that moral influence of his which used to crush me having suddenly disappeared) and yet to love him better and more independently than before, that I could not understand what drawbacks he could see for me in society life. It was a new feeling of pride and self-satisfaction when all eyes were turned in my direction as we entered a ball-room, while he, as though ashamed to acknowledge his ownership of me in public, made haste to leave my side and lose himself in the crowd of black coats. 'Wait a little!' I often thought, as my eyes sought his inconspicuous and sometimes woebegone figure at the other end of the ball-room. 'Wait till we get home! Then I will show you for whose sake I tried to be beautiful and brilliant, and what it is I love best in all that surrounds me this evening!' I really believed that my triumphs gave me pleasure only because thus I would be in a position to sacrifice them to him. The only way, I thought, in which society life could do me harm was in the possibility it offered of my being attracted by one of the men I met at parties, and arousing my husband's jealousy. But his trust in me was so absolute, he seemed so tranquil and indifferent, and all the young men I met were so insignificant in comparison with him, that I was not alarmed by what I considered to be society's one risk for me. All the same, the attention of so many men in the social world afforded me gratification, flattered my vanity and led me to imagine that there was a sort of merit in my love for my husband, and made me treat him in a bolder and more casual way.

'Ah, I saw you carrying on a very animated conversation with Madame N.,' I said, shaking a finger at him, one night as we were coming home from a ball. He had indeed been talking to this lady, who was a well-known figure in Petersburg society. He was more silent and depressed than usual, and I said this to rouse him.

'Oh, why say things like that? And you, Masha, especially!' he said through half-closed teeth and frowning as though something pained him physically. 'How little that sort of thing suits you and me. Leave that to others: such false relations may spoil the true ones between us, which I still hope may come back.'

I felt ashamed, and was silent.

'Will they come back, Masha? What do you think?' he asked.

'They have never been spoilt, and never will be,' I said; and at that moment I really believed it.

'Please God you are right,' he commented, 'or else it is high time we went back to the country.'

But he only spoke so that once – for the rest he seemed as well-content as I, and I was so delighted and happy. 'And even if he is bored occasionally,' I consoled myself, 'I endured boredom for his sake in the country; and if our relationship has changed a little, everything will come back once we're alone again with *maman* in the summer at Nikolskoe.'

So the winter slipped by, and we stayed on, regardless of our plans, and spent Eastertide too in Petersburg. In the following week when we were making preparations for our departure and had finished our packing, and my husband, who had bought things – plants for the garden and presents for people at home – was in a particularly gay and affectionate frame of mind, his cousin, Princess D., unexpectedly arrived and begged us to stay till the Saturday, in order to go to a *soirée* at Countess R.'s. She urged that the Countess was very anxious to have me, because a certain foreign prince who was visiting Petersburg had wanted to be introduced ever since the last ball I had been at, and was going solely for that purpose, saying that I was the prettiest woman in Russia. All Petersburg was to be there, and, in short, it would really be a shame if I refused.

My husband was talking to someone at the other end of the drawing-room.

'So you will come, won't you, *Marie?*' said his cousin.

'We were meaning to start for the country the day after tomorrow,' I replied doubtfully, glancing over at my husband. Our eyes met, and he hurriedly looked away.

'I will persuade him to stay,' she said, 'and then we can go on Saturday and break all hearts. Agreed?'

'It would mean upsetting our plans, and besides we are all packed,' I answered, beginning to give way.

'Why, she had better drive round this evening and make her curtsey to the Prince,' my husband called out from the other end of the room in a tone of repressed anger which I had never heard from him before.

'Aha, he's jealous! It's the first time I've seen that,' his cousin laughed. 'But I'm not trying to persuade her for the Prince's sake, Sergei Mihailovich, but for all our sakes. The Countess is so anxious to have her.'

'It rests with her entirely,' my husband said frigidly, and then left the room.

I saw that he was more than usually upset, which distressed me and I made no promise to his cousin. As soon as she had gone I went to my husband. He was pacing up and down absorbed in thought, and neither saw nor heard me come into the room on tiptoe.

'There he is – thinking of our dear house at Nikolskoe,' I said to myself as I looked at him, 'and our morning coffee in the bright drawing-room, and his land and the peasants, our evenings in the music-room, and our secret midnight suppers ... Yes!' I said to myself decidedly, 'I'd give up all the balls in the world, and the flattery of all the princes on earth, in exchange for his timid happiness, his gentle affection.' I was on the point of telling him that I did not want to go to the *soirée* when he suddenly looked round, saw me and frowned. His face lost its sweet dreamy expression and assumed its old appraising soundness of judgement and patronizing composure. He did not care for me to see him as an ordinary person: he had always to be a demigod on a pedestal to me.

'What is it, my dear?' he asked, turning towards me with a casual, unconcerned air.

I did not answer. It annoyed me that he should conceal his true self from me, and not want to remain the man I loved.

'Do you want to go to this *soirée* on Saturday?' he asked.

'I did, but you disapprove. And anyway, our things are all packed,' I added.

Never had he looked at me so coldly, never had he spoken to me so coldly.

'I will order the things to be unpacked,' he said, 'and I shall stay until Tuesday. So you can go if you want to. I hope you will; but I shall not go.'

As always when he was upset, he took to striding jerkily about the room, not looking at me.

'I simply can't understand you,' I said, following him with my eyes from where I stood. 'You say you are always so calm' (he had never said so); 'so why do you talk to me in this odd way? I am ready on your account to sacrifice this pleasure, and then you, in a sarcastic tone which you've never used to me before, insist on my going.'

'So you make a *sacrifice*!' – he threw special emphasis on the word – 'well, so do I. What could be better? We compete in generosity. What an example of domestic bliss!'

It was the first time I had heard such harsh, contemptuous language from his lips. And his sarcasm did not put me to shame, but hurt me, and the bitterness did not alarm me but infected me. How could *he* speak thus, who was always so frank and open and dreaded insincerity between us? And what was it all about? What had I done except want to sacrifice for him a pleasure in which I could see no harm? And a moment ago I had loved and understood him so well. We had changed rôles: he avoided direct and plain words, while I sought them.

'You have altered a great deal,' I said, with a sigh. 'What am I guilty of? It is not this *soirée* – you have something else, some old count against me. Why be insincere? Wasn't it you who was always so afraid of insincerity before? Tell me straight out: what have you against me?' ('What can he say?' I wondered, reflecting complacently that he had had no cause to find fault with me all the winter.)

I came forward into the middle of the room, so that he was obliged to pass close to me, and looked at him. 'He will come up and clasp me in his arms, and all will be over,' I thought, and even began to feel sorry that I should not have the chance of proving him wrong. But he paused at the far end of the room, and stared at me.

'Do you still not understand?' he said.

'No, I don't.'

'Well then, I will tell you. What I feel, what I cannot help feeling, positively disgusts me for the first time in my life.' He stopped, evidently startled by the harsh sound of his own voice.

'What *do* you mean?' I asked, with tears of indignation in my eyes.

'It's disgusting that the Prince should think you pretty and that you therefore run after him, forgetting your husband and yourself and your womanly dignity, and refuse to understand what your husband must feel for you, if you are so devoid of self-respect as to come to your husband and speak of the "sacrifice" you are making, by which you mean: "It would be a great pleasure to me to exhibit myself to His Highness, but I *sacrifice* it".'

The longer he spoke, the more the sound of his own voice inflamed him, and his voice had a rough, biting, cruel note in it. I had never seen, had never thought of seeing him like this. The blood rushed to my heart, and I was frightened; but I felt that I had nothing to be ashamed of, and injured pride incited me to punish him.

'I have long been expecting this,' I said. 'Go on, go on.'

'I don't know what you expected,' he continued. 'But I had good reason to expect the worst, seeing you day after day in the filth, idleness and luxury of that idiotic society life, and I got what I expected ... so that now I am filled with shame and pain, as I have never been before – pain for myself, when your friend probes my heart with her nasty fingers, and begins talking about jealousy – my jealousy; and of whom am I supposed to be jealous? Of a man whom neither you nor I know. And you, on purpose it seems, refuse to understand me and want to sacrifice to me – what? I am ashamed for you, ashamed of your degradation! . . . Sacrifice!' he repeated again.

'Ah, here we have it, the power of the husband,' thought I, 'to insult and humiliate a perfectly innocent woman. Such may be a husband's rights, but I will not submit to them.'

'No, I shall make no sacrifice on your account,' I said, feeling my nostrils dilating unnaturally and the blood deserting my face. 'I shall go to the *soirée* on Saturday – most certainly I will.'

'And I wish you joy of it – only all is over between us!' he shouted in a burst of unrestrained fury. 'But you shall not torture me any longer! I was a fool to . . .' he started again, but his lips quivered, and with a visible effort he forbore finishing his sentence.

I feared and hated him at that moment. I wanted to say a great deal to him and be revenged for all his insults; but if I had opened my mouth I should have lost my dignity by bursting into tears. I walked out of the room without a word. But as soon as I ceased to hear his footsteps I was aghast at what we had done. I was in terror that the bond which made up my whole happiness might really be severed for all time, and I thought of going back. But then I wondered: 'Has he sufficiently recovered his composure to understand me when I mutely hold out my hand to him and look at him? Will he realize my generosity? What if he should call my grief a pretence? Or with a sense of his own righteousness calmly and aloofly accept my repentance and forgive me? And why, oh why, did he whom I loved so much insult me so cruelly?'

I went not to him but to my own room, where I sat for a long while and cried. With horror I recalled each word of our conversation, and substituted different words, added other, kind words – and then the memory of what had happened would return to appal me, and my feelings would be outraged again. In the evening when I went down to tea and met my husband in the presence of a friend who was our guest I felt that a wide gulf had opened between us from that day. Our friend asked me when we were leaving, and before I had time to answer, my husband replied: 'On Tuesday. We have still to go to a *soirée* at Countess R.'s. You are going, aren't you?' he turned to me.

I was frightened by his matter-of-fact tone, and looked at him timidly. His eyes were directed straight at me with a malicious, mocking expression; his voice was cold and even.

'Yes,' I answered.

In the evening when we were alone he came up to me and held out his hand.

'Please forget what I said to you today,' he said.

I took his hand, a smile faltering on my face and the tears ready to flow; but he withdrew his hand and sat down in an arm-chair some distance away from me, as if afraid of a sentimental scene. 'Can it be that he still considers himself in the right?' I wondered; and though I had it on the tip of my tongue to explain and to beg that we might not go to the party, the words died on my lips.

'I must write to *maman* that we have put off our departure,' he said; 'otherwise she will be uneasy.'

'When were you thinking of leaving?' I asked.

'On Tuesday after the *soirée*,' he replied.

'I hope it's not on my account?' I said, looking into his eyes; but his eyes merely looked back, and said nothing, as though they were somehow shrouded from me. His face suddenly struck me as old and unpleasant.

We went to the *soirée*, and it seemed that good, friendly relations between us had been restored; but those relations were quite different from what they had once been.

At the *soirée* I was sitting with other ladies when the Prince came up to me, so that I was obliged to stand to talk with him. As I rose my eyes involuntarily sought my husband, and I saw him looking at me from the other end of the room, and then turn away. I suddenly felt such a sense of mortification and hurt that I became painfully confused and blushed from my neck to the roots of my hair under the Prince's gaze. But I was forced to stand and listen while he spoke and surveyed me from his superior height. Our conversation was soon over: there was no room for him to sit beside me, and he, no doubt, was conscious that I felt very ill at ease with him. We talked of the last ball, of where I should spend the summer, and so on. As he left me, he expressed a desire to be introduced to my husband, and I watched them meet and begin to talk together at the far end of the room. The Prince must have said something about me, for in the middle of their conversation he smiled over in my direction.

My husband all at once flushed hotly, made a low bow and walked away from the Prince, without waiting to be dismissed. I blushed in my turn: I was ashamed of the impression which I – and, still more, my husband – must have made upon His Highness. Everyone, I thought, must have noticed my own awkward embarrassment, and my husband's eccentric behaviour. Heaven only knew what interpretation they would put on it. Perhaps they were already aware of the scene between us.

Princess D. drove me home, and on the way I spoke of my husband. I could not contain myself and told her the whole story of what had taken place between us thanks to this luckless *soirée*. She tried to be comforting, assuring me that our quarrel would have no after-effects. She explained to me her view of my husband's character, and said that she thought he had become very stiff and unsociable. I agreed with her, and felt that I now understood him better and more dispassionately myself.

But afterwards, when I was alone with Sergei Mihailovich, the fact of having discussed him lay heavy on my conscience like a crime, and I felt that the gulf which now separated us had widened still further.

3

FROM that day our life and our relationship completely changed. We were no longer as happy when we were alone together as before. There were subjects to which we gave a wide berth, and conversation flowed more easily in the presence of a third person. When talk turned on life in the country or on a ball we felt that we were treading on dangerous ground and we avoided each other's eye. Both of us knew where the gulf between us lay, and shrank from approaching it. I was convinced that he was proud and hot-tempered, and I must be careful not to come up against his weak spots. He was equally sure that I disliked the country and was dying for social distractions, and that he must give in to this unfortunate taste of mine. And we both avoided plain speech on these topics, and each misjudged the other. We had long ceased to think each other the most perfect people in the world, but made comparisons with others and secretly passed judgement on each other. I fell ill just before our departure, and instead of going back to the country we moved to our summer villa, from which my husband went on alone to join his mother at Nikolskoe. By that time I was sufficiently recovered to have gone with him, but he persuaded me to stay behind on the pretext that he was worried about my health. I knew it was not my health that worried him but the thought that we should not get on together in the country. I did not insist much, and he went off alone. I felt empty and lonely without him, but when he returned I did not find that he added to my life as in the past. Our old relationship – when every idea, every experience not shared with him oppressed me like a crime, when his every word and deed seemed to me models of perfection, when merely to look at one another made us want to laugh for joy – this relationship had changed so imperceptibly that we did not even notice that it was no longer there. Each of us had acquired our separate interests and occupations, which we no longer thought of sharing. It had even ceased to trouble us that each had a separate private world from which the other was shut out. We became used to the idea, and before a year had passed we could look at each other without embarrassment. His moods of wild gaiety when he was with me, his boyish pranks, had completely vanished, along with his careless readiness to forgive everyone and everything which had formerly displeased me. Gone were the searching looks that had once both disconcerted and delighted me. There were no more prayers, no more transports of joy together. We did not even meet often: he was constantly away, and was neither afraid nor sorry to leave me alone; while I was continually going to parties where I did not need him.

There were no further scenes or quarrels between us: I tried to please him, he did his best to fulfil my wishes, and we appeared to love each other.

When we were by ourselves – which we seldom were – I felt neither joy nor excitement nor embarrassment in his company: it seemed like being alone. I knew very well that this was my husband and not some stranger but a good man – my husband, whom I knew as well as I knew myself. I was certain that I knew everything he would do or say, and how he would look; and if anything he did surprised me I decided that he had done it by mistake. I expected nothing from him. In a word, he was my husband – and that was all. It seemed to me that this was as it should be, that it could never be and had never been otherwise. When he left home, especially at first, I was lonely and nervous, and recognized more keenly my need of his support. When he returned I flung myself on his neck in delight, though two hours later my delight would be entirely forgotten and I would find nothing to say to him. Only in the moments of quiet, undemonstrative affection which we occasionally had would it seem to me that something was wrong, and my heart ached, and in his eyes I seemed to read that it was the same with him. I was conscious of limits set to our affection – frontiers which he apparently would not, and I could not, cross. Sometimes this made me sad, but I had no leisure for reflection and the regrets that these dimly-felt changes caused me I tried to forget in the distractions with which I was always surrounded. Society life, which from the first had dazzled me with its glitter and its power to flatter my conceit, soon had me completely in its power. It became a habit, fastened its shackles upon me and monopolized my capacity for feeling. I now could not bear solitude and was afraid to reflect on my position. All my time, from late in the morning until late at night, was taken up by the claims of society; even when I stayed at home my time was not my own. I was neither happy nor unhappy: it seemed to me that it must always be this way and not otherwise.

So three years passed, during which our relations remained unchanged, stood still as it were, and crystallized, unable to become either better or worse. Though there were two important events in our family during that time, neither of them altered my life. They were the birth of my first child and the death of Tatiana Semeonovna. At first I was so carried away by the feeling of motherhood, which gave me such unexpected ecstasy, that I thought it would prove to be the beginning of a new life for me; but within a couple of months I started to go out again and the feeling grew weaker and weaker until it was transformed into mere habit and the cold performance of a duty. My husband, on the contrary, with the birth of our first son became his old self again – quiet, unruffled and content to stay at home – and poured out all his tenderness and gaiety upon the child. Often when I went into the nursery dressed for a ball to make the sign of the cross over the baby before he slept I would find my husband there and feel his eyes fixed on me, as it were reproachfully and sternly scrutinizing. Then I was ashamed and suddenly horrified at my indifference to the child, and asked myself if I was worse than other women. 'But it can't be helped,' I thought. 'I love my son, but I can't sit day in and day out beside him: it would be too tedious, and I'm not going to pretend about it.'

His mother's death was a great grief for my husband. It was painful for him, as he said, to go on living at Nikolskoe without her; but for myself, although I missed her and sympathized with my husband's sorrow, life in the country was now pleasanter for me and I felt more at home. The greater part of those three years we spent in town, and I only went to the country once, for two months, and the third year we went abroad.

We spent the summer at a watering-place.

I was then twenty-one; our circumstances were, I supposed, flourishing; I asked no more of my life than it already gave me; everyone I knew, it seemed to me, loved me; my health was excellent; I was the best-dressed woman at the spa; I knew that I was good-looking; the weather was magnificent; a peculiar atmosphere of beauty and elegance surrounded me, and I felt very light-hearted. I was not as light-hearted as I had been in the old days at Nikolskoe, when my happiness was in myself and came from the feeling that I deserved to be happy, and from the anticipation of still greater happiness to come. That was a different state of things, but this summer, too, I was well content. There was nothing I desired, nothing I hoped for, nothing I feared. My life, it seemed, was full and my conscience easy. Among the young people that season there was not one man I preferred in any way to the rest – not even to old Prince K., our ambassador, who paid me marked attention. One was young and another old; one was English and fair, another French and wore a beard – to me they were all alike, but all indispensable. Individually indistinguishable, together they made up the atmosphere which I so enjoyed. Only one of them, an Italian marquis, especially attracted my attention by the boldness with which he expressed his admiration for me. He seized every opportunity of being with me – danced with me, rode with me, met me at the casino, and so on, and on every occasion spoke to me of my charms. Several times from the windows I caught sight of him outside our house, and often the unpleasant, intent stare of his brilliant eyes would make me blush and look away. He was young, handsome, elegant, and, above all, in his smile and the shape of his forehead he resembled my husband, but he was far better-looking. I was struck by this resemblance although in his general appearance – in his lips, his eyes and long chin – there was something coarse and animal in place of my husband's charming expression of kindliness and noble serenity. I imagined at the time that the marquis was passionately in love with me, and occasionally thought of him with proud commiseration. At times I tried to pacify him, to bring him round to a state of half-friendly, quiet trust, but he sharply repelled these attempts and continued to disturb me disagreeably by his smouldering passion that threatened every moment to break out. I did not acknowledge it to myself but I was afraid of this man, and against my will often thought of him. He was an acquaintance of my husband's, who treated him even more coldly and disdainfully than he did those others who regarded him merely as his wife's husband. Towards the end of the season I fell ill and stayed indoors for a fortnight. The first evening that I went out again to hear the band I learnt that the long-expected Lady S., a famous English beauty, had arrived in my absence. A group gathered round me, and I was greeted warmly; but a more distinguished group gathered round the beautiful stranger. She and her beauty were the sole topic of conversation. She was pointed out to me, and she certainly was lovely, but I was disagreeably impressed by the self-satisfied expression on her face, and I said so. That day everything that had formerly seemed amusing I found dull. On the next day Lady S. got up a party to visit the castle, which I declined to join. Practically everyone else went; and my opinion of the spa completely changed. Everything and everybody seemed stupid and boring. I wanted to cry, to finish the cure quickly and return to Russia. At the bottom of my heart there was a strange wicked feeling but I had not yet acknowledged it to myself. Pretending that I was not strong, I gave up appearing in society; if I went out, it was only now and then alone in the mornings, to drink the waters. Otherwise, my only companion was Mme. M., a Russian lady with whom I would go for a drive in the surrounding countryside. My husband was away at this time: he had gone to Heidelberg for a few days while I finished my cure, when he intended to return to Russia, and he only came to see me occasionally.

One day when Lady S. had carried off the entire company on a shooting expedition Mme. M. and I drove in the afternoon to the castle. While we were driving slowly in our carriage up the winding road, bordered by century-old chestnut-trees and commanding a vista of the pretty, elegant environs of Baden, lit by the rays of the setting sun, we talked more seriously than we ever had before. I had known my companion for a long while but she appeared to me now in a new light, as a well-principled and intelligent woman, to whom it was safe to speak without reserve, and whose friendship was worth having. We spoke of our families, of our children, of the emptiness of life in Baden; we longed to get back to Russia, to the country, and fell into a mood of pleasant melancholy. Still feeling pensive, we went into the castle. Inside the walls it was shady and cool, overhead the sun played about the ruins, and we could hear steps and voices. The gateway served as a frame through which we could look back and see a typical Baden view, exquisite, though cold to a Russian eye. We sat down to rest, and watched the setting sun in silence. The voices reached us more distinctly, and I thought I heard my own name. I listened and could not help overhearing every word. I recognized the voices: they belonged to the Italian marquis and a French friend of his whom I also knew. They were discussing me and Lady S., and the Frenchman was comparing our respective charms. Though he said nothing derogatory his remarks made the blood rush to my heart. In detail he enumerated my good points and hers. I was already a mother, while Lady S. was only nineteen; I had prettier hair, my rival a more graceful figure. Lady S. was a woman of birth, 'whereas your fair lady,' he said, 'is really nothing much – just another of those little Russian princesses who are beginning to flock here nowadays'. He ended by saying that I was wise not to enter the lists with Lady S., and that my day was definitely over, so far as Baden was concerned.

'I am sorry for her – unless, of course, she takes it into her head to console herself with you,' he added with a ringing laugh of amusement.

'If she goes away, I go after her!' coarsely articulated the voice with the Italian accent.

'Happy mortal! He can still fall in love!' laughed the Frenchman.

'Love!' said the other voice, and was silent for a moment. 'It's a necessity to me: I cannot live without it. To turn life into a romance is the one thing worth while. And with me romance never breaks off in the middle, and this affair I shall carry through to the end.'

'Bonne chance, mon ami!' said the Frenchman.

We did not hear any more, for they passed round the corner and soon their steps sounded on the other side. Then we heard them coming down the stairs and a few minutes later they emerged through a side door and were most surprised to see us. I blushed when the marquis approached me, and was dismayed when we left the castle and he offered me his arm. I could not refuse, and we set off for the carriage, behind Mme. M. who was walking with his friend. I was mortified by what the Frenchman had said about me, though I secretly owned to myself that he had only put into words what I had felt myself; but the marquis's plain speaking had astounded and shocked me by its coarseness. I was disquieted by the thought that, though I had overheard him, he showed no fear of me. It was repulsive to have him so close, and without looking at or answering him, and trying to put up my hand so as not to hear what he was saying, I hurried after the couple in front. The marquis remarked on the fine view and said something about the unexpected happiness of meeting me, and so on, but I was not listening to him. My thoughts were with my husband, my child, my country; I was filled with a confused sense of shame, regret and longing, and I was in a hurry to get home to my solitary room in the Hôtel de Bade, there to consider at leisure the storm of feeling that had just risen in my heart. But Mme. M. walked slowly, it was still some distance to the carriage, and my escort, it seemed to me, stubbornly slacked his pace as though with the express purpose of detaining me. 'No, no!' I said to myself, and resolutely walked faster. But it soon became unmistakable that he was holding me back and even pressing my arm. Mme. M. turned a corner, and we were quite alone. I was frightened.

'Excuse me,' I said coldly and tried to free my arm, but the lace of my sleeve caught in a button of his coat. Bending towards me, he began to disentangle it, and his ungloved fingers touched my arm. A feeling new to me, half horror, half pleasure, sent an icy shiver down my spine. I looked at him, intending to convey by one cutting glance all the contempt I felt. But my eyes expressed something different: they expressed apprehension and excitement. His liquid, burning eyes close to my face stared strangely at me, at my neck, at my bosom; both his hands fingered my arm above the wrist; his parted lips were saying something – were saying that he loved me, that I was all the world to him – and those lips were coming nearer and nearer, and those hands were squeezing mine more and more tightly, burning me. Fire ran through my veins, there was a mist before my eyes, I trembled, and the words with which I meant to stop him dried in my throat. Suddenly I felt a kiss on my cheek. Shaking and going cold all over, I stood and stared at him. Unable to speak or move, I stood there, terrified, expectant, and desirous. All this lasted but a second. But it was a horrible second. In that brief spell I saw him exactly as he was. I could read his face so easily – the low craggy forehead (so like my husband's) under the straw hat; the handsome straight nose with the wide nostrils; the little beard and the long moustaches waxed into points; the smooth shaven cheeks and sun-burned neck. I hated him, I feared him, he was utterly repugnant and alien to me; and yet at that moment the excitement and passion of this odious stranger raised a powerful echo in my own heart. I felt an irresistible desire to surrender myself to the kisses of that coarse handsome mouth, to the caresses of those white hands with their delicate veins and jewelled fingers. Such a craving possessed me to fling myself headlong into the abyss of forbidden delights that had suddenly opened at my feet! ...

'I am so unhappy already,' I thought. 'What does more unhappiness matter?'

He put one arm round me and bent towards my face. 'All right, why not let sin and shame overwhelm me still further,' I said to myself.

'*Je vous aime,*' he whispered in the voice which was so like my husband's. I remembered my husband and child as once precious beings who had now quite passed out of my life. But suddenly at that moment I heard Mme. M.'s voice calling me round the corner. I came to myself, tore my hand away and without looking at him almost ran after her. We took our seats in the carriage, and only then did I glance at him. He lifted his hat and asked me something with a smile. He little knew the inexpressible loathing I felt for him at that moment.

My life seemed to me so miserable, so wretched, the future so hopeless, the past so black! Mme. M. talked to me but I did not take in what she said. It seemed to me she only spoke out of pity, to hide the contempt I aroused in her. In every word, in every look, I fancied I detected this contempt and insulting pity. The shame of that kiss burned my cheek, and the thought of my husband and child was more than I could bear. Alone in my room I had hoped to think over my position, but I was afraid to be alone. I did not finish the tea they brought me, and, not knowing why I did so, I packed with feverish haste to catch the evening train and join my husband in Heidelberg.

I found seats for myself and my maid in an empty compartment, and when the engine started and the fresh air blew on my face from the window I began to recover, and to have a clearer vision of my past and my future. All my married life, from the day of our first visit to Petersburg, suddenly presented itself to me in a new light, and lay like a reproach on my conscience. For the first time I vividly recalled our early days at Nikolskoe and our plans for our life together and for the first time it occurred to me to wonder what happiness had my husband had all this time. And I felt that I had wronged him. 'But why didn't he stop me? Why did he pretend? Why did he always avoid any frank discussion? Why did he humiliate me?' I asked myself. 'Why did he not make use of the power over me that his love gave him? Or did he not love me?' But however much he might be to blame, I still felt the imprint of another man's kiss on my cheek. The nearer we got to Heidelberg the more distinctly I saw my husband in my imagination, and the more I dreaded our meeting. 'I'll tell him everything,' I thought. 'Everything. I will weep tears of repentance, and he will forgive me.' But I did not know myself what I meant by 'everything', and I did not believe in my heart that he would forgive me.

But as soon as I entered my husband's room and saw his calm, if surprised expression, I felt that I had nothing to tell him, no confession to make, and nothing to ask forgiveness for. My grief and remorse must remain locked within me.

'What put this into your head?' he asked. 'I was intending to join you tomorrow.' But looking more closely into my face he seemed to become alarmed. 'What is it? What has happened?' he exclaimed.

'Nothing,' I answered, with difficulty restraining my tears. 'I have come away for good. Let us go home to Russia – tomorrow, if possible.'

He was silent for a space, looking at me thoughtfully.

'But won't you tell me what has happened?' he said.

Involuntarily I blushed and looked down. There was a flash of injured pride and anger in his eyes. Afraid of what he might imagine, I said with a ready hypocrisy which I had never suspected in myself:

'Nothing at all has happened. It was merely that I got bored and depressed by myself, and I have been thinking a great deal about our way of life and about you. I have been to blame towards you for so long now! Why do you take me to places you don't care for yourself? I have been to blame for so long,'

I repeated, and again the tears started to my eyes. 'Let us go back to the country and stay there for ever.'

'Oh, my dear, spare us sentimental scenes,' he said coldly. 'So far as wanting to return to the country goes, it is a good idea, for our money is running short; but the notion of staying there "for ever" is a delusion. I know you would never be able to settle down there. And now, have some tea and you will feel better,' he concluded, getting up and ringing for the waiter.

I imagined all he might be thinking of me, and I was outraged by the dreadful thoughts that I attributed to him as I saw the uncertain and, as it were, shamefaced way he looked at me. No, he could not and would not understand me. I said I would go and have a look at the baby, and I left the room. I wanted to be alone, and to cry and cry and cry . . .

4

THE house at Nikolskoe, so long empty and unheated, came to life again, but not so those who had lived in it. *Maman* was no more, and my husband and I were alone together. But now, far from desiring such close companionship, we even found it irksome. The winter was all the more difficult for me as I was unwell, and I only recovered my health after the birth of my second son. My husband and I continued on the same coldly amicable terms established when we were in Petersburg; but in the country every room, every wall, every sofa reminded me of what he had once been to me, and of what I had lost. It was as if some unforgiven injury lay between us, as though he were punishing me for some offence and affecting not to be aware of what he was doing. There was nothing to beg forgiveness for, no penalty to deprecate: he punished me only by not giving me all of himself, his whole heart and mind as he used to do; but he did not give it to anyone or anything else: it was as though he no longer had a heart to give. Sometimes it occurred to me that he was only pretending to be like this in order to hurt me, and that the old feeling was still alive in him, and I would try to bring it out. But he always seemed to shun frankness, as though he suspected me of insincerity and dreaded any ludicrous display of emotion. His look and the tone of his voice said: 'What is the good of talking? I know it all, chapter and verse, already. I know all you want to say – and I know, too, that you will say one thing and do another.' At first I was offended by this dread of frankness, but later I became used to the idea that it was not any dread but rather the absence on his part of any need of frankness. I could never have brought myself now to tell him suddenly that I loved him, or ask him to repeat prayers with me or listen while I played the piano. Our behaviour with each other was regulated by certain fixed rules of propriety. We lived our separate lives: he had his occupations in which I had now no need or wish to share, while I continued my idle existence which no longer vexed or grieved him. The children were still too young to form a bond between us.

But spring came round and brought Katya and Sonya to spend the summer with us in the country. As the house at Nikolskoe was under repair we moved over to Pokrovskoe. My old home was unchanged – there was the veranda, the folding table and the piano in the sunny drawing-room, and my old room with its white curtains and the dreams of my girlhood which I seemed to have left behind me there. Two little beds stood in the room now. One of them had been mine, and here every evening I made the sign of the cross over my sprawling, chubby little Kokosha. The other was a crib, where Vanya's baby face peeped from the midst of his night-clothes. After saying good-night to them I often used to stand still in the middle of the quiet room, and suddenly from every corner, from the walls, from the curtains, old forgotten visions of youth crept out. Old voices began to sing the songs of my girlhood. What had become of those visions now, of those dear, sweet songs? All that I had hardly dared to hope for had materialized. My vague confused dreams had become a reality, and reality had become an oppressive, difficult joyless life. And yet everything here was just the same: the garden I saw from the window, the grass, the path, the very same bench over there at the edge of the dell, the same song of the nightingale by the pond, the same lilac in full flower, and the same moon above the house – and yet all so dreadfully, so desperately changed!

Everything so cold and distant that might have been so near and dear! Just as in the old days Katya and I sit in the parlour talking softly together, and we talk of him. But Katya has grown wrinkled and yellow, her eyes no longer sparkle with joy and hope but express sympathetic distress and commiseration. We do not go into raptures as we used to, we criticize him; we do not wonder what we have done to deserve such happiness; nor long, as of old, to cry our thoughts to all the world. No! We whisper together like conspirators and ask each other for the hundredth time why everything is so sadly changed. And he is just the same too, except for a deeper furrow between his eyebrows and more grey hair about his temples; but the profound, intent look in his eyes is veiled from me for ever by a cloud. And I, too, am the same woman, only there is no love in my heart, or desire for love, no interest in work, no contentment in myself. And how remote and impossible my old religious enthusiasms seem now, and the love I had felt for him, and my former abounding life! What once seemed so plain and right – that happiness lay in living for others – is unintelligible now. Why live for others, when life has no attractions even for oneself?

I had completely given up my music ever since the time of our first visit to Petersburg; but now the old piano, the old albums of music tempted me to begin again.

One day I was not well and stayed indoors by myself. My husband had taken Katya and Sonya to see the new buildings at Nikolskoe. Tea was laid; I went downstairs and, while I was waiting for them, sat down at the piano. I opened the Moonlight Sonata and began to play. There was no one about to see or hear, the windows were open on to the garden, and the familiar notes floated through the room, plaintive and solemn. I finished the first movement and looked round instinctively to the corner where he used to sit listening to my music. But he was not there: his chair, untouched this long while, was still in its place; through the window I could see a lilac-bush against the light of the setting sun; and the cool of the evening flowed in through the open windows. I rested my elbows on the piano and covered my face with both hands. I sat like that for a considerable time, thinking with anguish of the days which would never return, and with apprehension imagining the future. But there seemed to be only a blank before me, I had no desires and no hopes. 'Can it be that my life is finished?' I pondered, and then, appalled, I raised my head and began to play the same *andante* through again, so as to forget and not to think. 'Oh God!' I prayed. 'Forgive me if I have sinned, or restore to me all that once blossomed in my heart, or teach me what to do and how to live now.' I heard the sound of wheels on the grass and the carriage drawing up before the porch; then careful, familiar footsteps on the veranda, and silence. But the old feeling no longer stirred in me in response to that well-known tread. When I stopped playing, I heard the steps behind me, and a hand was laid on my shoulder.

'What a clever girl you are to play that sonata,' he said.

I did not speak.

'Haven't you had tea?'

I shook my head without looking round at him lest he see the traces of emotion on my face.

'They'll be here directly: the horse gave trouble, and they got out to walk back from the high-road,' he said.

'Let's wait for them,' I suggested, and went out on to the veranda, hoping that he would follow; but he asked after the children and went upstairs to see them. Once more his presence and simple, kindly voice made me doubt that I had really lost anything. What more could I wish for? 'He is kind and gentle, a good husband, a good father – I don't know myself what more I want.' I went out on to the balcony and sat under the veranda awning on the very bench on which I had sat the day we became engaged. The sun had set now, it was beginning to grow dark, and a little spring rain-cloud hung over the house and garden; only low in the west, through the trees, could be seen the clear rim of the sky touched with the fading glow and the faint golden light of the evening star. The shadow of the little cloud lay over all the landscape, and everything seemed to be waiting for the soft spring shower. There was not a breath of wind; not a leaf, not a blade of grass stirred; the scent of lilac and wild cherry filled the garden and the veranda as if all the air were in flower – it came in waves, now stronger, now weaker, making one want to close eyes and ears, and shut out everything but that sweet fragrance. The dahlias and rose-bushes, not yet in bloom, stood motionless in the dark, newly turned soil of the flower-bed, looking as if they were growing slowly up the white supports of whittled stick. Beyond the dell the frogs were making the most of their time before the rain drove them to the pond, croaking in piercing chorus with all their might. Only the high continuous note of water falling at a distance rose above their croaking. From time to time the nightingales called to one another, and I could hear them flitting restlessly from bush to bush. Again this spring a nightingale had tried to build in a bush under the window, and when I came out on the veranda I heard her fly across to the other side of the avenue. From there she called once and was silent; she, too, was expecting the rain.

It was in vain that I tried to lull myself quiet: I was full of waiting and longing.

He came back from upstairs and sat down beside me.

'I am afraid they will get wet,' he said.

'Yes,' I answered; and we sat for a long time without speaking.

The cloud sank lower and lower in the windless sky. The air grew stiller and more fragrant. Then suddenly a drop fell and appeared to skip along the sailcloth awning of the veranda; then another splashed on the gravel path; soon there was a patter on the burdock leaves, and now the heavy cool drops fell faster and faster. The nightingales and frogs ceased their clamour; only the thin sound of water still persisted – although it, too, sounded farther away because of the rain – and some bird, which must have sheltered in the dry leaves not far from the veranda, steadily repeated its two monotonous notes. My husband rose to go in.

'Where are you off to?' I asked, trying to keep him. 'It is so nice here ...'

'We ought to send them an umbrella and goloshes,' he replied.

'There's no need – it will soon be over.'

He agreed, and we remained together by the balustrade of the veranda. I rested one hand on the wet slippery rail and leaned my head out. The cool rain sprinkled my hair and neck. The little cloud, growing lighter and thinner, emptied itself overhead; the steady patter of the rain gave place to occasional drops that fell from the sky or dripped from the trees. The frogs began to croak again below, the nightingales shrilled into song again, calling from the dripping bushes first on one side then on the other. The whole scene before us suddenly cleared.

'How lovely it is!' he exclaimed, sitting on the balustrade and passing his hand over my wet hair.

The simple caress affected me like a reproach: I wanted to cry.

'What more can a man desire?' he said. 'I am so contented now that I don't need anything – perfectly happy I am.'

'It was a different story once,' I thought. 'Then you used to say, however great your happiness was you wanted more and more. But now you are tranquil and resigned, while my heart is bursting with unspoken repentance and unshed tears.'

'I feel that too,' I said, 'but the very beauty of it all makes me sad. Inside me everything is so confused, so incomplete, so troubled with vague longings and dissatisfactions, whereas outside all is so peaceful and fair. Is there no element of pain, no yearning after bygone things, in your delight in nature?'

He took his hand off my head and was silent for a while.

'Yes, I used to feel that,' he said, as if he were searching his memory, 'especially in spring. I used to sit up all night too, with my yearnings and hopes for company – and good company they were! . . . But life was all before me then. Now it is behind me, and I am content with what I have; and find it excellent,' he added with such convincing nonchalance that, painful as it was for me to hear it, I could not help believing that he spoke the truth.

'And is there nothing you wish for?' I asked.

'I don't ask for impossibilities,' he said, guessing my thoughts. 'You go getting your head wet,' he went on, stroking me as he would a child, and again passing his hand over my damp hair. 'You envy the leaves and the grass because the rain wets them, and you want to be the grass and the leaves and the rain too. But I am content to enjoy them and everything else in the world that is good and young and happy.'

'And you are not homesick for the past?' I persisted, my heart growing heavier and heavier.

He pondered and was silent again. I saw that he was anxious to reply in all sincerity.

'No,' he answered briefly.

'That's not true – it's not true!' I cried, turning towards him and looking into his eyes. 'Do you really not regret the past?'

'No,' he repeated. 'I am grateful for it, but I don't regret it.'

'But would you not like to have it back?' I asked.

He swung round and looked out over the garden.

'I might as well wish I had wings. It would be equally impossible.'

'And would you not like to alter the past? Have you no reproaches for yourself – or me?'

'Never! It was all for the best.'

'Listen!' I said, touching his arm to make him turn and look at me. 'Listen – why did you never say you wanted me to live your way, in the way you wanted? Why did you give me a freedom which I didn't know how to use? Why did you give up teaching me? If you had cared, if you had managed me differently, none of this would have happened,' said I in a voice more and more expressive of cold vexation and reproach, and without a trace of my old love.

'What wouldn't have happened?' he asked, turning to me in surprise. 'Nothing did. Things are all right, quite all right,' he added, smiling.

'Does he really not understand?' I thought. 'Or, worse still, doesn't he want to understand?' And the tears welled into my eyes.

Then I suddenly blurted out: 'I'll tell you what wouldn't have happened. Had you acted differently, I should not now be punished – though I have done you no wrong – by your indifference, your contempt even! It wouldn't have happened that for no fault of mine you took away all that was precious to me.'

'What do you mean, my dear?' he said – he seemed not to understand.

'No, let me speak . . . You have taken from me your trust, your love, even your respect; for I cannot believe, when I think of how it was in the past, that you still love me. No, I must get it all off my chest now – all that has been making me miserable for so long,' I exclaimed, interrupting him again. 'Was it my fault that I knew nothing of life, and you left me to find out for myself? . . . Is it my fault that now, when I have learned the lesson I needed and for nearly a year been struggling to come back to you, you push me away and pretend not to understand what I want – and all in such a manner that it is impossible for you to be blamed, while I am left guilty and unhappy! Yes, you would drive me back to the sort of life which could make us both wretched.'

'But how have I ever shown any such thing?' he asked, in real dismay and amazement.

'Didn't you say to me only yesterday – and aren't you for ever saying – that I could never settle down here, and that we shall have to go back to Petersburg for the winter, Petersburg which I detest?' I went on. 'Instead of giving me some support you avoid all plain speaking: you never say a single frank affectionate word to me. And then, when my failure is complete, you will reproach me and rejoice at my fall.'

'Stop, stop!' he said with calm severity. 'You have no right to say that. It only proves that you bear me ill will, that you don't . . .'

'That I don't love you? Say it, say it!' I said, taking the words out of his mouth, and bursting into tears. I sat down on the bench and hid my face in my handkerchief.

'So this is how he understands me!' I thought, trying to restrain the sobs that choked me. 'Gone, gone is our old love,' a voice in my heart was saying. He did not come over to me, or try to comfort me. He was hurt by what I had said. His voice was dry and composed.

'I don't know what it is you reproach me with,' he began. 'If you mean that I don't love you as I once did . . .'

'Once did!' I murmured into the handkerchief, while the bitter tears soaked it more and more.

'Time is to blame for that, and we ourselves. Each stage in life has its own kind of love . . .' He paused. 'Shall I tell you the whole truth, if you still wish for plain speaking? Just as that first year when I first got to know you I used to lie awake at nights thinking of you and creating my ideal of love, a love which grew and grew in my heart – so in Petersburg and abroad

I spent horrible sleepless nights trying to shatter and destroy the love which was a torment to me. I did not destroy it but I destroyed that part of it which gave me pain. I regained my peace of mind and I still love you, only it is a different kind of love.'

'Yes, you call it love but I call it torture,' I said. 'Why did you let me go into society if you thought it so evil that you ceased to love me because of it?'

'It was not society, my dear,' he said.

'Why did you not use your authority?' I went on. 'Why didn't you lock me up or kill me? I would be better off than I am now, deprived of all that made up my happiness. I should have been happy, instead of being ashamed.'

I began to sob again and hid my face.

At that moment Katya and Sonya, wet and cheerful, came out on to the veranda, full of noisy talk and laughter; seeing us they fell silent and went in again immediately.

For a long time after they had gone we did not speak. I had had my cry, and felt better. I glanced at him. He was sitting leaning his head on his hand, and he tried to make some response to my look, but only sighed deeply and again leaned on his elbow.

I went up to him and took his hand away. His eyes rested musingly on me.

'Yes,' he began, as though continuing his thoughts aloud, 'all of us, and especially you women, must discover for ourselves all the futilities of life in order to come back to life itself: the experience of other people is no good. At that time you were far from having got to the end of that sweet and charming nonsense that I used to enjoy in you, and I left you to have your fill of it, feeling that I had no right to stand in your way, although for me the time for that sort of thing was long past.'

'If you loved me,' I said, 'why did you stand by and allow me to go through with it?'

'Because even if you had wanted to accept my experience you would not have been able to: you had to find out for yourself – and you did.'

'You thought it all out – thought it all out very carefully,' I said. 'You did not love very much.'

We relapsed into silence again.

'That was harsh, what you said just now, but it is the truth,' he exclaimed, suddenly rising to his feet and beginning to walk about the veranda. 'Yes, it's the truth. I was to blame,' he added, stopping opposite me. 'Either I ought not to have allowed myself to love you at all, or I ought to have loved you in a simpler way.'

'Shall we forget it all?' I said timidly.

'No, what's past can never come back – you can never bring it back,' and his voice softened as he spoke.

'It is restored already,' I said, laying a hand on his shoulder.

He took my hand and pressed it.

'I was wrong when I said that I did not regret the past. I do regret it. I weep for that past love which can never return. Who is to blame, I do not know. Love remains, but not the same love; its place remains, but it is all wasted away – there is no strength and substance in it. Memories are left, and gratitude, but . . .'

'Don't say that!' I broke in. 'Let it all be as it was before. It could be, couldn't it?' I asked, looking into his eyes. But his eyes were serene and placid, and did not look deeply into mine.

Even as I was speaking I knew that what I wished and was asking him for was impossible. He smiled a quiet, gentle smile – the smile, it seemed to me, of an old man.

'How young you are still, and I am so old!' he said. 'What you seek in me is no longer there. Why deceive ourselves?' he added, still with the same smile.

I stood beside him in silence, and my heart began to feel more at peace.

'Don't let us try to repeat life,' he went on. 'Don't let us deceive ourselves. And if the old heartaches and emotions no longer exist – well, thank God for that! The excitement and anxiety of searching is over for us: our quest is done and happiness enough has fallen to our lot. It's for us to stand aside now and make way for – yes, look for whom,' he said, pointing to Vanya in the arms of the nurse, who was standing at the veranda door. 'That's the way of it, my dear one,' he concluded, drawing my head towards him and kissing it. It was not a lover, but an old friend who kissed me.

And from the garden the cool fragrance of the night rose sweeter and stronger, the sounds and the stillness fell ever more solemn, star after star began to twinkle in the sky overhead. I looked at him, and suddenly my heart felt easier, as though the sick moral nerve, the cause of my suffering, had been removed. I suddenly realized clearly and calmly that the passionate feeling of that time had passed irrevocably away, like the time itself, and that it would be not only impossible but painful and uncomfortable to bring it back. And indeed had it been so perfect, that time which had seemed to be so happy? And it was all so long, long ago.

'It's time for tea, though!' he said, and we went together to the parlour. At the door we met the nurse with the baby again. I took the child in my arms, covered up his bare little red legs, hugged him to me and brushed my lips against him. Half asleep, he moved his tiny hand with outspread wrinkled fingers, and opened vague eyes, as though seeking or trying to remember. All at once his eyes rested on me, the spark of a thought flashed in them, the chubby pouting lips met and parted into a smile. 'Mine, mine, mine!' I repeated to myself, with a blissful tension in all my limbs, trying not to press him too closely to my breast and hurt him. And I began to kiss the cold little feet, his tummy, his hands and the tiny head with its thin covering of soft hair. My husband came towards me, and I quickly covered the child's face and uncovered it again.

'Ivan Sergeich!' said my husband, chucking him under the chin with a finger. But I made haste to cover Ivan Sergeich up again. None but I should look at him for long. I glanced at my husband; his eyes were laughing as they met mine, and for the first time for many a long month I found it easy and a happiness to look into them.

That day ended the romance of our marriage; what was past became a precious, irrecoverable memory, while a new kind of love for my children and the father of my children laid the foundation of a new life and a quite different happiness which I am still enjoying at the present moment...

—

[*1859*]

THE DEATH OF IVAN ILYICH

I

In the great building of the Law Courts, during an interval in the hearing of the Melvinsky affair, the members of the Court and the public prosecutor gathered together in Ivan Yegorovich Shebek's private room, and the conversation turned on the celebrated Krasovsky case. Fiodr Vassilyevich maintained hotly that it was not subject to their jurisdiction, Ivan Yegorovich argued the contrary, while Piotr Ivanovich, not having entered into the discussion at the start, was taking no part in it but looking through the *Gazette* which had just been brought in.

'Gentlemen!' he exclaimed, 'Ivan Ilyich is dead!'

'No. Really?'

'Here, read for yourself,' replied Piotr Ivanovich, handing Fiodr Vassilyevich the paper fresh from the press and still smelling of ink.

Surrounded by a black border were the words:

With profound sorrow Praskovya Fiodorovna Golovin informs relatives and friends of the demise of her beloved husband, Ivan Ilyich Golovin, member of the Supreme Court, who departed this life on the 4th of February of this year 1882. The funeral will take place on Friday at one o'clock in the afternoon.

Ivan Ilyich had been a colleague of theirs, and they had all liked him. He had been ailing for several weeks with an illness said to be incurable. His post had been kept open but it was generally considered that in the case of his death Alexeyev might be appointed as his successor, with either Vinnikov or Shtabel to succeed Alexeyev. So that on hearing of Ivan Ilyich's death the first thought of each of those present was its possible effect in the way of transfer or promotion for themselves or their associates.

'I am sure to get Shtabel's place, or Vinnikov's, now,' thought Fiodr Vassilyevich. 'I was promised that long ago, and the promotion means another eight hundred roubles a year for me, as well as the allowance for office expenses.'

'I must apply for my brother-in-law's transfer from Kaluga,' thought Piotr Ivanovich. 'My wife will be very pleased. She won't be able to say then that I never do anything for her relations.'

'I thought all along that he would never leave his bed again,' said Piotr Ivanovich aloud. 'A sad business.'

'What exactly was the matter with him?'

'The doctors couldn't say – at least they could, but each of them said something different. When I saw him last, it seemed to me he was improving.'

'And I haven't called once since the holidays. I kept meaning to go.'

'Did he have means?'

'I believe his wife has something. But precious little.'

'Well, we shall have to go and see her. They live a frightful distance off.'

'You mean a long way from you. Everything's a long way from your place.'

'Hear that? – he can never forgive me for living on the other side of the river!' said Piotr Ivanovich, smiling at Shebek. And talking of the distances from one part of the city to another, they returned to court.

Besides the reflections upon the transfers and possible changes in the department likely to result from Ivan Ilyich's decease, the mere fact of the death of an intimate associate aroused, as is usual, in all who heard of it a complacent feeling that 'it is he who is dead, and not I'.

'Now he had to go and die but I manage things better – I am alive,' each of them thought or felt; while Ivan Ilyich's closer acquaintances, his so-called friends, could not help reflecting that now they would have to fulfil the exceedingly tiresome demands of propriety by attending the requiem service and paying a visit of condolence to the widow.

Fiodr Vassilyevich and Piotr Ivanovich had been his nearest acquaintances. Piotr Ivanovich had been a fellow student when they were studying law and considered himself under obligations to him.

Having told his wife during dinner of Ivan Ilyich's death and of his idea that it might be possible to get her brother transferred to their circuit, Piotr Ivanovich, foregoing his customary nap, put on his frock-coat and drove off to Ivan Ilyich's.

Outside Ivan Ilyich's house stood a carriage and two cabs. Leaning against the wall downstairs in the hall near the hat-stand was a coffin-lid covered with a tasselled cloth of gold, the braid of which had been freshened up with metal powder. Two ladies in black were removing their fur cloaks. One of them, Ivan Ilyich's sister, Piotr Ivanovich knew but the other was a stranger to him. His colleague Schwartz was just about to come downstairs but on seeing Piotr Ivanovich he stopped short on the top stair and winked at him as much as to say: 'Ivan Ilyich has made a mess of things – not like you and me.'

Schwartz' face with his Piccadilly whiskers, and his spare figure in the frock-coat, had, as always, an air of elegant solemnity which contrasted with his rollicking nature and had a special piquancy here, or so it seemed to Piotr Ivanovich.

Piotr Ivanovich allowed the ladies to precede him and slowly followed them upstairs. Schwartz did not make any move to descend but waited at the top. Piotr Ivanovich knew why: he obviously wanted to arrange where they should play whist that evening. The ladies went upstairs to the widow; while Schwartz with his firm lips gravely compressed but with a mischievous look in his eyes indicated to Piotr Ivanovich by a twitch of his eyebrows the room to the right where the body lay.

Piotr Ivanovich went in, feeling uncertain, as people always do in such circumstances, as to what would be the proper thing to do there. He only knew that crossing oneself never came amiss on these occasions. But he was not quite sure whether it was also necessary to bow down, so he adopted a middle course: on entering the room he began crossing himself and making a slight movement resembling a bow. At the same time, as far as the movement of hands and head permitted, he surveyed the scene. Two young men, one a high school boy, nephews probably, were coming out of the room, crossing themselves as they did so. An old woman was standing perfectly still, and a lady with queerly arched eyebrows was saying something to her in a whisper. A Church reader in a frock-coat, resolute and hearty, was reading something in a loud voice with an expression that forbade contradiction. The butler's assistant, Gerassim, stepping lightly in front of Piotr Ivanovich, was strewing something on the floor. Noticing this, Piotr Ivanovich was instantly aware of a faint odour of decomposing body. On his last visit to Ivan Ilyich, Piotr Ivanovich had seen Gerassim in the study, acting as sick-nurse, and Ivan Ilyich had been particularly fond of him.

Piotr Ivanovich continued crossing himself and inclining his head in an intermediate direction between the coffin, the reader and the ikons on the table in the corner. Presently, when this action of making the sign of the cross with his hand seemed to him to have gone on quite long enough, he stood still and began to look at the dead man.

The dead man lay, as dead men always do lie, in a peculiarly heavy, dead way, his stiffened limbs sunk in the padding of the coffin, with the head bent back forever on the pillow. His yellow waxen brow with bald patches over the sunken temples was thrust up, after the fashion of dead men, and the prominent nose appeared to press tight down on to the upper lip. He was much altered and had grown even thinner since Piotr Ivanovich had last seen him, but as always is the case with the dead the face was handsomer and, above all, more impressive than it had been when alive. The expression on the face signified that what required to be done had been done, and done rightly. There was reproach, too, in that expression, and a reminder to the living. This reminder seemed out of place to Piotr Ivanovich, or at least to have nothing to do with him. It gave him an unpleasant sort of feeling, and so he hastily crossed himself once more and, as it seemed to him, too hastily and incompatibly with decent observance, turned and went to the door. Schwartz was waiting for him on the landing, standing with legs wide apart and both hands toying with the top hat held behind his back. The mere sight of that sprightly, sleek, elegant figure restored Piotr Ivanovich. He felt that Schwartz was above all these happenings and would not surrender to any depressing influences. His very look said that the incident of a requiem service for Ivan Ilyich could not possibly constitute sufficient grounds for interrupting the recognized order of things – in other words, that nothing could interfere with the unwrapping and cutting of a new pack of cards that very evening while a footman set out four fresh candles; in fact that there was no reason to suppose that this incident could hinder their spending the evening as agreeably as any other evening. Indeed, he said this in a whisper as Piotr Ivanovich passed him, proposing that they should meet for a game at Fiodr Vassilyevich's. But apparently it was not Piotr Ivanovich's destiny to play whist that evening. Praskovya Fiodorovna, a short, fat woman who despite all efforts to the contrary had continued to broaden steadily from the shoulders downwards, all in black, with lace covering her head, and her eyebrows as queerly arched as those of the lady who had been standing beside the coffin, came out of her own apartments with some other ladies, and conducting them to the door of the dead man's room said: 'The service will begin immediately: please go in.'

Schwartz, making a vague bow, remained where he was, obviously neither accepting nor declining this invitation. Praskovya Fiodorovna, recognizing Piotr Ivanovich, sighed, went close up to him, took his hand and said: 'I know you were a true friend of Ivan Ilyich's ...' and looked at him, awaiting some suitable response to her words. Piotr Ivanovich knew that just as it had been the right thing before, in that room, to cross himself, now it was necessary to press the widow's hand, sigh and say: 'Yes, indeed!' And he did so. And as he did so he felt that the desired result had been achieved: that he was moved and she was moved.

'Come,' said the widow. 'They haven't begun yet: I want to have a talk with you. Give me your arm.'

Piotr Ivanovich offered her his arm and they moved towards an inner apartment, passing Schwartz who winked compassionately at Piotr Ivanovich.

'So much for our game! Don't complain if we find another partner. Perhaps you can cut in when you do get away,' said his quizzical glance.

Piotr Ivanovich sighed still more deeply and despondently, and Praskovya Fiodorovna gratefully pressed his arm. When they reached her drawing-room, which was upholstered in pink cretonne and lighted by a dismal-looking lamp, they sat down at the table – she on a sofa and Piotr Ivanovich on a low pouffe with broken springs which yielded spasmodically under his weight. Praskovya Fiodorovna had been on the point of warning him to take another seat but felt that such a remark would have been out of keeping with her situation, and thought better of it. As he sat down on the pouffe Piotr Ivanovich remembered how Ivan Ilyich had arranged this drawing-room and had consulted him about this very pink cretonne with the green leaves. The whole room was full of knicknacks and furniture, and on her way to the sofa the widow caught the lace of her black fichu on the carved edge of the table. Piotr Ivanovich rose to detach it, and the pouffe, released from his weight, bobbed up and bumped him. The widow began detaching the lace herself, and Piotr Ivanovich sat down again, suppressing the mutinous springs of the pouffe under him. But the widow could not quite free herself and Piotr Ivanovich rose again, and again the pouffe rebelled and popped up with a positive snap. When this was all over she took out a clean cambric handkerchief and began to weep. But the episode with the lace and the struggle with the pouffe had put Piotr Ivanovich off, and he sat looking sullen. This awkward situation was interrupted by Sikolov, Ivan Ilyich's butler, who came in to report that the plot in the cemetery which Praskovya Fiodorovna had selected would cost two hundred roubles. She left off weeping and, looking at Piotr Ivanovich with the air of a victim, remarked in French that it was very terrible for her. Piotr Ivanovich made a silent gesture signifying his undoubted belief that it must indeed be so.

'Pray smoke,' she said in a voice at once magnanimous and disconsolate, and began to discuss with the butler the question of the price of the plot for the grave.

Lighting a cigarette, Piotr Ivanovich heard her very circumstantially inquiring into the prices of different plots and finally decide which one to have. When that was done she gave instructions about engaging the choir. The butler departed.

'I see to everything myself,' she said to Piotr Ivanovich, pushing to one side the albums that lay on the table; and noticing that the table was in danger from his cigarette ash she quickly passed him an ash-tray, saying as she did so: 'It would be hypocritical of me to pretend that my grief prevents me from attending to practical affairs. On the contrary, if anything could – I won't say console me but – distract me, it is this seeing after everything to do with him.' She took out her handkerchief again as though preparing for tears but suddenly, as if struggling with her feelings, she shook herself and began to speak calmly: 'However, there is something I want to talk to you about.'

Piotr Ivanovich bowed, keeping control of the springs of the pouffe, which had immediately begun quivering under him.

'The last few days his sufferings were dreadful.'

'He suffered very much?' asked Piotr Ivanovich.

'Oh, dreadfully! At the last he screamed, not for minutes, but for hours on end. During three days and nights he screamed incessantly. It was unendurable. I don't know how I bore it: you could hear him three rooms away. Oh, what I have gone through!'

'And was he really conscious all that time?' asked Piotr Ivanovich.

'Yes,' she whispered, 'to the very end. He said good-bye to us a quarter of an hour before he died, and even asked us to take Volodya away.'

The thought of the sufferings of the man he had known so intimately, first as a light-hearted child, then a youngster at school, and later on, when they were grown up, as a partner at whist, suddenly struck Piotr Ivanovich with horror, in spite of the unpleasant consciousness of his own and this woman's hypocrisy. He again saw that brow, and the nose pressing down on the lip, and was overcome with a feeling of dread on his own account.

'Three days and nights of awful suffering and then death. Why, it might happen to me, all of a sudden, at any moment,' he thought, and for an instant he was terrified. But immediately, he could not have explained how, there came to his support the old reflection that this thing had befallen Ivan Ilyich and not him, and that it ought not and could not happen to him, and that to think that it could meant that he was falling into a melancholy frame of mind, which was a mistake, as the expression on Schwartz' face had made quite clear. After which reflection Piotr Ivanovich cheered up and began to ask with interest about the details of Ivan Ilyich's end, as though death were some mischance to which only Ivan Ilyich was liable, but he himself was not.

After describing at length the really dreadful physical suffering endured by Ivan Ilyich (the details of which Piotr Ivanovich learned only through the effect Ivan Ilyich's agonies had had on the nerves of Praskovya Fiodorovna) the widow apparently thought it time to get to business.

'Ah, Piotr Ivanovich, how distressing it is, how terribly, terribly distressing!' and she burst into tears again.

Piotr Ivanovich sighed and waited for her to finish blowing her nose. When she had done so he said, 'Believe me . . .', and again she began to talk, coming to what was evidently her chief concern with him – namely, to question him as to how she could obtain a grant of money from the government on the occasion of her husband's death. She made it appear that she was asking Piotr Ivanovich's advice about her pension, but he soon realized that she already knew all about it down to the smallest particular, knew more even than he did himself. She knew how much could be got from the government in consequence of her husband's death, but wanted to find out if it would be possible to extract a little more. Piotr Ivanovich tried to think of some way of doing so, but after pondering a while and, out of politeness, condemning the government for its niggardliness, he said it seemed to him nothing more could be got. Then she sighed and was unmistakably beginning to cast about for some means of release from her visitor. Noticing this, he put out his cigarette, rose, pressed her hand and went into the ante-room.

In the dining-room where the clock stood which Ivan Ilyich had liked so much that he bought it in an antique shop Piotr Ivanovich met the priest and a few acquaintances come to attend the service; also a handsome young woman who was Ivan Ilyich's daughter. She was all in black and her slim figure appeared slimmer than ever. She had a gloomy, determined, almost angry expression, and bowed to Piotr Ivanovich as though he were in some way at fault. Behind the daughter, with the same aggrieved look, stood a wealthy young man, whom Piotre Ivanovich also knew, an examining magistrate and her fiancé, as he had heard. He bowed mournfully to them and was about to pass on into the dead man's room, when from under the staircase appeared Ivan Ilyich's schoolboy son, who was extraordinarily like his father. It was Ivan Ilyich over again, as Piotr Ivanovich remembered him when they studied law together. His eyes were red with weeping and had the look seen in the eyes of nasty-minded boys of thirteen or fourteen. When he saw Piotr Ivanovich he scowled morosely and diffidently. Piotr Ivanovich nodded to him and entered the dead man's room. The service began: candles, sighing, incense, tears and sobs. Piotr Ivanovich stood frowning down at his feet. He did not once look at the body, right through to the very end refusing to give way to depressing influences, and was one of the first to leave. There was nobody in the ante-room, but Gerassim, the butler's assistant, came darting out of the dead man's room, tossed over with his strong hands all the fur cloaks to find Piotr Ivanovich's and helped him on with it.

'Well, Gerassim, my friend,' said Piotr Ivanovich, for the sake of saying something. 'A sad affair, isn't it?'

'It's God's will. We shall all come to it some day,' said Gerassim, showing the even white teeth of a peasant – and like a man in the thick of urgent work he briskly opened the front door, hailed the coachman, saw Piotr Ivanovich into the carriage and sprang back to the porch as though occupied with the thought of what he had to do next.

Piotr Ivanovich found the fresh air particularly pleasant after the smell of incense, dead body and disinfectant.

'Where to, sir?' asked the coachman.

'It's not too late. I've still time to call round on Fiodr Vassilyevich.'

And Piotr Ivanovich drove there, and did, in fact, find them just finishing the first rubber, so that he arrived at a quite convenient moment to take a hand.

2

THE story of Ivan Ilyich's life was of the simplest, most ordinary and therefore most terrible.

He had been a member of the Court of Justice and died at

the age of forty-five. He was the son of an official whose career in Petersburg in various ministries and departments had been such as leads men to positions from which, by reason of their long service and the official rank they have attained, they cannot be discharged, although it is obvious that they are unfit to perform any useful duty, and for whom, therefore, posts are specially created, which though fictitious carry salaries of from six to ten thousand roubles that are not fictitious and on which they go on living to an advanced age.

Of such was the Privy Councillor, the superfluous member of various superfluous institutions, Ilya Yefimovich Golovin.

He had three sons, of whom Ivan Ilyich was the second. The eldest son was following in his father's footsteps, only in another ministry, and was already approaching that stage in the Service when inertia is rewarded by a sinecure. The third son was a failure. He had ruined his prospects in a number of positions and was now employed in the department of railways. His father and brothers, and still more their wives, not merely disliked meeting him but avoided remembering his existence unless compelled to do so. His sister had married Baron Greff, a Petersburg official of the same stamp as his father-in-law. Ivan Ilyich was *le phénix de la famille*, as people said. Neither so cold and formal as his elder brother nor as wild as the younger, he was the happy mean between them – an intelligent, polished, lively and agreeable man. He had been educated for the law, along with his younger brother, but the latter had not finished the course, being expelled when in the fifth class. Ivan Ilyich, however, had graduated well. As a student he was already just what he was to remain for the rest of his life: a capable, cheerful, good-natured and sociable fellow, though strict in the performance of what he considered to be his duty; and he considered as his duty whatever was so considered by those in authority over him. Neither as a boy nor as a man had he been one to curry favour, yet there was that about him that from his very earliest years he was attracted, as a fly to the light, by people of high station. He adopted their ways and views on life, and established friendly relations with them. All the enthusiasms of childhood and youth passed without leaving much mark on him; he succumbed to sensuality, and to vanity, and, towards the end of his schooldays, to the idea of liberalism, but always within limits which his instinct unfailingly indicated to him.

As a law student he had done things which had before that seemed to him vile and at the time had made him feel disgusted with himself; but later on when he saw that such conduct was practised by people of high standing and not considered wrong by them, he came not exactly to regard those actions of his as all right but simply to forget them entirely or not be at all troubled by their recollection.

Having taken his degree and qualified for the tenth rank of the Civil Service, and receiving from his father a sum of money for his outfit, Ivan Ilyich ordered clothes for himself at Scharmer's, hung on his watch-chain a medallion inscribed *Respice finem*, took leave of his professor and the prince who was patron of the school, had a farewell dinner with his comrades at Donon's, and with his new fashionable belongings – a trunk, linen, uniform, shaving and toilet requisites and a travelling rug – all ordered and purchased at the very best shops, he set off for one of the provinces to take up the post of confidential clerk and emissary to the governor which had been obtained for him by his father.

In the province Ivan Ilyich soon arranged as easy and agreeable a position for himself as he had enjoyed at the School of Law. He attended to his duties, advanced his career and at the same time led a life of well-bred social gaiety. Now and then he paid official visits to country districts, bearing himself with dignity alike with superiors and inferiors, and fulfilling every commission entrusted to him, which generally related to sectarians, with a scrupulous and incorruptible integrity of which he could only feel proud.

In official matters, despite his youth and taste for frivolous amusements, he was exceedingly reserved, business-like, even severe; but in society he was often amusing and witty, and always good-natured, gentlemanly and *bon enfant*, as the governor and his wife – to whom he was like one of the family – used to say of him.

In the province he had an affair with a lady who threw herself at the elegant young lawyer. There was also a little milliner, and drinking bouts with visiting aides-de-camp, and after-supper excursions to a certain outlying street; and there were, too, some rather dubious efforts to ingratiate himself with his chief, and even his chief's wife; but all this was carried off with such an air of good breeding that no hard names could be applied to it. It all came under the heading of the French saying, '*Il faut que la jeunesse se passe*'.* It was all done with clean hands, in clean linen, with French phrases and, what was of most importance, in the very highest society and consequently with the approval of persons of rank.

Such was Ivan Ilyich's career for five years, and then came a change in his official life. New judicial institutions were introduced, and new men were needed.

Ivan Ilyich became one of these new men.

Ivan Ilyich was offered the post of examining magistrate, and he accepted it in spite of the fact that the post was in another province and he would have to give up the connexions he had formed, and make new ones. His friends who went to see him off had a group photograph taken, and presented him with a silver cigarette-case; and away he went to his new appointment.

As an examining magistrate Ivan Ilyich was just as *comme il faut*, as decorous, as adroit in keeping official duties apart from private life, and as successful in inspiring general respect as he had been as a confidential clerk and emissary. The duties of his new office were vastly more interesting and attractive than those of his previous appointment. In his old post it had been pleasant to stroll from Scharmer's in undress uniform through the crowd of petitioners and petty officials timorously awaiting an audience with the governor, and envying him as he marched with his easy swagger straight into the governor's private room, to sit down with him to tea and a cigarette. But there had been very few people who directly depended upon his good pleasure – only police officials and the sectarians when he went on special missions; and he liked to treat such dependent folk affably, almost as comrades. He liked to make them feel that here was he, who had the power to crush, treating them in this simple, friendly way. Such people were then few in number. But now that he was an examining magistrate Ivan Ilyich felt

* Youth must have its fling. [*Translator's note*]

that everyone – everyone without exception, even the most important and self-sufficient – was in his hands, and that he had only to write certain words on a sheet of paper with a printed heading, and this or that important, self-sufficient person would be brought before him in the capacity of defendant or witness, and if he did not choose to allow him to sit down would have to stand in his presence and respond to his interrogation. Ivan Ilyich never abused his authority: on the contrary, he tried to temper the expression of it. But the consciousness of this power and of the possibility of tempering its effect supplied the chief interest and attraction of his office. In the work itself – in his judicial investigations, that is – Ivan Ilyich very soon acquired the art of eliminating all considerations irrelevant to the legal aspect, and reducing even the most complicated case to a form in which the bare essentials could be presented on paper, with his own personal opinion completely excluded and, what was of paramount importance, observing all the prescribed formalities. The work was new and Ivan Ilyich was one of the first men to put into operation the Code of 1864.

On taking up the office of examining magistrate in a new town Ivan Ilyich made new acquaintances and connexions, established himself anew and adopted a somewhat different tone. He preserved a rather dignified aloofness towards the provincial authorities, while he singled out the top circle among the legal gentlemen and wealthy gentry living in the town with whom his attitude was one of easy-going criticism of the government, together with a moderate form of liberalism and enlightened citizenship. At this time, without making any change in the elegance of his toilet, Ivan Ilyich, in his new dignity, ceased shaving his chin and allowed his beard to grow as it pleased.

Ivan Ilyich settled down once more to a very pleasant existence in the new town. The society in which he moved, and which had a tendency to raise its voice against the governor, was amiable and upper class; his salary was larger, and he began to play whist, which he found added not a little to his enjoyment of life. A good-humoured player, able to think quickly and calculate with finesse, he almost invariably found himself on the winning side.

After a couple of years in the new town Ivan Ilyich met his future wife, Praskovya Fiodorovna Mikhel, who was the most fascinating, clever and brilliant girl in the set in which he moved, and among other recreations and relaxations from his labours as examining magistrate Ivan Ilyich started a light, playful flirtation with Praskovya Fiodorovna.

When he had been a confidential clerk and emissary Ivan Ilyich had hardly missed a dance; now as examining magistrate he danced only as an exception – as if to show that though he served under the reformed order of things, and had reached the fifth official rank, yet when it came to dancing he could still do better than most people. So now and then at the end of the evening he danced with Praskovya Fiodorovna, and it was during these dances that he made his conquest. She fell in love with him. At first Ivan Ilyich had no clearly defined intention of marrying, but when the girl fell in love with him he said to himself: 'After all, why not marry?'

Praskovya Fiodorovna came of a good family, was not bad looking; and there was a little bit of property. Ivan Ilyich might have aspired to a more brilliant marriage, but even this was quite a worthy match. He had his salary, and her private income, he hoped, would come to as much. She was well connected, and was a sweet, pretty and perfectly *comme il faut* young woman. To say that Ivan Ilyich married because he fell in love with his betrothed and found that she sympathized with his views of life would be as untrue as to say that he married because his social circle approved of the match. Ivan Ilyich was influenced by both these considerations: the marriage afforded him personal satisfaction and at the same time he was doing what persons of the loftiest standing looked upon as the correct thing.

So Ivan Ilyich got married.

The wedding ceremony itself and the start of married life with the conjugal caresses, the new furniture, new crockery, new linen, right up to the time his wife became pregnant, were all that could be desired, so that Ivan Ilyich had really begun to think that marriage so far from impairing his easy-going, agreeable, light-hearted and always respectable mode of existence, so approved of by society and regarded by himself as natural, would even add to its charms. But at that point, with the first months of his wife's pregnancy, there appeared a new element, unexpected, unpleasant, tiresome and unseemly, which could never have been anticipated and from which there was no escape.

His wife, without any reason, or so it seemed to Ivan Ilyich, from *gaîté de cœur*,* as he expressed it to himself, began to disturb the enjoyable and decent current of his life. Without any sort of justification she began to be jealous, demanded that he should devote his whole attention to her, found fault with everything and made disagreeable, ill-mannered scenes.

At first Ivan Ilyich hoped to escape from the unpleasantness of this state of affairs by taking the same light-hearted and correct line that had served him so well formerly: he tried to ignore his wife's bad-tempered moods, continued to live in his usual free and easy fashion, invited his friends to the house for a game of cards and tried going to the club and accepting invitations himself. But one day his wife abused him so coarsely and energetically, and so persistently continued thus to abuse him every time he failed to comply with her demands, evidently determined not to stop until he gave in, or in other words agreed to stay at home and be as bored as she was, that Ivan Ilyich's heart sank. He realized that matrimony – at any rate with Praskovya Fiodorovna – was not always conducive to the pleasures and amenities of life but, on the contrary, often infringed both comfort and propriety, and that he must therefore protect himself against such infringement. And Ivan Ilyich began to cast about for means of protection. His official position was the one part of his life which impressed Praskovya Fiodorovna, and Ivan Ilyich began to use his official position and the duties attached to it in this struggle with his wife for independence.

The birth of their child, the attempts to feed it and the various failures to do so, and the real and imaginary illnesses of infant and mother, in which Ivan Ilyich's sympathy was demanded but about which he understood nothing, all made it more and more urgent for Ivan Ilyich to fence off a world for himself outside his family life.

* Sheer wantonness. [*Translator's note*]

As his wife grew more irritable and exacting, so Ivan Ilyich transferred the centre of gravity of his existence from his home life to his work. He became increasingly fond of his official functions, and more ambitious than he had ever been before.

Very soon, within a year of his wedding, Ivan Ilyich had realized that marriage, while affording certain advantages, was in fact a very intricate and difficult business with regard to which, in order to perform one's duty, that is, to lead the decorous life approved by society, one must work out for oneself a definite attitude, just as he had done for his official existence.

And such an attitude Ivan Ilyich did work out for himself in regard to his married life. He required of it only those conveniences – a wife to manage his house, meals and a bed – which it could give him and, in particular, the keeping up of appearances as ordained by public opinion. For the rest he looked for cheerful amiability and if he found it was very grateful: but if he encountered antagonism and peevishness he promptly retreated into his other world of official duties, and there found satisfaction.

Ivan Ilyich was esteemed an excellent magistrate and after three years he was appointed assistant public prosecutor. His new functions, their importance, the possibility of indicting and imprisoning anyone he chose, the publicity his speeches received and the success which attended Ivan Ilyich in this field – all made his work the more attractive.

Children were born to him. His wife grew ever more querulous and ill-tempered, but the line Ivan Ilyich had mapped out for himself so far as his home life was concerned rendered him almost impervious to her grumbling.

After seven years of service in the same town he was transferred to another province with the post of public prosecutor. They moved, money was short and his wife did not like their changed surroundings. Though his salary was higher living was more expensive, besides which two of their children died, and thus family life became still more disagreeable to Ivan Ilyich.

Praskovya Fiodorovna blamed her husband for every reverse that befell them in their new home. Most of the conversations between husband and wife, especially those concerning the children's education, led to topics recalling previous disputes, so that quarrels were apt to flare up at any moment. There remained only those rare periods of amorousness which still came to them at times but which did not last. These were islets at which they put in for a while, only to embark again upon that ocean of concealed hostility that was made apparent in their estrangement from one another. This estrangement might have grieved Ivan Ilyich had he believed that it should not have existed but he had come to regard the situation, not only as normal, but as the goal he aimed at in his domestic life. He aspired to free himself more and more from all the unpleasantnesses and give them a semblance of being decently innocuous. And this he attained by spending less and less time with his family, and when obliged to be at home he tried to safeguard himself by the presence of outsiders. The great thing for Ivan Ilyich, however, was that he had his office. His whole interest now centred in the world of his duties and this interest absorbed him. The sense of his own power, the feeling of being able to ruin anybody he wished to ruin, even the external dignity of his position, when he made his entry into the court or met with his subordinates, the fact that he was successful in the eyes of superiors and subordinates, and, above all, his masterly handling of cases, of which he was conscious – in all these he rejoiced as he did in the chats with his colleagues, the dinners and whist which filled his time. So that, on the whole, Ivan Ilyich's life continued to flow as he considered it should – pleasantly and properly.

Thus things continued for another seven years. His eldest daughter was already sixteen, another child had died, and there remained only one son, a schoolboy and the object of their wrangling. Ivan Ilyvich wanted the lad to study law but to spite him Praskovya Fiodorovna sent him to the high school. The daughter had been educated at home and had turned out well: the boy, too, was not doing badly with his studies.

3

SUCH was the course of Ivan Ilyich's life for seventeen years after his marriage. He was now a public prosecutor of long standing and had declined several offers of transfer in the hope of a still more desirable opening, when an unlooked-for and disagreeable incident quite destroyed the peaceful tenor of his existence. He was expecting to be appointed presiding judge in a university town but Hoppe somehow stole a march on him and secured the nomination. Ivan Ilyich was nettled, accused Hoppe and quarrelled both with him and with his immediate superiors. A coolness sprang up towards him and he was again passed over when the next appointment was made.

This was in 1880, the hardest year of Ivan Ilyich's life. In this year it became evident, on the one hand that his salary was insufficient and on the other that he had been forgotten by everybody, and that what seemed to him the most monstrous and cruellest injustice appeared to others as a perfectly usual occurrence. Even his father did not feel called upon to help him. Ivan Ilyich felt that every one had deserted him, and that they all regarded his position with a salary of three thousand five hundred roubles as quite normal, even fortunate. He alone knew that, what with the injustices he had suffered, his wife's everlasting nagging, and the debts that were beginning to accumulate through living beyond his means – he alone knew that his position was far from being a normal one.

In order to ease his expenses that year he obtained leave of absence and went with his wife to spend the summer in the country at her brother's.

In the country, with no official duties to occupy him, Ivan Ilyich for the first time in his life experienced not merely *ennui* but intolerable depression, and decided that things could not go on like that, and that he absolutely must take immediate and energetic measures.

After a sleepless night passed pacing up and down the veranda he made up his mind to go to Petersburg and bestir himself, in order to get transferred to another ministry and punish *them*, meaning the people who had not known how to appreciate him.

Next day, in spite of all the efforts of his wife and her brother to dissuade him, he departed for Petersburg.

He went with a single object in view : to obtain a post with a salary of five thousand roubles. He was not particular now about any special ministry, or about following any special bent or about the sort of work that would be required of him. All he wanted was an appointment to another post with a salary of five thousand, either in the administrative services, in the banking department, with the railways, in one of the Empress Maria's institutions, even in the Customs – so long as it carried with it a salary of five thousand roubles and took him away from the department where he had not been appreciated.

And behold, this excursion of Ivan Ilyich's was crowned with amazing, unlooked-for success. At Kursk an acquaintance of his, F. S. Ilyin, got into the same first-class carriage and told him of a telegram just received by the governor of Kursk announcing a change about to take place in the ministry – Piotr Ivanovich was to be superseded by Ivan Semeonovich.

The proposed change, apart from its significance for Russia, had a special significance for Ivan Ilyich inasmuch as by bringing to the front a new man, Piotr Petrovich, and no doubt with him his friend Zahar Ivanovich, it was highly favourable for Ivan Ilyich, since Zahar Ivanovich was a friend and colleague of his.

In Moscow the news was confirmed, and on reaching Petersburg Ivan Ilyich sought out Zahar Ivanovich and received a definite promise of an appointment in his old department, the Ministry of Justice.

A week later he telegraphed to his wife : '*At first opportunity Zahar to appoint me Miller's place.*'

Thanks to this change of personnel, Ivan Ilyich unexpectedly obtained in his old ministry an appointment which placed him two ranks above his former colleagues, besides providing him with an income of five thousand roubles plus three thousand five hundred for the expenses connected with his move. All his grievances against his former enemies and the whole department were forgotten, and Ivan Ilyich was completely happy.

He returned to the country in better spirits and more contented than he had been for a long time. Praskovya Fiodorovna cheered up too, and a truce was concluded between them. Ivan Ilyich had a lot to tell about the respect with which he had been treated in Petersburg, how all those who had been his enemies had been humbled and now fawned on him, how envious they all were of his appointment, and, in particular, how much everybody in Petersburg had liked him.

Praskovya Fiodorovna listened to all this and pretended to believe it, not contradicting him in anything but confining herself to making plans for their new life in the city to which they were going. And Ivan Ilyich perceived with delight that these plans were his plans, that he and his wife were in agreement and that his life after the disturbing hitch in its progress was about to regain its true and natural character of gaiety and decorum.

Ivan Ilyich had come back to the country for a short stay only: he had to enter upon his new duties on the 10th of September. Moreover, he needed a little time to settle into the new place, move all his belongings from the province, and order a good many other things: in short, to establish himself in the fashion he had already decided on and which coincided with Praskovya Fiodorovna's ideas too.

And now that everything had happened so fortunately, and he and his wife were at one in their aims and, in addition, were so little together, they got on better than they had done since the first years of their marriage. Ivan Ilyich had thought of taking his family with him at once but his wife's brother and her sister-in-law, who had suddenly become extraordinarily cordial and friendly to them all, would not hear of it, so Ivan Ilyich had to go alone.

So Ivan Ilyich departed, and the happy frame of mind induced by his success and the harmony between him and his wife, the one intensifying the other, did not leave him. He found a charming set of apartments, the very thing husband and wife had dreamed of. Spacious, lofty reception-rooms in the old style, a comfortable, impressive-looking study, rooms for his wife and daughter, a schoolroom for his son – it might have been expressly designed for them. Ivan Ilyich himself superintended the arrangements, selected the wallpapers, bought more furniture (generally antiques which he considered particularly *comme il faut*) and supervised the upholstering; and it all progressed and progressed and approached the ideal he had set himself. Even when things were only half finished they exceeded his expectations. He saw what a refined character, elegant and free from vulgarity, it would all have when completed. As he fell asleep at night he would picture to himself how the reception-room would look. Surveying the as yet unfinished drawing-room he could see the hearth, the screen, the *étagère* and the little chairs dotted here and there, the dishes and plates on the walls, and the bronzes, as they would appear when everything was in place. He was delighted with the thought of how struck his wife and daughter would be, both of whom were also possessed of taste in these matters. They would never expect anything like this. He had been particularly successful in discovering and buying for a song old pieces of furniture which gave an exceptionally aristocratic air to the whole place. In his letters he purposely disparaged everything so as to give them a surprise. All this so absorbed him that his new duties, much as he liked his official work, interested him less than he had expected. Sometime he even had moments of inattention during the Sessions because he was pondering whether to have straight or curved cornices with his curtains. He was so taken up with it all that he often did things himself, rearranging the furniture or the hangings. Once when mounting a step-ladder to show a workman, who did not understand, how he wanted some material draped, he made a false step and slipped, but being a strong and agile person he clung on and only knocked his side against the knob of the window frame. The bruise was painful but it soon passed off. All this time, indeed, Ivan Ilyich felt particularly alert and well. 'I feel fifteen years younger,' he wrote. He thought to have everything finished and ready by September but it dragged on till mid-October. Still, the result was charming – it was not only his opinion but that of everyone who saw it.

In reality it was just what is commonly seen in the houses of people who are not exactly wealthy but who want to look like wealthy people, and so succeed only in looking like all the others of their kind: there were damasks, ebony, plants, rugs and bronzes, everything sombre and highly polished – all the things people of a certain class have in order to resemble other people of that class. And in his case it was all so like that it made no impression at all; but to him it all seemed to be something special. When he met his family at the railway-station and brought them to the newly decorated apartments, all lighted up in readiness, and a footman in white tie opened the door into the hall which was arranged with flowers, and then they walked into the drawing-room and the study, uttering cries of delight, he was very happy, conducting them everywhere and drinking in their praises eagerly, beaming with pleasure. At tea that evening when Praskovya Fiodorovna among other things asked about his fall he laughed and showed them how he had gone flying and how he had frightened the upholsterer.

'It's a good thing I'm a bit of an athlete. Another man might have killed himself, whereas I got nothing worse than a knock here. It hurts if you touch it, but it's wearing off already – it's merely a bruise.'

So life began in their new abode, and, as always happens, when they were thoroughly settled in they found they were just one room short; and with their increased incomes – although they found, as always happens, that another five hundred roubles would have made all the difference – everything was very nice. Things went particularly well at first, before everything was finally arranged, and there was still something to do to the place: this to buy and that to order, this piece of furniture to be moved and that adjusted. And although there were occasional disputes between husband and wife, both were so well satisfied, and there was so much to do, that it all went off without any serious quarrels. When, however, there was nothing left to decide it became rather dull and something seemed to be lacking, but by then they were making new acquaintances, getting into a routine, and their lives were full.

Ivan Ilyich, after spending the morning at the Law Courts, came home to dinner, and at first he was generally in a good humour, although this was apt to be upset a little, and precisely on account of the new house. (Every spot on the tablecloth or the upholstery, a frayed tassel on the window-blind, irritated him: he had taken such trouble to arrange it all that it hurt him to have things spoiled.) But on the whole Ivan Ilyich's life ran its course as he believed life should: easily, agreeably and decorously. He got up at nine, drank his coffee, read the newspaper, then donned his undress uniform and went to the Law Courts. There he fell instantly into his well-worn harness and prepared to deal with petitions, inquiries in the office, the office itself, and the sessions – public and administrative. In all this the thing was to exclude everything with the sap of life in it, which always disturbs the regular round of official business, and not to admit any sort of relations with people except official relations, and then only on official grounds. For instance, a man might come anxious for certain information. Ivan Ilyich, not being the functionary in whose sphere the matter lay, would have nothing to do with him; but if the man had business that came within his official competence, something that could be committed to officially stamped paper, then within the limits of such official relations Ivan Ilyich would do everything he could, and in doing so would maintain the semblance of friendly human relations, that is, would observe the courtesies of social intercourse. But where official relations ended, so did every other form of human contact. This art of isolating the official part of his life from his real life, Ivan Ilyich possessed in the highest degree, and long practice combined with natural aptitude had developed it to such a pitch of perfection that at times in the manner of a virtuoso he would permit himself, in short, as it were, to intermingle his human and his official relations. He allowed himself to do this just because he felt that he could at any time he chose resume the purely official line and drop the human attitude. And Ivan Ilyich did it all not only smoothly, pleasantly and correctly but even artistically. In the intervals between sessions he smoked, drank tea, chatted a little about politics, a little about affairs in general, a little about cards, but most of all about appointments in the Service. And tired but feeling like some artist – one of the first violins in the orchestra – who has given a perfect performance, he would return home. At home mother and daughter had been out paying calls, or had a visitor, and his son had been to school, had been preparing his lessons with his tutor and was duly learning what it is they teach at high schools. Everything was as it should be. After dinner, if there were no visitors, Ivan Ilyich sometimes read some book that was being talked about, and in the evening would settle down to work, that is, read official papers, consulted the statute books and examined witnesses' statements, noting down the paragraphs of the Code which applied to them. This he found neither tiresome nor entertaining. It was tiresome when he might have been playing whist but if no whist was available it was at any rate better than doing nothing or sitting with his wife. Ivan Ilyich's chief pleasure was giving the little dinners to which he invited ladies and gentlemen of good social position, and just as his drawing-room resembled all other drawing-rooms, so did his enjoyable little parties resemble all other such parties.

Once they even gave an evening party with dancing. Ivan Ilyich himself enjoyed it, and everything went well, except that it led to a violent quarrel with his wife over the refreshments. Praskovya Fiodorovna had her own ideas but Ivan Ilyich insisted on getting everything from an expensive confectioner and ordered too many cakes, and the quarrel arose because cakes were left over and the confectioner's bill came to forty-five roubles. It was a violent and disagreeable quarrel, inasmuch as Praskovya Fiodorovna called him 'a fool and an imbecile', and he clutched at his head and muttered angrily about a divorce. But the evening itself was enjoyable. The best people were there, and Ivan Ilyich danced with Princess Trufonov, a sister of the one so well known in connexion with the charitable institution 'Bear my Burden'. His pleasures where his work was concerned lay in the gratification of ambition; his social pleasures lay in the gratification of his vanity; but his real delight was playing whist. He was ready to confess that whatever disagreeable incident happened in his life, the joy which beamed bright as a flame over all the others came of sitting down to whist with good players, not noisy partners, and of course to four-handed whist (with five players it was annoying to have to stand out, though one pretended not to mind a bit), to play an intelligent, serious game (when the cards allowed), then supper and a glass of wine. And when he went to bed after whist, especially if he had won a little (to win a large sum is uncomfortable), Ivan Ilyich would lie down to sleep in a particularly happy frame of mind.

So they lived. They moved in the very best circles, and were visited by persons of consequence and by young people.

As regards the circle of their acquaintances husband, wife and daughter were quite agreed, and by tacit consent they shook off and rid themselves of various shabby friends and relatives who came fawning around them in their drawing-room with the Japanese plates on the walls. Very soon these down-at-heel persons ceased to flutter round them and only the very best people were seen at the Golovins'. Young men came courting Liza, and an examining magistrate, Petrishchev, Dmitri Ivanovich Petrishchev's son and sole heir, began to be so attentive to her that Ivan Ilyich started to consult his wife as to whether it would not be a good plan to arrange a sledge drive for them, or get up some private theatricals. So they lived. And everything continued in the same way, without a reverse, and it was all very pleasant.

4

THE whole family was in good health. Ivan Ilyich sometimes complained of a queer taste in his mouth and a sort of uncomfortable feeling on the left side of the stomach, but one could hardly call that illness.

But this uncomfortable feeling got worse and, though not exactly painful, grew into a sense of pressure in his side accompanied by low spirits and irritability. The irritability became worse and worse and began to mar the agreeable, easy, seemly existence the Golovins had settled down to. Husband and wife quarrelled more and more frequently, and before long all the easiness and amenity of life had fallen away and it was with difficulty that they managed to preserve appearances. As before, there were repeated scenes, until very few of those islets in the sea of contention remained on which husband and wife could meet without an explosion. And Praskovya Fiodorovna said, not without justification now, that her husband had a trying temper. With characteristic exaggeration she maintained that he had always had a dreadful temper, and that it had needed all her good nature to put up with it for twenty years. It was true that now he was the one to begin the quarrels. His gusts of temper always broke out as they were sitting down to dinner, often just as he was beginning the soup. He would observe that a plate or dish had been chipped, or the food did not taste as it should, or his son put his elbow on the table, or his daughter's hair was not done properly. And whatever it was, he blamed Praskovya Fiodorovna. At first she had answered in kind, and said disagreeable things to him, but once or twice, just at the start of dinner, he had flown into such a frenzy that she realized it was due to some physical derangement brought on by eating, and so she restrained herself and did not reply but simply made haste to get the meal over. Praskovya Fiodorovna took great credit to herself for this exercise of self-control. Having come to the conclusion that her husband had a frightful temper and made her life wretched, she began to feel sorry for herself. And the more she pitied herself the more she detested her husband. She began to wish he would die, yet she did not want him dead because then there would be no salary. And this made her still more exasperated with him. She regarded herself as terribly unhappy precisely because not even his death could bring deliverance, and, though she concealed her irritation, that hidden bitterness of hers increased his irritability.

After one scene in which Ivan Ilyich had been particularly unfair, and after which he had said in explanation that he certainly was irritable but that it was due to his not being well, she had told him that if he were ill it should be attended to, and had insisted on his going to see a celebrated doctor.

He went. The whole procedure followed the lines he expected it would; everything was as it always is. There was the usual period in the waiting-room, and the important manner assumed by the doctor – he was familiar with that air of professional dignity: he adopted it himself in court – and the sounding and listening and questions that called for answers that were foregone conclusions and obviously unnecessary, and the weighty look which implied, You just leave it all to us, and we'll arrange matters – we know all about it and can see to it in exactly the same way as we would for any other man. The entire procedure was just the same as in the Law Courts. The airs that he put on in court for the benefit of the prisoner at the bar, the doctor now put on for him.

The doctor said that this and that symptom indicated this and that wrong with the patient's inside, but if this diagnosis were not confirmed by analysis of so-and-so, then we must assume such-and-such. If then we assume such-and-such, then ... and so on. To Ivan Ilyich only one question was important: was his case serious or not? But the doctor ignored this misplaced inquiry. From the doctor's point of view it was a side issue not under consideration: the real business was the assessing of probabilities to decide between a floating kidney, chronic catarrh or appendicitis. It was not a question of Ivan Ilyich's life or death but one between a floating kidney or appendicitis. And this question the doctor, in Ivan Ilyich's presence, settled most brilliantly in favour of the appendix, with the reservation that analysis of the urine might provide a new clue and then the case would have to be reconsidered. All this was to an iota precisely what Ivan Ilyich himself had done in equally brilliant fashion a thousand times over in dealing with persons on trial. The doctor summed up just as brilliantly, looking over his spectacles triumphantly, gaily even, at the accused. From the doctor's summing-up Ivan Ilyich concluded that things looked bad, but that for the doctor, and most likely for everybody else, it was a matter of indifference, though for him it was bad. And this conclusion struck him painfully, arousing in him a great feeling of pity for himself, and of bitterness towards the doctor who could be unconcerned about a matter of such importance.

But he said nothing. He rose, placed the doctor's fee on the table and remarked with a sigh, 'We sick people no doubt often put inappropriate questions. But tell me, in general, is this complaint dangerous or not?'

The doctor regarded him sternly over his spectacles with one eye, as though to say, 'Prisoner at the bar, if you will not keep to the questions put to you, I shall be obliged to have you removed from the court.'

'I have already told you what I consider necessary and proper,' said the doctor. 'The analysis may show something more.' And the doctor bowed.

Ivan Ilyich went out slowly, seated himself dejectedly in his sledge and drove home. All the way home he kept going over what the doctor had said, trying to translate all those involved, obscure, scientific phrases into plain language and find in them an answer to the question, 'Am I in a bad way – a very bad way – or is it nothing after all?' And it seemed to him that the upshot of all that the doctor had said was that he *was* in a very bad way. Everything in the streets appeared depressing to Ivan Ilyich. The sledge-drivers looked dismal, so did the houses, the passers-by and the shops. And this pain, this dull gnawing ache that never ceased for a second, seemed, when taken in conjunction with the doctor's enigmatical utterances, to have acquired a fresh and far more serious significance. With a new sense of misery Ivan Ilyich now paid constant heed to it.

He reached home and began to tell his wife about it. She listened but in the middle of his account his daughter came in with her hat on, ready to go out with her mother. Reluctantly she half sat down to listen to this tiresome story, but she could not be patient for long, and her mother did not hear him to the end.

'Well, I am very glad,' she said. 'You must be careful now and take the medicine regularly. Give me the prescription: I will send Gerassim to the chemist's.' And she went away to dress.

He had hardly paused to take breath while she was in the room, and he heaved a deep sigh when she was gone.

'Well,' he said to himself, 'perhaps it's nothing after all ...'

He began taking the medicine and to carry out the doctor's instructions, which were altered after analysis of the urine. But it was just at this point that some confusion arose in connexion with the analysis and what ought to have followed from it. The doctor himself, of course, could not be blamed, but the fact was that things had not gone as the doctor had told him, and that he had either forgotten, or blundered, or was hiding something from him.

Nevertheless, Ivan Ilyich still continued to obey the doctor's orders, and at first found some comfort in so doing.

From the time of his visit to the doctor Ivan Ilyich's principal occupation became the exact observance of the doctor's prescriptions regarding hygiene and the taking of medicine, and watching the symptoms of his malady and the general functioning of his body. His chief interests came to be people's ailments and people's health. When sickness, deaths or recoveries were mentioned in his presence, especially when the illness resembled his own, he would listen, trying to conceal his agitation, ask questions and apply what he heard to his own case.

The pain did not grow less but Ivan Ilyich made great efforts to force himself to believe that he was better. And he was able to deceive himself so long as nothing happened to excite him. But the moment there was any unpleasantness with his wife, or he suffered any rebuff in court or held bad cards at bridge, he was at once acutely sensible of his illness. In former days he had borne with such mishaps, hoping soon to correct what was wrong, to master it and be successful, to make a grand slam. But now every reverse upset him and plunged him into despair. He would say to himself: 'There now, no sooner do I feel a little better, no sooner does the medicine begin to take effect, than I have this cursed piece of bad luck, this disappointment ...' And he would break out against his bad luck or against the people who were causing him the disappointment and killing him, and he felt how these bursts of passion were killing him but he could not restrain himself. One would have thought it ought to have been quite obvious to him that this exasperation with circumstances and people could only aggravate his illness, and therefore he ought not to pay any attention to disagreeable incidents. But he came to exactly the opposite conclusion: he said to himself that he needed peace, and was on the watch for everything that disturbed this peace, and flew into a rage at the slightest infringement of it. His condition was rendered worse by the fact that he read medical books and consulted doctors. The progress of his disease was so gradual that, comparing one day with another, he was able to deceive himself, so slight was the difference. But when he consulted the doctors it seemed to him that he was getting worse, and very rapidly worse. Yet despite this he was continually consulting doctors.

That month he went to see another medical celebrity. The second celebrity said pretty much the same as the first, only he propounded his questions differently; and the interview with this celebrity only redoubled Ivan Ilyich's doubts and fears. Then a friend of a friend of his, a very good doctor, diagnosed his malady quite otherwise, and, though he predicted recovery, his questions and hypotheses still further confused Ivan Ilyich and increased his scepticism. A homoeopath made a different diagnosis still, and gave him a medicine which Ivan Ilyich took secretly for a week; but at the end, not feeling any relief and losing confidence both in his former drugs and this new treatment, he became more despondent than ever. One day a lady of his acquaintance mentioned a cure effected by means of wonder-working ikons. Ivan Ilyich caught himself listening intently and beginning to believe in the story as actual fact. This incident alarmed him. 'Can my mind have degenerated to such a point?' he asked himself. 'It's all nonsense, rubbish! I mustn't give way to nervous fears but choose a single doctor and keep strictly to his treatment. That's what I will do. Now it's settled. I will think no more about it but stick to the treatment until the summer, and then we shall see. From now on there must be no more of this wavering!' This was easy to say but impossible to put into practice. The pain in his side harassed him and seemed to grow worse and more incessant, while the taste in his mouth grew more and more peculiar. It seemed to him that his breath smelled very nasty, and his appetite and strength continually dwindled. There was no deceiving himself: something terrible, new and significant, more significant than anything that had ever happened in his life, was taking place within him of which he alone was aware. Those about him did not understand, or refused to understand, and believed that everything in the world was going on as usual. This thought tormented Ivan Ilyich more than anything. He saw that his household, especially his wife and daughter who were absorbed in a perfect whirl of visiting, had no conception at all and were annoyed with him for being so depressed and exacting, as though he were to be blamed for that. Even though they tried to disguise it he could see that he was in their way; but that his wife had taken up a definite line in regard to his illness and adhered to it, no matter what he might say or do. Her attitude was this: 'You know,' she would say to her friends, 'Ivan Ilyich can't do as other people do, and keep to the treatment prescribed for him. One day he'll take his drops and keep carefully to his diet and go to bed at the right time; but the next day, if I don't see to it, he will suddenly forget his medicine, eat sturgeon – which is forbidden him – and sit up playing cards until one in the morning.'

'Oh come, when did I do that?' Ivan Ilyich would ask in vexation. 'Only once at Piotr Ivanovich's.'

'What about yesterday with Shebek?'

'It makes no difference, I couldn't have slept for pain ...'

'Be that as it may, but you'll never get well like that, and you make us wretched.'

Praskovya Fiodorovna's attitude to Ivan Ilyich's illness, openly expressed to others and to himself, implied that the whole illness was Ivan Ilyich's own fault and just another of the annoyances he was causing his wife. Ivan Ilyich felt that this opinion escaped her involuntarily, but it was none the easier to bear for all that.

At the Law Courts, too, Ivan Ilyich noticed or fancied he noticed the same strange sort of attitude to himself. At one time it would seem to him that people were watching him inquisitively, as a man who would shortly have to give up his post. Then all at once his friends would begin to rally him in an amicable way about his nervous fears, as though that nightmare thing that was going on inside him, incessantly gnawing at him and irresistibly dragging him away, were the pleasantest subject in the world for raillery. Schwartz in particular irritated him with his high spirits, vitality and correctness, which reminded him of what he himself had been ten years before.

Friends would drop in for a game of cards. They sat down at the card-table; they dealt, bending the new cards to soften them, and he sorted the diamonds in his hand and found he had seven. His partner said, 'No trumps' and supported him with two diamonds. What could be better? It should have been jolly and lively – they would make a grand slam. And suddenly Ivan Ilyich is conscious of that gnawing ache, that taste in his mouth, and it strikes him as grotesque that in such circumstances he could take any pleasure in making a grand slam.

He would look at his partner Mihail Mihailovich tapping on the table with his confident hand, and instead of snatching up the tricks pushing the cards politely and condescendingly towards Ivan Ilyich that he might have the satisfaction of gathering them up without the trouble of stretching out his hand for them. 'Does he suppose I'm so weak that I can't stretch my arm out?' thinks Ivan Ilyich, and he forgets the trumps, and trumps his partner's cards and misses the grand slam by three tricks. And the most awful thing of all is that he sees how upset Mihail Mihailovich is about it, whereas he does not care at all. And it is awful to think why he doesn't care.

They all see that he is in pain, and say to him: 'We can stop if you are tired. You go and lie down.' Lie down? No, he's not in the least tired, and they finish the rubber. They are all gloomy and silent. Ivan Ilyich feels that it is he who has cast this gloom upon them, and he cannot disperse it. They have supper, and the party breaks up, and Ivan Ilyich is left alone with the consciousness that his life is poisoned for him and that he is poisoning the lives of others, and that this poison is not losing its force but is working its way deeper and deeper into his whole being.

And with the consciousness of this, and with the physical pain in addition, and the terror in addition to that, he must go to bed, often to lie awake with the pain for the greater part of the night. And in the morning he must needs get up again, dress, go to the Law Courts, speak, write, or, if he does not go out, stay at home for all the four-and-twenty hours of the day and night, each one of which is torture. And he had to live thus on the edge of the precipice alone, without a single soul to understand and feel for him.

5

So one month succeeded another. Just before the New Year his brother-in-law arrived in town and came to stay with them. Ivan Ilyich was at the Law Courts. Praskovya Fiodorovna had gone out shopping. Coming home and going into his study, Ivan Ilyich found his brother-in-law there, a healthy, florid man, unpacking his portmanteau himself. He raised his head on hearing Ivan Ilyich's footsteps and for a second stared up at him without a word. That look told Ivan Ilyich everything. His brother-in-law opened his mouth to utter an exclamation of dismay but checked himself. That movement confirmed everything

'Changed, have I?'

'Yes . . . there is a change.'

And after that, try as he would to get his brother-in-law to return to the subject of his looks, the latter maintained an obstinate silence. Praskovya Fiodorovna came back, and her brother went to her room. Ivan Ilyich locked the door and began to examine himself in the glass, first full face, then in profile. He picked up a portrait of himself taken with his wife, and compared it with what he saw in the glass. The change in him was enormous. Then he bared his arms to the elbow, looked at them, pulled down his sleeves, sat down on the ottoman and felt blacker than night.

'No, no, this won't do!' he said to himself, sprang to his feet, went to the table, opened some official document and began to read, but could not go on with it. He unlocked the door and went into the drawing-room. The parlour door was shut. He approached it on tiptoe and listened.

'No, you are exaggerating,' Praskovya Fiodorovna was saying.

'Exaggerating? Why, surely you can see for yourself – he's a dead man! Look at his eyes – there's no light in them. But what is it that is wrong with him?'

'Nobody knows. Nikolayev' (that was another doctor) 'said something, but I don't know what. Leshchetitsky' (this was the celebrated specialist) 'says the opposite.'

Ivan Ilyich walked away, went to his own room, lay down and began to think: 'The kidney, a floating kidney.' He recalled all that the doctors had told him of how it had detached itself and was floating about. And by an effort of imagination he tried to catch that kidney and arrest and make it firm. So little was needed for this, it seemed to him. 'No, I must go and see Piotr Ivanovich again.' (This was the friend who had a friend who was a doctor.) He rang, ordered the carriage and got ready to go out.

'Where are you off to, *Jean*?' asked his wife, with a peculiarly melancholy and unusually gentle expression.

This unusual gentleness infuriated him. He looked at her grimly.

'I want to see Piotr Ivanovich.'

He drove off to the friend who had a friend who was a

doctor, and together they went to the doctor's. He was in, and Ivan Ilyich had a long conversation with him.

Reviewing the anatomical and physiological details of what in the doctor's opinion was going on inside him, he understood it all.

There was just one little thing – the least trifle – wrong in the intestinal appendix. It might all come right. Stimulate one sluggish organ, check the activity of another – secretion ensues, and everything would come right. He was a little late for dinner. He ate and talked cheerfully but it was a long time before he could bring himself to go back and work in his own room. At last he went to his study and at once sat down to his official papers. He read his legal documents and laboured over them, but he was conscious all the time that he had put something aside – an important, private matter – which he would revert to when his work was done. When he had finished he remembered that this private matter was the thought of his intestinal appendix. But he did not give himself up to it: he went into the drawing-room for tea. Visitors had called, among them the examining magistrate who was a desirable match for his daughter, and they were conversing, playing the piano and singing. Ivan Ilyich, as Praskovya Fiodorovna remarked, spent the evening in better spirits than on other occasions, but he never forgot that there was that important matter of the intestinal appendix waiting to be considered. At eleven o'clock he said good-night and went to bed. He had slept alone since his illness in a little room adjoining his study. He undressed and took up a novel by Zola, but instead of reading it he fell to thinking. And in his imagination that desired improvement in the intestinal appendix took place. Secretion, evacuation were stimulated: regular action re-established. 'Yes, that's it!' he said to himself. 'One only has to assist nature, that's all.' He remembered his medicine, sat up, swallowed it and lay down on his back, watching for the medicine to have its salutary effect and stop the pain. 'All I have to do is to take it regularly and avoid harmful influences. Why, I am better already, much better.' He began to feel his side: it was not painful to the touch. 'There, I really don't feel it. It's much better already.' He put out the light and turned on his side ... 'The appendix is righting itself, secretion is occurring.' Suddenly he felt the old familiar, dull, gnawing pain, the same obstinate, steady, serious pain. In his mouth there was the same familiar loathsome taste. His heart sank, his brain felt dazed. 'O God, O God!' he whispered. 'Here it is again! And it will never cease.' And in a flash the trouble presented itself in quite a different guise. 'Intestinal appendix! The kidney!' he said to himself. 'It's not a question of appendix or kidney but of life and ... death. Yes, once there was life, and now it is drifting away, drifting away, and I can't stop it. Yes. Why deceive myself? Isn't it obvious to everyone but me that I am dying, and that it's only a matter of weeks, days ... it may happen this very moment. There was light but now there is darkness. I was here but now I am going. Where?' A cold chill came over him, his breathing ceased, and he heard only the throbbing of his heart.

'I shall be no more, then what will there be? There will be nothing. Then where shall I be when I am no more? Can this be dying? No, I will not have it!' He jumped up and tried to light the candle, fumbled about with trembling hands, dropped candle and candlestick on the floor and fell back upon the pillow. 'What's the use? It makes no difference,' he said to himself, staring with wide-open eyes into the darkness. 'Death. Yes, death. And they none of them understand, or want to understand, and they feel no pity for me. They are enjoying themselves.' (He heard through the closed door the distant cadence of a song and its accompaniment.) 'They don't care, but they will die too. Fools! 'Twill be a little sooner for me and a little later for them, that's all; their turn will come. But now they are making merry. The brutes!' Anger choked him. And he was agonizingly, intolerably wretched. 'It cannot be that all men always have been doomed to suffer this awful horror!' He raised himself.

'I ought not to go on like this: I must be calm, I must think it all over from the beginning.' And here he began to reflect. 'Yes, the beginning of my illness. I knocked my side but I was still all right that day and the next. It hurt a little, then it got worse, then I went to doctors, then there followed depression, misery and more doctors; and all the time I got nearer and nearer to the abyss. My strength began to fail. Nearer and nearer! And now I have wasted away and there is no light in my eyes. Death is here, and I am thinking of an appendix! I am thinking of how to get my bowels in order, while death knocks at the door. Can it really be death?' Terror seized him again and he gasped for breath. He leant down and began feeling for the matches, pressing with his elbow on the little pedestal table beside the bed. It was in his way and hurt him, he lost his temper with it, pressed upon it still harder in his anger and overturned it. Breathless and in despair, he fell back, expecting death that instant.

Meanwhile the visitors were departing. Praskovya Fiodorovna was seeing them off. She heard something fall and came in.

'What is the matter?'

'Nothing. I accidentally knocked it over.'

She went out and returned with a candle. He lay there panting heavily, like a man who has run a mile, staring at her with fixed eyes.

'What is it, *Jean*?'

'No-othing. I up-set it.' ('Why speak of it? She won't understand,' he thought.)

And, indeed, she did not understand. She picked up the candle and lit it for him, and hurried away to say good-night to another visitor.

When she came back he was lying in the same position on his back, gazing at the ceiling.

'What is the matter? Are you feeling worse?'

'Yes.'

She shook her head and sat down.

'Do you know, *Jean*, I think we had better ask Leshchetitsky to come here.'

That meant, send for the celebrated specialist and not mind the expense. He smiled venomously and said 'No.' She sat a moment longer and then came up to him and kissed his forehead.

He hated her from the bottom of his soul while she was kissing him, and with difficulty refrained from pushing her away.

'Good-night. Please God you'll sleep.'

'Yes.'

6

IVAN Ilyich saw that he was dying, and he was in continual despair.

In the depths of his heart he knew he was dying but, so far from growing used to the idea, he simply did not and could not grasp it.

The example of a syllogism which he had learned in Kiezewetter's *Logic*: 'Caius is a man, men are mortal, therefore Caius is mortal,' had seemed to him all his life to be true as applied to Caius but certainly not as regards himself. That Caius – man in the abstract – was mortal, was perfectly correct; but he was not Caius, nor man in the abstract: he had always been a creature quite, quite different from all others. He had been little Vanya with a mamma and a papa, and Mita and Volodya, with playthings and the coachman and nurse; and afterwards with Katya and with all the joys and griefs and ecstasies of childhood, boyhood and youth. What did Caius know of the smell of that striped leather ball Vanya had been so fond of? Was it Caius who had kissed his mother's hand like that, and had Caius heard the silken rustle of her skirts? Was it Caius who had rioted like that over the cakes and pastry at the Law School? Had Caius been in love like that? Could Caius preside at sessions as he did?

And Caius was certainly mortal, and it was right for him to die; but for me, little Vanya, Ivan Ilyich, with all my thoughts and emotions – it's a different matter altogether. It cannot be that I ought to die. That would be too terrible.

That was the way he felt inside himself.

'If I had to die like Caius I should have known it was so, some inner voice would have told me. But there was nothing of the sort in me, and I and all my friends, we knew that it was quite different in our case. And now here it is!' he said to himself. 'It can't – it can't be, and yet it is! How has it happened? How am I to understand it?'

And he could not understand it, and tried to drive this false, erroneous, morbid thought away and supplant it with other proper, wholesome thoughts. But the idea, and not the idea only but as it were the reality itself, kept coming back again and confronting him.

And he summoned in place of this thought other thoughts, one after another, in the hope of finding succour and support. He tried to get back into former trains of thought which in the old days had screened him from the notion of death. But strangely enough all that used to cover up, obscure and obliterate the feeling of death no longer had the same effect. Ivan Ilyich now spent most of his time in these attempts to restore the former mental screen which had kept death out of sight. He would say to himself: 'I will take up my duties again – after all, I used to live for my work.' And banishing all doubts he would go to the Law Courts, enter into conversation with his colleagues and take his seat with an absent-minded air, as was his wont, scanning the crowd with a thoughtful look and resting his two emaciated hands on the arms of his oak chair just as he always did, and leaning over to a colleague and drawing his papers nearer, he would interchange whispers with him, and then suddenly raising his eyes and sitting erect he would pronounce the traditional words that opened the proceedings. But abruptly in the midst of it all the pain in his side, regardless of the stage the proceedings had reached, would begin its own gnawing work. Ivan Ilyich, becoming aware of it, would try to drive the thought of it away, but it went on with its business. It would come and stand before him and look at him, and he would find himself rigid with fear and the light would die out of his eyes, and he would begin asking himself again whether *It* alone was true. And his colleagues and his subordinates would notice with surprise and distress that he, the brilliant, discriminating judge, was getting confused and making mistakes. He would shake himself, try to pull himself together, manage somehow to bring the sitting to a close, and return home with the sorrowful consciousness that his judicial labours could not as of old hide from him what he wanted to be hidden, and that his official work could not deliver him from *It*. And, worst of all, *It* drew his attention to itself not in order to make him take some action but simply that he might look at it, look at it straight in the face, and without doing anything suffer unspeakably.

And to save himself from this condition of mind Ivan Ilyich sought relief – new screens – and new screens were found and for a while seemed to save him, but very soon they would not so much fall to pieces as become transparent, as if *It* penetrated them and nothing could shut *It* out.

Sometimes of late he would go into the drawing-room he had furnished and decorated – that drawing-room where he had had the fall and for the sake of which (how bitterly ludicrous it seemed) he had sacrificed his life, for he knew that his illness had originated with that bruise. He would go in and see that something had scratched the polished table. He would look for the cause and find that it was the bronze ornamentation of an album which had been bent back at the corner. He would pick up the expensive album which he had arranged with such affection, and feel vexed with his daughter and her friends for their carelessness – here a page was torn, there some photographs were upside down. He would tidy it up and put it to rights, and bend the metal back into position.

Then it would occur to him to move all this *établissement* of albums over into another corner of the room where the plants were. He would call the footman: either his daughter or his wife would come to his assistance; they did not agree with him, contradicted him, and he argued and got angry. But that was all right, since he did not think of *It*. *It* was not in sight.

But then his wife would say, when he was moving something himself: 'Do let the servants do it, you'll hurt yourself again,' and immediately *It* peeped through the screen; he caught a glimpse of *It*. It just peeped through, and still he hoped it would disappear but involuntarily he would watch for the pain in his side – there it was, the same as before, aching, aching all the time, and now he can forget it no longer, and *It* is staring at him from behind the flowers. 'What's the use of it all?

'And it's a fact that I lost my life here over that curtain, just as I might have done storming a fort. Can it be possible? How terrible and how ridiculous! It cannot be! It cannot be, but it is.'

He would go to his study, lie down, and again be alone with *It*. Face to face with *It*. And nothing to be done with *It*. Only look and shudder.

7

How it happened it is impossible to say because it came about step by step, imperceptibly, but in the third month of Ivan Ilyich's illness his wife, his daughter, his son, the servants, his acquaintances, the doctors and above all he himself were aware that the whole interest he had for other people was concentrated solely in this one thing – how soon he would vacate his place and at last release the living from the constraint of his presence and himself be released from his sufferings.

He slept less and less; they gave him opium and began injections of morphine, but this did not relieve him. The dull distress which he experienced in his half drowsy condition at first merely afforded the relief of change, but soon it became as distressing as the pain itself or even more so.

Special foods were prepared for him according to the doctors' directions; but these dishes struck him as being more and more tasteless, more and more nauseating.

Special arrangements, too, had to be made to assist his evacuations, and this was a continual misery to him: misery from the uncleanliness, the unseemliness and the smell, and from knowing that another person had to assist in it.

Yet this very unpleasant business brought some comfort to Ivan Ilyich. Gerassim, the peasant who waited at table, always came to clear up for him.

Gerassim was a clean, fresh young peasant lad, grown stout on the good fare in town and always cheerful and bright. At first the sight of him, in his clean Russian peasant costume, engaged on that disgusting task embarrassed Ivan Ilyich.

Once when he got up from the commode too weak to pull up his trousers, he dropped into a soft low chair and surveyed with horror his bare, enfeebled thighs with the muscles so sharply marked on them.

Gerassim came in, with a firm light tread, diffusing a pleasant smell of tar from his boots and of fresh winter air. He was wearing a clean hessian apron and clean cotton shirt, with his sleeves rolled up over his strong bare young arms. Without looking at Ivan Ilyich – out of consideration for the sick man's feelings – and restraining the joy of life that beamed from his face, he went up to the commode.

'Gerassim,' said Ivan Ilyich in a weak voice.

Gerassim started, evidently afraid that he had done something wrong and with a swift movement turned towards the invalid his fresh, good-natured, simple young face on which a beard was just beginning to sprout.

'Yes, sir?'

'This must be very disagreeable for you. You must forgive me. I can't help it.'

'Oh, why, sir,' and Gerassim's eyes shone and he showed his white young teeth in a smile. 'What's a little trouble? It's a case of illness with you, sir.'

And his deft strong hands performed their usual office, and he went out of the room, stepping lightly. And five minutes later he as lightly returned.

Ivan Ilyich was still sitting in the same position in the armchair.

'Gerassim,' he said, when the latter had replaced the night-stool all washed and clean. 'Please come here and help me.' Gerassim went to him. 'Lift me up. It's difficult for me alone, and I have sent Dmitri away.'

Gerassim went up to him; as lightly as he moved he put his strong arms round him, skilfully and gently lifted and supported him with one hand while with the other he pulled up his trousers and would have set him down again. But Ivan Ilyich asked to be helped to the sofa. Gerassim, without effort and without seeming to hold him tightly, led him, almost carrying him, to the sofa and settled him there.

'Thank you. How neatly and well you ... do everything.'

Gerassim smiled again and turned to leave the room. But Ivan Ilyich felt his presence such a comfort that he did not want to let him go.

'One more thing: move that chair near me, please. No, the other one – under my feet. I feel more comfortable when my legs are raised.'

Gerassim brought the chair, put it down noiselessly in the right place and lifted Ivan Ilyich's legs on to it. It seemed to Ivan Ilyich that he felt easier while Gerassim was lifting his legs higher.

'It's better when my legs are up,' he said. 'Put that cushion under me.'

Gerassim did so. Again he lifted his legs to put the cushion under them, and again Ivan Ilyich felt better while Gerassim held his legs. When he set them down Ivan Ilyich fancied he felt worse.

'Gerassim,' he said, 'are you busy just now?'

'Not at all, sir,' said Gerassim, who had learnt from the town-bred servants how to speak to gentlefolk.

'What have you got to do still?'

'What have I still got to do? I've done everything, except chop the wood for tomorrow.'

'Then hold my legs up a bit higher, can you?'

'Of course I can.' And Gerassim raised his master's legs higher and it seemed to Ivan Ilyich that in that position he did not feel any pain at all.

'But how about the wood?'

'Don't you trouble about that, sir. There's plenty of time.'

Ivan Ilyich told Gerassim to sit down and hold his legs, and began to talk to him. And, curiously to say, it seemed to him that he felt better while Gerassim had hold of his legs.

After that Ivan Ilyich would sometimes call Gerassim and get him to hold his legs on his shoulders, and he liked to talk with him. Gerassim did everything easily, willingly, simply, and with a good nature that touched Ivan Ilyich. Health, strength and vitality in other people were offensive to him, but Gerassim's strength and vitality did not fret but soothed him.

What tormented Ivan Ilyich most was the pretence, the lie, which for some reason they all kept up, that he was merely ill and not dying, and that he only need stay quiet and carry out the doctor's orders, and then some great change for the better would result. But *he* knew that whatever they might do nothing would come of it except still more agonizing suffering and death. And the pretence made him wretched: it tormented him that they refused to admit what they knew and he knew to be a fact, but persisted in lying to him concerning his terrible condition, and wanted him and forced him to be a party to the lie. Deceit, this deceit enacted over him up to the very eve of his death: this lying which could only degrade the awful, solemn act of his death to the level of their visitings, their curtains, their sturgeon for dinner ... was horribly painful to Ivan Ilyich. And it was a strange thing – many a time when they were playing their farce for his benefit he was within a hair's breadth of shouting at them: 'Stop lying! You know, and I know, that I am dying. So do at least stop lying about it!' But he had never had the spirit to do it. The awful, terrible act of his dying was, he saw, reduced by those about him to the level of a fortuitous, disagreeable and rather indecent incident (much in the same way as people behave with someone who goes into a drawing-room smelling unpleasantly) – and this was being done in the name of the very decorum he had served all his life long. He saw that no one felt for him, because no one was willing even to appreciate his situation. Gerassim was the only person who recognized the position and was sorry for him. And that was why Ivan Ilyich was at ease only when Gerassim was with him. He felt comforted when Gerassim supported his legs – sometimes all night long – and refused to go off to bed, saying: 'Don't you worry, Ivan Ilyich. I'll get sleep enough later on,' or suddenly dropped into the peasant *thou* instead of *you*, and added: 'If thee weren't sick 'twould be another matter but as things are 'twould be strange if I didn't wait on thee.' Gerassim alone told no lies; everything showed that he alone understood the facts of the case, and did not consider it necessary to disguise them, and simply felt sorry for the sick, expiring master. On one occasion when Ivan Ilyich was for sending him away to bed he even said straight out:

'We shall all of us die, so what's a little trouble?' meaning by this that he did not mind the extra work because he was doing it for a dying man and hoped someone would do the same for him when his time came.

Apart from this lying, or in consequence of it, the most wretched thing of all for Ivan Ilyich was that nobody pitied him as he yearned to be pitied. At certain moments, after a prolonged bout of suffering, he craved more than anything – ashamed as he would have been to own it – for someone to feel sorry for him just as if he were a sick child. He longed to be petted, kissed and wept over, as children are petted and comforted. He knew he was an important functionary, that he had a beard turning grey, and that therefore what he longed for was impossible; but nevertheless he longed for it. And in Gerassim's attitude towards him there was something akin to what he yearned for, and so Gerassim was a comfort to him. Ivan Ilyich feels like weeping and having someone to pet him and cry over him, but in comes his colleague Shebek and instead of weeping and being petted Ivan Ilyich puts on a grave, stern, profound air, and by force of habit expresses his opinion on a decision of the Court of Appeal, and obstinately insists on it. This falsity around and within him did more than anything else to poison Ivan Ilyich's last days.

8

It was morning. He knew it was morning because Gerassim had gone and Piotr the footman had come and put out the candles, drawn back one of the curtains and begun quietly tidying up the room. Whether it was morning or evening, Friday or Sunday, made no difference, it was all one and the same: gnawing, agonizing pain never ceasing for an instant, the consciousness of life inexorably ebbing away but not yet gone; the relentless approach of that ever dreaded and hateful death, which was the only reality, and all this lying going on at the same time. What were days, or weeks, or hours of the day to him?

'Wouldn't you like your tea, sir?'

'He wants things done properly, and that requires the gentry to take tea in the morning,' thought Ivan Ilyich, and only said 'No.'

'Wouldn't you care to move on to the sofa, sir?'

'He has to make the room tidy, and I'm in his way. I am dirt and disorder,' he thought to himself, and said merely: 'No, leave me alone.'

The man still moved busily about his work. Ivan Ilyich stretched out his hand. Piotr came up, ready to do his bidding.

'What is it, sir?'

'My watch.'

Piotr picked up the watch, which lay just under his hand, and gave it to his master.

'Half-past-eight. Are they up yet?'

'No, sir, except for Vladimir Ivanovich' (Ivan Ilyich's son) 'who has gone off to school. Madam left orders to wake her if you asked for her. Shall I do so, sir?'

'No, no need.'

'Should I try some tea?' he wondered. 'Yes, ... bring me some tea.'

Piotr went to the door. The idea of being left alone filled Ivan Ilyich with dread. How should he keep the man a little longer? Oh yes, there was the medicine. 'Piotr, give me my medicine.' The medicine might help after all, there was no knowing. He took the spoon and swallowed a dose. No, it was no good. It was all rubbish and delusion, he decided as soon as he tasted the familiar, insipid, hopeless taste. No, I can't believe in it any longer. But the pain – why should I have this pain? If it would only stop just for a moment!' And he groaned. Piotr turned round. 'No, go along. Bring the tea.'

Piotr went out. Left alone, Ivan Ilyich groaned not so much from the pain, terrible though it was, as from mental anguish. Always and for ever the same, always these endless days and nights. If only it would come quicker. If only *what* would come quicker? Death, darkness. No, no! Anything rather than death!

When Piotr returned with the tea on a tray, Ivan Ilyich stared confusedly at him for a long time, not comprehending who he was and what he wanted. Piotr was disconcerted by this stare and his embarrassment brought Ivan Ilyich to himself again.

'Oh yes,' he said, 'tea ... good, put it down. Only help me to wash and put on a clean shirt.'

And Ivan Ilyich began to wash. With pauses for rest, he washed his hands and then his face, cleaned his teeth, brushed his hair and looked in the glass. His heart went cold at what he saw, especially at the limp way in which his hair clung to his pallid forehead.

While his shirt was being changed he knew that he would be still more frightened at the sight of his body, so he avoided looking at it. But at last it was all done. He put on his dressing-gown, wrapped himself round with a rug and sat down in the arm-chair to drink his tea. For a moment he felt refreshed, but no sooner had he begun to drink the tea, than back came that taste and the pain. He finished the tea with an effort, and then lay down, stretching out his legs. He lay down and let Piotr go.

It was always the same. At one moment a gleam of hope, the next a raging sea of despair, and always pain, always misery and pain, over and over again. All this lonely misery was terrible: he would have liked to call someone but he knew beforehand that with others in the room with him it would be still worse. 'If only I might have some more morphine, I might lose consciousness a little. I will tell him, tell the doctor, that he must think of something else. It's impossible to go on like this., quite impossible.'

An hour passes in this way, and then a second. But now there is a ring at the front door. Perhaps it's the doctor? It is the doctor, spruce and hearty, fat and cheerful, with that look on his face that seems to say: 'The patient a little bit nervous, eh? But we'll very soon set all that to rights.' The doctor is aware that this expression is not appropriate here but he has put it on once and for all and can't take it off – like a man who has got into his frock-coat in the morning to pay a round of calls.

The doctor rubs his hands in a brisk and reassuring manner.

'Brr, it's cold! There's a sharp frost. Just let me warm myself,' he says, as though it were only a matter of waiting a second or two till he was warm, and then he would straighten things out.

'Well now, how are we?'

Ivan Ilyich feels that the doctor would like to say, 'Well, how's the little trouble?' but even he feels that this would not do, and asks instead: 'What sort of a night did you have?'

Ivan Ilyich looks at the doctor as much as to say: 'Will you never be ashamed of prevaricating, I wonder?' But the doctor has no desire to understand, and Ivan Ilyich says: 'Just as awful as ever. The pain never stops, never leaves me alone. If only you could give me something ...'

'Ah, you sick folk are all the same ... There now, I do believe I've thawed out, and even Praskovya Fiodorovna, who is so particular, could find no fault with my temperature. Well, now I can say good morning,' and the doctor shakes hands with his patient.

And, dropping his former levity, he begins with serious face to examine the patient, feeling his pulse and taking his temperature before beginning the tappings and soundings.

Ivan Ilyich knows quite well and beyond doubt that all this is nonsense and empty deception, but when the doctor, getting down on his knees, leans over him, applying his ear now higher up, now lower down, and with most sapient countenance performs various gymnastic evolutions over him, Ivan Ilyich submits to it all as he once submitted to the speeches of the lawyers in court, though he was perfectly well aware that they were lying all the time, and also why they were lying.

The doctor, kneeling on the sofa, is still sounding him when Praskovya Fiodorovna's silk skirt rustles at the door and she is heard scolding Piotr for not having let her know of the doctor's arrival.

She comes in, kisses her husband, and immediately proceeds to explain that she has been up a long time and only through a misunderstanding failed to be there when the doctor arrived.

Ivan Ilyich looks at her, scans her from head to foot and chalks up against her the whiteness and plumpness and cleanness of her arms and neck, her glossy hair and the lively sparkle in her eyes. With his whole soul he detests her. And when she touches him he is swept by a paroxysm of hate.

Her attitude towards him and his illness is still the same. Just as the doctor had adopted a certain line with his patient which he could not now drop, so she, too, had taken a line with him – that he was not doing something he ought to be doing, and was himself to blame, and she was lovingly reproaching him for this – and now she could not relinquish that attitude.

'You see he doesn't listen to me, and doesn't take his medicine at the proper time. And what's worse, he will lie in a position which must be very bad for him – with his legs in the air.'

She described how he made Gerassim hold his legs up.

The doctor smiled with a bland condescension that said: 'What can we do? These sick people, you know, do sometimes get such foolish fancies, but we must forgive them.'

When the examination was over, the doctor looked at his watch, and then Praskovya Fiodorovna announced to Ivan Ilyich that it was, of course, as he pleased, but she had sent that day for a celebrated specialist who would examine him and have a consultation with Mihail Danilovich (their regular doctor).

'Now please don't raise any objections. I am doing it for my own sake,' she said ironically, letting it be understood that she was doing it all for his sake, and was only saying the opposite to leave him no right to refuse. He was silent, knitting his brows. He felt himself enveloped and caught in such a mesh of falsity that it was difficult to disentangle anything.

Everything she did for him was entirely for her own sake, and she told him she was doing for herself what in fact she was doing for herself, as if it were such an incredible thing that it could only mean the contrary.

And, indeed, at half-past-eleven the celebrated specialist arrived. Once more there were soundings, and earnest conversations in his presence and in another room about the kidney and the appendix, and questions and answers with such an air of importance that again, instead of the real question of life and death which now alone confronted him, the question that came uppermost concerned the kidney and the appendix which were not behaving as they should and would now be attacked by Mihail Danilovich and the specialist and forced to mend their ways.

The celebrated specialist took his leave with a serious but not a hopeless expression of countenance, and to the timid question that Ivan Ilyich, looking up at him with eyes glistening with fear and hope, put to him, Was there a chance of recovery? he answered that he could not vouch for it but there was a possibility. The look of hope with which Ivan Ilyich watched the doctor out was so pathetic that seeing it Praskovya Fiodorovna even burst into tears as she passed through the study door to hand the celebrated doctor his fee.

The gleam of hope kindled by the doctor's encouragement did not last long. The same room, the same pictures, curtains, wall-paper, medicine bottles were all there, and the same aching, suffering body. And Ivan Ilyich began to moan. They gave him a subcutaneous injection and he sank into oblivion.

It was dark when he came to. They brought him his dinner and he forced himself to swallow a little beef tea; and again everything was the same, with another night approaching.

After dinner, at seven o'clock, Praskovya Fiodorovna came into the room dressed for a party, her exuberant bosom pushed up by her stays, and with traces of powder on her face. She had reminded him in the morning that they were going to the theatre. Sarah Bernhardt was visiting the town and they had a box, which he had insisted on their taking. He had forgotten all about this now and her attire offended him. But he concealed his vexation when he remembered that he had himself insisted on their securing a box and going because it would be an aesthetic pleasure and good for the children's education.

Praskovya Fiodorovna came in well satisfied with herself but yet with a slightly guilty air. She sat down, asked how he was, as he saw, simply for the sake of asking and not in order to find out, knowing very well that there was nothing to find out – and then went on to say what was incumbent upon her to say: that she would not have gone on any account but the box had been taken, and Ellen and her daughter were going, as well as Petrishchev (the examining magistrate, their daughter's suitor) and that it was out of the question to let them go alone. But she would have much preferred to sit with him for a while, and he must be sure to carry out the doctor's orders while she was away.

'Oh, and Fiodr Petrovich' (the suitor) 'would like to come in. May he? And Liza.'

'All right, let them in.'

His daughter came in in full evening dress, her fair young flesh exposed, while his flesh made him suffer so. But she paraded it: she was strong, healthy, clearly in love and impatient with illness, suffering and death because they interfered with her happiness.

Fiodr Petrovich came in too, in evening dress, his hair curled *à la Capoul*, his long sinewy neck encased in a white collar, with an enormous expanse of white shirt-front and narrow black trousers tightly stretched over strong thighs. One hand was smoothly gloved in white, and he carried an opera hat.

Behind him crept in unnoticed the little high school boy in his new uniform, poor little chap, wearing gloves and with that terrible blue circle under the eyes, the meaning of which Ivan Ilyich knew too well.

His son had always seemed pathetic to him, and now it was dreadful to see the boy's frightened look of pity. With the exception of Gerassim, it seemed to Ivan Ilyich that Vassya was the only one who understood and felt sorry for him.

They all sat down and again inquired how he was. A silence followed. Liza asked her mother if she had the opera-glasses, and there was an argument between mother and daughter as to who had had them and where they had been put. This occasioned some unpleasantness.

Fiodr Petrovich inquired of Ivan Ilyich whether he had ever seen Sarah Bernhardt. Ivan Ilyich did not at first catch the question but after a moment he said, 'No, have you seen her before?'

'Yes, in *Adrienne Lecouvreur*.'

Praskovya Fiodorovna mentioned some rôles in which Sarah Bernhardt was particularly good. Her daughter disagreed. A discussion began about the grace and naturalness of her acting – the sort of conversation that springs up repeatedly and is always the same.

In the middle of the conversation Fiodr Petrovich glanced at Ivan Ilyich and relapsed into silence. The others looked at him and fell silent. Ivan Ilyich was staring with glittering eyes straight before him, obviously furious with them. Here was something to be rectified but there was no means whatever of doing so. The silence had somehow to be broken but nobody ventured to speak and panic seized them all that the conventional deception was suddenly about to be shattered and the truth become plain to all. Liza was the first to pluck up courage and break the silence, but by trying to cover up what they were all feeling she betrayed it.

'Well, if we *are* going it's time to start,' she said, glancing at her watch, a present from her father; and with a scarcely perceptible smile to the young man, referring to some secret between them, she got up with a rustle of her skirts.

They all rose, said good-night and went away.

When they had gone Ivan Ilyich fancied that he felt better: there was no more falsity – that had gone with them – but the pain remained. That continual pain, that continual terror, made nothing harder, nothing easier. Everything always grew worse.

Again minute after minute, hour after hour, dragged by, always the same and always interminable – and the inevitable end of it all becoming more and more terrible.

'Yes, send Gerassim to me,' he replied to a question from Piotr.

9

LATE at night his wife returned. She came in on tiptoe but he heard her, opened his eyes and made haste to close them again. She wanted to send Gerassim away and sit with him herself. He opened his eyes and said, 'No, go away.'

'Are you in great pain?'

'The same as usual.'

'Take some opium.'

He agreed and drank a dose. She went away.

Until about three in the morning he slumbered in a state of stupefied misery. It seemed to him that he and his pain were being thrust somewhere into a narrow, deep black sack, but though they kept forcing him farther and farther in they still could not push him to the bottom. And this horrible state of affairs was accompanied by agony. And he was frightened and yet wanted to fall into the sack, he struggled and at the same time co-operated. Then quite suddenly he burst out of the sack and fell, and regained consciousness. There was Gerassim still sitting at the foot of the bed, dozing peacefully and patiently, while he himself lay with his wasted, stockinged legs resting on Gerassim's shoulders. The same candle was there, with its shade, and the same unceasing pain.

'Go away, Gerassim,' he whispered.

'It's all right, sir. I'll stay a bit longer.'

'No, go away.'

He removed his legs from Gerassim's shoulders, turned sideways on to his arm, and began to feel sorry for himself. He waited only until Gerassim had gone into the next room and then restrained himself no longer but wept like a child. He wept at his own helplessness, at his terrible loneliness, at the cruelty of man, the cruelty of God, at the absence of God.

'Why hast Thou done this? Why hast Thou brought me to this? Why, why dost Thou torture me so dreadfully?'

He did not expect any answer, and yet wept because there was no answer and could be none. The pain flared up more acutely again but he did not stir and did not call. He said to himself: 'Go on, smite me! But why? What have I done to Thee? What is it for?'

Then he was still and not only ceased weeping but even held his breath and became all attention: he listened, as it were, not to an audible voice but to the voice of his soul, to the tide of his thoughts that rose up within him.

'What is it you want?' was the first clear conception capable of expression in words that he heard. 'What is it you want? What is it you want?' he repeated to himself.

'What do I want? Not to suffer. To live,' he answered.

And again he listened with such concentrated attention that even his pain did not distract him.

'To live. Live how?' asked his inner voice.

'Why, to live as I used to – well and pleasantly.'

'As you used to live – well and pleasantly?' queried the voice. And he began going over in his imagination the best moments of his pleasant life. But oddly enough none of those best moments of his pleasant life now seemed at all what they had seemed at the time – none of them except his earliest memories of childhood. There, in childhood, there had been something really pleasant with which it would be possible to live if it could return. But the person who had experienced that happiness was no more: it was like a memory of someone else.

As soon as the period began which had produced the present Ivan Ilyich everything that had seemed a joy at the time now dwindled away before his eyes and was transformed into something trivial and often disgusting.

And the farther he departed from childhood and the nearer he came to the present, the more worthless and doubtful were the joys. This began from the time he was a law student. There was still something then that had been genuinely good – gaiety, friendship, hopes. But in the upper classes these good moments were already becoming rarer. Later on, during the first years of his official career, when he was in the service of the Governor, there were again some good moments: they were the memories of love for a woman. Afterwards it all became mixed up, and less and less of it was good. And the farther he went the less good he found.

His marriage ... as gratuitous as the disenchantment that followed, and his wife's bad breath, and the sensuality, the hypocrisy! And that deadly official life and the preoccupation with money, a year of it, two years, ten, twenty, and always the same thing. And the longer it lasted the more deadly it became. 'As though I had been going steadily downhill while I imagined I was climbing up. And that is really how it was. In public opinion I was going up, and all the time my life was sliding away from under my feet ... And now it's all done and I must die.

'But what is it all about? Why is it like this? It can't be – it can't be that life is so senseless and loathsome. And if it really has been so loathsome and senseless, why must I die and die in agony? There is something wrong!

'Maybe I did not live as I should,' the thought suddenly occurred to him. 'But how could that be, when I have always done my duty,' he answered himself, and immediately dismissed from his mind this, the sole solution of all the enigma of life and death, as something quite impossible.

'Then what do you want now? To live? Live how? Live as you lived in court when the usher boomed out: "The Court sits! The Court sits!" ... The Court sits, the Court sits!' he repeated to himself. 'Here's my sentence. But I am not guilty!' he shrieked in fury. 'What is it for?' And he left off crying but, turning his face to the wall, fell to pondering one and the same question: Why, and wherefore, all this horror?

But however much he pondered he could find no answer. And when the thought occurred to him, as it often did, that it all came of his not having lived as he ought to have lived, he at once recalled the orderliness of his life and dismissed so strange an idea.

10

ANOTHER fortnight passed. Ivan Ilyich now no longer left his sofa. He would not lie in bed but lay on the sofa. And facing the wall most of the time he lay and in solitude suffered all the inexplicable agonies, and in solitude pondered always the same insoluble question: 'What is it? Can it be true that it is death?' And the inner voice answered: 'Yes, it is true.' – 'Why these agonies?' And the voice answered, 'For no reason – they just are so.' Beyond and besides this there was nothing.

From the very beginning of his illness, ever since he had first gone to see the doctor, Ivan Ilyich's life had been divided between two contrary and alternating moods – now despair and the expectation of an unintelligible and terrible death; now hope and an intently interested observation of the functioning of his organs. At one moment he was merely confronted with a kidney or an intestine that temporarily evaded its duty; at the next death loomed before his eyes, incomprehensible and terrible, death from which there was no escaping.

These two states of mind had alternated from the very beginning of his illness; but the farther the malady progressed the more doubtful and fantastic became his conception of the kidney, and the more real the sense of impending dissolution.

He had but to call to mind what he had been three months before and what he was now, to reflect how steadily he was going downhill, for every possibility of hope to be shattered.

Of late, in the loneliness in which he found himself, lying with his face to the back of the sofa, a loneliness in the midst of a populous town and surrounded by numerous acquaintances and relations – loneliness more complete than could be found anywhere, be it at the bottom of the sea or in the bowels of the earth – of late in this fearful loneliness Ivan Ilyich had lived only in memories of the past. One after another pictures of his past presented themselves to him. They always began with what was nearest in time and then went back to what was most remote – to his childhood – and rested there. If he thought of the stewed prunes that had been offered him for dinner that day, his mind went back to the raw, wrinkled French plums of his childhood, their peculiar flavour and the flow of saliva when he got down to the stones, and along with this recollection of the taste of a plum there arose a whole series of other memories of the same period – his nurse, his brother, his toys. 'But I mustn't think of all that . . . it's too painful,' and Ivan Ilyich brought himself back to the present – to the button on the back of the sofa and the creases in the morocco. 'Morocco is expensive and doesn't wear well. There had been a quarrel about it. But it was a different morocco and a different quarrel when we tore father's portfolio and were punished, and mamma brought us some tarts.' And again his thoughts dwelt on his childhood, and again it was painful and he tried to banish them and think of something else.

And now again, together with this chain of memories another series came into his mind – of how his illness had developed and grown worse. This time, too, the farther he looked back the more life there had been. There had been more of what was good in life and more of life itself. And the two merged together. 'Just as the pain goes from worse to worse so my whole life has gone from worse to worse,' he reflected. 'There is one bright spot far back, right at the beginning of life, but after that it kept getting blacker and blacker and going faster and faster – in inverse ratio to the square of the distance from death,' thought Ivan Ilyich. And the comparison of a stone falling downwards with increasing velocity fastened upon his mind. Life, a series of increasing sufferings, speeds swifter and swifter to the end, and that end – the most terrible suffering. 'I am falling . . .' He shuddered, shifted himself and tried to resist but was already aware that resistance was impossible, and again, with eyes wearied of gazing but unable not to look at what was before him, he stared at the back of the sofa and waited, waited expecting the fearful fall, the jolt, and destruction. 'It's no good resisting,' he said to himself. 'Yet if only I could understand what it is all for. Even that's impossible. It might be explained if it could be said that I have not lived as I ought to have lived. But that could not possibly be said,' he told himself, thinking of all the law-abidingness, uprightness and respectability of his life. 'That at any rate can certainly not be admitted,' he said to himself, his lips smiling ironically as though someone could see that smile and be taken in by it. 'There is no explanation! Agony, death . . . Why?'

II

ANOTHER two weeks went by after this manner, and during that fortnight an event occurred that Ivan Ilyich and his wife had desired: Petrishchev made a formal proposal. It happened in the evening. The next day Praskovya Fiodorovna came into her husband's room, cogitating how best to inform him of it, but that very night Ivan Ilyich's condition had taken a fresh turn for the worse. Praskovya Fiodorovna found him still on the sofa but in a different position. He lay on his back, groaning and gazing straight in front of him with a fixed stare.

She began to speak about his medicines. He turned his glance upon her. She did not finish what she was saying, such bitter animosity, to her in particular, did that look express.

'For Christ's sake let me die in peace!' he said.

She would have gone away but at that moment their daughter came in and went up to say good morning to him. He looked at his daughter as he had looked at his wife, and in reply to her inquiry about his health said coldly that he would very soon relieve them all of his presence. Both women were silent and after sitting for a little went out.

'Why are we to blame?' said Liza to her mother. 'It's as though it were our fault. I am sorry for papa, but why should he torment us?'

At his usual hour the doctor came. Ivan Ilyich replied 'Yes' and 'No', never taking his infuriated eyes from him, and towards the end said: 'You know very well you can do nothing for me, so leave me alone.'

'We can ease your suffering,' said the doctor.

'Even that you can't do. Let me be.'

The doctor went into the drawing-room and told Praskovya Fiodorovna that the case was very serious and that the only resource left was opium to allay her husband's sufferings, which must be terrible.

It was true, as the doctor said, that Ivan Ilyich's physical sufferings were terrible, but worse than his physical sufferings were his mental sufferings, which were his chief torture.

His mental sufferings were due to the fact that in the night as he looked at Gerassim's sleepy, good-natured face with its prominent cheek-bones the thought had suddenly come into his head: 'What if in reality my whole life has been wrong?'

It occurred to him that what had appeared utterly impossible before – that he had not lived his life as he should have done – might after all be true. It struck him that those scarcely detected inclinations of his to fight against what the most highly placed people regarded as good, those scarcely noticeable impulses which he had immediately suppressed, might have been the real thing and all the rest false. And his professional duties, and his ordering of his life, and his family, and all his social and official interests might all have been false. He tried to defend it all to himself. And suddenly he realized the weakness of what he was defending. There was nothing to defend.

'But if that is so,' he said to himself, 'and I am leaving this life with the consciousness that I have lost all that was given me and there's no putting it right – what then?' He lay flat on his back and began going over his whole life entirely anew. In the morning when he saw first the footman, then his wife, then his daughter, then the doctor, every movement they made, every word they uttered, confirmed for him the awful truth that had been revealed to him during the night. In them he saw himself – all that he had lived for – and saw plainly that it was all wrong, a horrible, monstrous lie concealing both life and death. This consciousness increased his physical suffering tenfold. He groaned and tossed about and threw off the clothes. It seemed to him that they were choking and stifling him. And he hated them on that account.

They gave him a large dose of opium and he lost consciousness; but at dinner-time the whole thing began all over again. He drove everybody away and tossed from side to side.

His wife came to him and said:

'*Jean*, my dear, do this for me.' (For her?) 'It can't do any harm and it often helps. It is really nothing, you know. People in good health often ...'

He opened his eyes wide.

'What? Take the Sacrament? What for? It's not necessary. However ...'

She burst into tears.

'Yes, do, my dear. I'll send for our priest, he's such a nice man.'

'All right, very well,' he said.

When the priest came and confessed him he felt quieter and knew a sort of relief from his doubts and consequently from his sufferings, and for a moment hope returned to him. He again began to think of the intestinal appendix and the possibility of curing it. He received the Sacrament with tears in his eyes.

When they laid him down again afterwards he felt easier for a moment, and the hope that he might live reappeared. He began to think of the operation which had been suggested to him. 'To live – I want to live!' he said to himself. His wife came in to felicitate him: she uttered the customary formula and added:

'You feel better, don't you?'

Without looking at her he said, 'Yes.'

Her dress, her figure, the expression of her face, the tone of her voice – all told him the same thing. 'Wrong! All you have lived for and are living for is a lie and a deception, hiding life and death from you.'

And as soon as he admitted that thought his exasperation returned and with it the agonizing physical suffering and with the suffering a consciousness of the unavoidable, approaching end. To this was added a new sensation of grinding shooting pain and a feeling of suffocation.

The expression of his face when he uttered that 'Yes' was dreadful. Having pronounced it, he looked at her straight in the eye, turned on his face with a rapidity extraordinary in his weak state and shouted:

'Go away, go away. Leave me alone!'

12

FROM that moment the screaming began that continued for three days and was so awful that one could not hear it through closed doors two rooms away without horror. At the moment when he answered his wife he realized that he was lost, that there was no return, that the end had come, the very end, while his doubts were still unsolved and remained doubts.

'Oh! Oh! Oh!' he cried in varying intonations. He had begun by screaming 'I won't!' and so had gone on screaming on the same vowel sound 'o'.

For three whole days, during which time did not exist for him, he struggled in that black sack into which he was being forced by an unseen, invincible power. He fought as a man condemned to death fights in the hands of the executioner, knowing that he cannot save himself. And every moment he felt that, notwithstanding all his struggles, he was drawing nearer and nearer to what terrified him. He felt that his agony was due both to his being thrust into that black hole and, still more, to his not being able to get right into it. What hindered him from getting into it was his claim that his life had been good. That very justification of his life held him fast and prevented him from advancing, and caused him more agony than everything else.

Suddenly some force smote him in the chest and side, making it still harder to breathe; he sank through the hole and there at the bottom was a light. It had happened to him as it had sometimes happened to him in a railway-carriage, when he had thought he was going forwards whereas he was actually going backwards, and all of a sudden became aware of his real direction.

'No, it was all wrong,' he said to himself, 'but no matter.' He could, he could do the right thing. 'But what *is* the right thing?' he asked himself, and abruptly grew quiet.

This was at the end of the third day, an hour before his death. At that very moment his schoolboy son had crept into the room and gone up to his father's bedside. The dying man was still shrieking desperately and waving his arms. His hand fell on the child's head. The boy seized it, pressed it to his lips and burst into tears.

It was at this very same moment that Ivan Ilyich had fallen through the hole and caught sight of the light, and it was revealed to him that his life had not been what it ought to have been but that it was still possible to put it right. He asked himself : 'But what *is* the right thing ?' and grew still, listening. Then he felt that someone was kissing his hand. He opened his eyes and looked at his son. He felt sorry for him. His wife came up to him. He looked at her. She was gazing at him with open mouth, the tears wet on her nose and cheeks, and an expression of despair on her face. He felt sorry for her.

'Yes, I am a misery to them,' he thought. 'They are sorry but it will be better for them when I die.' He wanted to say this but had not strength to speak. 'Besides, why speak, I must act,' he thought. With a look he indicated his son to his wife and said :

'Take him away ... sorry for him ... sorry for you too ...' He tried to add 'Forgive me' but said 'Forego' and, too weak to correct himself, waved his hand, knowing that whoever was concerned would understand.

And all at once it became clear to him that what had been oppressing him and would not go away was suddenly dropping away on one side, on two sides, on ten sides, on all sides. He felt full of pity for them, he must do something to make it less painful for them : release them and release himself from this suffering. 'How right and how simple,' he thought. 'And the pain ?' he asked himself. 'What has become of it ? Where are you, pain ?'

He began to watch for it.

'Yes, here it is. Well, what of it ? Let the pain be.

'And death ? Where is it ?'

He searched for his former habitual fear of death and did not find it. 'Where is it ? What death ?' There was no fear because there was no death either.

In place of death there was light.

'So that's what it is!' he suddenly exclaimed aloud. 'What joy!'

To him all this happened in a single instant, and the meaning of that instant suffered no change thereafter. For those present his agony lasted another two hours. There was a rattle in his throat, a twitching of his wasted body. Then the gasping and the rattle came at longer and longer intervals.

'It is all over!' said someone near him.

He caught the words and repeated them in his soul. 'Death is over,' he said to himself. 'It is no more.'

He drew in a breath, stopped in the midst of a sigh, stretched out and died.

[25 *March 1886*]

THE COSSACKS

I

ALL is hushed in Moscow. At long intervals a solitary carriage creaks along the wintry streets. Every window is dark and the street lamps are extinguished. Only the church bells echoing over the slumbering city tell of the approach of morning. The streets are deserted. Very occasionally a sledge, its narrow runners cutting through the sanded snow, ploughs across to another corner, where the driver falls asleep waiting for a fare. An old woman passes by on her way to church. Inside the church the gilded mountings of the ikons reflect the flickering red flames of a few irregularly placed wax candles. The workers are beginning to get up after the long winter night, and set off for work.

But for the gentry it is still the evening before.

At Chevalier's lights, illegal at this hour, show through a slit in one of the closed shutters. A private sledge, a carriage and some cabs are drawn up in a bunch at the entrance, the drivers standing back to back for warmth. A troika from the post-station is also waiting. The yard-porter, muffled up and pinched with cold, tries to shelter round the corner of the building.

'What's the sense of all this fiddle-faddle?' thinks a haggard-faced attendant sitting in the hall. 'And it's always when I am on duty.' The voices of three young men are heard at supper in the lighted room adjoining. Their table is littered with the remains of food and wine. One of the three, a thin, ill-favoured, trim little man, sits looking with kindly, tired eyes at his companion who is about to start on a journey. The second, a tall youth, reclines on a settee near the bottle-strewn table, toying with his watch-key. The third, the one who is leaving, in a new sheepskin coat, paces about the room, stopping every now and then to crack an almond between his fingers, which are strong and rather thick, with carefully tended nails. A smile hovers about his flushed face, and his eyes glow. He speaks with warmth, and gesticulates; but it is evident that the words he wants evade him, and those that do come to him seem inadequate to express all that fills his heart. He smiles continually.

'Now I can speak out,' says the traveller. 'I am not trying to defend myself, but I should like you, at least, to understand me as I understand myself, and not in the way the vulgar herd look upon the affair. You say I have treated her badly,' he continues, turning to the little man who looks at him with affection.

'Yes, certainly,' replies the little man, and his eyes seem to express more affection and weariness than ever.

'I know why you say that,' pursues the traveller. 'You think that to be loved is as great happiness as being in love, and should suffice for a whole lifetime, once a man has attained it.'

'Undoubtedly, my dear boy – more than enough!' insists the plain little man, blinking.

'But why shouldn't the man love as well?' begins the traveller, looking at his friend thoughtfully and with something like commiseration. 'Why? Because love doesn't come . . . Oh no, it is a misfortune to be loved – a misfortune when you feel guilty because you don't give something which you cannot give. Oh Lord!' and he waves his arm. 'If only these things happened logically, but it's all topsy-turvy: things don't happen the way we want them but in some crazy fashion of their own. Why, it is as if I had stolen that love! Even you think so. Don't deny it – you must think so! And yet, would you believe it, of all the foolish and disgusting things I have found time to do in my life, this is one I do not and cannot repent of. Neither at first nor afterwards did I deceive either myself or her. At first I honestly believed I was in love, but afterwards I discovered that I had unconsciously deceived myself, that it was not possible to love like that, and I couldn't go on with it. But she persisted. Am I to blame for not being able to love? What was I to do?'

'Well, anyhow, it is all over now!' said his friend, lighting a cigarette to keep himself awake. 'This is what it amounts to, then: you have never loved and you don't know what it is to love.'

The traveller in the sheepskin clasped his head in his hands and wanted to say something, but words failed him.

'Never loved! Yes, quite true, I have never loved. But I want to love. No desire could be stronger. But then again, does love exist? Something always remains incomplete. Ah well, what is the use of talking? I have messed up my life. But it's all over now, you are right. And I feel that a new life is about to begin.'

'Which you will again make a mess of,' put in the tall man who lay on the sofa toying with his watch-key. But the traveller ignored him.

'I am both sad and glad to go,' he continued. 'Why I am sad, I don't know.'

And he went on talking about himself, unaware that his interest in himself was not shared by the others. A man is never such an egoist as at moments of spiritual exaltation, when it seems to him that there is nothing in the world more splendid and fascinating than himself.

'Dmitri Andreyevich, the driver won't wait any longer!' said a young man-servant in a sheepskin coat with a scarf tied round his head, who came in at this moment. 'The horses have been standing since eleven o'clock, and now it is four in the morning.'

Dmitri Andreyevich looked at his servant, Vanyusha. The scarf round Vanyusha's head, his felt boots and sleepy face seemed to beckon his master to a new life of toil, privation and activity.

'Yes, it is time to say good-bye,' he conceded, feeling for the unfastened hook and eye on his coat.

Disregarding the suggestion that he should appease the coachman with another tip, he pulled on his cap and stood in the middle of the room. The friends kissed once, then again, and after a pause a third time. The man in the sheepskin coat went up to the table, emptied a glass of champagne he found there, then seized the plain little man by the hand, a flush spreading over his face as he did so.

'Ah well, I'll speak out all the same ... I must, and can be frank with you because I am very fond of you ... You love her, don't you? I always thought you did ... Am I right?'

'Yes,' answered his friend, smiling still more gently.

'And perhaps ...'

'Excuse me, gentlemen, I have orders to snuff the candles,' said the sleepy waiter, who had been listening to the last part of the conversation and wondering why the gentry were always talking about one and the same thing. 'Shall I have the bill made out to you, sir?' he added, knowing whom to address and turning to the tall man.

'Yes, to me,' replied the tall man. 'How much is it?'

'Twenty-six roubles.'

The tall man considered for a moment but said nothing and slipped the bill into his pocket.

The other two were still talking.

'Farewell, you're a good fellow!' said the ugly little man with the kindly eyes.

Tears welled up into the eyes of both. They went out on to the porch.

'Oh, by the way,' said the traveller, reddening as he turned to the tall man, 'you settle Chevalier's bill, and then write and let me know.'

'Yes, all right,' answered the tall man, pulling on his gloves. 'How I envy you!' he added quite unexpectedly when they got outside.

The traveller took his seat in the sledge, wrapped his coat round him and said, 'Well then, come with me!' and even moved a little to make room for the man who said he envied him. His voice trembled.

But the tall man only said: 'Good-bye, Dmitri, God bless you. I wish you –' But as his only wish was that his friend would go away quickly he did not finish the sentence.

For a moment all were silent. Then someone said again: 'Good-bye,' and a voice cried 'Ready!', and the coachman touched up the horses.

'Right, Elizar!' called one of the friends, and the other coachman and the sledge-drivers began to move, clicking their tongues and tugging at the reins. The frozen carriage-wheels creaked over the snow.

'Nice chap, Olenin,' said one of the friends. 'But what an idea to go to the Caucasus – and as a cadet, too! I wouldn't do it for anything. Are you dining at the Club tomorrow?'

'Yes.'

They parted at that.

The traveller felt warm, even too hot in his sheepskin. He sat on the floor of the sledge, his coat unfastened, and the three shaggy post-horses dragged themselves out of one dark street into another, past houses he had never seen before. It seemed to Olenin that only travellers bound on a long journey ever went through such streets as these. All about him was dark, silent and dismal, while his soul was full of memories, love and regrets, and the pleasant constriction of tears.

2

'I'M fond of them, extremely fond of them. Nice fellows! Very nice!' he kept repeating to himself and felt tearful. But why did he want to cry? Who were the nice fellows he was so fond of? He was not too sure. Now and then he looked round at some house and wondered why it was so curiously built; sometimes he began wondering why the coachman and Vanyusha, who were such different beings from him, sat so near and why they all swayed and jolted as the side-horses tugged at the frozen traces; then again he exclaimed: 'First-rate fellows! I am so fond of them!' Once he even said aloud: 'Drives like Jehu! How splendid it all is!' and wondered what made him say it. 'Dear me, am I drunk?' he asked himself. True, he had put away a couple of bottles of wine, but it was not the wine alone that was having this effect. He remembered the words of farewell, spoken warmly, shyly and, as it seemed to him, sincerely. He remembered the handclasps, the glances, the silences, the voice calling, 'Good-bye, Dmitri!' after he had taken his seat in the sledge. He remembered his own determined frankness. And all this had a touching significance for him. Not only friends and relatives, not only people who hitherto had been indifferent, but even those who did not like him, seemed suddenly to have agreed to become fonder of him, or to forgive him, before his departure, as one does before going to confession or dying. 'Perhaps I am not to return from the Caucasus,' he thought. And he felt his heart swell with affection for his friends and for someone else besides. A wave of self-pity came over him. But it was not love for his friends that so stirred and uplifted his heart that he could not repress the meaningless words that rose to his lips of their own accord; nor was it love for a woman (he had never yet been in love) that induced this mood. It was love for himself, love full of hope – warm young love for all that was good in him (and at that moment he felt that there was nothing but good there) – that compelled him to weep and mutter disjointed words.

Olenin was a young man who had left the university before completing his course, who had never worked (he held only a nominal post in some government office or other), who had squandered half his fortune and reached the age of twenty-four without doing anything or even choosing a career. He was what in Moscow society is called *un jeune homme*.

Since his eighteenth year he had been as free as only a wealthy young Russian in the 'forties, who had lost his parents at an early age, could be. Neither physical nor moral fetters of any kind existed for him; he could do as he pleased, lacking nothing and bound by nothing. He had no family, no country, no religion, no wants. He believed in nothing and accepted nothing. But though he acknowledged no belief he was not a morose, blasé, argumentative youth: on the contrary, he continually allowed himself to be carried away. He had decided there was no such thing as love, yet his heart missed a beat whenever he found himself in the presence of a young and attractive woman. He had long regarded honours and rank as mere dross, yet he could not help feeling gratified if at a ball Prince Sergey came up and spoke to him affably. However, he would surrender to his enthusiasms only in so far as they did not commit him to anything. As soon as he began to suspect that some impulse to which he had yielded might involve him in exertion or strife – even in one of the petty conflicts of everyday life – he instinctively hastened to extricate himself from the interest or activity, and regain his freedom. In this way he had toyed with society life, the Civil Service, farming, music – to which at one time he had thought of devoting himself – and with love, in which he did not believe. He meditated on the use to which he should put all the energy of youth which comes to a man only once in life. Should he devote this power, which is not the strength of intellect or heart or education, but an urge which once spent can never return, the power given to a man once only to make himself, or even – so it seems to him at the time – the universe into anything he wishes: should he devote it to art, to science, to love, or to practical activities? True, there are people who never have this urge: at the outset of life they place their necks under the first yoke that offers itself, and soberly toil away in it to the end of their days. But Olenin was too acutely conscious of the presence within himself of that all-powerful god of Youth, of his capacity to be entirely transformed into an aspiration or an idea, the capacity to will and to do, the capacity to hurl himself headlong into a bottomless pit without knowing the why or wherefore. He carried this consciousness within himself with pride and, unknowingly, was happy in it. Up to this time he had loved only himself, and could not help it, for he expected nothing but good of himself and had not yet had time for disillusion. He was leaving Moscow in that happy youthful state of mind in which a young man, while recognizing mistakes, suddenly confesses to himself that he has not been on the right track but that all that has gone before was accidental and unimportant. Till then he had not really tried to live *properly*, but now, with his departure from Moscow, a new life was beginning, in which there would be no more mistakes, no more remorse and, of course, nothing but happiness.

It is always the case on a long journey that during the initial stages the imagination lingers behind on the place one has left, but with the first morning on the road it leaps forward to the end of the journey, and there begins building castles in the air. So it was with Olenin.

When the city had been left behind and he saw the wide stretch of snow-covered fields he was glad to be alone in their midst. Wrapping himself in his fur coat, he lay down on the floor of the sledge, settled himself comfortably and dozed. The parting with his friends had moved him deeply, and he began to go over the winter he had just spent in Moscow, while images of the past, mixed with confused thoughts and regrets, rose unbidden in his imagination.

He remembered the friend who had seen him off, and his relations with the girl they had talked about. The girl was rich. 'How could he love her, knowing that she loved me?' he thought, and ugly suspicions crossed his mind. 'Men are very dishonourable, when one comes to think of it.' Then he asked himself, 'But why is it that I have never been in love? Everyone tells me I never have. Am I an unnatural monster?' And he began to recall all his infatuations. He recalled his début into society and a girl, the sister of a friend of his, with whom he had spent several evenings with the table-lamp lighting up her slender fingers busy with their needlework, and the lower part of her pretty, delicate face. He remembered the conversations that dragged on like a game of *kurilka* in which the players have to pass a stick of burning wood backwards and forwards, keeping it alight as long as possible, and the general awkwardness and embarrassment, and his continual feeling of rebellion at all that stiffness. Some voice had always whispered: 'Not this one, not this one,' and the voice had proved to be right. Then he remembered a ball, and the mazurka he had danced with the lovely D—. 'How much in love I was that night, how happy! And how upset and disappointed the next morning when I woke up and found that I was heart-free again! Why doesn't love come and bind me hand and foot? No, there is no such thing as love. That woman in the country who kept telling me – as she had told Dubrovin and the marshal of the Nobility – how much she loved the stars wasn't *the* one either. And this brought to his mind his experiment in managing his estate in the country, and again his reflections gave him no pleasure. 'Will they have much to say about my departure?' he wondered, but who 'they' were he did not quite know. Next came a thought which made him wince and mutter to himself: it was the recollection of M. Cappel, the tailor, and the six hundred and seventy-eight roubles he still owed him, and he recalled the words in which he had begged him to wait another year, and the doubtful look of resignation which had appeared on the tailor's face. 'Oh Lord, oh Lord!' he repeated, frowning and trying to drive away the uncomfortable picture. 'And yet she loved me in spite of it all,' he said to himself, thinking of the girl they had talked about at the farewell supper. 'Yes, if I had married her I'd have got out of debt, but now I still owe money to Vassilyev.' And he recalled the last night he had played cards with Vassilyev at the Club (just after leaving her), and his humiliating entreaties for one more hand, and Vassilyev's cold refusal. 'One year of strict economy, and I'll pay off the whole damn lot ...' But in spite of this assurance he fell to calculating his debts again, the dates they were due for payment and when he could hope to pay them off. 'Let me see. Of course – I still owe Morel something as well as Chevalier,' and he recalled the night when he had run up so large a debt. It was a gipsy party arranged by some fellows from Petersburg: Sashka B—, an aide-de-camp to the Emperor, and Prince D—, and that pompous old ass —. 'And why should these gentlemen be so pleased with themselves?' he thought. 'What grounds have they for forming a clique to which they think others must be highly flattered to be admitted? Because they are on the Emperor's staff? It is really revolting, the way they look upon everyone else as fools and scoundrels! However, I jolly well showed them I wasn't in the least anxious to be one of them. All the same, I fancy Andrei, my bailiff, would be amazed to know I am on familiar terms with a man like Sashka B—, colonel and aide-de-camp to the Tsar .... Yes, and nobody drank more than I did that evening, and I taught the gipsies a new song and had the whole room listening. I may have done all sorts of stupid things,' he reflected, 'but I am still a very good fellow, a very good fellow indeed.'

Morning found Olenin at the third post-station. He drank some tea, helped Vanyusha rearrange his packages and trunks, and settled down among them, clear-headed, erect and meticulous, knowing where all his belongings were – how much money he had, and where it was, where he had put his passport, where his travelling papers – and everything seemed so well arranged that his spirits rose and the long journey before him appeared like an extended pleasure-trip.

All that morning and during the early part of the afternoon he sat engrossed in calculations: how many miles he had already travelled, how far was it to the next post-station, to the next town; how many miles to go before he would dine, or drink tea, or reach Stavropol, and what proportion of the journey was now behind him. At the same time he was working out how much money he had, how much would be left over, how much was needed to pay off all his debts, and what portion of his income he would be obliged to disburse each month. By tea-time he had reckoned that to Stavropol there remained seven-elevenths of the whole journey, that his debts would require seven months' economizing and represented one-eighth of his entire fortune; and having thus satisfied his mind he wrapped himself up, stretched out on the floor of the sledge and dozed off again. This time his imagination turned to the future, to the Caucasus, and his dreams were all of Amalat-Beks,* Circassian women, mountains, precipices, fearful torrents, and danger. Everything was hazy and confused but the lure of fame and the threat of danger made that future interesting. Now, with unprecedented courage and a strength that astounded everybody, he was slaying and subduing an innumerable host of hillsmen; now he was himself a hillsman, and was fighting on their side for independence from Russian dominion. When the picture became more detailed, familiar Moscow figures appeared on the scene. Sashka B— was there waging war with the Russians or the hillsmen against him. Even his tailor, M. Cappel, in some inexplicable way was taking part in the conqueror's triumph. If occasionally amid all this the recollection of his former humiliations, weaknesses and mistakes cropped up, the recollection was pleasant rather than otherwise. It was clear that there among the mountains, waterfalls, the Circassian girls and the perils, such mistakes could not recur. Having once made full confession to himself, there was an end of it. One other dream, the dearest of them all, was associated with the young man's every thought of the future: the vision of a woman among the mountains, a young Circassian slave with a slim waist, long braided hair and deep submissive eyes. He pictured a lonely hut in the mountains with *her* on the threshold, waiting for him to return, covered with dust, blood and glory, and he marvels at her kisses, her shoulders, her sweet voice and her docility. She is enchanting but unlettered, wild and rough. In the long winter evenings he would begin to educate her. She is quick, receptive and gifted, and soon acquires all the essential elements of knowledge. Why not? She could easily learn foreign languages, read the masterpieces of French literature and appreciate them. *Notre Dame de Paris*, for example, was sure to impress her. She can even speak French. In a drawing-room she would display more natural dignity than a lady of the highest society. She can

* A character in a Russian novel of the Caucasus by Marlinsky. [*Translator's note*]

sing too – simply, but with feeling and passion. 'Oh, what nonsense!' he suddenly said to himself, and just then they arrived at a post-station and had to change into another sledge and tip the men. But again his fancy began searching for the 'nonsense' he had relinquished and again he imagined fair Circassians and himself, crowned with glory, returning to Russia with an appointment as aide-de-camp to the Emperor, and a lovely wife. 'But we know there is no such thing as love,' he told himself again, 'and honours are rubbish. But what about those six hundred and seventy-eight roubles? ... The conquered land will have put into my hands more money than I need for a lifetime. It would not be right, though, to keep all that wealth for myself. I shall have to distribute it. But to whom? Well, six hundred and seventy-eight roubles to Cappel, and then we'll see ...' And now his thoughts become confused and disconnected, and only Vanyusha's voice and the feeling of the sledge stopping disturb the healthy slumber of youth. Half asleep he climbs into another sledge at the next stage and continues his journey.

Next morning it was the same all over again: post-stations, tea-drinking, the jogging backs of the horses, brief chats with Vanyusha, hazy visions and drowsiness towards evening, and the same tired, healthy, youthful sleep at night.

3

THE farther Olenin travelled from the centre of Russia the farther he left his memories behind, and the nearer he drew to the Caucasus the lighter his heart became. At times the idea of going away for good and never coming back or appearing in society again occurred to him. 'The people I see here are not really *people*. None of them knows me, none of them will ever go to Moscow and move in the circles in which I moved, and learn about my past. And no one in Moscow will ever know what I may do when I live among these others.' And a quite novel sense of freedom from his entire past came over him among the uncouth humanity he encountered on the road and whom he did not regard as *people* in the way that his Moscow acquaintances were people. The rougher they were, and the fewer were there any signs of civilization, the freer he felt. Stavropol, through which he had to pass, irked him. The sign-boards over the shops – some of them were even in French – the ladies in their barouches, the cabs drawn up in the square, a gentleman in a cloak and tall hat strolling along the boulevard and staring at the passers-by, quite upset him. 'Perhaps some of these people and I have mutual acquaintances,' he thought; and the Club, his tailor, card-playing, society life ... came back to his mind. After Stavropol, however, all was satisfactory: wild and, to boot, beautiful and warlike. Olenin's spirits soared higher and higher. All the Cossacks, post-boys and the station-masters seemed simple folk with whom he could jest and converse simply, without having to consider their class. They all belonged to the human race which he now loved whole-heartedly, and they all treated him as a friend.

Already in the province of the Don Cossacks his sledge had been exchanged for a post-chaise, and beyond Stavropol it became so warm that Olenin took off his sheepskin coat. It was spring here – a radiant, unexpected spring for Olenin. At night they were warned not to leave the Cossack villages, and it was said to be dangerous to travel after sundown. Vanyusha was uneasy and a loaded musket lay ready to hand. Olenin grew gayer and gayer. At one of the post-stations the post-master told them of a horrible murder that had recently been committed on the highway. They began to meet men carrying weapons. 'So now we've come to it!' thought Olenin, and kept looking for the snow-clad mountains of which he had heard so often. Once, towards evening, the Nogay driver pointed with his whip to peaks behind the clouds. Olenin looked eagerly but the sky was overcast and the mountains were almost hidden by the clouds. All he could make out was something grey and white and fleecy: try as he would, he could discover nothing beautiful about these mountains of which he had read and heard so much. Mountains and clouds appeared alike to him, and he began to suspect that the special beauty of snowy peaks, of which he had so often been told, was as much a figment of the imagination as the music of Bach, or love, in neither of which did he believe – and so he gave up looking forward to the mountains. But early next day, awakened in his post-chaise by the freshness of the air, he glanced casually to the right. The morning was crystal-clear. Suddenly he saw, at what seemed to him at first glance to be about twenty paces away, gigantic pure white masses with gentle curves and fantastical airy summits minutely outlined against the distant sky. When he realized the distance between himself and them and the sky, and the whole immensity of those mountains, and their infinite beauty, he feared lest it prove to be a mirage or a dream. He gave himself a shake, but the mountains were still there.

'What's that? What is it?' he asked the driver.

'Why, the mountains,' answered the Tartar indifferently.

'I've been looking at 'em for a long time too,' said Vanyusha. 'Ain't they fine? They won't ever believe me at home when I tell 'em.'

With the swift movement of the troika over the smooth road the mountains appeared to run along the horizon, their rose-coloured crests glittering in the light of the rising sun. At first Olenin only marvelled at the towering masses, then delighted in them; but later on, gazing more and more intently at that snow-peaked chain that seemed to rise not from other, black masses but straight out of the plain, and to glide away into the distance, he began gradually to take in their beauty and *feel* the mountains. From that moment whatever he saw, whatever he thought, whatever he felt, acquired a new character, sternly majestic, like the mountains. All his recollections of Moscow, his shame and repentance, all his trivial fantasies about the Caucasus – vanished never to return. A solemn voice seemed to say, 'It has begun.' And the road, and the Terek, just then coming into sight, and the Cossack villages and the people no longer seemed unreal and not to be taken seriously. He looked at the sky and thought of the mountains. He looked at himself or Vanyusha, and still thought of the mountains. Two Cossacks rode by, their guns in their holsters swinging rhythmically behind their backs, the white and bay legs of their horses intermingling ... and the mountains. Beyond the Terek smoke was rising from a Tartar hamlet ... and the mountains. The sun has risen and glitters on the waters of the Terek now visible beyond the reeds ... and the mountains. From the village comes a Tartar wagon, and women, young, beautiful women walk by ... and the mountains.

'Abreks * canter about the steppe, and here am I, driving along, unafraid: I have a gun, and strength, and youth ... and the mountains!'

4

THE whole line of the Terek, along which, for some fifty miles, are scattered the villages of the Greben Cossacks, is uniform in character, both as to landscape and inhabitants. The Terek, which separates the Cossacks from the hill-tribes, flows still turbid and swift but broad now, and smooth, continually depositing grey silt on its low reedy right bank, and washing away the steep, though not high, left bank with its tangled roots of century-old oaks, rotting plane-trees and young underbrush. On the right bank lie the villages of the pro-Russian but still somewhat restless Tartars; along the left, half a mile back from the river and five or six miles apart from one another, lie the Cossack villages. In former times the majority of these villages were on the edge of the river; but the Terek, year after year shifting northwards from the mountains, washed away its banks and now all that remains are the ruins of old settlements and the gardens of pear and plum trees and poplars, thickly overgrown with blackberry bushes and wild vines. The place is no longer inhabited and the only signs of life are the tracks made on the sand by deer, wolves, hares and pheasants, who have learned to love the spot. A road runs from village to village, cut in a bee-line through the forest. Along the road are cordons of Cossacks, and watch-towers with sentinels on guard. Only a narrow strip of some seven hundred yards of fertile wooded land belongs to the Cossacks. To the north begin the sand drifts of the Nogay or Mozdok steppe, stretching away and merging, heaven knows where, into the steppes of Turkmenia, Astrakhan and Kirghiz-Kaisatsk. Southwards, beyond the Terek, run the Great Chechnya river, the Kochkalykov range, the Black Mountains, yet another range, and at last the snowy mountains, which can just be seen but have never yet been

* Hostile Circassians who cross the Terek to raid the Russian side of the river. [*Translator's note*]

scaled. In this fertile wooded belt, rich in vegetation, has lived since time immemorial a warlike, handsome, prosperous Russian population of Old Believers, called the Greben Cossacks.

Long, long ago their ancestors had fled from Russia and settled among the Chechens on the Greben, the first stretch of wooded mountains beyond the Terek. Dwelling among the Chechens, the Cossacks intermarried with them and adopted the manners and customs of the hill tribes, though they still retained the Russian language and the Old Faith in all their purity. According to a tradition still existing Tsar Ivan the Terrible came to the Terek, sent for the Cossack elders and gave them the land on this side of the river, exhorting them to remain friendly to Russia and promising not to enforce his rule upon them nor oblige them to change their faith. Ever since, the Cossacks have claimed relationship with the Chechens, and love of freedom, of leisure, plunder and war have been their most notable traits. Russian influence shows itself only in a detrimental way, by interference at elections, the confiscation of church-bells and the presence of troops who are quartered in the country, or march through it. A Cossack is less inclined to hate the Chechen brave, the *dzhigit*, who may well have killed his brother, than the Russian soldier billeted on him for the defence of his village but who has fouled his cottage by smoking in it. He respects his enemy the hillsman, but despises the soldier, who is in his eyes an alien and an oppressor. In fact, the Cossack regards the Russian peasant as a foreign, outlandish, despicable creature, of whom he sees specimen enough in the hawkers and Ukrainian immigrants whom he contemptuously calls 'wool-combers'. For the Cossack, to be smartly dressed means to be dressed like a Circassian. The best weapons are obtained from the hillsmen, and the best horses are bought or stolen from them. The young Cossack brave prides himself on his knowledge of the Tartar language, and when carousing talks Tartar even to his fellow Cossack. In spite of all this, this small Christian clan, stranded in a tiny corner of the earth, surrounded by half-savage Mohammedan tribes and Russian soldiers, considers itself highly advanced, acknowledges none but Cossacks as human beings and despises everybody else. The Cossack spends most of his time in the outposts, in action, or in hunting and fishing. He hardly ever works at home, and when he is in the village, which is exceptional, he carouses and makes merry. All Cossacks produce their own wine and drunkenness is not so much a general tendency as a rite which it would be apostasy not to observe. The Cossack looks upon a woman as an instrument for his well-being. As long as she is single she is allowed to enjoy life but once married a wife must toil for her husband from her youth to the end of her days, and is expected to be as hard-working and submissive as an Oriental woman. In consequence the Cossack woman is powerfully developed both physically and morally, and though to all appearances in subjection possesses – as is usually the case in the East – incomparably greater influence and weight in family affairs than her Western sister. Their exclusion from public life and inurement to heavy manual labour give the women all the more authority and importance at home. The Cossack, who in the company of strangers considers it improper to speak affectionately or without reason to his wife, is very conscious of her superiority when they are alone. His house and all his property – in fact, the entire homestead – have been acquired and are kept together solely by her diligence and care. Though he is obstinately convinced that work is degrading to a Cossack, and is a proper occupation only for a Nogay labourer or a woman, he is vaguely aware of the fact that all he enjoys and calls his own is the result of that toil, and that although he considers both wife and mother his slaves, it lies in the power of the women to deprive him of all that makes life agreeable. Added to this, constant hard manual work and the responsibilities entrusted to them have endowed the Greben women with a peculiarly independent, masculine outlook and developed in them physical strength, common sense, resolution and stability of character to a remarkable degree. The women are in most cases stronger, more intelligent, more developed and handsomer than the men. The combination of the purest Circassian type of face with the broad and powerful build of the Northern woman makes the beauty of the Greben women particularly striking. Cossack women wear the Circassian dress: a Tartar smock, the *beshmet* * and soft leather slippers; but they tie kerchiefs round their heads in the Russian

* Under-tunic. [*Translator's note*]

fashion. Elegance, neatness and good taste in their dress and in the arrangement of their homes are a custom and a necessity with them. In their relations with men the women, and especially the unmarried girls, are completely free.

The village of Novomlinsk is accepted as the metropolis of the Greben Cossacks. Here more than anywhere else the old Greben customs have been preserved, and for generations its women have been renowned all over the Caucasus for their beauty. The Cossacks live on the products of their vineyards and orchards, water-melon and pumpkin plantations, on fishing and hunting, maize and millet growing, and the spoils of war.

Novomlinsk village is separated from the Terek by about two-and-a-half miles of dense forest. On one side of the road which runs through the village is a stream; on the other side green vineyards and orchards gradually give way to the drift-sands of the Nogay steppe. The township is surrounded by earth banks and thorn hedges, and is entered at either end through tall gates hung on posts and protected by little reed-thatched roofs. On a wooden gun-carriage near one of them stands an unwieldy cannon captured by the Cossacks at some time or other, which has not been fired for a century. A Cossack in uniform, with cap and gun, is sometimes found and sometimes not found on guard beside the gate; sometimes he presents arms to a passing officer, and sometimes does not. A white board hangs under the roof of the gateway with an inscription in black letters: 'Houses 266; male inhabitants 897; female inhabitants 1012'. The Cossacks' cottages are all raised on posts two-and-a-half feet from the ground. They have large carved gables and are neatly thatched with reeds. If not new, they are at least all straight and clean, with high porches of different shapes; and they are not huddled close together but picturesquely placed, with ample space between them, alongside streets and lanes. In front of the large clear windows of many of the houses, beyond the kitchen gardens, dark poplars and acacias with their tender pale-green leaves and scented white blossoms overtop the roofs, and beside them grow flaunting yellow sunflowers and the twining tendrils of the wild pea and grapevines. On the wide square three little shops display haberdashery side by side with sunflower and pumpkin seeds, locust beans and gingerbread; and behind a tall fence and a row of ancient poplars stands the colonel's house, loftier and larger than all the others and having leaded windows. The streets, especially in summer, are generally deserted on week-days. The Cossacks are away on duty, the young men in the outposts or on military expeditions, the older ones hunting or fishing or helping the women in the orchards and gardens. Only the very old, the children and the sick remain at home.

5

It was one of those evenings that are peculiar to the Caucasus. The sun had gone down behind the mountains but it was still light. An evening glow had spread over a third of the sky and against its radiance the dull white immensity of the ranges was sharply outlined. The air was rarified, motionless and full of sound. The mountains cast long shadows over several miles of steppe. The steppe, the opposite bank of the river and the roads were all deserted. If, very occasionally, horsemen appeared, the Cossacks in the cordon and the Chechens from their villages watched with suspicion, trying to guess who such questionable people could be. At nightfall the inhabitants, fearful of one another, flock to their dwellings, and only wild beasts and birds, unafraid of man, are left to prowl unhindered about the wilderness. Women who have been tying up the vines hurry home before sunset, talking gaily together, and the surrounding stretches of garden and field are empty. But the villages at this time of day become extremely animated, people thronging in from every side, on foot, on horseback or in their creaking ox-carts. Girls with their skirts tucked up and switches in their hands run chattering merrily to the village gates to meet the cattle crowding together in a cloud of dust and mosquitoes which have followed them from the steppe. The well-fed cows and buffaloes scatter over the streets, and the women in their coloured *beshmets* wander in and out among them, their squeals and happy laughter mingling with the lowing of the cattle. There an armed and mounted Cossack, on leave from the cordon, rides up to a hut and, leaning down, taps on the window, whereupon the pretty head of a young woman appears and one hears the murmur of caressing, laughing voices. There a ragged high-cheekboned Nogay labourer brings a load of reeds from the marshes, turns his creaking cart into the wide clean courtyard of the captain's house, lifts the yoke off the oxen, who stand tossing their heads, while he and his master shout to one another in Tartar. Past a puddle that spreads nearly the width of the street – a puddle crossed by so many people for so many years – a barefooted woman with a bundle of faggots on her back picks her way laboriously, clinging to the fences and holding her petticoats high above her white ankles, while a Cossack back from hunting calls out in jest, 'Higher with 'em, you shameless hussy!' and points his gun at her. The woman lets down her skirts and drops the wood. An old Cossack, returning home from fishing, with his trousers rolled up and his grey hairy chest uncovered, has a net across his shoulder full of flapping silvery fish, and to make a short cut crawls through his neighbour's broken fence, giving a tug to his coat as it catches on a splinter. Yonder an old woman drags a dry branch along, and from nearby echo the blows of an axe. Children screech as they whip their tops wherever they can find a bit of level ground in the streets. Women clamber over hedges to save themselves the trouble of walking round. From every chimney rises the pungent smoke of *kizyak*.* From every homestead comes the sound of urgent bustle which precedes the stillness of the night.

Old Mother Ulitka, the wife of the ensign who is also the teacher in the regimental school, has, like the other women, come out to the gate of her yard to watch for the cattle which her daughter Marianka is driving down the street. Almost before she can get the wicket gate open an enormous buffalo cow with gnats swarming about her rushes bellowing into the yard. Several fat cows follow her slowly, their large eyes recognizing their mistress as they lazily swish their sides with their tails. Marianka, a comely beauty, approaches the yard and, throwing down her stick, slams the gate and scampers round to separate the cattle and drive them into their stalls. 'Take off your shoes, you spawn of the devil!' shouts her mother. 'You've worn them to shreds as it is.' Marianka is not in the least affronted at being

* Dung mixed with straw. [*Translator's note*]

called devil's spawn: she accepts it as a term of endearment and gaily continues her work. Her kerchief has slipped down over her forehead. She is wearing a pink smock and a green *beshmet*. She disappears into the byre after the big fat cattle, and then her voice is heard coaxing the buffalo cow. 'There now, stand still, my lovely. What a creature! There, there, come now, old lady.' Soon the girl and her mother cross from the byre to the dairy, each carrying two brimming crocks of milk, the day's yield. A cloud of smoke rises from the clay chimney of the dairy-house: the milk is being boiled for clotted cream. While the girl makes up the fire the mother goes back to the gate. Dusk has fallen on the village. The air is full of the smell of vegetables, cattle and pungent *kizyak* smoke. Women come running along the streets, carrying flaming rags. The beasts, eased of their milk, stand snorting and peacefully chewing in their byres, and the only other sound comes from the women and children calling out shrilly to one another in the streets and yards. Very rarely on a week-day does one hear the drunken voice of a man.

A tall masculine-looking old woman with a rag in her hand comes across from the homestead opposite to ask Goody Ulitka for a light.

'Well, friend, do you reckon you're finished now?'

'The girl is seeing to the fire. Is it fire you want?' says Goody Ulitka, proud of being able to oblige a neighbour.

The two women go into the cottage. Clumsy fingers, unused to handling small objects, tremblingly remove the lid of the precious match-box, for matches are few and far between in the Caucasus. The masculine-looking visitor sits down on the doorstep, with the evident intention of having a gossip.

'So your good man is away at the school, eh?' she asks.

'Yes, he's still learning the youngsters. But he wrote me he'll be here come the holiday,' said the teacher's wife.

'There's a mighty learned man for you! That's useful work, that is.'

'Aye, indeed.'

'My Luka, he's at the cordon, and they don't allow him to come home,' says the visitor, though well aware that this is no news to the teacher's wife. She wants to talk about her Luka, whom she has recently put into the Cossacks and whom she would like to marry to the teacher's daughter, Marianka.

'So he's at the cordon?'

'At the cordon, friend. He's not been home since last holiday. T'other day I sent him some shirts by Fomushkin. The lad's all right, he tells me, and the officers are pleased with him. He says they're on the look out for *abreks* again. The lad's happy, he says.'

'Ah well, thank the Lord for that,' answers the teacher's wife. 'Snatcher's the name for him all right.'

Luka had earned the nickname 'Snatcher' because of his bravery in snatching a boy from drowning, and the teacher's wife alluded to this as she wished to say something pleasant to Luka's mother.

'I bless the Lord every day of me life, friend, that he's such a good son. He's a fine lad, everybody speaks well of him,' says Luka's mother. 'Me one wish is to see him wed, and then I could die in peace.'

'Well, aren't there girls and to spare in the village?' retorts the teacher's wife slyly, with her gnarled fingers carefully replacing the lid on the match-box.

'Plenty, friend, plenty,' remarks Luka's mother, nodding her head. 'Your Marianka now, there's a fine lass for you! A body'd have to go a long way afore finding another like her.'

The teacher's wife knows what Luka's mother is after, and though she approves of Luka she hangs back: first because she is the teacher's wife and well-to-do, whereas Luka is the son of a mere Cossack, and a dead one at that; secondly, because she does not feel ready to part with her daughter; but chiefly because propriety demands it.

'Yes, when Marianka grows up 'twill be time enough to think of getting her wed,' she says with sober discretion.

'I'll go send the matchmakers round, that's what I'll do. Just let me get the vineyards done and then we'll come and wait on you,' says Luka's mother. 'We'll come and talk things over with your good man.'

'What's he got to do with it? I am the one you'll have to speak to,' says the teacher's wife haughtily. 'But all in good time.'

Seeing by the severe expression on her neighbour's face that she has said enough, the visitor lights her rag with the match and rising to her feet ends the conversation with 'Well, don't forget, friend. Think over what I've said. I must be going now. 'Bout time I got me fire started.'

As she crosses the road, swinging the burning rag in her outstretched hand, she meets Marianka, who greets her with a nod.

'Ah, she's a reg'lar queen, a splendid worker, that girl!' she thinks, following the beauty with her eyes. 'How much more has she got to grow, I should like to know? 'Tis high time she was wed and in a nice home of her own, married to my Luka.'

Goody Ulitka has preoccupations of her own and remains sitting on the step, deep in thought until Marianka came to call her.

6

THE men of the village spend their time on military expeditions and in the cordon – or 'at the posts', as the Cossacks call it. Towards evening that same Luka the Snatcher of whom the old women had been talking was standing on the watch-tower of the Nizhne-Prototsk outpost, situated right on the bank of the Terek. Leaning on the railing of the tower and screwing up his eyes, he stared now into the distance beyond the Terek, now below at his fellow Cossacks, with whom he occasionally exchanged a stray remark. The sun was already sinking towards the snow-covered peaks which gleamed white above the fleecy clouds. The sea of clouds at the foot of the mountains became increasingly dark. The cool of the evening spread through the air. A breath of freshness came from the thick, wild forest but round the post it was still hot. The voices of the Cossacks rang out clear and loud, seeming to hover in the air. The moving mass of the Terek's swift brown waters contrasted sharply with its still banks. It was now beginning to fall and here and there the wet sands showed grey on the banks and in the shallows. The shore directly opposite the outpost was deserted; only an immense waste of low-growing reeds stretched far away to the very foot of the mountains. On the low bank, a little to one side, could be seen the flat-roofed mud huts and the funnel-shaped chimneys of a Chechen village. The alert eyes of the young Cossack standing on the watch-tower gazed through the evening smoke of the pro-Russian village at the moving figures of the Chechen women in their clothes of red and blue.

Although the Cossacks were expecting the *abreks* to sweep across the river and attack them from the Tartar side – especially as it was in May when the woods along the Terek are so dense as to be almost impassable on foot and the river is shallow enough in certain places for a horseman to ford; and a couple of days earlier a messenger had arrived from the commander of the regiment, warning them that according to a report from their scouts a party of eight *abreks* were preparing to cross the Terek, and advising special vigilance – no special vigilance was being observed in the cordon. The Cossacks, unarmed and their horses unsaddled, spent their time some fishing, some drinking, some hunting, just as though they were at home. Only the horse of the sentry on duty was saddled and, with its feet hobbled, was moving about the brambles near the wood; and the sentry himself was the only man to have his uniform on and carry his musket and sabre. The sergeant, a tall thin Cossack with an extraordinarily long back and small hands and feet, was sitting on a bank of earth round one of the huts. His *beshmet* was unbuttoned, there was an overall expression of lazy boredom on his face as he rocked his head from one hand to the other, with closed eyes. An elderly Cossack with a broad greyish-black beard, clad only in a shirt belted with a black leather strap, was lying at the edge of the water, indolently watching the waves of the Terek as they monotonously foamed and swirled past him. Others, likewise overcome by the heat and half naked, were rinsing clothes in the river, or plaiting a string bridle, or humming a tune as they lay stretched out on the hot sand. One Cossack with a thin face burnt black by the sun, and evidently dead drunk, lay flat on his back under a wall which had been in the shade an hour or two earlier but was now exposed to the fierce slanting rays of the sun.

Luka the Snatcher, who stood on the watch-tower, a tall, handsome lad of about twenty, was very like his mother. His face and his whole figure, in spite of the angularity of youth, indicated great strength, both physical and moral. Though but recently enrolled with the Cossacks on active service his expression and the calm assurance of his attitude showed that already he had acquired the somewhat haughty warlike bearing peculiar to Cossacks and military men generally, and that he was a Cossack and held his head high in consequence. His ample Circassian coat was torn in places, his cap sat awry on the back of his head, Chechen fashion, his long leggings were pushed down below the knees. His garments were poor but Luka wore them with the jaunty air of the Cossack imitating the Chechen brave. About the latter everything is bunchy, torn and untidy: only his weapons are costly. But he wears his ragged clothes and adjusts his weapons in his belt with a certain distinction not given to everybody and which is immediately apparent to the eye of Cossack or hillsman. Luka had the swagger of a genuine brave. With his hands on his sabre and his eyes screwed up he was watching the Tartar village in the distance. His features were not beautiful individually but his superb physique and his intelligent face with its dark eyebrows would cause the involuntary exclamation 'What a fine lad!'

'Why are all them women spilling out of the village, I wonder?' he said in a sharp voice, languidly showing his gleaming white teeth and addressing no one in particular.

Nazar, who was stretched out below, lifted his head at once and observed:

'Going for water most likely.'

'What if I rattles 'em with a shot?' said Luka, laughing. 'I reckon that'd scare 'em right enough!'

'You couldn't reach that far.'

'You say so? My gun'll carry further than that,' said Luka, testily beating off the gnats clinging about him. 'When their feast-day comes round I must drop in on Girey Khan and get a drink o' their beer.'

A rustling in the thicket drew the Cossacks' attention. A spotted mongrel setter with nose to the ground ran up to the cordon, wagging a mangy tail. Luka recognized his neighbour's, Gaffer Yeroshka's, dog, and directly after saw the hunter himself approaching through the thicket.

Gaffer Yeroshka was a gigantic Cossack with a thick snow-white beard and such breadth of chest and shoulder that in the forest away from comparison with other men he appeared to be but little above average height, so well was his powerful figure proportioned. He wore a tattered peasant coat bunched up at the waist and a crumpled lamb-skin cap. Sandals of undressed deer-hide were tied on with string over his leg bands. Over one shoulder he carried a screen to hide himself when shooting pheasants, and a bag containing a hen and a small falcon for luring hawks; a wild cat he had just shot was slung on a strap over his other shoulder, and stuck in his belt behind were various little pouches containing bullets, gunpowder and bread, a horse's tail for swishing off mosquitoes, a large dagger in a torn sheath smeared with old bloodstains, and a couple of dead pheasants. When he saw the cordon he halted.

'To heel, Lyam!' he shouted to the dog in a ringing bass that echoed far through the forest. Then, hitching over his shoulder an enormous musket of the kind the Cossacks call a 'flint', he raised his cap.

'Had a good day, lads, eh?' he asked, addressing the Cossacks in the same strong, cheerful voice which without any effort on his part boomed out as though he were calling to someone on the other bank of the river.

From all sides young voices gaily answered, 'Yes, Gaffer, fine!'

'What news?' shouted Gaffer Yeroshka, wiping the sweat from his broad red face with the sleeve of his coat.

Nazar gave a wink. 'I'll tell you,' he said, jerking his shoulder and leg. 'There's a vulture here in the plane-tree. Comes out and hovers round so soon as it's night-time.'

'Go on now,' said the old man incredulously.

'It's a fact all right. You just wait and see,' insisted Nazar, grinning.

The other Cossacks laughed.

The wag had not seen any vulture but the young Cossacks in the cordon had long since taken to teasing and misleading Gaffer Yeroshka every time he came to see them.

'The fool – lies like a trooper, he does!' shouted Luka from the tower, whereupon Nazar relapsed into silence.

'If there's anything to watch for, I'll watch,' rejoined the old man to the great delight of all the Cossacks. 'But have you seen any boars?'

'What do you think! Us look out for boars!' said the sergeant, bending forward and scratching his back with both hands, very pleased at the chance of a little distraction. 'It's *abreks* we're after, not boars. You don't happen to have heard anything, have you?' he added, needlessly screwing up his eyes and showing his close-set white teeth.

'*Abreks*, you mean?' said the old man. 'No, I ain't. Say, got any *chikhir*? * I could do with a drink. I'm proper fagged. One of these days I'll bring you some game, honest I will. Come on, give us a drink, there's me good lad.'

'So you're out after game, eh?' inquired the sergeant as though he had not heard what the other said.

'I did think to stay out tonight,' replied Yeroshka. ' "Maybe," I says to meself, "maybe I'll bag something for the holiday." Then you'd get your share, honest to God.'

'Hi, Gaffer!' Luka called down sharply, attracting general attention so that everybody looked up at him. 'You jus' go upstream and you'll find a fine herd of boars. Cross me heart. T'other day one of our chaps shot one there. It's true what I'm telling you,' he concluded, readjusting the musket at his back and speaking in a tone that showed he was not joking.

'Ah, so Luka the Snatcher's 'ere,' said the old man, looking up. 'Where did you say the boar were shot?'

'So you didn't notice me then? So small, aren't I?' said Luka. 'Close by the ditch, it was,' he continued earnestly, with a shake of his head. 'We was walking along the ditch an' all on a sudden we hear a crackling noise in the bushes. But my gun was in its case, so Ilya fired . . . I can show you the very spot – it ain't far. Just you wait. Man, I knows every one of their trails. . . . It's time to be changing guard!' he added, turning resolutely and almost commandingly to the sergeant; and, picking up his gun, he began to descend from the watch-tower, without waiting for any order.

Luka was already on his way when the sergeant called to him to come down.

* Home-made Caucasian wine. [*Translator's note*]

' 'Tis your turn now, Gurka, ain't it?' said the sergeant, glancing round. 'Get moving, lad.' Then, to the old man: 'This here Luka of yours has got to be a fair dab. He's for ever prowling, same as you. There's no keeping him chained up at home. Why, only t'other day he killed a boar.'

7

THE sun had now set and the shades of night were sweeping swiftly over from the forest. The Cossacks finished their duties at the cordon and assembled in the hut for supper. Only the old man still stayed under the plane-tree, watching for the vulture and tugging at the string tied to the falcon's leg. But though there actually was a vulture perched among the branches it declined to swoop down on the hen. Luka, singing one song after another, was leisurely setting pheasant snares in the very thick of the brambles. In spite of his great height and big hands it was plain to see that any kind of work, rough or fine, prospered once he put his hand to it.

'Hi, Luka!' came a piercing call from Nazar in the nearby thicket. 'Seems everybody's gone in for supper.' And Nazar, with a live pheasant under his arm, struggled through the brambles and emerged on to the footpath.

'Oh!' cried Luka, breaking off his song. 'Where did you come by that bird? In one of my snares, I'll lay.'

Nazar was the same age as Luka, and had also been serving in the cordon since the previous spring. He was a puny little lad with a shrill voice that rang in one's ears. He and Luka were neighbours and chums.

' 'Dunno for sure whose it was. Maybe 'tis one of yours.'

'If 'twas over by the pit, under the plane-tree, 'twas mine right enough, I set the nets last night.'

Luka was sitting on the grass, cross-legged like a Tartar, fixing up a snare. He got up and examined the pheasant, which was stretching out its neck and rolling its eyes in terror. He took it in his hands and stroked the dark-blue head.

'We'll make him into a pilaff for supper. Here, you kill and pluck him.'

'Shall you and me eat him, or give him to the sergeant?'

'He's had his fill.'

'I don't like killing 'em,' said Nazar.

'Here, give him to me.'

Luka drew a clasp-knife from behind his dagger and gave it a swift jerk. The bird fluttered, but before it had time to spread its wings the bleeding head sagged and quivered.

'There you are!' said Luka, throwing the bird on the ground. ''Twill make a nice fat pilaff.'

Nazar shuddered as he picked up the pheasant.

'I say, Luka, that old devil'll be sending us on patrol again tonight,' he said, meaning the sergeant. ''Tis Fomushkin's turn, but he's been despatched to fetch wine. How many more times? He's for ever coming down on us.'

Luka went whistling along the cordon.

'Take a hold of this line!' he shouted.

Nazar obeyed.

'I'm giving him a bit of me mind today, that I am,' continued Nazar. 'Let's say as we ain't going. We'll tell him we're dog-tired, and there's an end of it. You tell him, he'll listen to you. It's a sight too bad!'

'Get along with you! What a thing to make a fuss about!' said Luka, his mind evidently on something else. 'Stuff and nonsense! If we was in the village now, and he turned us out at night, that would be hard luck, because there we might be having a bit of fun. But what difference do it make here whether we're in the cordon or out on patrol? You are a ...!'

'Was you thinking of going to the village?'

'I'll be going for the holiday.'

'Gurka says your Dunayka is carrying on with Fomushkin,' Nazar said suddenly.

'Well, let her go to the devil,' said Luka showing his regular white teeth, though he did not laugh. 'As if I couldn't find another!'

'Gurka says he went to her home, and her husband was out, and there was Fomushkin sitting eating some pie. Gurka hung about a bit and then went off, and as he was passing under the window he heard her say, "Thank goodness the old devil's gone. Why don't you eat your pie, my pet? No need for you to go home tonight," says she. And Gurka under the window calls out "That's right!" '

'You're pulling me leg.'

' 'Tis a fact, cross me heart.'

'Well, if she's found another, let her go to the devil,' said Luka, after a pause. 'There're plenty of girls about, ain't there? An' I was sick to death of her, anyway.'

'You're a devil of a fellow, ain't you? Say, why don't you go for the cornet's girl, Marianka? She ain't fixed up with anyone.'

Luka frowned. 'Why Marianka special? All them girls is the same as one another.'

'Well, you just try your hand on her . . .'

'Maybe I will. But you wouldn't say girls was scarce in the village, would you?'

And Luka started whistling again and moved towards the post, stripping leaves from the branches as he passed. Suddenly, catching sight of a smooth sapling, he stopped, drew the knife from the handle of his dagger, and cut it down. 'There's a fine ramrod for you,' he said, swishing the stick through the air.

The Cossacks were at supper, sitting round a low Tartar table on the earth floor of the clay-plastered outer room of the hut, when the question of whose turn it was to do patrol was raised.

'Who's on tonight?' shouted one of the Cossacks through the open door to the sergeant inside.

'Yes, whose turn is it?' the sergeant called back. 'Old Burlak has been, same as Fomushkin,' (this not quite confidently). 'It had better be you two – you and Nazar,' he went on, addressing Luka. 'Yes, and Yergushov can go. He must have slept it off by now?'

'You don't sleep it off that quick yourself, so why should he?' Nazar muttered under his breath.

His companions laughed.

Yergushov was the Cossack who had been lying in a drunken sleep under the wall of the hut. At that moment he staggered into the room, rubbing his eyes.

Luka had got to his feet and was slinging his musket over his shoulder.

'And get a move on, lads. Finish your food and be off,' said the sergeant. And without waiting for any acknowledgement of the order he shut the door, evidently very doubtful of being obeyed. 'I have me orders, or I wouldn't send no one out. But the captain might turn up any minute. Besides, they say eight *abreks* are over the river already.'

'Well, I suppose as we'd better make a start,' said Yergushov. 'Orders is orders. Can't be helped in times like these. Come on.'

Meanwhile Luka, with both hands holding a great chunk of pheasant to his mouth, and glancing now at the sergeant, now at Nazar, apparently quite indifferent to what passed, only laughed at them both. Before the Cossacks had time to start, Yeroshka, who had been waiting in vain for the hawk under the plane-tree till night fell, entered the dimly lit outer room.

'Well, lads,' boomed his bass voice in the low porch, drowning all the rest. 'I'll be coming along with you. You can watch for *abreks* and I'll keep a lookout for boars.'

8

IT was quite dark when Gaffer Yeroshka and the three Cossacks in felt cloaks and their muskets over their shoulders left the cordon and went down along the Terek to the spot where they were to lie in ambush. Nazar was very loath to go, but Luka shouted at him and they quickly got under way. After a few steps in silence they turned aside from the ditch and followed a footpath almost hidden by reeds, till they reached the river. On the bank lay a big, black log washed up by the water and surrounded by recently crushed reeds.

'What about this spot?' asked Nazar.

'Why not?' replied Luka. 'You stay here, and I'll come back in no time. I'll just show Yeroshka where to go.'

'This is the best place there is,' said Yergushov. 'We can see without being seen. So here we are and here we stays. It's a grand place.'

Nazar and Yergushov spread out their cloaks and settled down behind the log, while Luka went on with Gaffer Yeroshka.

' 'Tain't far,' whispered Luka, stepping noiselessly ahead of the old man. 'I'll show you where they was. I'm the only one as knows.'

'You show us. You're a good lad, Snatcher,' the old man whispered back.

After they had gone a few steps Luka halted, stooped down over a puddle and whistled. 'This here's where they comes to drink, see?' he said, so softly that he could hardly be heard, and pointed to some fresh hoof-prints.

'Bless you,' answered the old man. 'The boar'll be in the hollow t'other side of the ditch,' he added. 'I'll watch, and you go along now.'

Luka hitched up his cloak and walked back alone, casting a swift glance now to the wall of reeds on his left, now to the Terek rushing by below the bank. 'For all I knows some *abrek*'s watching me or slinking about somewhere,' he thought. A sudden loud rustling and a splash in the water made him start and seize his musket. A wild boar dashed panting from the shore, his dark outline showing for a moment against the glassy surface of the water and then disappearing among the reeds. Quickly Luka raised his gun and took aim, but before he could fire the boar had disappeared in the thicket. Luka spat in disgust and went on his way. On approaching the ambuscade he halted again and whistled softly. His whistle was answered and he joined his comrades.

Nazar, curled up, was sound asleep. Yergushov was sitting cross-legged on the ground and moved slightly to make room for Luka.

'Proper sort of a place this is, 'tis real nice sitting here,' he said, 'Well, an' did you take him there?'

'Yes, I did,' Luka answered, spreading out his cloak. 'An' what a huge boar I started up just now, right by the river. It must have been the very same one. I reckon you heard the crash?'

'Aye, an' I knows at once 'twas an animal. I thinks to meself, "Luka's started a boar moving," ' said Yergushov, wrapping his cloak round him. 'I'll get some sleep now,' he continued. 'Wake us soon as cock crow: we must have things regular. I'll have a nap, we'll both get a nap; and while you're sleeping I'll keep watch ... That's the way we'll do it.'

'I thank you, but I don't want no sleep,' answered Luka.

It was a dark, warm night, and there was no breeze. Only in one quarter of the sky the stars were shining: all the rest was overcast by one huge cloud that rested on the mountain-tops. This black cloud, coalescing with the mountains, in the absence of wind moved slowly onwards, its wavy edges sharply outlined against the deep starry heavens. Only in front of him could Luka discern the Terek and the distance beyond: behind and on both sides he was surrounded by a wall of reeds. Occasionally, without any apparent cause, the reeds would sway and rustle against one another. Seen from below, against the clear section of the sky, their quivering tufts looked like the feathery branches of trees. The river bank was at his very feet, and below that the rushing torrent of the Terek. Farther away the flowing mass of glassy brown water eddied rhythmically along the bank and round the shallows. Farther still, water, bank, clouds all merged together in impenetrable gloom. On the surface of the river black shadows floated past, which the experienced eyes of the Cossack recognized as fallen trees being carried down by the current. Now and again summer lightning, reflected in the black mirror of the water, disclosed the sloping bank opposite. The measured sounds of night: the rustling of the reeds, the snoring of the men, the hum of mosquitoes, the gurgling of the river were broken every now and then by a shot fired in the distance or the squelch when a piece of the bank slipped down, the splash of a big fish, or the crashing of an animal through the thick undergrowth in the forest. Once an owl flew by along the Terek, flapping its wings together at every second beat. Just above Luka's head it turned towards the forest and then, flapping its wings together at every stroke instead of every other, it circled round an old plane-tree, where it fussed about for a long time before settling down among the branches. At every one of these sudden sounds the watching Cossack strained his ears, screwing up his eyes and quietly fingering his musket.

Night was nearly over. The black cloud that had moved westward now revealed behind its broken edges the clear starry sky, and the yellow upturned crescent of the moon shone above the mountains with a pinkish light. It began to get cold. Nazar woke, muttered a word or two and fell asleep again. Luka, feeling bored, got up, drew the knife from his dagger-sheath and set to to whittle his stick into a ramrod. His head was full of the Chechens who lived over there in the mountains – how their braves came across the river and were not afraid of the Cossacks, and might even now be crossing at some other spot. Then he would push out of his hiding-place and scan the river, but there was nothing to be seen. Gradually, looking at the water and the distant bank, now dimly visible in the faint moonlight, he ceased to think of the Chechens and simply waited for the hour to wake his comrades and the day when he could go home to the village. Thinking of the village brought Dunayka to his mind, his darling, as the Cossacks call a man's mistress, and felt angry and bitter. Morning gave signs of approaching: a silvery mist began to rise white over the water, and not far from Luka young eagles whistled shrilly and flapped their wings. At last the first cock crowed far away in the village, followed by another, long and loud, and then others all around.

'Time to wake 'em,' thought Luka, who had finished his ramrod and felt his eyes growing heavy. He turned to his comrades and had just made out which pair of legs belonged to whom when suddenly he thought he heard a splash on the other side of the Terek. He swung round again to look at the horizon beyond the hills, where day was breaking under the horned crescent of the moon; he saw the outline of the opposite bank, the river and the floating driftwood, which was now plainly visible. For a moment it seemed to him that he was gliding along and that the Terek and the drifting wood were stationary. Again he peered out intently. One large black log with a projecting branch especially attracted his attention. There was something odd about the way it swam down the middle of the stream without rolling or swerving. Indeed it seemed to him that it was not floating with the current but was coming across the river in the direction of the shallows. He craned his neck and watched it closely. The log floated to the shallows, stopped and shifted in a peculiar manner. Luka thought he saw an arm appear from underneath the log. ''Ere's a chance to kill an *abrek* all by meself!' he thought, and seized his gun. With swift but unhurried movements he set up the gun rest, rested the barrel on it, noiselessly raised the hammer and with bated breath took aim, still peering out intently. 'I won't wake 'em,' he said to himself. But his heart throbbed so violently that he paused and listened. Suddenly the log gave a plunge and again began to float across stream to our bank. 'If only I don't miss him!' he thought, and now by the faint light of the moon he caught a glimpse of a shaven Tartar head in front of the floating tree-trunk. He aimed straight at the head, which appeared to him very near – just at the end of his barrel. He glanced across. ' 'Tis an *abrek* right enough,' he thought gleefully, and suddenly jerking to his knees he took aim again. Having sighted his target, just visible in a line with the end of the long barrel, he whispered, 'To the Father and the Son!' (according to the Cossack custom he had learned as a child), and pulled the trigger. A blinding flash lit up the reeds and the water; and the sharp, abrupt report rang out across the river, changing to a rumbling echo in the far distance. The log no longer swam across the current but floated with the stream, twisting and rolling.

'Hold him, I tell you!' shouted Yergushov, groping for his musket and rising up from his hiding-place.

'Shut up, you fool!' whispered Luka through clenched teeth. ' 'Tis *abreks*!'

'Who have you shot?' Nazar kept asking. 'Who have you shot, Luka?'

Luka did not answer. He was reloading his gun and watching the log as it floated away. A little distance off it ran aground on a sand-bank and from behind it something large appeared which bobbed up and down in the water.

'What'd you shoot? You dumb or something?' insisted the Cossacks.

' 'Tis *abreks*, I'm telling you!' said Luka.

'Stop your nonsense! Did the gun go off?'

'I've killed an *abrek*! That's what I fired at!' muttered Luka, his voice breaking with excitement. He leapt to his feet and pointed to the sank-bank. 'A man come swimming ... I shot him. See over there.'

'Stop fooling,' said Yergushov again, rubbing his eyes.

'What are you talking about? Have a look over there!' said Luka, grabbing him by the shoulders and pulling him with such force that Yergushov grunted.

He looked in the direction where Luka was pointing and seeing the body suddenly changed his tone.

'Oh my! I reckon more of they will be coming now,' he said

softly and began to examine his musket. 'That there must have been a scout swimming across; either t'others are here already, or not far off on t'other side, make no mistake.'

Luka unbuckled his belt and began to take off his coat.

'What are you up to, you fool?' exclaimed Yergushov. 'Show yourself and you're a goner, I tell you. If you killed him, he won't run away. Give us a spot of powder. You got some, haven't you? Nazar, you run back to the cordon, and look lively – only don't be going along the bank or they'll get you, mark my words.'

'Catch me going alone! Go yourself!' said Nazar angrily.

Luka had taken off his coat and was walking towards the river.

'Don't go in, I tell you,' insisted Yergushov, busy pouring powder into the pan of his gun. 'Look, he's not moving. I can see. 'Tis near morning, wait till they comes from the cordon. Run along, Nazar. What you frightened of? There ain't nothing to be frightened of, I'm telling you.'

'Luka, I say, Luka, quick now, tell us how you did it!' said Nazar.

Luka had changed his mind about going into the water just then.

'Hurry up to the cordon, both of you, while I waits here. And tell 'em to send out the mounted patrol. If the *abreks* are on this side we must try and catch 'em.'

'That's what I'm telling you. They'll get away,' said Yergushov, jumping to his feet. 'Of course we must do all to catch 'em.'

Yergushov and Nazar rose and, crossing themselves, started off for the cordon – not along the river bank but breaking their way through the brambles to reach a path in the woods.

'Now mind, Luka, don't you budge,' Yergushov called back, 'or they'll come and you'll have your throat slit. Look out, keep your eyes open, I tell you.'

'Go on, I know what I'm doing of,' muttered Luka, and having re-examined the gun he settled down again in his hiding-place.

He sat alone, staring at the sand-bank and listening for the Cossacks; but it was some distance to the cordon and he was frantic with impatience. He kept worrying that the *abreks* who had been with the dead man would get away. Just as he had been annoyed with the boar that had escaped the evening before he was annoyed now with the *abreks* who were going to escape. He continually glanced now about him, now at the bank opposite, expecting every moment to see someone appear, and with his musket on the rest he was ready to fire. The idea that he might get killed never entered his head.

9

IT was growing quite light now. The *abrek*'s body, gently rocking in the shallow water, was plainly visible. Suddenly the reeds rustled not far from Luka, and he heard steps and saw the feathery tops of the rushes moving. He set his gun at full cock and muttered, 'To the Father and the Son,' but when the cock clicked the sound of the steps ceased.

'Hey, Cossacks, don't go shooting Uncle,' a deep voice said calmly, and, parting the reeds, old Yeroshka appeared close to Luka.

'I almost killed you, by God I did!' Luka exclaimed.

'What have you shot?' asked the old man.

His sonorous voice ringing through the forest and down along the river suddenly dispelled the silence and the mystery that surrounded Luka. All at once everything seemed lighter and more distinct.

'There now, while you didn't see nothing I killed a wild beast,' said Luka, uncocking his gun and standing up with unnatural composure.

The old man was staring fixedly at the *abrek*'s white back, now absolutely visible, with the water rippling around it.

'He was swimming with a log on his back. I spotted him, and ... Look there. See? Blue drawers, and a gun seemingly ... Over there, can't you see?' inquired Luka.

''Course I can see!' growled the old man, and his face was half grave, half stern. 'You've gone and killed a brave,' he said, almost regretfully.

'Well, I was sitting here, looking about me, and suddenly I see something dark on t'other side. I spotted him while he was still over there. It looked as if a man had fallen into the water. That's funny, I thinks. And a piece of driftwood, a good-sized piece, comes floating along, not with the current but acrost it; and what do I see but a head appearing from under it. What the devil's this? I wanted to take aim but couldn't see nothing for the reeds. So I stands up, and he must have heard, the brute – he crawls up on to the sand-bank, and looks round. "No, you ain't getting away!" I thinks. Well, he crept out and looked about. (Fair choked me to see him!) I cocked me gun and watched without stirring. He waited and waited and after a time swims out again, and when he comes out into the moonlight I could see his whole back. "To the Father and the Son and the Holy Spirit" ... and when the smoke cleared a bit I sees him floundering in the water. I thinks I hear him moan. "Glory be!" thinks I. "I've killed him!" And when he drifted on to the sand-bank I could see him quite plain: he tried to get up but couldn't. He struggled a bit, and then lay still. I could see it all plain as daylight. Look, he ain't moving, he must be dead. The Cossacks have dashed back to the cordon, so as the rest of 'em shan't escape!'

'So you got him,' said the old man. 'He's far away now, my lad ...' And again he shook his head sadly.

Just then they heard branches snapping and the loud voices of Cossacks approaching along the bank on horseback and on foot. 'Are you bringing the skiff?' shouted Luka. 'You're a smart lad, Luka!' one of the Cossacks shouted back. 'Lug him to the shore!'

Luka began to undress, without waiting for the skiff and keeping an eye all the while on his prey.

'Hold on, Nazar is bringing the skiff,' shouted the sergeant.

'Don't be a fool! Maybe he's still alive and shamming! Take your dagger with you!' called another Cossack.

'I wasn't born yesterday!' cried Luka, pulling off his trousers. Undressing quickly, he crossed himself, skipped and plunged into the river with a splash. Then with powerful strokes of his white arms, breathing deeply and lifting his back high out of the water, he struck out across the current to the shallows. The Cossacks crowded on the bank, all talking and shouting. Three horsemen rode off to patrol. The skiff appeared round a bend. Luka climbed on to the sand-bank, leaned over the body and shook it twice. 'He's dead, right enough!' he cried in a shrill voice.

The Chechen had been shot through the head. He wore a pair of blue drawers, a shirt and a Circassian coat, and he had a gun and a dagger fastened to his back. On top of these was tied the large branch which at first had misled Luka.

'That's the way to catch carp!' said one of the circle of Cossacks as the body was dragged out of the skiff and laid on the ground, flattening the grass.

'How yellow he is!' said another.

'Where have our fellows gone looking for the others? I reckon the rest of 'em is over there on the other bank.'

'This here must have been a scout, or he wouldn't have swum acrost like that. Why else should he come by hisself?' said a third.

'He were a clever one, to offer hisself afore the others: a reg'lar brave!' said Luka derisively, wringing the water out of his wet garments and shivering with the cold as he stood on the shore. 'Look, his beard's dyed and clipped.'

'And he's got a bag tied on his back with a coat in it,' pointed out one of the Cossacks. 'That'd make it easier for him to swim.'

'Listen, Luka,' said the sergeant, holding the dead man's dagger and gun in his hands. 'You keep this here dagger and the coat, and I'll give you three silver roubles for the gun. See, it's got a hole in it,' he added, blowing into the muzzle. 'I just want it for a keepsake.'

Luka did not answer. It was obvious that this sort of cadging was not to his liking but he could not avoid it.

'Devil take him!' he said, scowling and throwing down the Chechen's coat. 'If only it was a good coat, but 'tis just a rag.'

' 'Twill do for going to fetch firewood in,' remarked someone.

'Mosev, I'm going home,' said Luka, evidently forgetting his vexation and determined to get something in return for his present to the sergeant.

'All right, you can go!' replied the sergeant, still examining the gun. 'Lug the body beyond the cordon, lads – and don't forget to put a shelter over him to keep the sun off. Maybe they'll come down from the mountains to ransom him.'

'It ain't hot yet,' said someone.

'But supposing a jackal digs him out?' ventured one of the Cossacks. 'That wouldn't do, would it?'

'We'll put a guard over him. They might come down to ransom him, and 'twould be bad if anything happened to him.'

'Well, Luka,' added the sergeant gaily, 'you'll have to stand a bucket of vodka for the lads, there's no getting away from it.'

'Aye, 'tis the custom,' chimed in the Cossacks. 'A bit of luck for a raw lad – to kill an *abrek* so easy as that!'

'Well, who'll buy the dagger and the coat?' said Luka. 'And don't be stingy. And you can have the trousers too. Worse luck, they're too tight for me: he was a skinny devil.'

One Cossack bought the coat for a rouble, and another gave the price of two buckets of vodka for the dagger.

'Now, boys, you'll have a drink,' said Luka. 'I'll stand you a bucket. I'll fetch it to you meself from the village.'

'Why not cut up them trousers into kerchiefs for the girls?' suggested Nazar.

The others burst out laughing.

'That's enough of that,' ordered the sergeant. 'Take the body away. The idea of putting the filthy thing by the hut ...'

'What are you waiting for? Haul him along, lads!' Luka shouted peremptorily to the Cossacks, who reluctantly took hold of the corpse, obeying him as though he were their leader. After lugging the body along for a few yards they let fall the legs which dropped with a lifeless jerk. Stepping back, they stood silent for a moment. Nazar approached and straightened the head so as to see the dead man's face with the round blood-stained bullet-hole above the temple. 'Marked him all right, didn't it? Right through the brain,' he said. 'He'll not get lost – his masters'll recognize him when they see him.' No one said anything to that, and again the angel of silence sped over the Cossacks.

The sun had risen high and its spreading rays were lighting up the dewy grass. Near by, the Terek murmured in the awakened forest, and on all sides the pheasants cried to one another, greeting the morning. The Cossacks, still and silent, stood round the dead man, looking at him. The brown body with nothing on except the wet blue drawers belted tightly over the hollow stomach was well-proportioned and comely. The muscular arms lay rigidly along the sides. The livid, freshly-shaven, round head with the clotted wound on the temple was thrown back. The smooth tanned forehead contrasted sharply with the shaven part of the head. The open glassy eyes with lowered pupils stared upwards, away and beyond everything. Under the clipped moustaches, dyed red, the thin lips, drawn at the corners, had stiffened into a good-natured, faintly mocking smile. The fingers of the small hands covered with ginger hairs were bent inward, and the nails were dyed red.

Luka had not yet dressed. He was still wet. His neck was redder and his eyes brighter than usual; his broad jaws twitched; and from his healthy white body it was just possible to see the steam rising in the fresh morning air.

'He, too, were a man,' he muttered, evidently admiring the corpse.

'Aye, if he'd a caught you, you wouldn't have stood much chance,' said one of the Cossacks.

The angel of silence had taken wing. The Cossacks began bustling about and talking. Two of them went to cut branches for the shelter, others strolled towards the cordon. Luka and Nazar hurried to get ready for their visit to the village.

Half an hour later the pair were on their way home, talking all the time and almost running through the dense forest which separated the Terek from the village.

'Mind, don't say I sent you, but just go and find out if her husband's at home,' Luka was saying in his harsh voice.

'And I'll go round to Yamka as well. We'll have a good fling, shall we?'

'Today's the day if ever there was one,' replied Luka.

As soon as they reached the village the two Cossacks filled themselves up with drink and then slumped down to sleep till evening.

10

A COUPLE of days after the event just described two companies of a Caucasian infantry regiment arrived at the Cossack village of Novomlinsk. The horses had been unharnessed, and the baggage-wagons were standing in the square. The cooks had dug a pit and collected bits of wood from various yards where they were lying about, and were now busy preparing gruel. The pay-sergeants were calling the roll. The Service Corps men were driving stakes into the ground for hitching the horses to. The quarter-masters sauntered about the streets as if they were at home, assigning billets to officers and men. On one side green ammunition boxes were lined up in a row. On another stood artillery-wagons and horses. Here were the cauldrons in which the porridge was cooking. Over there were the captain and the lieutenant and the sergeant-major, Onisim Mihailovich. And all this array found itself in the Cossack village where it was reported that the companies had been ordered to take up their quarters; therefore the place was now their home. But why they were stationed there; who the Cossacks were; and whether they liked having the troops in their village; and whether they were Old Believers* or not – was all quite immaterial. Having received their pay and been dismissed, tired out and caked with dust, the soldiers in noisy disorder, like a swarm of bees about to settle, poured out in the squares and streets. Determinedly ignoring the villagers' resentment, they marched into the cottages in twos and threes, chattering cheerfully and with their muskets clinking, hung up their accoutrements, unpacked their haversacks and jested with the women. Gathered round the soup-kettles – a favourite spot with all soldiers – was a large group with little pipes between their teeth. They gazed at the

* If they were Old Believers they would strongly disapprove on religious grounds of, for instance, the use of tobacco (cf. Matt. xv, 11: 'Not that which goeth into the mouth defileth a man; but that which cometh out of the mouth, this defileth a man'). The presence, therefore, of Russian soldiers smoking and chewing tobacco would be particularly objectionable. [*Translator's note*]

smoke rising into the hot sky, at first in thin, almost invisible spirals, and then thickening into white clouds higher up; at the flames of the camp-fire quivering like molten glass in the pure air; and they bantered and made fun of the Cossack men and women because they did not live at all like the Russians. There were soldiers to be seen in every yard, and one could hear their boisterous laughter and the exasperated, shrill cries of the Cossack women trying to protect their homes and refusing to give up water or cooking utensils. Little boys and girls clinging to their mothers and to each other watched every movement of the troopers (whom they were seeing for the first time in their lives), with frightened curiosity, or ran after them at a respectful distance. The old Cossacks came out of their cottages and sat in despondent silence on the earthen embankment outside, surveying the soldiers' activity with a puzzled air of resignation.

Olenin, who had joined the Caucasian army as a cadet three months before, was quartered in one of the best houses in the village – the house of the army teacher, Ilya Vassilyevich: that is to say, at Goody Ulitka's.

'Goodness knows what it'll be like, Dmitri Andreich,' said the panting Vanyusha to Olenin, who, dressed in a Circassian coat and mounted on a Kabarda* horse which he had bought in Groznyi, was, after a five-hours' march, riding gaily into the yard of the quarters assigned to him.

'Why, what's the matter?' he asked, caressing his horse and watching with amusement the sweating, dishevelled, worried lad, who had arrived with the baggage-wagons and was now unpacking.

Olenin looked an absolutely different man. Instead of clean-shaven lips and chin he now had youthful moustaches and a small beard. Instead of the sallow complexion of one whose nights are spent in dissipation his cheeks, his forehead and the skin behind his ears were red with healthy sunburn. Instead of brand-new morning coat he wore a dirty white Circassian tunic with wide skirts, and carried arms. Instead of a freshly-starched

*Kabarda horses are famous for their powers of endurance – Kabarda is a district in the Terek territory of the Caucasus. [*Translator's note*]

collar his tanned neck was tightly clasped by the red band of his silk *beshmet*. He wore Circassian dress but he did not wear it well: anyone would recognize him at once for a Russian and not a Tartar brave. It was all right – but it looked wrong. But for all that his whole person radiated health, joy and satisfaction.

'Yes, it may seem funny to you,' said Vanyusha; 'but just try talking to these people yourself! They spike your guns, and there you are. You can't get so much as a word out of them. They don't seem to like Russians somehow,' concluded Vanyusha, angrily throwing an iron pail towards the door of the cottage.

'You should speak to the chief of the village.'

'I don't know where to find him,' said Vanyusha in an offended tone.

'What has upset you so much?' asked Olenin, looking round.

'Everything, the devil take them! The master of the house isn't here: gone down to the *kriga*,* they say. And the old woman's a proper witch, God help us!' answered Vanyusha, clasping his head in his hands. 'How we're going to live here, I don't know. They're worse than Tartars, I do declare, though they call theirselves Christians. Why, next to them a Tartar's a gentleman. "Gone to the *kriga*," they say. A *kriga* – what's that? Who's ever heard of such a thing?' cried Vanyusha finally as he turned away.

'So you don't feel altogether at home here then?' chaffed Olenin without dismounting.

'Can I have the horse, please?' said Vanyusha, evidently perplexed by this new order of things but resigning himself to his fate.

'So a Tartar is more of a gentleman, eh, Vanyusha?' repeated Olenin after him, dismounting and slapping the saddle with his hand.

'Yes, you laugh! You think it's funny,' muttered Vanyusha angrily.

'Come, don't be angry, Vanyusha,' Olenin replied, continuing to smile. 'Wait till I've spoken to the people of the house. You'll

* An enclosure of stakes made in a river for catching fish – a weir. [*Translator's note*]

see, I'll arrange everything. You don't know what a happy time we shall have here. Only don't upset yourself.'

Vanyusha made no reply but merely screwed up his eyes and, shaking his head, looked witheringly after his master. Vanyusha regarded Olenin as no more than his master. Olenin regarded Vanyusha as no more than his servant. They would have been greatly surprised had anyone told them they were friends. And yet they were friends, without either of them knowing it. Vanyusha had been taken into the house when he was a boy of eleven, and Olenin just about the same age. When Olenin was fifteen he gave Vanyusha lessons for a time and taught him to read French, of which Vanyusha was inordinately proud; and still, when he felt in particularly good spirits, he would come out with a French word or two, accompanying them with a foolish laugh.

Olenin ran up the steps of the porch and pushed open the door of the cottage. Marianka, wearing nothing but a pink smock such as Cossack women usually wear when at home, sprang back from the door in fright and pressed herself against the wall, covering the lower part of her face with her flowing sleeve. Opening the door wider, Olenin in the semi-darkness of the passage saw the young Cossack girl's tall, shapely figure. With the quick avid curiosity of youth he noticed the firm girlish form under the thin cotton smock, and the beautiful black eyes fixed on his with childlike terror and wild interest. 'This is *she*!' said Olenin to himself, but his next thought was: 'But there will be many others like her,' and he opened the inner door. Marianka's mother, likewise wearing nothing but a smock, was stooping down with her back to him, sweeping the floor.

'Good day to you, mother! I have come about my lodgings ...' he began.

The Cossack woman, without straightening up, turned her austere but still handsome face towards him.

'What are you doing here?' she screamed, looking askance at Olenin from under frowning brows. 'Come to laugh up your sleeves at us, have you? I'll teach you to laugh up your sleeves! May the black plague take you!'

Olenin had always imagined that the way-worn gallant Caucasian army (to which he belonged) would be given a warm welcome everywhere, especially by the Cossacks, their comrades in the war, and therefore such a reception as this disconcerted him. Without letting himself be abashed, however, he tried to explain that he meant to pay for his lodgings, but the old woman would have none of it.

'What are you here for?' she shrieked in a piercing voice, interrupting Olenin. 'Who wants a pest like you with your ugly shaved mug! Just wait till my man comes home – he'll show you your place. I don't want your dirty money. D'you suppose we've never seen money? You'll stink the house out with your filthy tobacco, and then expect to make it right with money! We know a pest when we see one! I hopes they shoot your heart into your guts! . . .'

'It seems Vanyusha was right!' thought Olenin. 'A Tartar would be more of a gentleman,' and he walked out of the hut, followed by the woman's abuse. As he was leaving, Marianka, still only in her pink smock but with her face hidden right up to her eyes by a white kerchief, suddenly slipped past him out of the door. Pattering swiftly down the steps in her bare feet, she ran from the porch, stopped, looked round impetuously with laughing eyes at the young man and vanished round the corner of the cottage.

Her firm youthful step, the untamed look, the flashing eyes under the white kerchief and the lithe body of the beautiful girl made an even greater impression on Olenin than before. 'Yes, it must be *she*,' he thought, and forgetting the difficulty over lodgings, and continually looking round at Marianka, he went back to Vanyusha.

'There you see, the girl's just as savage!' said Vanyusha, still busy with the baggage-cart but now in a more cheerful frame of mind. 'Like a wild colt. *La fam!*' he added in a loud, triumphant voice, and roared with laughter.

II

In the late afternoon the master of the house returned from his fishing and, finding that he would be paid for the rooms, pacified his wife and came to an agreement with Vanyusha.

Soon everything was in order in the new quarters. The family moved into the winter hut, and let Olenin have the summer one for three roubles a month. Olenin had some food and lay down for a nap. Towards evening he woke, washed and made himself tidy, ate his dinner and, lighting a cigarette, sat down by the window that looked on to the street. It had grown cooler. The slanting shadow of the hut with its carved gables fell across the dusty road and bent upwards at the base of the cottage opposite, whose reed-thatched roof shone in the rays of the setting sun. The air became fresher. In the village everything was quiet, the soldiers having found their billets and settled down. The cattle had not yet been driven in, and the villagers were still out at work.

Olenin's lodgings were almost at the end of the village. From time to time he heard a muffled shot from somewhere far beyond the Terek, in the direction from which he had come (the Chechnya or the Kumytsk plain). He was feeling very well-contented after three months of bivouac life. His skin felt fresh, his rested limbs relaxed, his muscular body clean and comfortable after the march. His mind, too, was untroubled and serene. He thought of the campaign and the dangers that he had encountered. He remembered that he had faced them no worse than other men, and that he was now accepted into the comradeship of the gallant Caucasian army. His Moscow memories were left heaven knows how far behind. The old life was wiped out, and a completely new one had begun in which so far there had been no mistakes. Here, a new man among new men, he could gain a new and good reputation. He was conscious of a youthful sensation of unaccountable *joie de vivre*. Looking out of the window at the boys spinning their tops in the shadow of the house, or round his tidy little lodging, he thought how agreeably he would settle into this novel life in a Cossack village. Now and then he glanced at the mountains and the sky, and a compelling awareness of the grandeur of nature came into all his reminiscences and dreams. His new life had begun, not as he imagined it would when he left Moscow, but unexpectedly well all the same. 'The mountains, the mountains, the mountains!' – they permeated his every thought, his every feeling.

'He kissed his bitch good-bye, then drained the pitcher dry.

Gaffer Yeroshka's kissed his bitch good-bye and all for a drink of liquor!' the children who had been spinning their tops under the window suddenly shouted in chorus, running towards the corner of the street. 'He's sold his bitch! He's sold his dagger – swapped 'em for a drink of liquor!' they screamed, crowding together and retreating.

These cries were directed to old Yeroshka who, with his gun on his shoulder and some pheasants hanging at his belt, was returning from a shooting expedition.

'Ah, 'twas a shame, lads, 'twas indeed!' he said, swinging his arms vigorously and looking up at the windows on both sides of the street. ' 'Twas a sin to let the bitch go for a drop a drink!' he reiterated, evidently vexed but pretending not to care.

Olenin was surprised at the way the urchins behaved towards the old hunter, but he was still more struck by the expressive, intelligent face and powerful build of the man whom they called Gaffer Yeroshka.

'Hey, Gaffer! Hey, Cossack!' he called. 'Come over here!'

The old man looked into the window and stopped.

'Good evening, me worthy friend,' he said, lifting his cap from his cropped head.

'Good evening, my worthy friend,' replied Olenin. 'What is it the youngsters are shouting at you?'

Yeroshka came up to the window. 'They was just a-teasing of an old man. 'Tis no matter. I don't mind. Let 'em have their bit of fun with an old 'un,' he said with the firm, musical intonations characteristic of sedate old age. 'Are you the commander, eh?'

'No, I'm a cadet. But where did you get those pheasants?'

'Them three hens I bagged in the forest,' answered the old man, turning his broad back to the window to show the three hen-pheasants which were hanging with their heads tucked into his belt and staining his coat with blood. 'Not seen none yet?' he asked. 'Have a brace if you'd care for 'em. Here you are,' and he handed two of the birds in at the window. 'You a sportsman yourself?' he inquired.

'I am. During the campaign I got four pheasants on my own.'

'Four? That's a lot!' said the old man sarcastically. 'And do you drink too? D'you like our Caucasian wine?'

'What do you suppose? Of course I enjoy drinking.'

'Ah, you're a fine young fellow, I can see. Us'll be sworn friends, you and me.'

'Step in,' said Olenin. 'We'll try some of that Caucasian wine.'

'I wouldn't say no to it. But you must take them pheasants.'

It was plain by the old man's face that he liked the cadet; also he was quick to see that here was someone he could get free drinks from, and therefore he could afford to present him with a brace of pheasants.

A few moments later Gaffer Yeroshka's figure appeared in the doorway of the hut, and it was only then that Olenin realized the enormous size and sturdy build of the man, whose red-brown face with its bushy snow-white beard was all furrowed by heavy lines and wrinkles, the result of hard work and age. His legs, arms and shoulders displayed the fine muscular development of a young man. There were deep scars on his head under the short-cropped hair. His thick, sinewy neck was checkered with criss-cross folds, like the neck of a bull. His horny hands were bruised and scratched. He stepped lightly and easily over the threshold, divested himself of his gun which he stood in a corner, and casting a quick glance round the room shrewdly estimated the value of its contents; then with out-turned toes and treading softly in his rawhide sandals he came into the middle of the room, bringing with him a penetrating but not unpleasant smell compounded of wine, vodka, gunpowder and dried blood. He bowed towards the ikons, smoothed his beard, and then, approaching Olenin, held out a thick black hand.

'*Koshkildy*,' he said. 'That's "Good-day to you" in Tartar, or "Peace to you," as they say.'

'*Koshkildy*, I know,' answered Olenin, giving him his hand.

'Ah, but you don't know. You don't know the right order, you ignoramus!' said Yeroshka, shaking his head reproachfully. 'If anyone says "*Koshkildy*" to you, you must answer "*Alla rasi bo sun*" – "God save you". That's how it goes, brother, and not "*Koshkildy*". But I'll teach you all of that. We had a lad here, Ilya Moseich, one of your Russians, and he and me was bosom pals. A fine fellow he was – drunk, thief and hunter. Ah, what a hunter, by heaven! I taught him everything.'

'And what will you teach me?' asked Olenin, who was becoming more and more interested in the old man.

'I will take you out hunting, and learn you to fish. I will show you the Chechens, and if you wants to find a girl I will do that for you too. That's the sort I am! ... A wag I am.' And the old man laughed. 'I'll sit me down. I'm tired. *Karga?*' he added inquiringly.

'And what does "*Karga*" mean?' asked Olenin.

'It means "All right" in Georgian. I'm always a-saying of it – it's a saying of mine, me favourite word: *karga, karga,* I sez it like that, and it means I'm not serious. Now, what about the wine, brother? Ain't you a-sending out for some? You got an orderly, haven't you? Hey, Ivan?' he shouted. 'All your soldiers is Ivan. Is yours Ivan?'

'Yes, he's Ivan – Vanyusha.* Here, Vanyusha, go and get some Caucasian wine from our landlady, please, and bring it here.'

'Ivan or Vanyusha, 'tis all the same. Why are all your soldiers called Ivan? Listen, Ivan, me lad, tell 'em to give you some from the cask they've just started on. They have the best wine in the village. But don't pay no more than thirty kopecks the pint, mind, because that old witch would be all too glad ... Our people are a cursed stupid lot,' he continued in a confidential tone after Vanyusha had gone. 'They don't look on you as human beings: you're worse nor a Tartar in their eyes. "Heathen Russians," they calls you. But to my way of thinking though you're a soldier, you're still a man, with a soul in your body same as everyone else. Ain't I right? Ilya Moseich, for instance – that pal of mine – he were a soldier but he had a heart of gold. Ain't that so, me dear? That's why our people here don't like me; but I don't care. I'm a cheerful customer, and I likes everybody, I'm Yeroshka: yes, my dear fellow!'

And the old Cossack patted the young man affectionately on the shoulder

* 'Vanyusha' is a diminutive form of 'Ivan'. [*Translator's note*]

12

VANYUSHA, who meanwhile had succeeded in getting his housekeeping arrangements in running order, was in excellent spirits. He had even had a shave by the company's barber, and had pulled his trousers out of his high boots as a sign that he was now taking things easy. He gazed at Yeroshka attentively but without benevolence, as though he were some strange wild animal never been seen before, shook his head at the dirty marks the old man had made on the floor and, taking two empty bottles from under a bench, went to the landlady.

'Good evening, kind people,' he said, having made up his mind to be particularly mild. 'The master sent me to buy some red wine from you. Will you draw some for me, good folk?'

The old woman made no reply. The girl, who was standing before a little Tartar mirror arranging a kerchief on her head, looked round and said nothing.

'I'll pay you money, honoured people,' continued Vanyusha, jingling the coins in his pocket. 'You treat us well, and we'll treat you well, and that'll be best for all of us.'

'How much d'you want?' the old woman asked abruptly.

'A quart.'

'Go and draw it for him, dearie,' said Goody Ulitka to her daughter. 'Take it from the cask that's tapped, my love.'

Marianka picked up the keys and a decanter and went out of the hut followed by Vanyusha. As she passed the window Olenin pointed to her and asked:

'Tell me, who is that young woman?'

Yeroshka winked and nudged the young man with his elbow.

'Wait a bit,' said he, and leaned out of the casement. 'Hem, hem!' he coughed, and bellowed: 'Marianka, my pet! Hey, Marianka, don't you love me, girlie! I'm a one, I am,' he added in a whisper to Olenin.

The girl passed on, walking with the peculiarly bold, dashing gait of the Cossack woman, swinging her arms evenly and vigorously. Without turning her head she gave the old man a slow glance of her dark-shadowed black eyes.

'Love me and I'll make you happy!' shouted Yeroshka, winking at Olenin and giving him an inquiring look. 'I'm a dog! I'm a wag, I am,' he added. 'A regular queen, that girl, eh?'

'A beauty,' agreed Olenin. 'Call her here.'

'Oh no,' said the old man. 'She's to be wedded to Luka, a fine Cossack lad, a brave – the one who killed an *abrek* t'other day. I'll find you a better one. I'll find you a girl dressed in silks and silver. Once I've said it, I'll do it. I'll get you a reg'lar beauty.'

'You, an old man, talking like that! Why, it's sinful.'

'Sinful? Where's the sin?' demanded the old man. 'A sin to look at a pretty girl? A sin to walk out with one? A sin to love one? Be that a sin where you come from? No, my dear boy, that ain't no sin, 'tis salvation. God made you, and God made the girl, too. He made everything there is. So 'tain't no sin to look at a pretty wench. That's what she were made for, to be loved and to give happiness. That's the way I sees it, my good fellow.'

Crossing the yard and entering a dark cool store-room filled with barrels, Marianka went up to one of them and murmuring the customary prayer plunged a dipper into it. Vanyusha stood in the doorway and watched her with a grin. It seemed very comical that she had only a smock on, close fitting behind and tucked up in front, and still more comical that she wore a necklace of silver roubles. He was thinking that this was quite un-Russian, and that in the serfs' quarters at home they would die of laughter if they saw a girl like that. 'All the same for a change *la fille comme c'est très bienne*,' he thought. 'I must tell the master.'

'What are you standing in the light for?' the girl suddenly shouted. 'Why don't you pass me the bottle?'

She filled it with cool red wine and handed it back to Vanyusha.

'Give the money to Mammy,' she said, pushing back his hand with the coins.

Vanyusha grinned. 'Why so cross, my pretty one?' he said good-naturedly, shuffling his feet while the girl was covering the cask.

She began to laugh.

'What about you? Are you good people?'

'My master and me, we're right good people,' Vanyusha answered decidedly. 'We're so nice that wherever we've lived they have liked us. He's a nobleman, you see.'

The girl stood listening.

'And is he married, your master?' she asked.

'No. The master's too young to marry – gentry can't wed when they are still young,' Vanyusha informed her sententiously.

'A likely story! Big as a buffalo but too young to wed! Is he the commander of you all?'

'My master is a cadet. That means he isn't an officer yet. But he's a person of quality, more important than a general. Because not only our colonel, but the Tsar himself, knows him,' proudly explained Vanyusha. 'We are not like the other poor beggars in the line regiment, the old master was a senator. He had more than a thousand serfs, he had, and we get a thousand roubles sent to us at a time. That's why everybody likes us. Even a captain with no money – what's the good of that?'

'Come on. I'm going to lock up,' said the girl interrupting him.

Vanyusha brought Olenin the wine and announced '*la fille c'est très joulie*,' laughed his inane laugh and immediately departed.

13

MEANWHILE the tattoo had sounded in the village square. The people had returned from their work. The herds were lowing as they crowded at the village gates, raising a cloud of golden dust. Girls and women bustled about the streets and yards, getting their cattle home. The sun had entirely disappeared behind the distant snowy peaks. One pale bluish shadow spread over land and sky. Above the darkened orchards faint stars began to kindle, and the sounds of life in the village gradually died away. After they had housed the cattle for the night the women came out and gathered at the street corners, and settled down on the earth embankments of the houses, crunching sunflower seeds. Marianka, after milking the two cows and the buffalo, also joined one of these groups where several women and girls and one old man were talking about the dead *abrek*. The old Cossack was telling the story and the women were questioning him.

'I reckon he'll get a great reward, won't he?' said one of the women.

'That he will, and a decoration, too, they say.'

'That Mosev tried to cheat him. Took the gun away from him, but the officers at Kizlyar heard of it.'

'A mean creature, that Mosev is!'

'They say Luka's home in the village,' remarked one of the girls.

'He and Nazar are drinking at Yamka's.' (Yamka was a wanton Cossack woman who kept an illicit pot-house.) 'I was told they've drunk half a bucketful already.'

'The Snatcher snatches all the luck!' said someone. 'Snatcher's the name for him all right. But he's a fine lad, there's no denying. Sharp as a needle, and a good, upright boy. His father was the same: he's the very spit of his dad. When he was killed the whole village went to the wake . . . Look, there they are,' added the speaker, pointing to three Cossacks coming down the street. 'That Yergushov has managed to hitch hisself on to 'em. What a toper he is!'

Luka, Nazar and Yergushov, having finished half a pail of vodka, were approaching the girls. The faces of all three were more flushed than usual, especially the old Cossack's. He was reeling, and kept laughing loudly and poking Nazar in the ribs.

'What about a song, you wenches?' he shouted to the girls. 'Come on, sing to our roistering, I tell you!'

'Bin enjoying yourselves, have you? Bin enjoying yourselves?' greeted the women.

'What have we got to sing for? Not a holiday, is it?' called a worthy housewife. 'You're tipsy, you go and sing.'

Yergushov roared with laughter and nudged Nazar. 'You're the one to start. And I'll join in. I'm a dab at singing, I can tell you.'

'Well, you beauties, have you all gone to sleep?' said Nazar. 'We come from the cordon to drink your health. We've already drunk Luka's health.'

Coming up to the group, Luka slowly pushed back his cap and stopped in front of the girls. His broad cheek-bones and neck were red. He stood still, speaking softly and sedately; but under his quiet gravity there lay more strength and life than in all Nazar's chatter and bustle. He reminded one of a playful colt which with a snort and a flourish of its tail suddenly stops short, as though rooted to the ground with all four legs. He stood mildly in front of the girls, saying hardly a word and looking with laughing eyes now at them, now at his drunken companions. When Marianka joined the group he lifted his cap with a steady, deliberate movement, stepped aside and then stood in front of her with one foot thrust slightly forward. He had his thumbs in his belt and was fingering his dagger. Marianka replied to his salutation with a leisurely inclination of the head, settled down on the embankment and took some sunflower seeds from the bosom of her smock. Without taking his eyes off her Luka cracked seeds and spat out the husks. Everybody stopped talking when Marianka appeared.

'Well, have you come for long?' asked one of the women, breaking the silence.

'Till tomorrow morn,' replied Luka gravely.

'Well, God grant you good fortune,' said the old Cossack. 'I was just saying, I'm very glad for your sake.'

'I says the same,' put in the tipsy Yergushov, laughing. 'Look at our visitors!' he added, pointing to a soldier passing by. 'Soldiers' vodka is good stuff – I likes it.'

'We got three of 'em devils in our place,' said one of the women. 'Grandad went to the village elder but he says there's nothing can't be done about it.'

'Aha! Met with trouble, have you?' said Yergushov.

'Do they stink your place out with their tobacco?' asked another woman. 'Smoke as much as you please out of doors, I always say, but we won't have it in the house. I won't allow it, not even if the elder came in person. They steal everything too. He's not quartered any of 'em on hisself, no fear, the son of a devil.'

''Tis plain you don't like 'em,' Yergushov began again.

'And then they say as the girls'll have to make the soldiers' beds for 'em, and serve 'em our red wine and honey,' said Nazar, putting one foot forward and tilting his cap in imitation of Luka.

'That's right,' bellowed Yergushov, roaring with laughter and seizing the girl who sat nearest to him and putting his arms round her.

'Now then, you black pitch!' squealed the girl. 'I'll tell your old woman.'

'Go on, tell her,' he shouted. ' 'Tis quite true what Nazar says. There was a paper sent round. He can read letters, you know. 'Tis true.' And he proceeded to hug the girl next in turn.

'Keep your hands off of me, you wretch!' shrieked the plump, rosy-cheeked Ustenka, laughing and lifting her arm to hit him.

Yergushov stepped aside and nearly fell. 'There, they say as girls have no strength, and she well-nigh killed me.'

'Get off, you black pitch, what devil brought you from the cordon?' cried Ustenka and turned away with a giggle. 'So you went to sleep and missed the *abrek*, eh? He might have got you; and that'd be a good riddance.'

'You'd have howled your eyes out, I expect!' laughed Nazar.

'About as much as I should have howled for you!'

'There you are, she ain't got no heart,' said Yergushov. 'But she would howl, wouldn't she, Nazar?'

All this time Luka was silently looking at Marianka. His gaze evidently embarrassed the girl.

'Well, Marianka, I hear they've quartered one of the officers with you?' he said, drawing nearer to her.

Marianka, as usual, did not reply at once, and only slowly raised her eyes to the Cossack's. Luka's eyes were laughing, as though something special, something apart from what was being said, was taking place between himself and the girl.

'Yes, it's all right for them, they have two huts,' an old woman broke in, speaking for Marianka. 'But at Fomushkin's now, they've got one of the chiefs quartered on 'em, and they say the whole place is crammed with his things and no room left for themselves anywhere. Whoever heard the like – turning a horde like that loose on the village! But there's naught we can do about it,' she said. 'And what the plague have they come here for, I'd like to know!'

'I heard they're going to build a bridge across the Terek,' said one of the girls.

'And I was told,' said Nazar, going up to Ustenka, 'they means to dig a pit to put the girls in who don't love the lads,' and again he made his favourite bow and scrape, which set them all laughing, while Yergushov, passing over Marianka, who was next in turn, began to embrace an old Cossack woman.

'Why don't you kiss Marianka? You oughter take each in turn,' said Nazar.

'No, my old 'un is sweeter,' cried the Cossack, kissing the struggling old woman.

'He's strangling me,' she screamed, laughing.

The measured tread of feet at the end of the street interrupted their laughter. Three soldiers in great-coats, with their muskets over their shoulders, were marching in step to relieve guard by the ammunition wagon. The corporal, an old cavalry man, looked irately at the Cossacks and led his men straight down the road, intending to make Luka and Nazar move out of the way. Nazar stepped to one side but Luka only screwed up his eyes, averted his head and his broad back, and never stirred.

'There are people standing here, you'll have to go round,' he muttered, only half turning his head and tossing it contemptuously in the direction of the soldiers.

The soldiers went by in silence, marching in step along the dusty road.

Marianka began laughing, and all the other girls laughed too.

'Smart boys, ain't they?' said Nazar. 'Just like long-skirted choir-singers!' and he walked a few steps down the road, imitating the soldiers.

Again everyone went into peals of laughter.

Luka slowly went up to Marianka.

'And where have you put the officer quartered on you?' he asked.

Marianka deliberated before answering.

'In the new hut,' she said.

'Is he old or young?' asked Luka, sitting down beside her.

'D'you suppose I asked?' retorted the girl. 'I went to get him some *chikhir* and saw him sitting in the window with Gaffer

Yeroshka. A red-headed fellow. He's brought a whole cart-load of baggage.'

And she lowered her eyes.

'I'm right glad I got leave from the cordon!' said Luka, drawing closer to the girl and all the time looking straight in her eyes.

'And how long can you stay?' asked Marianka, smiling slightly.

'Till morn. Give me some seeds,' he said, holding out his hand.

Marianka now smiled outright and unfastened the neckband of her smock. 'Don't take them all,' she said.

'I was very lonesome away from you, really and truly I was,' Luka said in a slow quiet whisper, helping himself to some sunflower seeds out of the bosom of the girl's smock. Then moving still closer he began to murmur something in her ear, looking at her with laughing eyes.

'I won't come, I tell you,' Marianka suddenly said aloud, leaning away from him.

'Honest,' he went on in a whisper, 'I want to tell you ... Honest to God ... Please come, Marianka.'

Marianka shook her head, but she still smiled.

'Sis! Marianka! Mammy's calling! Supper time!' shouted Marianka's little brother, running towards the group.

'Coming,' replied the girl. 'You go on by yourself, there's a good boy. I'm just coming.'

Luka stood up and raised his cap.

'I reckon I'd better go home too, 'tis getting late,' he said, trying to appear indifferent but hardly able to repress a smile; and he disappeared round the corner of the house.

Meanwhile night had settled over the village. Bright stars spangled the sable sky. The streets were dark and empty. Nazar remained with the women on the earth-bank, and their laughter still rang out, but Luka, moving quietly away from the girls, crouched down like a cat and, holding his dagger so that it should not rattle, suddenly started running noiselessly, not homeward but in the direction of the cornet's house. After traversing two streets he turned into a lane and, gathering up his coat, sat down on the ground in the shadow of a fence. 'A real cornet's daughter!' he said to himself, thinking of Marianka. 'Won't even have a bit of fun. But just wait a bit!'

The sound of approaching footsteps attracted his attention. He began listening, and laughed silently to himself. Marianka, with bent head, was coming straight towards him with quick even strides, letting her switch clatter against the palings of the fence. Luka got to his feet. Marianka started and stopped short.

'Oh, you brute, you frightened me! So you didn't go home?' she said, with a loud laugh.

Luka put one arm round the girl and with the other hand lifted her face towards him. 'There's something I want to say to you ... as true as I live! ...' His voice trembled and broke.

'What are you talking about at this time of night?' answered Marianka. 'Mammy's waiting for me, and you'd better go to your sweetheart.'

And freeing herself from his arms she ran a few steps. When she had reached the wattle fence of her home she stopped and turned to the Cossack, who was running beside her and still trying to persuade her to stay awhile with him.

'Well, and what is it you want to tell me, you night-prowler?' And again she laughed.

'Give over laughing at me, Marianka! Please. What if I do have a sweetheart? The devil take her. Only say, and I'll love you – I'll do anything you want. Listen to this!' (He jingled the money in his pocket.) 'Now we could set up house together. Other people enjoy theirselves; why can't I? Why don't you make me happy, Marianka?'

The girl did not answer. She stood in front of him, breaking her switch into pieces with rapid movements of her fingers.

Luka suddenly doubled his fists and set his teeth. ' 'Tis nothing but wait, wait, wait! Don't I love you enough? You can do what you like with me,' he said suddenly with an angry frown, seizing both her hands.

There was no change in Marianka's quiet expression as she answered gently:

'Don't get excited, Luka, but listen to me.' She left her hands in his but pushed him a little away from her. ' 'Tis true I'm only a girl, but you listen to me. 'Tis not for me to say, but if you love me I'll tell you this. Let go my hands, I can speak without that. I will marry you, but you'll never get any of that from me,' she concluded, keeping her face turned towards him.

'How do you mean, you'll marry me? Marriage don't depend on us. But I want you to love me yourself, my little Marianka,' said Luka, suddenly mild and docile and tender instead of sullen and violent. And smiling he looked deeply into her eyes.

Marianka pressed close to him and kissed him warmly on the lips. 'My dearie lad!' she whispered, clinging to him convulsively. Then, suddenly tearing herself away, she ran to the gate of her house without looking round.

In spite of the Cossack's entreaties to wait one more minute and hear what he had to say Marianka did not stop.

'Go away,' she cried. 'They'll see us. There's that devil of a lodger of ours walking about the yard, I do believe.'

'The cornet's daughter!' thought Luka. 'So she will marry me, will she? Marriage is all very well, but she shall love me first.'

He found Nazar at Yamka's house, and after drinking awhile with him he went on to Dunayka, where, in spite of her recent infidelity, he spent the night.

14

OLENIN was indeed strolling about the yard when Marianka came in at the gate, and he heard her say 'That devil of a lodger of ours is in the yard'. He had spent the whole evening with Yeroshka on the porch of his new lodging. He had had a table, a samovar, wine and a lighted candle brought out, and over a glass of tea and a cheroot he listened to the tales of the old man seated on the steps at his feet. Although the air was still, the candle dripped and the flame flickered, bending this way and that and lighting up in turn the newel-post, the table and the crockery, and the old man's close-cropped white head. Moths, circling round the light, shed the dust of their wings as they dashed against the table and the glasses. Some flew into the candle flame, others disappeared into the black space beyond. Olenin and Yeroshka emptied five bottles of *chikhir*. Each time Yeroshka filled the glasses he held one up to Olenin and drank his health. He talked untiringly, telling Olenin about Cossack life in the old days, about his father, the 'Broad-Back', who could carry on his shoulders the carcass of a boar weighing three hundred pounds, and drink two pails of *chikhir* at a sitting. He told of his own days and his friend Girchik, and how together they had smuggled felt cloaks across the Terek in the time of the plague. He told Olenin about his hunting and the two deer he had killed in one morning; and about his 'sweetheart' who used to run out to him at the cordon at night. And he recounted it all with such picturesque eloquence that Olenin did not notice the passing of time.

'Ah yes, my dear, you're come too late. You missed me in me golden days. Then I'd have shown you a thing or two. Today it's "Yeroshka's licked the pitcher dry" but in those days Yeroshka was famous throughout the regiment. Who had the finest horse? Who had a real *Gurda* sword? Who was always open-handed? Who was the merriest chap to go on a spree with? Who should be sent to the mountains to kill Ahmet Khan? Why Yeroshka, acourse. Who did the girls love best of all? Always 'twas Yeroshka. Because I were a real brave: I could drink and thieve – I used to steal droves of horses in the mountains – I could sing ... There were naught I couldn't turn me hand to. There ain't no Cossacks like me nowadays. Fair makes me sick to set eyes on 'em. They're 'bout as tall as that' (Yeroshka held his hand two-and-a-half feet from the ground.) 'They wears silly boots and keeps looking at 'em – that's all the joy they have in life. Or else they drink theirselves stupid – they don't drink like men but like I don't know what. But what was I? I were Yeroshka, the thief, famous not only in the villages but in the mountains too. Tartar princes used to come an' visit me, my friends they was. Tartar or Armenian, soldier or officer – 'twas all one to me. I didn't trouble so long as they knew how to drink. "You should keep clear of the world," they sez, "and not drink with soldiers or eat with Tartars." '

'Who says that?' asked Olenin.

'Why, our preachers do. But you listen to a Mullah or a Tartar Cadi, and he'll say, "You unbelieving giaours, why do you eat pig?" Just goes to show as everyone has his own law. But I thinks 'tis all one. God created everything for the joy of man. There's no sin in any of it. Take a wild animal, for instance. It lives in the Tartar reeds or in ours. Wherever it happens to be, there's its home. Whatever God gives it to eat, so it eats. But our people sez we shall be made to lick red-hot frying-pans in hell for things like that. I reckon 'tis all humbug,' he added after a pause.

'What's humbug?'

'Why, what the preachers say. We had a Cossack captain once who was a friend of mine. A fine fellow he was, just like me. He was killed in Checheny. Well he always said the preachers made it all up out of their own heads. "When you die," he used to say, "grass'll grow up on your grave, and that be all."' The old man laughed. 'A desperate fellow, he were.'

'How old are you?'

'The Lord only knows. Must be seventy anyways. When you had a Tsartiza* reigning in Russia I wasn't little any more. So you can reckon it out. Would it be around seventy?'

'About that. But you're still hale and hearty.'

'Yes, thank the Lord, I'm sound, sound all through. Except that a woman harmed me, the witch –'

'How was that?'

'Oh, just harmed me ...'

'And so when you're dead the grass will grow over you?' repeated Olenin.

Yeroshka evidently had no desire to express his thoughts more clearly. He was silent for a while.

'And what are your ideas about it? Come, have a drink!' he suddenly cried, smiling and filling Olenin's glass.

15

'LET me see, what were I a-saying?' he continued. 'Ah yes, that's the man I am! I'm a huntsman – there's no hunter to equal me in the regiment. I'll find you any sort of animal, any sort of bird; and what and where – I knows it all. I have dogs and two guns and nets and a screen and a hawk. I have everything, thank the Lord. If you really are a huntsman, and not just bragging, I'll show you everything. D'you know what sort of man

* Catherine the Great, on the throne from 1762 to 1796. [*Translator's note*]

I am? Once I've found a track I knows the animal – knows where he'll sleep and where he'll come to drink or roll about. Then I makes meself a perch and sits there all night, watching. What's the good of staying at home, anyway? You only falls into mischief and gets drunk. And the women come cackling round, and the children yell at you, and you're choked with charcoal smoke. 'Tis another thing altogether when you goes out at nightfall, selects a nice little place for yourself, stamps down the reeds and there you sits and waits like a good 'un. In the woods you knows all what's going on. You looks up at the sky, the stars pass over and you can tell from them how the time goes. You looks round you: there's a rustling in the wood and you waits and you hears a crashing, and a boar comes out to roll in the mud. You listens to the young eagles screeching or the cocks in the village begins to crow, or the geese will be honking: if you hears geese you knows it ain't come midnight. And all these things I knows. Then if I hears a shot somewhere in the distance, it sets me thinking. Who is that firing, I thinks to meself. Maybe 'tis a Cossack like me who has been watching for some animal? And did he get it, or only wound it, so that the poor thing'll go crawling through the reeds, smearing 'em with its blood, and all for nothing? I hates that, I does. Why injure a beast, you fool? Or I thinks to meself, perhaps 'tis an *abrek* killed some little fool of a Cossack. All them thoughts goes through your head. And once as I sat watching by the river I see a cradle floating down – quite all right, it were, except for one corner which was broke off. The thoughts that come to me that time! Whose cradle could it be? It must be some of them devils, your soldiers, I thinks, got into a Tartar village and grabbed the women, and one of the brutes has killed the baby: taken it by its little legs and hit its head against the wall. That's the sort of thing they do, ain't it? Ah, men have no hearts! And thoughts come to me that made me full of pity. I sez to meself: "The cradle thrown away and the mother carried off, the home burnt to the ground and her man taken his gun and come over to our side to rob us. Aye, I sits thinking. And then when I hears a litter of wild pigs breaking through the thicket, something begins to knock inside of me. "Come this way, me darlings!" No, I thinks, they'll scent me, and I sits without stirring and me heart goes thump, thump, thump, so hard it fairly lifted me off the ground. This spring now I see something black in the distance and a fine litter comes along. "To the Father and the Son . . ." and I was just about to fire when the sow sniffs and grunts to her piglets: "Careful, children, there's a man here," and off they scampered, crashing through the bushes. Vexatious it was, just when I'd almost got me teeth into her.'

'How did the sow tell her gruntlings there was a man there?'

'No doubt of it. D'ye suppose the animal's a fool? No, he's wiser nor a man, even though he is called a pig. There ain't nothing he don't know. For instance: a man will come across your tracks and not notice, but a hog now turns and makes off at once: that shows there's sense in him, since he scents a man's smell and you don't. And there's this to be said too: you are out to kill the hog, but he wants to run about the wood alive. You have one law, and he has another. He's a hog but he's no worse nor you are – he's one of God's creatures same as you. Oh dear, 'tis man that's stupid – very, very stupid, he is!' The old fellow repeated this several times and then with drooping head sat thinking.

Olenin became thoughtful too, and getting down from the porch he began to walk up and down the yard, his hands behind his back.

Yeroshka suddenly roused himself, lifted his head and started gazing intently at the moths circling round the flickering flame of the candle and falling into it.

'Little fools, little fools!' he said softly. 'Where are you flying, you silly creatures?' He rose to his feet and started to drive the moths away with his thick fingers.

'You'll burn yourselves, you little fools,' he muttered tenderly, trying with his clumsy hands to catch them gently by the wings. 'Here, fly this way, there's plenty of room. You'll be the death of yourselves, but I would spare you.'

He sat on a long time, chattering and taking an occasional sip from the bottle, while Olenin paced about the yard. Suddenly Olenin's attention was attracted by the sound of whispering outside the gate. Involuntarily holding his breath, he heard a woman's laugh, a man's voice, and then the sound of a kiss.

Purposely scuffling his feet on the grass, he crossed to the opposite side of the yard. Presently the wattle fence creaked. A Cossack in a dark Circassian coat and a white sheepskin cap walked along outside the fence (it was Luka), and a tall woman with a white kerchief on her head passed Olenin. 'I have nothing to do with you, and you have nothing to do with me,' Marianka's firm step seemed to say. Olenin followed her with his eyes to the porch of the hut, and he could even see her through the window take off her kerchief and sit down. And suddenly his heart was swept with a sense of loneliness, vague longings and hopes, and envy of someone for something he could not define.

The last lights had been extinguished in the cottages. The last sounds had died away in the village. The wattle fences and the dim white forms of the cattle in the yards, the roofs of the houses and the tall graceful poplars – all seemed to be sleeping the healthy, peaceful sleep of the labourer who has earned his rest. Only the incessant croaking of frogs from the distant swamps reached the attentive ear. In the east the stars seemed to melt away, one by one, in the increasing light; but overhead they were denser and deeper than before. The old man dozed with his head on his arm. A cock crowed in the yard opposite. But Olenin still walked up and down, back and forth, thinking and pondering. The sound of voices singing in chorus reached him, and he moved up to the fence and listened. Some young Cossacks were carolling a merry song, with one clear youthful voice ringing out strongly above the rest.

'D'you know who that is singing?' said the old man, rousing himself. ' 'Tis Luka, the brave. He's happy because he's killed an *abrek*. But is that anything to be happy about? The young fool –'

'And have you ever done any killing?' asked Olenin.

The old man lifted himself abruptly on both elbows and brought his face close to Olenin's. 'You devil!' he shouted. 'What are you asking? 'Tis wrong to talk like that. 'Tis a serious matter to destroy a human being – aye, a very serious matter. Well, good-bye to you for now,' he said, rising to his feet. 'I've had me fill of food and drink. Shall I take you out hunting tomorrow?'

'Yes, come and fetch me.'

'Mind you're up on time. If you oversleeps you'll be punished and fined!'

'Never fear, I'll be up before you are,' answered Olenin.

The old man went off. The song had ceased but the sound of footsteps could be heard, as well as cheerful talk. After a while the song broke out again, but farther away, and Yeroshka's loud bass chimed in with the others.

'What men! What a life!' thought Olenin with a sigh, as he went back alone into the cottage.

16

Gaffer Yeroshka was past active service, and lived by himself. Some twenty years back his wife had gone over to the Orthodox Church, deserted him and married a Russian sergeant-major. He had no children. It was no idle boast when he spoke of himself as having been the dare-devil of his village when he was young. Everybody in the regiment knew of his old-time exploits. The death of more than one Chechen and of more than one Russian lay on his conscience. He used to go plundering in the mountains, and he had robbed the Russians too, and twice he had been in prison. Now most of his time was spent hunting in the forest. He could live for days on a crust of bread and nothing but water. But he made up for it when he came back to the village, and drank from morning to night. After leaving Olenin he slept for a couple of hours and awoke before it was light. He lay on his couch thinking of the man he had become acquainted with the evening before. He liked Olenin's 'simplicity' – by that he meant his generosity with the wine – and he liked Olenin himself. He wondered why the Russians were all so 'simple' and so rich, and why, although they were so learned, they knew nothing at all. He reflected on all these points, and also considered what he might get out of Olenin. Yeroshka's hut was a tolerable size and not old, but the absence of a woman's hand was very noticeable. Cossacks are usually scrupulously clean, but his whole place was filthy and superlatively untidy. A blood-stained coat had been thrown on the table, together with the remains of a dough-cake and a plucked and mangled crow for his hawk. Sandals of raw-hide, a dagger, a little bag, wet clothes and sundry rags lay scattered on the benches. A tub of stinking water, in which another pair of sandals were being soaked, stood in a corner, beside a gun and a hunting-screen. A net with several dead pheasants in it had been flung on the floor, while a hen tied by its leg to the table wandered about pecking among the dirt. Inside the unheated oven was a chipped pot full of some kind of milky liquid, and on top of the oven a falcon was screeching and trying to break loose from the cord which fastened it. A moulting hawk sat quietly on the edge of the oven, looking sideways at the hen and occasionally twisting its head to right or left. Yeroshka himself, in his shirt, was lying flat on his back on the short bed he had rigged up between the wall and the oven. His powerful legs were drawn up with his feet resting on the oven, while his thick fingers picked at the scabs made on his hands by the hawk which he always carried without wearing gloves. The whole room, especially the corner by the bed, was filled with the strong but not unpleasant conglomeration of odours which accompanied the old man everywhere.

'*Uidye-ma,* Daddy?' ('Are you in, Gaffer?'), he heard a clear voice calling through the window, which he at once recognized as Luka's.

'*Uidye, uidye,* come in,' shouted the old man. 'Come along in, neighbour Marka, Luka Marka. Come to see old Gaffer, eh? On your way to the cordon, are you?'

At the sound of his master's voice the hawk flapped its wings and tugged at the cord.

The old man was fond of Luka, who was the only man he excepted from the general contempt in which he held the younger generation of Cossacks. Besides which, Luka and his mother, who were his nearest neighbours, often brought him *chikhir,* clotted cream and other home produce such as Yeroshka did not have. Gaffer Yeroshka, who all his life had followed the dictates of his heart, liked to find a practical explanation for his actions. 'Well, why not?' he would say to himself. 'They're well-to-do people. I'll give them some fresh meat, or a bird, and they won't forget Gaffer: they'll bring him a dough-cake or a piece of pie once in a while.'

'Morning, Marka! Glad you're come!' he shouted cheerfully, and quickly putting down his bare feet he jumped off the bed and took a step or two across the creaking floor, looking down at his out-turned toes. Suddenly, amused at the appearance of his feet, he grinned, stamped with his bare heels on the ground, stamped a second time, and cut a comic little caper. 'Pretty good, eh?' he asked, his small eyes twinkling. Luka smiled faintly. 'Well, going back to the cordon?' asked the old man.

'Here's the *chikhir* I promised you when we was at the cordon.'

'Bless you,' said the old man. He picked up his very wide trousers and *beshmet* from the floor, put them on, fastened a strap round his waist, poured some water over his hands from an earthenware pot, wiped them on his old trousers, ran a piece of ancient comb through his beard, and presented himself before Luka. 'Ready!' he said.

Luka fetched a cup, wiped it, filled it with wine and handed it to the old man.

'Here's to your health! To the Father and the Son!' said the old man, accepting the wine with solemnity. 'May all your desires come true, may you always be a hero and get a decoration!'

Luka also repeated a prayer before drinking a little of the wine and then setting it down on the table. The old man rose, got out some dried fish which he laid on the threshold and beat it with a stick to make it tender. Then he picked it up with his horny hands, put it on a blue plate (the only one he possessed) and placed it on the table.

'You see, I have everything I wants, victuals and everything, praise be to God,' he said proudly. 'Well, and how about Mosev?' he asked.

Luka, evidently anxious to know the old man's opinion, told him how the sergeant had taken the gun from him.

'Never mind the gun,' said the old man. 'Let him keep it or you won't get your reward.'

'But they say 'tis little reward a green lad can get who hasn't yet seen mounted service. But the gun was a beauty, a real Crimean gun, worth eighty roubles!'

'Aw, let it go, I tell you! I had a quarrel like of that once with a capting: he wanted my horse. "Give us your horse," says he, "and I'll make you a cornet." I wouldn't, and so I never got on.'

'I see that, Gaffer. But I've got to buy a horse and they say as you can't get one across the river for less than fifty roubles. And mother hasn't sold our wine yet.'

'Aw, we didn't bother about such trifles when Gaffer Yeroshka was your age: he stole whole herds from the Nogays and drove 'em across the Terek. Sometimes we sold a darn good horse for a cloak or a quart of vodka.'

'Why so cheap?' asked Luka.

'You're a fool, Marka, you're a fool!' said the old man contemptuously. 'Why, that's what a man steals for – so as not to be stingy! As for you lads, I reckon you've never so much as seen a herd of horses being driven off? Why don't you say nothing?'

'What can I say? It don't seem as we're the same sort of breed as you.'

'You're a fool, Marka, and no mistake! "Not the same sort of breed!"' retorted the old man, mimicking the Cossack lad. 'No, I should say not: when I were your age I were a different breed of Cossack.'

'What was you?' asked Luka.

The old man shook his head scornfully.

'Gaffer Yeroshka were *homely*, he didn't grudge nobody nothing. That's why I were good friends with the whole of Chechnya. If any of my friends come to see me I'd make him drunk and happy with vodka, and put him to sleep in my bed. And if I went to visit him I'd take him a present – *peshkesh*, they called it. That's the way to live, not like you lives nowadays. The only amusement you lads have is cracking seeds and spitting out the husks,' the old man concluded derisively, imitating present-day Cossacks cracking sunflower-seeds and spitting out the husks.

'Yes, I know,' said Luka. ''Tis so.'

'If you wants to be a fellow of the right sort, be a brave and not a peasant. A peasant can buy a horse – pay the money down and take the horse.'

Both were silent for a while.

'Well, of course, 'tis dull, Gaffer, both in the village and at the cordon. But there's nowhere a man can go for a bit o' sport. All our fellows are so funky. Take Nazar, now. T'other day we was in the Tartar village and Girey Khan wanted someone to go to Nogay after some horses, but no one would, and how was I to go alone?'

'And what about me? Do you think I'm quite done for? No, I'm not done for. Give me a horse and I'll be off to Nogay in a brace of shakes.'

'What's the use of talking nonsense,' said Luka. 'You'd better tell me what to do about Girey Khan. "Only get the horses down to the Terek," he says. "I'll always find a place for 'em, even if you brings a whole bunch." But he's a shaven-headed Tartar, and how can I trust him?'

'You may trust Girey Khan, all his kith and kin is good people. His father were a faithful friend of mine. But you listen to Gaffer: he won't give you no bad advice: make him take an oath, then everything will be all right. But if you goes with him, have your pistol ready; especially when it comes to dividing up the horses. I was nearly killed that way once by a Chechen. I asked him ten roubles for a horse. Trusting is all right, but don't go to sleep without a gun.'

Luka listened attentively to the old man.

'I say, Gaffer,' he began after a pause. 'I heard you've got some stone-break grass, is that true?'

'No such thing, but I'll tell you how to get some. You're a good lad, you don't forget old Gaffer. Shall I tell you?'

'Yes, go on.'

'Well, you know what a tortoise is? Well, she's a devil, is the tortoise.'

'Of course I know!'

'Find her nest and plait a little fence round it, so she can't get in. When she comes back she'll walk round it and then she'll go away again to find the magic grass to break the fence. Next morning you look in good time, and where the fence is broken you'll find the stone-break grass. Take it wherever you likes: no lock, no bar, will ever stop you.'

'Have you tried it yourself, eh Gaffer?'

'Well, no, I haven't. But I were told about it by worthy

people. I only used one charm meself – I said the "All hail" when I mounted me horse, and no one ever killed me.'

'What's the "All hail", Gaffer?'

'What, you don't know? Oh, what people! You do right to ask Gaffer. Well, listen, and repeat it after me:

All hail, ye inhabitants of Zion,
Behold your King!
Our steeds we shall mount
O Sophonios sing!
O Zachary speak!
O Father Mandricha!
Mankind-kind ever loving.

Kind ever loving,' the old man repeated. 'Do you know it now? Try.'

Luka laughed.

'Come, Gaffer, d'you mean to say as that's the reason you never got killed? Maybe it just happened so.'

'Oh all you are too clever by half. Just you learn it all through, and say it. It won't do you no harm. Once you've sung "O Mandricha" you'll be all right.' And the old man began laughing himself. 'But just one thing, Luka, don't go to Nogay, that's what I say.'

'Why not?'

'Times have changed, and you aren't the people. Rubbishy Cossacks, you are. Besides, look at all the Russians that have come down on us! You'd get yourself into gaol. Believe me, Luka, give it up. You can't do these things. 'Twere different with me and Girchik now ...'

And the old man was about to start on one of his endless stories but Luka glanced out of the window and interrupted him.

' 'Tis broad daylight, Gaffer, I must be off. Look us up some day.'

'Christ preserve you, Luka. I'll be going out too: I promised the army man to take him shooting. He seems a good fellow.'

17

FROM Yeroshka's Luka went home. As he returned, a raw, misty vapour was rising from the ground, enveloping the village. Invisible cattle began to stir in the various yards. Cocks crowed across to one another with increasing frequency and persistence. It was growing lighter and the villagers were getting up. Not till he was close to it could Luka discern the fence of his yard, all wet with dew, the porch of his hut and the open shed. The sound of an axe chopping wood came from the misty yard. Luka entered the cottage. His mother was up and stood at the oven, throwing wood into it. His little sister was still lying in bed asleep.

'Well, Luka, had enough holiday-making?' his mother asked quietly. 'Where did you spend the night?'

'In the village,' her son replied reluctantly, reaching for his musket which he drew from its cover and examined attentively.

His mother shook her head.

Pouring some gunpowder on to the pan, Luka took a few empty cartridge-cases out of a pouch and began filling them carefully, plugging each one with a bullet wrapped in a rag. Then, having tested the loaded cartridges with his teeth and inspected them, he put down the bag.

'I say, mother, I told you the nose-bags wanted mending. Have they been done?' he asked.

'Aye, dumb Stepka was doing some mending last night. Surely 'tisn't time for you to go back to the cordon? I haven't seen aught of you.'

'I must go soon as I'm ready,' replied Luka, tying up the powder-bag. 'Where's Stepka? Out o' doors already?'

'Chopping wood, I expect. She kept fretting because she wouldn't see you. She puts her hand to her face like this, and clicks her tongue, and presses both hands to her heart, to show as she is sad. Shall I go and call her? And you know, she understood all about the *abrek*.'

'Yes, you call her,' said Luka. 'And I had some tallow. Bring it here: I must grease my sabre.'

The old woman went out and a few minutes later Luka's deaf and dumb sister came up the creaking steps and entered the hut. She was six years older than her brother, and would have been extraordinarily like him had it not been for the dull expression of her face and the exaggerated grimaces characteristic of all deaf mutes. Her dress consisted of a coarse, patched smock, with an old blue kerchief round her head. Her feet were bare and dirty. Her neck, arms and face were sinewy like a man's. Her whole appearance denoted that she had always done the hard work of a man. She brought in an armful of logs which she threw down by the stove. Then she went up to her brother and with a delighted smile puckering up her face she patted him on the shoulder and began making rapid signs with her hands, her face and her entire body.

'That's right, that's right,' nodded Luka. 'Stepka is a good girl. She's fetched everything and mended everything, she's been very good. Here is something for her.' And he took two pieces of gingerbread out of his pocket and gave them to her.

Stepka's face flushed with pleasure and she began making weird noises to express her joy. Seizing the gingerbread, she started gesticulating still more rapidly, pointing frequently in one direction and drawing a thick finger over her eye-brows and face. Luka understood what she meant and kept nodding with a slight smile. She was telling him that he ought to give the dainties to the girls, and that the girls loved him, and that Marianka, who was the best of them all, loved him too. She indicated Marianka by pointing quickly in the direction of Marianka's house and to her own eyebrows and face, and by smacking her lips and wagging her head. 'She loves you,' Stepka expressed by pressing her hands to her bosom, kissing her hand and pretending to hug someone. The mother came back into the room and seeing what the deaf and dumb girl was trying to say smiled and shook her head. Stepka showed her the gingerbread and again squealed with joy.

'I told the cornet's wife t'other day as I'd send the matchmakers along,' said the mother. 'She took my words favourably.'

Luka looked at his mother without speaking.

'Well, mother, and how about selling the wine? I must have a horse.'

'I'll take it soon as I have time. I must get the barrels ready first,' his mother replied, obviously unwilling to have her son meddle in domestic matters. 'When you go out you'll find a bag in the passage. I borrowed it from the neighbours and got you a few things to take back to the cordon with you. Or will you put them in the saddle-bag?'

'All right,' answered Luka. 'By the way, if Girey Khan comes from across the river, send him up to the cordon. I have some business to talk over with him, and I shan't get no more leave for a long time.'

He began making ready to start.

'All right, I'll send him, Luka,' said the old woman. 'It seems as you spent all your time spreeing at Yamka's. Last night, when I got up to go out to the cattle, I listened and I thought as I heard you singing songs.'

Luka did not reply. He went out into the passage, threw his bags over his shoulder, tucked up the skirts of his coat, took his musket, and then paused on the threshold.

'Good-bye, mother!' he said as he closed the gate behind him. 'Send me a small barrel of *chikhir* by Nazar. I promised some to the lads. He'll call for it.'

'God be with you, Luka, God be with you! I'll send you some – I'll send from the new barrel,' said the old woman, following her son to the gate. 'And another thing,' she added, leaning over the hedge.

The Cossack stopped.

'You have been making merry. Well – that's all right. Why shouldn't a lad amuse himself? God sent you a piece of good fortune, and that's a fine thing. But now look out, son, and don't be overdoing it ... And above all keep on the right side of your superior. And I'll sell the wine and find money for a horse, and I'll arrange the match for you –'

'All right, all right!' Luka interrupted with a frown.

His deaf sister shouted to attract his attention. She pointed to her head and the palm of her hand, to indicate a shaven head – a Chechen. Then, contracting her brows, she made believe to aim a gun, gave a shriek and began to chirrup, rocking her head from side to side. She was telling Luka to kill another Chechen.

Luka understood. He smiled to her and, shifting the gun at his back under his cloak, walked away with quick, light steps, soon to disappear in the thick mist.

The old woman stood silently for a moment or two at the gate before returning to the hut and immediately falling to work.

18

LUKA started off for the cordon. At the same time Gaffer Yeroshka whistled to his dogs and, climbing over the wattle fence, went round to Olenin's lodgings, going by the back of the houses (he disliked meeting women when he was off hunting or shooting). He found Olenin still asleep, and even Vanyusha, though awake, was still in bed, looking around him, trying to make up his mind whether or not it was time to get up, when Gaffer Yeroshka, gun on shoulder and in full hunting attire, opened the door.

'To arms!' he bellowed in his deep voice. 'Sound the alarm! The Chechens are on us! Ivan! Put the samovar on for your master. And get yourself up – quick!' cried the old man. 'That's the way it is with us, my good fellow! Why, even the girls are up. Look out of the window – there's one going for water, and you still asleep!'

Olenin awoke with a start and jumped out of bed, feeling fresh and light-hearted at the sound of Yeroshka's voice.

'Quick march, hurry up, Ivan!' the old man shouted. 'Is this the way you go hunting? People having their breakfast, and you still asleep. Lyam, where are you?' he called his dog. 'Is your gun ready?' he went on at the top of his voice as though there were a whole crowd in the hut.

'I plead guilty, there's no denying it. The powder, Vanyusha, and the wads!'

'A penalty!' roared the old man.

'Doo tay voulay voo?' asked Vanyusha with a smirk.

'You b'ain't one of us. What lingo's that, you devil's spawn?'

the old man shouted at him, showing the stumps of his teeth.

'This is the first offence; you must let me off,' laughed Olenin, pulling on his high boots.

'Right 'tis, I'll forgive you this time,' said Yeroshka, 'but if you oversleeps again you'll be fined a bucket of *chikhir*. Once the sun is up you won't see no deer.'

'And even if we do find one, he'll be wiser than we are,' said Olenin, quoting the old man's words of the evening before. 'You can't deceive him.'

'Yes, laugh away! Kill one first, then you can talk. Now then, hurry up! Ah, here's your landlord coming to pay you a visit,' said Yeroshka, glancing out of the window. 'Look, he's been and dressed hisself up, new *beshmet* and all, so as you'd see he were an orficer. Oh, these people, these people!' And, sure enough, Vanyusha came in to announce that the master of the house wished to see Olenin.

'L'arjan!' Vanyusha remarked significantly, to prepare his master for the purpose of the visit. Immediately behind him the cornet himself entered in a new Circassian coat with an officer's stripes on the shoulders and polished boots – a quite exceptional thing among Cossacks. He swaggered into the room and with a smile offered his lodger the salutations of the day. The cornet was an 'educated' Cossack, who had been in Russia proper, was a school-teacher and, above all, was 'well-born'. He was anxious to appear 'well-born' but one could not help feeling that beneath his grotesque pretence of polish, his uneasy self-assurance and his absurdly affected manner of speaking, he was just the same as old Gaffer Yeroshka. This was evident alike in his sun-burned face, his hands and his red nose. Olenin begged him to be seated.

'Good morning, Ilya Vassilyevich, sir!' said Yeroshka, standing up and making what seemed to Olenin an ironically low bow.

'Good morning, old man. You are here early,' replied the cornet with a casual nod.

The cornet was a man of about forty with a grey pointed beard, skinny and lean but handsome and very fresh-complexioned for his age. Having come to see Olenin, he was evidently afraid of being taken for a common Cossack and was anxious at once to impress Olenin with his importance.

'There we have our Egyptian Nimrod,' he remarked with a self-satisfied smile, addressing Olenin and pointing to the old man. '*A mighty hunter before the Lord.* Foremost among us in everything. You have already been pleased to become acquainted with him?'

Yeroshka gazed at his feet in their sandals of wet rawhide, and shook his head thoughtfully, as though in amazement at the cornet's wit and learning, while he muttered to himself: ''Gyptian Nimrod! What will he think of next?'

'Yes, we are going off hunting together,' said Olenin.

'Just so, sir,' said the cornet. 'But I have a little business to discuss with you.'

'What is it?'

'Seeing that you are a gentleman,' began the cornet, 'and as I may likewise represent myself to be in the rank of an officer, and therefore we may always progressively negotiate, after the manner of gentlemen ...' (He paused and glanced with a smile at the old man and at Olenin.) 'Though, with my consent, you may nourish such an intention, my wife is a foolish woman according to our class, and at the time of speaking is unable to comprehend the meaning of your pronouncement of yesterday's date. Therefore my quarters can be let to the Regimental Adjutant for six roubles without the stables; but being a gentleman I can always avert it from myself free of charge. But, as you desire, I, as holding the rank of officer, can come to an agreement with you on every matter and subject personally. As an inhabitant of these regions I can comply with the conditions not so much according to our local customs but in every possible and conceivable respect ...'

'Put very clear!' muttered Yeroshka.

The cornet continued in the same strain for a long time. At last, and not without difficulty, Olenin gathered that the cornet wished to let his rooms to him for six roubles a month. He gladly agreed to this, and offered his visitor a glass of tea. The cornet declined.

'According to our foolish custom,' he said, 'we consider it a sin to drink out of a heathen tumbler. Though, of course, with my education I may understand, but my wife owing to her human frailty . . .'

'Well, anyway, will you have some tea?'

'With your permission I will use my own *private* tumbler,' replied the cornet, and went out on to the porch. 'Bring me my glass!' he shouted.

In a few moments the door opened and a young sunburnt arm in a print sleeve passed him a tumbler through the door. The cornet went up, took it and whispered something to his daughter. Olenin poured tea into the cornet's 'private' glass, and for Yeroshka into a 'heathen' glass.

'However, it is not my intention to detain you,' said the cornet, emptying the tumbler and scalding his lips. 'I likewise am partial to fishing, and I am here, so to say, only on leave of absence for recreation from my duties. I too have the desire to tempt fortune and see if some of the Terek's bounties will not fall to my lot. May I express the hope that you will come and visit us and partake of our native wine, as is the custom in our village?' he added.

The cornet bowed, shook hands with Olenin and departed. While Olenin was getting ready he heard the cornet giving orders to his family in a clear, authoritative voice, and a few minutes later he saw him go past the window in a tattered coat, his trousers rolled up to the knees and a fishing net over his shoulder.

'What a rogue!' said Gaffer Yeroshka, drinking the rest of the tea from his 'heathen' glass. 'Are you really going to pay him six roubles? Who ever heard of such a thing? The best cottage in the village wouldn't be no more than two. The cheat! Why, I'd let you have mine for three.'

'No, I'd rather stay where I am,' said Olenin.

'Six roubles! Seemingly you got money to burn. Ah me!' answered the old man. 'Hey, Ivan, let's have some *chikhir* here!'

Having had a snack and a drink of vodka to prepare themselves for the road, Olenin and the old man went out together soon after seven o'clock. At the gate they came up against a cart to which a pair of oxen were harnessed. Marianka, with a white kerchief pulled almost down to her eyes and a *beshmet* over her smock, and wearing high boots, was dragging the oxen by a cord attached to their horns.

'Sweetheart!' exclaimed the old man, pretending that he was going to seize her in his arms.

Marianka flourished her switch at him, and glanced merrily at the two men with her beautiful eyes.

Olenin felt more light-hearted than ever.

'Now then, come on, come on,' he said to Yeroshka, throwing his gun over his shoulder and conscious of the girl's eyes resting on him.

'Away with you, my beauties!' sounded Marianka's voice behind them, followed by the creak of the moving cart.

So long as their road lay through the pastures at the back of the village Yeroshka went on talking. He could not forget the cornet, and continued his railing.

'But why are you so angry with him?' asked Olenin.

'He's stingy. I can't abide stingy folk,' replied the old man. 'He'll leave it all behind come he pegs out. So who's he saving up for? He's built two huts, and he got a second orchard from his brother by a lawsuit. And you know, he's a devil for paper writing. They even comes to him from other villages so as he can write papers for 'em. And it all turns out just as he wrote it. He does it proper. But who's he storing it up for? He's only got one little lad and the girl. Come she's wed there won't be nobody.'

'Well, then, he's saving up for her dowry,' said Olenin.

'What dowry? The girl's sought after, she's a fine girl. But he's such a devil, he wants to marry her to a rich man. Wants to get a big price for her. There's a Cossack named Luka here, a neighbour and a nephew of mine, a fine, upstanding lad – the same who killed the Chechen. Well, he's been courting her this many a day, and still he hasn't let him have her. Makes one excuse after another – says the girl is too young, and such like. But I know what he's up to. He wants to keep them on their bended knees. What disgraceful goings-on there have been lately, to do with the girl. Still, Luka will get her in the end, because he's the best Cossack in the village, a brave who's killed an *abrek* and he'll have a medal for it.'

'But how about this? When I was walking up and down the yard last night I saw the girl kissing some Cossack,' said Olenin.

'You ain't serious!' cried the old man, stopping short.

'Upon my word.'

'Women are the devil,' said Yeroshka, pondering. 'But what Cossack was it?'

'I couldn't see.'

'Well, what was his cap like? A white one?'

'Yes.'

'An' did he have a red coat? Was he about your height?'

'No, a bit taller.'

'It's him all right!' Yeroshka burst out laughing. 'It's him, my Marka. Luka, I mean. I call him Marka for a joke. His very self! I'm that fond of him. I were just such a lad meself once. But what is the use of watching over women? My sweetheart slept in the hut with her mother and her sister-in-law, but I got in all right. She slept up above. The mother were a witch, devil take her. Couldn't abide the sight of me. Well, I used to come along with a chum of mine, Girchik his name were. We'd come under her window, and I'd climb on his shoulders, push up the window and grope me way in. Her used to sleep close by on the bench. Once I woke her up and she nearly cried out – she hadn't recognized me. "Who's there?" she cries. But how could I tell her? Her mother were beginning to stir anyhow. So I took off me cap and shoved it over her nose, and she knew whose it were all right, by the seam of it. She jumped up. I never wanted for nothing in them days. She'd fetch along clotted cream and grapes and everything,' added Yeroshka, who always brought in the practical side to his anecdotes. 'Aye, and she weren't the only one either. There were a life for you!'

'And what about now?'

'Now us'll follow the dog, get a pheasant to settle on a tree, and then you can have a shot.'

'If you were me, would you court Marianka?'

'You keep yer eye on the dogs. I'll tell you this night,' said the old man, pointing to his favourite Lyam.

Both were silent.

Then their talking was resumed while they proceeded another

hundred paces or so, when the old man stopped again and pointed to a twig lying across the path.

'What d'you make of that?' he said. 'You think it is just a twig. No, 'tis bad when it lies that way.'

'Why bad?'

'Ugh, you don't know nothing. Listen to me. When a stick lies that way, don't you be steppin' acrost it but go round, or fling it off the path like this, and say a prayer "To the Father and the Son and the Holy Spirit". Then you can go on with God's blessing, and you won't come to no harm. That's what the old folk learned me.'

'What nonsense!' said Olenin. 'You'd better tell me more about Marianka. So she's carrying on with Luka, is she?'

'Sssh . . . Be quiet now!' the old man again interrupted in a whisper. 'Just listen. Us'll go round by the wood.'

And the old man, stepping noiselessly in his soft sandals, led the way along a narrow path into the dense, wild, overgrown forest. Occasionally he looked round and scowled at Olenin, who rustled and clattered with his heavy boots and carried his gun carelessly so that several times it caught in the branches of the trees that grew across the path.

'Don't go making so much noise! Tread soft, soldier!' old Yeroshka kept whispering angrily.

They could feel by the air that the sun had risen. The mist was clearing but it still enveloped the tops of the trees, making the forest seem immensely high. With every successive step things changed: what had appeared to be a tree turned out to be a bush, and a reed looked like a tree.

19

THE mist had partly lifted, disclosing wet thatched roofs, and had partly changed to dew, which stood in big drops on the road and the grass along the hedges. Thick smoke rose from all the chimneys. People were pouring out of the village, some to the fields, others to the river, others still to the cordon. Olenin and Yeroshka walked together along the damp, grass-grown path, while their dogs trotted on either side of them, wagging their tails as now and again they looked up at their master. Myriads of gnats danced up and down in the air, following the huntsmen, covering their backs and hands, and flying into their eyes. The air smelled of grass and the humidity of the forest. Olenin kept glancing back at the ox-cart, in which Marianka sat, urging on the oxen with her switch.

It was very quiet all around. The sounds from the village now no longer reached the ears of the sportsmen, only brambles cracked as the dogs made their way through the thicket, and occasionally a bird would call to its mate. Olenin knew that it was dangerous in the forest, for *abreks* were always apt to hide in such places; but he knew too that in the forest, for a man on foot, a gun is a great protection. Not that he was afraid, but he felt that someone else in his place might be; and, looking ahead into the damp misty forest and listening to the rare and faint sounds with strained attention, he gripped his gun firmly and was aware of a pleasant sensation that was new to him. Gaffer Yeroshka went in front, stopping to examine every puddle where an animal had left a double track, and pointing it out to Olenin. He hardly spoke, except occasionally in a whisper. The track they were following had at one time been driven over by ox-carts but for long had been overgrown by grass. The forest of elms and plane-trees on either side of them was so dense with creepers that the eye could not penetrate its depths. Nearly every tree was draped from top to bottom with wild vines, while the ground below was covered with blackthorn. Every little glade was thick with blackberry bushes and grey feathery reeds. Here and there large hoofprints and small funnel-shaped pheasant trails led from the path into the thicket. Olenin, who had never seen anything like it, was amazed at the exuberance of this virgin forest. The dense vegetation, the danger, the old man with his mysterious whisperings, Marianka and her virile, graceful figure, and the mountains – all seemed like a dream to him.

'A pheasant settled a moment since,' whispered the old man, looking round and pulling his cap over his face. 'Look lively, cover your phiz.' He waved his arm impatiently at Olenin and crawled forward almost on all fours. 'They pheasants are scary of a man's phiz.'

Olenin was still in the rear when the old man suddenly halted and began examining a tree. A cock-pheasant up in the branches clucked at the dog that was barking at it, but just as Olenin caught sight of the bird a deafening report, like a cannon, came from Yeroshka's heavy fowling-piece. The pheasant fluttered up, scattering some feathers, and then plunged to earth. Coming up to the old man, Olenin disturbed another bird. Raising his gun, he took aim and fired. The pheasant darted into the air, and dropped like a stone, catching in the foliage as it fell into the thicket.

'Hooray!' cried the old man, laughing. (He could never bring down a bird on the wing.)

Picking up the pheasants, they continued. Olenin, excited by the exercise and the old man's praise, kept up a running conversation.

'Hold hard,' Yeroshka interrupted. 'Us'll go this ways now. Remarked the track of deer hereabouts yesterday, I did.'

They turned off into the thicket, and after a hundred yards or so scrambled through into a glade overgrown with weeds and partly under water. Olenin lagged behind the old sportsman, and presently he saw Gaffer Yeroshka, who was a short distance in front, stoop down, nod his head significantly and beckon with his arm. When he came up, he found the old man pointing at a human footprint.

'D'ye see?'

'Yes. Well?' said Olenin, trying to speak as calmly as possible. 'A man's been here.'

Cooper's *Pathfinder*, and *abreks*, flashed into his mind, but noticing Yeroshka's mysterious air he hesitated to ask any questions, and was therefore in doubt whether to attribute this hint of mystery to fear of danger or to the exigencies of sport.

'Nay, 'tis me own footprint,' the old man said quietly, pointing to some grass under which could be seen the almost obliterated track of an animal.

The old man went on, and Olenin kept up with him. Some twenty paces farther ahead they descended to lower ground and came upon a spreading pear-tree at the foot of which, on the black earth, lay the fresh droppings of an animal. The spot, surrounded with wild vines, was like a cosy arbour, dark and cool.

'He's been hereabout this morning,' said the old man with a sigh. 'Look, this lair here's still damp and fresh as anything.'

Suddenly they heard a tremendous crashing in the forest quite close to where they stood. Both started and seized their muskets, but they could see nothing and only heard the breaking of branches. Then for an instant came the rhythmical swift thud of galloping hoofs, which changed into a dull rumble echoing and re-echoing in wider and wider circles through the silent forest. Olenin's heart missed a beat. He peered in vain into the green of the thicket, and at last turned and looked at Yeroshka. The old man, with the butt of his gun pressed to his breast, stood motionless: his cap was thrust to the back of his head, his eyes gleamed unusually bright, and his open mouth, showing fierce yellow stumps of teeth, seemed to have stiffened wide open.

'A horned stag!' he muttered, and throwing down his gun in despair he began to tear at his white beard. 'He were a-standing right here. I should have come round by the path. Crazed I am, crazed!' And he gave his beard an angry tug. 'Crazed! Dolt!' he kept repeating, pulling at his beard until it hurt. Something seemed to be flying through the forest in the mist; the hoofs of the escaping stag echoed fainter and fainter, farther and farther away...

It was already dusk when Olenin, hungry and tired but in fine fettle, returned to his lodgings with the old man. Dinner was ready. They ate and drank until Olenin felt warmed and high-spirited, and he stepped out on to the porch. Again westwards before his eyes rose the mountains. Again the old man began telling his endless stories about hunting, about the *abreks*, about his sweethearts and his wild reckless life. Again Marianka passed to and fro across the yard, her cotton smock revealing the strong, virginal lines of her beautiful body.

20

NEXT morning Olenin went alone, without the old man, to the spot where they had disturbed the stag. Instead of leaving the village by the gates he climbed over the hedge as everybody else did, and before he had time to pull out the thorns caught in his coat his dog, which had run on ahead, started up two pheasants. No sooner had he got in among the blackthorns than pheasants began to rise at every step. (The old man had not shown him the place the day before because he meant to keep it for shooting from behind a screen.) Olenin killed five pheasants in twelve shots and got so exhausted clambering after them through the briars that the sweat rolled off him in large drops. He called off his dog, uncocked his gun, inserted a bullet above the small shot and, brushing away the mosquitoes with the wide sleeve of his Circassian coat, quietly set out for the spot they had visited the day before. But it was impossible to restrain the dog, who kept finding fresh trails on the path itself, and Olenin shot still another brace of pheasants, and being thus delayed it was nearly noon before he looked round for the place they had found the previous day.

It was a clear, soft, warm day. The morning dew had already dried even in the forest, and myriads of midges literally covered his face, his back and his arms. His dog had turned from black to grey, so thickly had they settled along its back, and it was the same with Olenin's coat, through which the insects stung him. Olenin was ready to take to his heels and run from the gnats, and was beginning to feel that life in this country in the summer was utterly impossible. He had turned for home when he bethought him that other people managed to endure and, deciding to continue, gave himself up to be devoured. And, strangely enough, by midday the sensation became almost pleasant. He even felt that without this mosquito-laden atmosphere around him, this taste of mingled insects and sweat which rolled up under his hand every time he wiped his perspiring face, without the intolerable itching of his whole body, the forest would lose its character and charm. These swarms of insects were so exactly suited to this monstrously lavish vegetation, to these multitudes of birds and beasts which filled the forest, to this dark foliage, the hot fragrant air, the tiny water-ways oozing through everywhere from the Terek and bubbling up under the overhanging leaves, that the very thing that at first seemed dreadful and unendurable he now began to enjoy. Going over the spot where they had come upon the stag the day before, and finding nothing, he felt inclined to take a rest. The sun was directly over the forest and its rays streamed perpendicularly down on his back and head whenever he came out into a clearing or on to a path. The seven heavy pheasants dragged painfully at his waist. Having found the traces of yesterday's stag, he crawled into the thicket and stretched himself out under a bush, in the actual spot where the stag had lain. He examined the dark foliage around him, the marks of sweat, the dry dung, the imprint of the animal's knees, the lump of black earth it had kicked up, and his own footprints of the day before. He felt cool and comfortable. He was not thinking about anything in particular, or wishing for anything. Suddenly there came over him such a strange feeling of overwhelming happiness and universal love that he began to cross himself as he did when a child, and murmur words of gratitude. With extraordinary clearness he started thinking: 'Here am I, Dmitri Olenin, a being quite distinct from every other being, now lying all alone heaven knows where – where a stag lived, an old stag, a beautiful stag, who perhaps has never seen a man; in a place where no human being has ever been before, or thought these thoughts. Here I sit, with trees young and old around me, one of them festooned with wild vines; and pheasants soar in the air about me, chasing each other and perhaps scenting their dead brothers.' He picked up his pheasants, examined them and wiped the warm blood off his hand on to his coat. 'Maybe the jackals sniff the smell of blood, and retire with disappointed faces. Everywhere around me, flying in and out among the leaves, which must seem to them like vast islands, mosquitoes hang and buzz in the air: one, two, three, four, a hundred, a thousand, a million mosquitoes, all for some reason making their buzzing noise near me, and each one of them as distinct and separate a Dmitri Olenin as I am.' Then he imagined he knew what the gnats were thinking and buzzing about. 'Here, this way, lads! Here's something good to eat,' they hum as they settle down upon him. And it was clear to him that he was not a Russian nobleman at all, a member of Moscow society, friend and relation of this person and that, but simply another mosquito or pheasant or stag like the mosquitoes, pheasants and stags having their haunts in the woods around him. 'Just like them, just like old Yeroshka, I shall live my little life and then die. And as he quite truly said: Grass will grow over me, and that will be all.

'But even if the end is grass growing over me,' his thoughts ran on, 'still I must live, and be happy, because happiness is all I desire. It doesn't matter what I am – an animal like all the rest over which the grass will grow and that will be the end, or a particle of Divinity – I must still live in the best possible way. How, then, must I live so as to be happy, and have I not been happy hitherto?' And he began to review his past life, and to feel disgust at himself. He saw himself as terribly exacting and selfish, although in reality wanting for nothing. And while he looked at the green leaves with the light shining through them, at the sun coming low in the clear sky, happiness suffused him as before. 'What makes me so happy and what did I live for until now?' he asked himself. 'How exacting I have been for my own interests, how I worried and schemed, yet all I gained was shame and sorrow. And now I find I don't need anything to make me happy!' And suddenly it seemed as though a new world were revealed to him. 'Now I know what happiness is,' he said to himself. 'Happiness lies in living for other people. And that's evident. The desire for happiness is innate in every human being: therefore it must be intended. Attempts to satisfy it selfishly – by pursuing wealth, fame, material well-being or love – may come to nothing, for circumstances may deny them. It follows, then, that it is these pursuits *per se* that are wrong: not the craving for happiness. What then are the cravings that can always be satisfied, independently of external circumstances? What are they? Love for others, and self-sacrifice.' He was so pleased and excited at this discovery, which seemed to him a new truth, that he sprang to his feet and began impatiently thinking to whom he could sacrifice himself, whom he could do good to, and love, immediately. 'Since I need nothing for myself,' he kept thinking, 'why not devote my life to others?'

Olenin picked up his gun and made his way out of the thicket, intending to return home quickly and think all this out and find an opportunity of doing good. When he came out into the clearing he looked about him: the sun was no longer visible above the tops of the trees. It had grown cooler, and the place seemed strange and not at all like the environs of the village. Everything – the weather and the forest – had suddenly changed. The sky was wrapped in cloud, the wind rustled in the treetops, and all around he saw nothing but reeds and decaying, fallen trees. When he called to his dog which had run off hunting, his voice echoed hollow in the wilderness. And all at once he was seized with a terrible sense of dread. He began to feel frightened. He remembered the *abreks* and the murderous deeds he had been told about, and behind every bush imagined an *abrek* ready to leap out at him, and he would either have to die fighting for his life or prove himself a coward. Then he began to think of God and of a future life in a way he had not done for a long time. And all around him was the same nature, wild, sombre and menacing. 'Anyhow is it worth while living for oneself,' he pondered, 'when at any moment one may die, and die without having done anything good, with nobody even knowing you're dead?' And pressing on in the direction he fancied the village lay, he gave no further thought to hunting. He felt desperately tired, and scrutinized every bush and tree almost with terror, expecting at any moment to have to fight for his life. After wandering in circles for a long time he came upon a ditch flowing with cold, sandy water from the Terek, and, fearful of getting still more lost, decided to follow it, though with no idea where it would lead him. Suddenly there was a crashing in the reeds behind. He started violently, clutching his gun. But when he turned round he felt ashamed of himself: it was only his dog, excited and panting, throwing itself into the ditch and lapping the cold water.

Olenin had a drink himself and then followed the dog in the hope that it would take him to the village. But despite the dog's company everything around him seemed to grow more and more sinister. The forest seemed darker and the wind blew with greater strength and fury in the tops of the old trees. Some large birds circled, screeching, round their nests in the hollow trunks. The vegetation thinned out, and increasingly he came upon rustling reeds and bare sandy patches marked by the tracks of wild beasts. To the howling of the wind was added another cheerless, monotonous drone which he could not define. His spirits were at a very low ebb. Feeling behind his back for the pheasants, he found one missing. It had got torn off and was lost: only a bleeding neck and head remained stuck in his belt. He felt more frightened than ever. He began to pray, and was obsessed by the fear lest he should die without having done any good in the world; he longed to live, and to live so as to achieve the renunciation of self.

21

SUDDENLY it was as if sunshine had flooded his heart. He heard voices speaking in Russian, heard the swift, even flowing of the Terek, and a few steps farther on saw the brown, moving surface of the river with the dun-coloured wet sand showing on the banks and in the shallows, saw the distant steppe, the cordon watch-tower rising above the water, a saddled, hobbled horse grazing among the brambles, and the mountains. The red sun peered for an instant from behind a cloud, and its last rays glittered gaily along the river, on the reeds, the watch-tower and a little knot of Cossacks, among whom Luka's stalwart figure attracted Olenin's involuntary attention.

For no apparent reason Olenin felt perfectly happy again. He had come upon the Nizhne-Prototsk post on the Terek, opposite a peaceable Tartar settlement on the other bank of the river. He saluted the Cossacks but, not yet having had an opportunity of doing anyone a kindness, went into the hut. Nor did he find the longed-for chance inside. The Cossacks received him coldly. Entering the mud-walled hut, he lit a cigarette. The Cossacks paid him little heed, in the first place because he was smoking a cigarette and in the second because they had other interests that evening. Some hostile Chechens, relatives of the shot *abrek*, had come from the hills with a scout to ransom the body, and the Cossacks were waiting for their commanding officer to arrive from the village. The dead man's brother, a tall, finely-proportioned brave with a short beard dyed red, was as dignified and stately as a king, despite his very ragged coat and lambskin cap. His features bore a striking resemblance to the dead *abrek*. He did not deign to look at anyone, nor once glance at the body, but squatting on his heels in the shade he spat as he smoked his short pipe, and occasionally uttered a few sharp guttural words to which his companion listened respectfully. It was plain that this was a brave who had more than once met with Russians in quite other circumstances, and nothing about them could surprise or even interest him. Olenin was about to go up and look at the dead body but the man's brother, glancing up at him with quiet contempt from under his brows, uttered an abrupt, angry exclamation and the scout hastened to cover the dead man's face with a coat. Olenin was struck by the brave's majestic, austere expression. He tried to speak to him, asking what village he came from, but the Chechen with barely a look spat scornfully and turned away. Olenin was so amazed at the man's indifference to him that he could only put it down to stupidity or ignorance of Russian, and addressed himself to the scout who acted as interpreter. The scout was as ragged as the other but his beard was black instead of red, and he was fidgety and all gleaming white teeth and flashing black eyes. He willingly entered into conversation, and asked for a cigarette.

'There was five brothers,' he began in broken Russian. 'This one make the third the Russians have killed, and now there is only two brothers left. He is brave, very much brave,' he said, pointing to the Chechen. 'When they shoot Akhmet Khan' (the name of the dead *abrek*) 'this one is hiding in the reeds on the bank opposite. He sees it all; sees them lay him in the skiff and bring him ashore this side. He stays there until nightfall: he wants to kill the old man but our others will not let him.'

Luka came up and sat down near the speakers.

'What village is he from?' he asked.

'From yonder in the mountains,' replied the interpreter, pointing to a bluish, misty gorge beyond the Terek. 'You know Suyuk-su? It is some eight miles beyond.'

'Did ever you know Girey Khan in Suyuk-su?' inquired Luka. 'He's a friend of mine.'

'He is my neighbour,' answered the scout.

'He's a good fellow!' And Luka, evidently much interested, began talking to the scout in Tartar.

Presently a Cossack captain and the village elder arrived on horseback with a suite of two Cossacks. The captain, one of the new type of Cossack officer, greeted the men but no one shouted 'Good health to your Honour!' as is customary in the Russian army, and only one or two responded with a nod. A few, among them Luka, got to their feet and stood to attention. The sergeant reported that everything was in order at the outpost. All this seemed laughable to Olenin, as if the Cossacks were playing at soldiers. However, the formalities soon gave place to simpler relations, and the captain, who was as alert and on the spot as the others, began speaking to the interpreter in fluent Tartar. A document was written and handed to the scout, money taken in exchange, and they approached the body.

'Which of you is Luka Gavrilov?' asked the captain.

Luka took off his cap and came forward.

'I have sent a report about you to the colonel. I don't know what will come of it. I have recommended you for a medal – you're too young to be made a sergeant. Can you read and write?'

'No, sir.'

'But you're a fine-looking lad,' said the captain, continuing to play the commander. 'You may put your cap on. Which of the Gavrilovs does he come from? The "Broad-Back", is it?'

'His nephew,' replied the sergeant.

'I know, I know ... Well, get moving, lend them a hand,' he said, turning to the Cossacks.

Luka's face shone with happiness and seemed handsomer than usual. Leaving the sergeant's side, he put on his cap and sat down near Olenin again.

When the body had been carried to the skiff, the dead man's brother descended to the bank. Involuntarily the Cossacks stepped aside to let him pass. With a powerful spring he jumped into the boat, and now for the first time surveyed the Cossacks with a swift glance and abruptly asked some question of the interpreter. The interpreter, answering, pointed at Luka. The Chechen's eyes rested briefly on Luka, and then turning slowly away gazed at the opposite bank, his look expressing not hate but chilling contempt. He spoke again.

'What did he say?' Olenin asked the fidgety scout.

'Yourn kills ourn, ourn kills yourn, the same old merry-go-round,' replied the scout, obviously making it up, and he laughed, his white teeth flashing, as he jumped into the boat.

The brother of the dead man sat motionless, his eyes fixed on the shore opposite. He was too full of hate and contempt to find anything to arouse his interest on this side of the river. The scout, standing in the stern and dipping his paddle alternately right and left, skilfully steered the boat across, and never left off talking. The current bore them obliquely down stream, the boat grew smaller and smaller, until the sound of voices was almost lost and at last, still within sight, they landed on the farther shore, where their horses stood waiting. There they lifted out the body and (though the horse shied) laid it across one of the saddles, mounted and rode along the road at foot-pace, past a Tartar village, from which a crowd came out to look at them. But the Cossacks on the Russian side of the river, cheerful and thoroughly pleased with themselves, laughed and joked. The captain and the village elder went into the hut to regale themselves. Luka, vainly striving to impart a staid expression to his beaming face, sat beside Olenin, his elbows on his knees, and whittled away at a stick.

'Why do you smoke?' he asked, as though he were curious to know. 'I'll lay t'ain't pleasant.'

He was evidently making conversation because he noticed Olenin felt ill at ease and cut off among the Cossacks.

'It's just a habit,' answered Olenin. 'Why do you ask?'

'I were only thinking, what a rumpus there'd be if any on us chaps started smoking. You see them mountains over yonder? They ain't far,' continued Luka, pointing to the defile, 'yet you can't never get to 'em ... But how you going to find yer way back come it be dark? Us'll take you, if you say. You ask the sergeant to let me come along a you.'

'What a fine lad!' thought Olenin, looking at Luka's animated face. He remembered Marianka and the kissing he had overheard at the gate, and suddenly he felt sorry for Luka and his ignorance. 'What folly and stupidity!' he thought. 'Here's a man who has killed a fellow being and is delighted with himself, as if he had done something magnificent. How is it he does not realize that he has no cause for rejoicing? That happiness lies not in killing others but in sacrificing oneself?'

'Look out he don't lay hold of you, mate!' said one of the Cossacks who had come down to see the skiff off, addressing Luka. 'Did you hear him ask after you?'

Luka raised his head.

'The one same as I christened?' he said, meaning the dead *abrek*.

'Him as you christened won't stand up no more, but yon red-'aired devil's his brother.'

'Let him praise God he got away whole,' said Luka with a laugh.

'Why are you so pleased?' asked Olenin. 'Supposing a brother of yours had been killed, would you be glad?'

The Cossack looked at Olenin with laughing eyes. He seemed to understand quite well what Olenin was trying to convey, but to be above such considerations.

'Aye, that happens too, don't it? Don't our fellows get killed sometimes?'

22

THE captain and the village elder rode away; and Olenin, to please Luka as well as to avoid going back alone through the dark forest, asked the sergeant to allow Luka to accompany him, which the sergeant did. Olenin thought that Luka wanted to see Marianka, and he was also glad of the company of such a pleasant-looking and sociable Cossack. Luka and Marianka were somehow united in his mind, and he found pleasure in thinking about them. 'He loves Marianka,' thought Olenin, 'and I could have loved her.' And he was swept by a warm, unfamiliar feeling of wistful tenderness as they walked homewards through the black forest. Luka too felt happy. Something akin to affection was springing up between these two very different young men. Every time their eyes met they wanted to laugh.

'Which is your gate?' asked Olenin.

'The middle one. But us'll see you so far as the marsh. After that you don't need to fear.'

Olenin laughed.

'Think I'm afraid? You go back, and much obliged to you. I can manage alone.'

'That's all right. I ain't got nothing to do. And how you going to help being affeared, even us chaps are,' said Luka, also laughing, and doing his best to save Olenin's face.

'Then come to my place, will you? We'll have a chat and a drink, and you can go back in the morning.'

'Couldn't I find somewheres to pass the night?' laughed Luka. 'Anyways the sergeant told me to return immediate.'

'I heard you singing yesterday evening, and I saw you too...'

'We're all human...' And Luka nodded his head.

'Is it true you're getting married?' asked Olenin.

'Mother's on for me marrying. But I haven't got no horse yet awhile.'

'Aren't you in the regular Service?'

'Not likely! Only just joined, haven't no horse yet, and don't know how I'll get one. Else I'd be marrying.'

'And what would a horse cost?'

'We was speaking for one t'other side of the river a day or so since. They was wanting more'n sixty roubles for 'un, and 'twere but a Nogay horse.'

'How would you like to come and be my *drabant*?'* Olenin asked suddenly. 'I can arrange it, and I'll give you a horse. Really now, I have two, and I don't need both.'

'What are you talking about – "don't need both"?' said Luka, laughing. 'What are you offering me presents for? I'll manage, I reckon, God 'elping.'

'No, really. Or don't you want to be my orderly?' insisted Olenin, glad that it had entered his head to give a horse to Luka, though at the same time he felt awkward and uncomfortable. He wanted to say something but did not know what to say.

*A *drabant* is a kind of orderly attached to an officer when campaigning. [*Author's note in the text.*]

Luka was the first to break the silence.

'Have you got a house of yourn in Russia?' he asked.

Olenin could not refrain from telling him that he had not only one but several houses.

'A proper house? Bigger'n ourn?' asked Luka good-naturedly.

'Much bigger – ten times as big, and three stories high,' replied Olenin.

'And have you got horses same as ourn?'

'I have a hundred horses, worth three or four hundred roubles each – silver roubles! But they're not like yours, they're trotters, you know . . . But still I like the horses here best.'

'How come it you had to come here? Was it yourn idea or was you made to come?' asked Luka, still with a touch of raillery. 'See, there's where you was lost,' he added, pointing to the footpath they were just crossing. 'You should have turned right.'

'I came by my own wish,' said Olenin. 'I wanted to see your country and take part in some expeditions.'

'I'd as lief join an expedition any day,' said Luka. 'D'you hear them jackals howling?'

'Tell me, didn't you feel terrible, killing a man?'

'How terrible? Aye, join an expedition,' Luka repeated. 'Give us the chance – aye, wouldn't I just!'

'Perhaps we'll be going together, you and I. Our company is off just before the holiday, and so is yours, I believe.'

'Anyways, fancy you coming here! You got a house, and horses, and serfs. I'd have a time of it if I was you. Day and night, I would. What be yer rank?'

'I'm a cadet, but I've been recommended for promotion.'

'Aye, suppose now you ain't bragging about your style of living at home – if I had it I'd have stayed there! Aye, us'd never have gone away anywheres. You likes it here with us then?'

'Yes, very much,' said Olenin.

It was quite dark by the time, thus talking confidentially together, they drew nearer the village. The deep gloom of the forest still surrounded them. The wind whistled in the tree-tops. The jackals seemed to be close at their heels, howling, chuckling and sobbing; but in the village ahead they could already hear the sound of women's voices and the barking of dogs, and see quite clearly the outline of the huts; lights gleamed and the air was heavy with the peculiar scent of *kizyak* smoke. Olenin felt more keenly than ever before that here in this Cossack village was his home, his family, his happiness, and that he never had lived and never would live so happily anywhere else. That evening he loved everybody, and Luka most of all. When they reached home Olenin went to a shed and to Luka's amazement led out a horse he had bought in Groznoe – it was not the one he usually rode himself but another and by no means a bad beast though no longer young – and presented it to Luka.

'What call have you to give me anything?' said Luka. 'I haven't done nothing for you this far.'

'Really, it's nothing,' replied Olenin. 'Take it, and one day you can give me something . . . I know, we'll go on an expedition against the enemy together.'

Luka was embarrassed.

'But what is it all about? How can you say as you don't need a horse?' he began, without looking at the creature.

'Take it, do take it! If you don't, you will offend me. Vanyusha, lead the grey home for him.'

Luka took hold of the halter.

'All right then, I thank you. This here's a fair surprise to me though; never so much as thought . . .'

Olenin was as happy as a twelve-year-old.

'Tie it up here. It's a good horse. I bought him in Groznoe, and he gallops beautifully. Vanyusha, bring us some *chikhir*. Let's go indoors.'

The wine was brought. Luka sat down and took the wine-bowl.

'Please God, I'll do something for you one day,' he said as he emptied the bowl. 'What might your name be?'

'Dmitri Andreich.'

'Well, 'Mitry Andreich, may God bless you. Us'll be brothers. I reckon you must come to our place. Us 'aven't got much but us knows 'ow to treat a friend. And I'll tell mother to give you anything you wants – curds or grapes – and if you comes to the cordon I'll be your servant: take you hunting, or acrost the river, any place you likes. If only I'd knowed t'other day. You should a seen the boar I killed – but I shared it out among us chaps. I'd have let you have it.'

'Fine, thank you. Don't harness the horse, by the way, it's never been in harness.'

'Harness a 'orse. Not much I shouldn't. And there's something else I'll tell you,' said Luka, bending his head. 'You might like to know, I have a friend, Girey Khan. He asked me if I'd come and lie in ambush on the road that leads down from the mountains. Shall us go together? I won't never let you down: I'll be yer bodyguard.'

'Yes, we'll go – we'll go along together some day.'

Luka seemed to be thoroughly at his ease now and to have understood Olenin's attitude towards him. The quiet simplicity of his manner surprised and even slightly shocked Olenin. They talked for a long time, and it was late when Luka, not tipsy (he never got tipsy) but having drunk a good deal, left Olenin after shaking hands.

Olenin looked out of the window to see what he would do. Luka walked slowly across the yard, with head bent. Then, as soon as he had led the horse out of the gate, he suddenly flung back his head, sprang on its back with the agility of a cat, gave the animal a free rein, and with a wild shout galloped down the street. Olenin had expected him to go and share his joy with Marianka, but though Luka did not do so Olenin felt more at peace with himself than ever before in his life. He was as blithe as a child, and could not refrain from telling Vanyusha not only that he had made Luka a present of the horse but also why he had done it, and expounded to him his whole theory of happiness. Vanyusha did not approve of the theory, and explained that he had no money to thrown away – '*l'arjan il n'y a pas*' – and therefore it was all sheer foolishness.

Luka rode home, and dismounting turned the horse over to his mother, telling her to put it out to grass with the other village horses. He himself had to report at the cordon that night. His deaf and dumb sister came to lead the horse away, and declared by signs that when she saw the man who had given the horse she would bow to the ground to him. Her son's story only made the old woman shake her head, convinced at the bottom of her heart that the animal must have been stolen. So she bade the girl take it to pasture before daybreak.

Luka went back alone to the cordon, pondering all the way over Olenin's action. Although in his opinion the horse was not much good, it was certainly worth at least forty roubles, and Luka was very glad to have such a present. But why it had been given him he could not understand, and not understanding he felt no sense of gratitude. On the contrary, his mind was full of vague suspicions as to the cadet's intentions. What those intentions might be he could not decide, but neither could he accept the idea that a perfect stranger would present him with a horse worth forty roubles for nothing, out of mere kindness; it seemed to him impossible. Had he been drunk now, he could have understood it – he would have been wanting to show off. But the cadet had been sober. Therefore it seemed probable he was trying to bribe Luka to do some dirty work. 'No fear!' thought Luka. 'I've got the horse, and I'll soon see what he's after. I ain't no fool. Us'll soon find out if he's more sharp than what I am. Us'll see right enough!' he thought, feeling that he must protect himself and so working up hostility against Olenin. He told no one how he had come by the horse. To some he said he had bought it, to others he replied evasively. In the village, however, the truth was soon known. Luka's mother, Marianka, her father and other Cossacks, when they learned about Olenin's gratuitous present, were bewildered and began to be on their guard against the Russian. But despite their fears the action aroused in them a great respect for what they called his 'simplicity' and wealth.

'Ever known the like of such a thing?' said one. 'That cadet quartered on Ilya Vassilich have chucked a horse worth fifty roubles at our Luka! He must be made of gold!'

'Yes, I heard of it,' replied another profoundly. 'Luka must have done something special for him. We shall see – we shall see what comes of it. He's lucky, Snatcher is.'

'Proper crafty lot, they Russians,' said a third. 'Capable of setting the village on fire, or something, I reckon.'

23

OLENIN'S life ran on smoothly and monotonously. He had little to do with his superior officers or his comrades. The position of a wealthy cadet in the Caucasus was peculiarly favourable in this respect. He was not required to do either work or training. In recognition of his service during the campaign he had been recommended for promotion, and meanwhile he was left in peace. The officers, regarding him as an aristocrat, were inclined to keep their distance. Their card-playing and carousals and sing-songs, of which he had had experience when with the detachment, held no attraction for him, and he, in his turn, avoided the officers' society and their life in the village. The existence of officers stationed in a Cossack village has long had its own invariable pattern. Just as every cadet or officer in a fort regularly drinks porter, plays faro and talks of decorations and promotions, so in a Cossack village he regularly drinks *chikhir* with his host, treats the girls to sweets and honey, flirts with the Cossack women, and falls in love; and occasionally even marries. Olenin had always lived after his own fashion, and had an unconscious aversion to beaten tracks. So here, too, he refused to walk in the ruts laid down for an officer in the Caucasus.

It came natural to him to wake at daybreak. After drinking his tea and from his porch admiring the mountains, the morning and Marianka, he would put on a tattered ox-hide coat, sandals of soaked rawhide, fasten a dagger to his belt, pick up his gun and a little bag containing lunch and some tobacco, call his dog and soon after five o'clock start for the forest beyond the village. Towards seven in the evening he would return tired and hungry, with half a dozen pheasants and occasionally some other small animal hanging from his belt, and with his bag of food and tobacco untouched. If the thoughts in his brain had been arranged like the cigarettes in his bag it could have been seen that during all those fourteen hours not one thought had been disturbed. He would come home morally fresh, full of vigour and completely happy. It would have been impossible for him to tell what he had been thinking about all that time. Were they ideas, memories or dreams that had been flitting through his mind? Frequently they were snatches of all three. Rousing himself, he would ask what he had been thinking about, and find himself in imagination a Cossack working in a vineyard with his Cossack wife, or an *abrek* in the mountains, or even a boar running away from him, Olenin. And all the time he would be listening and watching for a pheasant, a boar or a deer.

In the evenings Gaffer Yeroshka invariably came and sat with him. Vanyusha would bring a jug of *chikhir* and they would chat quietly, drink, and part contentedly to go to bed. Next day he would be off shooting again, there would be the same healthy tiredness, once more the after-dinner drinking and mutual satisfaction. Sometimes on a holiday or a day of rest he would spend all the hours at home. Then the chief occupation would be watching Marianka, whose every movement, without being aware of it himself, he would follow eagerly from his window or the porch. He contemplated Marianka and loved her (so he imagined) just as he loved the beauty of the mountains and the sky, and he had no thought of entering into any relations with her. It seemed to him that between the two of them such relations as existed between Marianka and the Cossack Luka were out of the question, to say nothing of the relations common between a wealthy officer and a peasant girl. He felt that if he attempted to follow the example of his fellow-officers the delights of contemplation would be exchanged for an abyss of suffering, disillusionment and remorse. Besides, in behaving as he did towards this woman, he had achieved a degree of self-denial which afforded him great satisfaction; but, above all, he was unaccountably afraid of Marianka and nothing would have induced him to venture an irresponsible word of love.

Once during the summer when Olenin had not gone shooting but was sitting at home a young man whom he had met in Moscow society quite unexpectedly came to call.

'Ah, *mon cher*, my dear fellow, how delighted I was when I heard that you were here!' he began in the mixture of Russian and French fashionable in Moscow, and he went on, interlarding his remarks with French words. 'They told me Olenin was here. *Quel* Olenin? I was so pleased ... Fancy fate bringing us together here! Well, how are you? What are you doing here, and why?'

And Prince Beletsky told his story: how he had temporarily entered the regiment, how the commander-in-chief had asked him to be his aide-de-camp, and how, although he was not at all keen on it, he had decided to accept the post after the campaign was over, although personally he did not care one way or the other.

'While I'm stranded in this hole I must at least look to my career – get a decoration, or promotion, or be transferred to the Guards. That is imperative, not so much for myself as for the sake of my family and friends. The prince received me very well; he is a very decent fellow,' Beletsky rattled on. 'I have been recommended for the St. Anna Cross, for the expedition. Now I'll be staying on till the next campaign. It's capital here. The women! Well, and how are you getting on? I was told by our captain – you know, Startsev, a kind-hearted stupid creat-ture ... he said you were living here like some awful savage, seeing no one. I can quite understand you don't care about being intimate with the set of officers we have here. I am so glad now, you and I will be able to see something of one another. I am lodging at the police sergeant's. You should see his daughter, Ustenka. She's *charmante*, I tell you!'

And faster and faster French and Russian words were bandied about, cascading from the world Olenin thought he had left for ever. In general people held the opinion that Beletsky was a nice, good-natured chap. Perhaps he was; but in spite of his handsome, friendly face Olenin found him extremely unpleasant. He seemed to exhale the filth that Olenin had rejected. What irritated Olenin particularly was that he could not – it was utterly beyond his powers to – give the cut direct to this man: it was as though the forgotten world from which he had escaped still had some irresistible claim on him. He was angry with Beletsky and with himself, and yet there he was against his will introducing French expressions into his conversation, displaying interest in the commander-in-chief and in their Moscow acquaintances and, because he and Beletsky in this

Cossack village both spoke French, running down their fellow-officers and the Cossacks, being friendly with Beletsky, promising to go along to him and giving an invitation to drop in to see him. Olenin, however, did not go to see Beletsky. Vanyusha for his part approved of Beletsky, declaring that he was a real gentleman.

Beletsky at once plunged into the usual routine of a wealthy officer in a Cossack village. Before Olenin's eyes within a month he was like an old resident of the place: he made the older men drunk, got up parties and himself went to parties arranged by the girls, bragged of his conquests and even progressed to the point where the girls and women for some reason addressed him as 'Daddy', while the Cossacks, who had no difficulty in understanding a man who loved wine and women, were soon won over and indeed came to prefer him to Olenin, who to them was an enigma.

24

It was five o'clock in the morning. Vanyusha was in the porch heating the samovar, using one of his high boots as a bellows to fan the coals. Olenin had already ridden away to bathe in the Terek. (He had recently invented a new sport – swimming his horse in the river.) His landlady was in her outhouse and dense black smoke from the kindling fire rose from the chimney. Marianka was in the byre milking the buffalo-cow. 'Oh stand still, you!' her impatient voice was heard protesting, followed by the rhythmical sound of milking. There was a brisk clattering of hoofs in the street outside, and Olenin, riding bareback on a handsome dark grey which was still wet and shining, rode up to the gate. Marianka's lovely head bound with a red kerchief appeared at the door of the byre and disappeared again. Olenin was wearing a red silk shirt, a white Circassian coat girdled with a strap which carried a dagger, and a tall lambskin cap. He sat his wet, well-fed horse with a slightly self-conscious swagger and, holding his gun at his back, bent down to open the gate. His hair was still wet, and his face shone with youthful vitality and health. He thought himself handsome, able and very much the brave, but he was mistaken, for one glance would have told any knowledgeable out-and-out Cossack that he was a mere Russian. When he noticed that the girl had put out her head he lent over with exaggerated verve, threw open the gate and swung into the yard, holding the reins high and flourishing the whip. 'Tea ready, Vanyusha?' he cried gaily, not looking at the byre door. It gave him great satisfaction to feel his splendid steed pressing down its flanks, pulling at the bridle and, with every muscle quivering, prancing on the hard clay of the yard, ready to take a standing leap over the fence. '*C'est prêt,*' replied Vanyusha. Olenin fancied that Marianka's beautiful eyes were still watching from the byre but he did not turn round to look. Then, jumping down from the horse, he caught his gun against the porch and made an awkward movement. He shot an anxious glance towards the cow-shed but no one was at the door and from inside came the rhythmical sound of milking.

He went into the cottage but soon emerged again with a book and his pipe, and sat down to a glass of tea in the corner of the porch not yet exposed to the slanting rays of the morning sun. He did not mean to go out before dinner that day, so as to write some long-neglected letters; but for some reason or other he felt disinclined to leave the porch and was as reluctant to go back to his room as if it were a prison. Dame Ulitka had got her stove alight, and Marianka, having driven the cattle to pasture, had come back and was collecting *kizyak* and sticking it in lumps along the fence to dry. Olenin read, but understood nothing of the book that lay open before him. He kept lifting his eyes from the page and looking at the vigorous young woman moving to and fro below. Whether she stepped into the damp morning shadow thrown by the house or walked out into the middle of the yard flooded with the cheerful brightness of the early sun – her lovely form in the gay dress shining in the dazzling light and casting a black shadow – he was afraid to miss a single one of her movements. It delighted him to see how freely and gracefully her figure bent; into what folds her pink smock, her only garment, draped itself on her bosom and clung to her shapely legs; how, when she drew herself up, the tightly gathered smock showed the firm outline of her breasts; how the soles of her narrow feet in their worn red slippers trod lightly on the ground without altering their shape; and the strong muscles of her arms (she had her sleeves rolled up) strained as she handled the spade almost impatiently; and how her black eyes occasionally glanced towards him. The delicate eyebrows were contracted in a frown and her eyes showed a conscious satisfaction in her own beauty.

'Hullo, Olenin, how long have you been up?' said Beletsky, entering the yard in the uniform of a Caucasian officer.

'Ah, Beletsky! How is it you are out so early?' Olenin asked, holding out his hand.

'There was no help for it. I was driven out – we are having a ball tonight. Marianka – you'll come to Ustenka's, won't you?'

Olenin was astonished at the familiarity with which Beletsky addressed the girl. But Marianka, as though not hearing, bent her head and throwing the spade across her shoulder went with her firm masculine tread towards the byre.

'She's shy, the wench is shy,' Beletsky called after her. 'Shy of you, Olenin,' he added as, smiling gaily, he ran up the steps of the porch.

'What is this party? Who kicked you out?'

'Ustenka's giving it – my landlady – and you are invited. A party means a pie and an assembly of girls.'

'Yes, but what are we expected to do?'

Beletsky smiled knowingly and winked, jerking his head in the direction of the outhouse into which Marianka had disappeared.

Olenin blushed and shrugged his shoulders.

'Really, Beletsky, you are a strange chap.'

'Oh come, out with it!'

Olenin frowned, and Beletsky noticing this smiled insinuatingly.

'Oh come, don't try to tell me ...' he said. 'Living in the same house ... and such a nice girl, a really nice girl and a perfect beauty ...'

'A remarkable beauty! I never saw such women!' exclaimed Olenin.

'Well then?' asked Beletsky, absolutely at a loss.

'It may sound strange to you,' Olenin answered, 'but why

not tell the truth? Since I've been here, women don't seem to exist for me. And that is the way it should be, I assure you! And besides, what can there be in common between us and these girls? Yeroshka now – that's different. He and I have a common passion – hunting.'

'Well, well! "In common," you say? What, I ask you, did I have in common with Amalia in Moscow? It's exactly the same here. You may say they're not very clean, but that's another matter. *A la guerre, comme à la guerre!*'

'But I've never had any Amalia,' said Olenin. 'And I wouldn't know how to behave with women of that sort. All I know is that I could have no respect for them, whereas I do respect these Cossack girls.'

'By all means, go on respecting them. Who's to stop you?'

Olenin did not reply. He evidently wanted to complete what he had begun to say. The subject lay too near his heart.

'I know I am an exception ...' (He was visibly embarrassed.) 'But my life here has shaped itself so well that I not only see no reason to renounce my precepts but I could not live here at all – let alone live as happily as I am doing – were I to follow your practice. And besides, I look for something quite different – I find something quite different in them from what you look for.'

Beletsky raised incredulous eyebrows. 'Anyhow, come to my place this evening. Marianka will be there too, and I'll make you acquainted. Please come! You can always leave if you find it tedious. Will you?'

'I would come, but to tell you the truth I am afraid of falling in love.'

'Oh! oh! oh!' cried Beletsky. 'But do come all the same. I will take care of you. You will come? Word of honour?'

'I would come, but really I'm not sure what we should have to do, what we should let ourselves in for.'

'Please, I beg you! You will?'

'Well ... perhaps.'

'For heaven's sake, Olenin, what's the idea of living like a monk among the loveliest women in the world? Why spoil your life and not enjoy things while you can? Have you heard our company is off to Vozdvizhensk?'

'Surely not? I was told the 8th Company were going,' said Olenin.

'No, I had a letter from the adjutant. He writes that the Prince himself will take part in the campaign. I shall be glad to see something of him. I'm beginning to get tired of this place.'

'They say we are preparing for a raid.'

'I haven't heard about that. But I have heard that Krinovitsin got the St. Anna Cross for the last one. Poor chap, he hoped he would be made a lieutenant. He's gone off to head-quarters ...'

Towards evening, when it was growing dusk, Olenin's thoughts turned to the party. The invitation worried him. He wanted to go but the idea seemed strange and he felt shy and half fearful. He knew there would be no Cossack men or older women there, but only the girls. What would it be like? How was he expected to behave? What would he say? What would they talk about? How would he get on with those wild Cossack girls? Beletsky had alluded to such curious, cynical and at the same time rigidly conventional relationships . . . It was queer to think of being in the same room as Marianka and even, perhaps, having to talk to her. It seemed impossible when he remembered her distant demeanour. Yet Beletsky spoke as if it were all perfectly simple. Was it possible Beletsky would treat Marianka as another Amalia? 'It would be interesting to find out,' thought Olenin. 'But no, I'd better keep away. The whole business is horrid, vulgar, above all of no earthly use.' But once more he was tormented by curiosity as to what it would be like. And besides, he felt bound by his promise. He went out without having made up his mind one way or the other, but having walked as far as Beletsky's he went in.

The cottage where Beletsky lived was exactly like Olenin's. It stood on wooden piles nearly five feet from the ground, and consisted of two rooms. In the first (which Olenin entered by a steep flight of steps) feather-beds, rugs, quilts and pillows were tastefully and decoratively arranged, Cossack fashion, along the front wall. On the side walls hung copper pans and weapons, while water-melons and pumpkins lay on the floor under a bench. In the second room there was a large stove, a table, a couple of benches and some ikons painted according to the canons of the Old Faith. This was where Beletsky was quartered, with his camp-bed and his various saddle packs. His weapons hung on the wall with a little rug behind them, and various toilet articles and some portraits were set out on the table. A silk dressing-gown had been thrown over a bench. Beletsky himself, looking spruce and handsome, lay on the bed in shirt and drawers, reading *Les Trois Mousquetaires*.

He jumped up.

'There, you see how I am established. Not bad, eh? I'm so glad you've come. By the way, the preparations are going ahead quite feverishly. Do you know what their pies are made of? Dough stuffed with pork and grapes. But that's not the important thing. Just look at the commotion out there!'

Indeed, as they looked out of the window they saw an extraordinary bustle going on in the other hut. Girls ran in and out, fetching and carrying.

'Will you be ready soon?' shouted Beletsky.

'In a minute. Why? Is our Daddy hungry?' And peals of laughter came from the hut.

Ustenka, plump, rosy-cheeked and pretty, with her sleeves rolled up, came running in to Beletsky's room to get some plates.

'Mind, or I'll go and drop 'em!' she squealed, dodging Beletsky. 'You'd better come and lend a hand,' she cried, laughing, to Olenin. 'And don't forget to bring a supply of sweeties for the girls.' (By 'sweeties' she meant gingerbread and bon-bons.)

'And has Marianka come?'

'Of course she has. She brought us some dough too.'

'You know,' said Beletsky, when Ustenka had left the room, 'if only one could dress her properly and clean and polish her up a bit, she'd be a sight better looking than all our beauties. Have you seen that Cossack woman who married Colonel Borshev? What *dignité*! Where do they get it? . . .'

'I don't know Borshev's wife, but I don't think anything could be more becoming than the clothes they wear here.'

'It's marvellous how I can adapt myself to any kind of life!' said Beletsky with a sigh of content. 'Well, I'll go and see what they are up to.' And throwing the dressing-gown over his shoulders he ran out, calling back to Olenin, 'And you look to the "sweeties"!'

Olenin despatched Beletsky's orderly to buy gingerbread and honey; but it suddenly seemed to him so abhorrent to be giving money (as if he were trying to bribe someone) that he made no definite reply to the orderly's question: 'How many cakes with peppermint and how many with honey?'

'Get what you think best.'

'Am I to spend all the money?' asked the old soldier meaningly. 'Them peppermint sort is dearer. They was charging sixteen kopecks t'other day.'

'Yes, spend the lot, by all means,' said Olenin, and sat down by the window, surprised to feel his heart thumping as though he were preparing some gravely discreditable venture.

He heard an uproar in the girls' hut as Beletsky entered, and a few minutes later saw Beletsky dash down the steps, accompanied by piercing shrieks and laughter. 'Thrown out!' he said.

Presently Ustenka came in and with great solemnity invited her guests to come over, saying that everything was ready.

When they went into the other hut they found all was ready indeed, and Ustenka rearranging the cushions along the wall. On the table, spread with a napkin that was too small for it, stood a decanter of red wine and some dried fish. The room smelled of dough and grapes. Half a dozen girls dressed in their best tunics and without the usual kerchief on their heads, huddled together in the corner behind the stove, whispering, giggling and spluttering with laughter.

'I humbly beg you to do honour to my patron saint,' said Ustenka, inviting her guests to the table.

When Olenin noticed Marianka among the group of girls, who were all without exception comely, he felt vexed and upset at meeting her in such cheap and uncomfortable circumstances. He was feeling foolish and out of place, and decided to watch Beletsky and do what he did. Somewhat solemnly, yet quite assured and at ease, Beletsky stepped forward to the table, drank a glass of wine to Ustenka's health and invited the others to do the same. Ustenka explained that young girls did not drink.

'With honey us might, though,' said a voice from among the girls.

The orderly, who had just returned with the honey and spice-cakes, was called in. He looked askance – was it with envy or contempt? – at the gentlemen, who in his opinion were out on the spree, and with scrupulous care handed them a piece of honeycomb and the cakes, wrapped in grey paper, and started on a detailed account of the price and the change, but Beletsky dismissed him.

After stirring honey into glasses of wine and scattering with a lavish gesture the three pounds of spice-cakes on the table, Beletsky proceeded literally to drag the girls from their corners, and making them sit round the table he began to distribute the cakes. Olenin could not help seeing how Marianka's small, sunburnt hand closed on two round peppermint cakes and one of cinnamon, and not know what to do with them. The conversation was halting and not pleasant despite the easy manner of Ustenka and Beletsky and their efforts to enliven the company. Olenin fidgeted and cudgelled his brains for something to say, feeling that he was exciting curiosity and perhaps provoking ridicule and infecting the others with his shyness. He blushed, and it seemed to him that Marianka in particular was feeling uncomfortable. 'Probably they are waiting for us to give them money,' he thought. 'But how is it done? If only we could do it quickly and get away!'

25

'MARIANKA, how is it you don't know your own lodger?' asked Beletsky.

'How am I to know him if he don't never come to see us?' answered Marianka with a glance at Olenin.

Olenin, startled, coloured up and replied at random:

'I'm scared of your mother. She gave us such a trimming the first time I presented myself.'

Marianka burst into a laugh.

'So you're scared, eh?' she said, looking at him and then turning away.

It was the first time Olenin had seen the whole of her face: till then she had always worn a kerchief pulled down almost over her eyes. Not without reason was she considered the belle of the village. Ustenka was a pretty, laughing chatterbox, plump and pink-cheeked with merry brown eyes and red lips perpetually parting in a smile. Marianka, on the contrary, could not be called pretty: she was beautiful. Her features might have been considered too masculine and almost hard had it not been for her tall stately figure, her magnificent shoulders and bust, and, especially, the stern and yet tender expression of her almond-shaped black eyes which shone dark from beneath the black brows, and the gentle curve of her mouth when she smiled. She seldom smiled but when she did one could not help being attracted. She radiated virginal strength and health. All the girls were good-looking but they themselves as well as Beletsky, and the orderly when he brought in the spice-cakes, were irresistibly drawn to Marianka, and anyone addressing the girls naturally turned to her. She was like a proud, joyous queen among them.

Beletsky, in his efforts to keep the party going, chattered without pause, made the girls hand round the wine, played the fool with them, and kept making improper remarks to Olenin in French about Marianka's beauty, referring to her as 'yours' ('*la vôtre*'), and inviting Olenin to behave as he was behaving. Olenin felt more and more uncomfortable. He had just thought out an excuse so that he could escape and get away when Beletsky proposed that Ustenka, whose saint's day they were celebrating, ought to offer wine to her guests accompanying it with a kiss. Ustenka agreed but only on condition they put money on her plate as is the custom at weddings. 'What the devil made me come to this disgusting affair?' wondered Olenin, rising to his feet.

'Where are you off to?'

'To fetch some tobacco,' he said, meaning to get away, but Beletsky caught him by the arm.

'I have some money,' he said in French.

'There's no avoiding it, I shall have to loose the purse strings,' thought Olenin bitterly, vexed at his own gaucherie. 'Why can't I behave like Beletsky? I oughtn't to have come, but now I am here I must not spoil their enjoyment. Let me at least try to drink like a Cossack,' and seizing a wooden bowl (it held about eight tumblers), he filled it with wine and practically drained it at a draught. The girls watched him doubtfully. It seemed a strange and unseemly thing to do, and they were a little shocked. Ustenka brought him and Beletsky another glass each, and kissed them both. 'Here we are, girls, now us can have a good time,' she said, jingling the four silver roubles the men put on her plate.

Olenin no longer felt any sense of constraint. He became talkative.

'Well, Marianka, it's your turn to offer us wine and a kiss,' said Beletsky, seizing her hand.

'I'll give you a kiss all right,' said Marianka, pretending to box his ears.

'Daddy can be allowed a kiss without paying for it,' one of the girls chimed in.

'There's a sensible child,' said Beletsky, grabbing the struggling girl and kissing her. 'Come, but you must pass the wine,' he insisted, turning to Marianka again. 'Come on, offer a glass to your lodger.'

And taking her by the hand he led her to the bench and made her sit down beside Olenin.

'Isn't she a beauty!' he said, turning her head round to show her profile.

Marianka did not resist but with a proud smile let her large eyes rest on Olenin.

'A perfect beauty!' said Beletsky again.

'Yes, see what a beauty I am!' Marianka's glance seemed to repeat.

Without considering what he was doing, Olenin threw his arms round her and was about to kiss her but she instantly tore herself free and sprang towards the stove, upsetting Beletsky and pulling the cloth off the table on the way. There were shrieks of laughter. Beletsky whispered something to the girls and suddenly he and they all ran out into the passage and locked the door behind them.

'Why is it that you kissed Beletsky but won't kiss me?' asked Olenin.

'I doesn't want to, that's all,' she answered, drawing up her underlip and frowning. 'He's our "Daddy",' she added with a smile. She went to the door and began to bang on it. 'What did you lock the door for, you devils?'

'It's all right, let them stay out there, and us be here,' said Olenin, drawing closer to her.

She frowned and pushed him severely away, and again she looked so dignified and beautiful that Olenin came to his senses and felt ashamed of what he was doing. He went to the door and tried to pull it open.

'Beletsky! Open the door! Stop these silly tricks!'

Marianka again broke into her gay, happy laugh. 'Aye, so you're afraid of me?' she said.

'I am. You're as hot-tempered as your mother.'

'Here, I'll tell you something: you keep on spending all yer time with old Yeroshka and of course the girls 'll love you more and more every day!' And she smiled, bringing her face close to his and looking him straight in the eyes.

He did not know what to say to that. 'And suppose I came to see you sometimes? ...' he ventured falteringly.

''Twould be a different matter,' she replied, with a toss of her head.

At that moment Beletsky pushed the door open and Marianka sprang away from Olenin. In doing so her thigh struck his leg.

'All that about love and self-sacrifice, and Luka, that I've been inventing for myself – it's all nonsense,' thought Olenin in a flash. 'Happiness is the thing. The man who is happy is the man who is right.' And with a vigour which surprised even himself he grabbed the beautiful Marianka and kissed her on the temple and the cheek. She was not angry, and only burst into a loud laugh and ran out to the other girls. With this the evening ended. Ustenka's mother came home from the vineyards, gave them all a scolding and turned the girls out.

26

'YES,' mused Olenin, as he walked homewards, 'if I don't keep a tight hold on myself I might fall madly in love with that Cossack girl.' He went to bed with this thought but expected it would all blow over and he would continue to live as before.

But the old life did not return. His relations to Marianka were changed. The wall that had separated them had broken down. Olenin now exchanged a word of greeting with her every time they met.

The owner of the house, who arrived to collect the rent, having learned of his lodger's wealth and generosity, hastened to invite him over to his own hut. The old woman received Olenin kindly, and from the day of the party he often went across of an evening and sat with them until late at night. To outward appearances his life in the village followed the same routine as before, but within him everything had changed. His days he spent in the forest but towards eight o'clock, when it was beginning to grow dark, he would drop in on his hosts, either alone or with Gaffer Yeroshka. Soon the family were so used to him that they were surprised if he did not come. He paid well for his wine and was a nice quiet fellow. Vanyusha would bring him his tea, and he would sit in a corner near the stove. The old woman went on with her work, unperturbed, and over tea or *chikhir* they would chat about local affairs and the neighbours, or Olenin would answer their questions and tell them about Russia. Sometimes he brought a book and spent the evening reading. Marianka, like a wild goat, with her feet drawn up under her, squatted on the stove * or crouched in some dark corner. She took no part in the conversation but Olenin saw her eyes and her face, and heard when she moved or cracked pumpkin seeds, and was aware of her listening with her whole being whenever he spoke, and felt her presence while he silently read to himself. Sometimes he fancied her gaze was fixed upon him, and when their eyes met he would keep still, looking at her; whereupon she would instantly hide her face, and he would pretend to be engrossed in conversation with the old woman, listening the while to her breathing, to her every movement, and waiting for her to look at him again. With others present she was generally gay and friendly with him, but when they were alone together she would be shy and abrupt. Sometimes he came before she had returned from work. Suddenly he would hear her purposeful step and glimpse her blue

* Russian stoves were tall and had a large flat top on which the peasants often made their bed. [*Translator's note*]

smock through the open door. Walking into the middle of the room, she would catch sight of him, her eyes would light up with a faint, tender smile – and Olenin would feel happy and afraid.

He asked for nothing and expected nothing from her, but every day her presence became more necessary to him.

Olenin had entered so thoroughly into the life of a Cossack village that his past seemed something quite foreign to him. As to the future – especially a future outside the world in which he was now living – it held not the slightest interest for him. When letters came from home he was indignant that his relatives and friends should mourn him as one dead and buried, while he, in his Cossack village, regarded as bereft of life those who did not live as he was living. He felt sure he would never regret having broken away from his former surroundings and arranged such solitary and unusual circumstances for himself. He had enjoyed the campaign and fortress life; but it was only here, under Gaffer Yeroshka's wing, in the forest, in his hut at the end of the village, above all when he thought of Marianka and Luka, that he realized with the utmost clearness all the falsity of his former existence, which had disturbed him even at the time and now seemed inexpressibly vile and preposterous. Here he felt freer and more of a man with every day that passed. The Caucasus appeared very different from what he had imagined. He found nothing at all resembling his dreams or the descriptions of the Caucasus he had heard or read. 'Here it is not a question of thundering cataracts, Amalat-Beks clad in romantic cloaks, heroes and villains,' he thought. 'People live as nature lives. They die, they are born, they mate and give birth – they fight, eat and drink, make merry and die, with no restriction beyond the immutable ones that nature imposes on sun and grass, on animal and tree. These people are subject to no other law ...' And therefore, compared to himself, they appeared beautiful, strong and free, and the sight of them caused Olenin to feel ashamed and sorry for himself. Often it quite seriously occurred to him to throw up everything, enrol with the Cossacks, buy a cottage and some cattle and marry a Cossack girl (only not Marianka, whom he conceded to Luka), and go hunting and fishing with Gaffer Yeroshka, and join the

Cossacks on their expeditions. 'Why ever don't I? What am I waiting for?' he would demand, and worry and try to shame himself. 'Am I afraid of doing what I hold to be sensible and right? Is the desire to live simply, like a Cossack, close to nature, harming nobody and even helping people – is that any more foolish than dreaming of becoming a minister, for instance, or commanding a regiment, as I used to do?' And yet a voice kept whispering that he should wait before taking any final decision. He was held back by a dim consciousness that he could not live altogether like Yeroshka and Luka, because his idea of happiness was different for theirs: he was held back by the thought that happiness lay in self-sacrifice. What he had done for Luka continued to give him deep satisfaction. He constantly sought for opportunities of sacrificing himself for others, but he did not meet with them. Sometimes he would forget his newly-discovered recipe for happiness and believe that he could identify his life with Gaffer Yeroshka's; but presently he would suddenly come to his senses and cling even more consciously than before to his ideal of self-sacrifice, from the heights of which he looked calmly and proudly at all men and on the happiness of others.

27

JUST before the vintage Luka rode over to see Olenin, looking more dashing than ever.

'Well, and when are you getting married?' asked Olenin, greeting him gaily.

Luka made no direct reply.

'See what I got in exchange for your horse,' he said. 'Ain't it a horse! A Kabarda from the Lov stud.* I knows a good horse when I sees 'un.'

They examined the new horse and put him through his paces in the yard. It was indeed an exceptionally fine animal, a bay

* The Lov Stud Farm was considered one of the best in the Caucasus. Kabarda horses – Kabarda is a district in the Terek Territory – were famous for their powers of endurance. [*Translator's note*]

gelding, broad and long, with a glossy coat, a thick tail and the soft silky mane and crest of a thoroughbred. He was so well fed that 'you could lie down and go to sleep on his back,' as Luka expressed it. His hoofs, eyes and teeth had the exquisite shape and clear outline only found in horses of the purest strain. Olenin could not help admiring the horse: he had never seen such a beauty in the Caucasus.

'And he can't half move!' said Luka, patting the creature's neck. 'What action! And knows everything – follows me about all the time!'

'Did you have to pay a lot extra?'

'I didn't never count,' Luka answered smiling. 'A friend of mine obliged me.'

'A wonderful horse, a beauty! How much would you take for it?'

'I've bin offered a hundred and fifty roubles but he's yourn for a gift like,' Luka said cheerfully. 'Say the word, and he's yourn. I'll unsaddle him, so as you can take him. Give us another in exchange – any old nag'll do.'

'Good heavens, no!'

'All right, then, I've brought this for you,' said Luka, unfastening his belt and taking out one of the two daggers that hung from it. 'I got it for you over the river.'

'Thank you very much.'

'An' mother's give her word to bring you some grapes herself.'

'She needn't do that. We'll settle up some day, you and I. After all, I'm not paying you anything for the dagger, am I?'

'Don't you never! We be pals. Just like when Girey Khan over the river took me into his hut and says, "Choose what you likes!" So I chooses this here sabre. Same as our custom is.'

They went into Olenin's hut and had a drink.

'Are you staying here awhile?' asked Olenin.

'Nay, I come to say good-bye to you. They're for sending me away from the cordon to a company t'other side of the Terek. I goes tonight along a my pal Nazar.'

'But what about the wedding? When is it to be?'

'Well, I'll be coming home for the betrothal, and then I goes back to the company again,' Luka replied reluctantly.

'But won't you see your girl today?'

'What's the good? Where is the use in just looking at her? Don't forget, when you starts out on a campaign to ask in our company for Luka, Broad-Back Luka. An' there are plenty o' wild boars in them parts, I may tell you. I've killed a couple already. I'll show you the places.'

'Well, good-bye, Luka. Good luck to you!'

Luka mounted his horse, and without calling at Marianka's rode jauntily down the street, where Nazar was waiting.

'What about it? Shall us go in?' asked Nazar, winking in the direction of Yamka's house.

'There is something in that,' said Luka. 'Here, take my horse to her, and if I doesn't turn up soon give him some hay. By morning I'll come to the company.'

'Get anything more out of the Russian?'

'Not likely. I were lucky to get off with giving him the dagger. He was beginning to ask for the horse,' said Luka, dismounting and handing the bridle to Nazar.

He darted back into the yard, past Olenin's very window, and crept to the window of Marianka's cottage. It was quite dark now. Marianka, wearing only her smock, was combing her hair and making ready for bed.

'Marianka – 'tis me, Luka!' whispered the Cossack.

Marianka's face had looked impassive and austere but it suddenly lighted up when she heard her name. She raised the sash and lent her head out, scared and happy.

'What is it? What do you want?' she asked quickly.

'Let us in,' muttered Luka. 'Only a minute now. I'm fair sick of all this here waiting. 'Tis terrible!'

He drew her head to him through the window and kissed her. 'Open up now, please.'

'You're wasting yer breath. I've told you I won't. How long are you here for?'

He did not answer and went on kissing her. She did not ask again.

'See, I can't even so far as put me arm round you proper through this here window,' said Luka.

'Marianka, who is it there with you, love?' came her mother's voice.

Luka took off his tall cap which might have given him away, and crouched down under the window.

'Go away quick!' whispered Marianka.

'It were Luka,' she called out to her mother. 'He wanted for to see Dad.'

'Well, send him in then.'

'He's gone. Said he had no time.'

Luka, still stooping, with swift strides made his way under the windows and ran out through the yard and towards Yamka's, unseen by anyone but Olenin. At Yamka's he and Nazar emptied a bowl or two of *chikhir* before setting out from the village. The night was warm, dark and still. They rode in silence, the tramp of their horses' hoofs being the only sound. Luka began to sing a song about the Cossack, Mingal, but before he had finished the first verse he stopped and turned to Nazar.

'You see, she wouldn't lemme go in.'

'Oh?' rejoined Nazar. 'I knew as she wouldn't. Yamka told me the Russian has started going to their house. And Yeroshka's bragging he got a gun from him for getting him Marianka.'

'Th'old devil's a liar,' Luka said angrily. 'She ain't that sort o' girl. He'd better watch out for hisself or I'll smash his ribs in,' and he began his favourite song:

'From the village of Ismailov,
From the master's beloved garden,
Once there flew a light-winged falcon
And after him a fair young hunter,
With right hand beckoned the keen-eyed falcon,
But the keen-eyed falcon then made answer:
"Your golden cage could never keep me,
Thy true right hand could never hold me –
So now I'll fly to the ocean blue;
And there a white, white swan I'll kill me
And of sweet swan's flesh I'll eat my fill." '

28

THE betrothal was being celebrated in the teacher's cottage. Luka had returned to the village but he did not come to see Olenin, and Olenin had not gone to the betrothal party though he had been invited. His heart was heavy, as it had never been since his arrival in the village. Earlier in the evening he had seen Luka, wearing his best clothes, entering the teacher's cottage, accompanied by his mother, and he was puzzled to understand why Luka was so cold to him. Olenin shut himself in his room and began to write in his journal:

'Many things have I pondered over lately, and much have I changed,' wrote he, 'only to come back to the copybook maxim: "The one and only way to be happy is to love, to love with a self-denying love – love everybody and everything, spread a web of love on all sides, catching in it all who come near." Thus have I caught Vanyusha, old Yeroshka, Luka, Marianka.'

As he was finishing this sentence old Yeroshka entered the room.

Yeroshka was in a hilarious frame of mind. A few evenings before this Olenin had gone to see him and had found him, proud and happy, in his yard, deftly skinning the carcass of a boar with a small knife. His dogs, including his favourite Lyam, were lying close by, wagging their tails as they watched him work. Some small boys looking through the fence were so impressed that they refrained from their usual teasing of him. His women neighbours, who were not too friendly with him as a rule, kept popping in with little presents – a jug of wine, some clotted cream or a little flour. On the following morning a blood-bespattered Yeroshka sat in his store-room and handed out boar flesh by the pound, taking in payment money from some and wine from others. The expression on his face said: 'God has sent me luck. I have killed a boar; so now they all want old Yeroshka.' After this, of course, he started drinking and kept it up steadily for four days, not setting foot outside the village. Besides which, he had been drinking at the betrothal, so by the time he came to Olenin he was blind drunk. His face was purple, his beard matted, but he was wearing a new tunic trimmed with gold braid and was carrying a balalaika made of a gourd which he had got from across the river. For a long time Olenin had been promised this treat, and now when he felt in the right mood to give him some music it was disappointing to find Olenin writing.

'Keep on writing, keep on writing, me lad!' he whispered, as if he thought some spirit were floating between Olenin and the paper and must not be frightened away, so that he cautiously and noiselessly settled down on the floor. The floor was his favourite place when he was drunk. Olenin looked round, told Vanyusha to bring some *chikhir* and went on writing. But Yeroshka did not care for drinking alone, and wanted to talk.

'I'sh been to the betrothal party,' he whispered. 'But I wouldn't shtay. They're shwine. I'd rather be here with you.'

'Where did you get the balalaika?' asked Olenin, still writing.

'I were over the river and got the inshtrument there, brother mine,' he answered, speaking as quietly as before. 'I'm a mashter at it. Tartar or Coshack shongs, gentlemen's or sholdiers' shongs – I can play you any shong you pleases.'

Olenin looked up again, smiled and proceeded with his journal.

The smile emboldened the old man.

'Come, leave off, me lad, leave off!' he said with sudden resolution. 'All right, they have hurt yer feelings. What of it? Shpit in their faces and forget it. But thish writing, writing, writing – where's the shense o' that?'

And he tried to mimic Olenin by scratching on the floor with his clumsy fingers and screwing up his large face into a grimace intended to express derision.

'Writing 'plaints and grumbles won't get a body nowheres. Better have a drink and show you're a man!'

Yeroshka could only associate writing with the composing of jeremiads.

Olenin burst out laughing. Yeroshka did the same. Then, jumping to his feet, he began to exhibit his skill on the balalaika, and sing Tartar songs.

'Ain't that better'n writing, me good lad? You'd a sight better listen while I shing. When you pegs out you won't hear no more shongs. Cheer up now!'

First he sang a song of his own composing, accompanying it with a dancing tune on the balalaika:

'Ah did-dee, did-dee, did-dee
When you saw him where was he?
In a booth 'twas at the fair,
Sellin' pins and brooches there.'

Then he sang a song he had learned from his old friend, the sergeant-major:

'I fell in love on Monday,
I suffered all day Tuesday,
I popped the question Wednesday
And waited all day Thursday.
Her answer came late Friday
All hope for me was over.
I determined like a man
Saturday my life to take
But for my salvation's sake
Sunday morning changed my plan.'

Then the refrain:

'Ah did-dee, did-dee, did-dee,
When you saw him where was he?'

After that, winking and jerking his shoulders and shuffling in time to the tune, he sang:

'I will kiss you and caress you,
A red ribbon I will give you,
And I'll call you little Hope,
Will you love me, little Hope?'

And he worked himself up into such a state of exhilaration that he pranced about the room as though he were a young brave again, all the time strumming on his instrument.

Songs like *Ah did-dee* – 'gentlemen's songs', he called them – he sang for Olenin's benefit but three or four more glasses of *chikhir* brought back the old days and he began singing real Cossack and Tartar songs. In the middle of one of his favourites his voice suddenly quavered and he stopped singing, and only continued to strum on the balalaika.

'Aye, me dear friend!' he said, and his voice sounded so strangely that Olenin looked up. The old man was weeping. Tears stood in his eyes, and one tear was rolling down his cheek. 'Me young days is gone, and won't never return!' he said, blubbering, and ceased playing. Suddenly, and without waiting to wipe away his tears, he roared out: 'Drink! Why don't you drink?'

There was one Tartar song which moved him especially. It had few words and its charm lay in its melancholy refrain, 'Ay, dy, dalaly!' Yeroshka translated the words of the song: 'A young man drove his sheep from the Tartar village to the mountains. The Russians came and burnt the village to the ground, killed the men and took the women into captivity. The young man returned from the mountains. Where the village had stood was an empty space. His mother was not there, his brothers were not there, his cabin was not there: only one tree was still standing. The young man sat beneath the tree and wept. "Alone like thee, alone am I left! Ay, dy, dalaly!"' And old Yeroshka repeated the wailing, heart-rending refrain several times. Then he suddenly snatched a gun from the wall, rushed out into the yard and fired both barrels into the air. After that he began again, even more dolefully. 'Ay, dy, dalaly – ah, aa-h!' and relapsed into silence.

Olenin followed him out on to the porch and silently gazed up at the dark starry sky in the direction where the shots had flashed. In the teacher's hut there were lights, and the sound of voices. In the yard girls swarmed round the other porch and the windows, and ran backwards and forwards between the hut and the outhouse. Some Cossacks dashed out from the hut, unable to restrain themselves, gave a wild shout and joined in Yeroshka's singing and shooting.

'Why aren't you at the betrothal?' asked Olenin.

'Never mind them! Never mind them!' muttered the old man, who had evidently in some way been affronted at the party. 'I don't like 'em, I don't. What people! Let you and me go back indoors. Leave 'em to their celebrations. You and me can celebrate by ourselves.'

Olenin followed him in.

'How's Luka? Is he happy? Isn't he coming to see me?' he asked.

'Luka?' growled the old man. 'D'you know what they told Luka? That I were trying to get his girl for you. What's so special about the girl, anyhow? She'll be ourn all right if we wants her: pay a bit more and she'll be ourn. I'll fix it for you, never you fear.'

'No, my good friend, money wouldn't do anything there if she doesn't love me. Let's not talk about it.'

'You're right, they don't love us poor beggars. Nobody don't love us,' said Yeroshka suddenly, and burst into tears again.

That evening Olenin drank more than usual as he listened to the old man's tales. 'So now my Luka is happy,' he said to himself; but his heart was heavy. Yeroshka drank so much that he finally collapsed on the floor and Vanyusha had to call some soldiers in to help, and he spat as they dragged the old man out. He was so incensed by Yeroshka's conduct that he could not utter a single word in French.

29

It was August. For days there had not been a cloud in the sky. The sun scorched unbearably, and from early morning the warm wind raised tornadoes of hot sand from the dunes and roads, whirling it through the air over reeds, trees and the village. Grass and foliage were covered with dust; the roads and salt-marshes were baked so hard that they rang when trodden on. The water had long since fallen in the Terek and the canals and ditches were dry. The village pond showed more and more of its slimy banks, trampled by the cattle, and all day long children shouted and splashed in the water. The reeds were withering in the steppe, and lowing cattle wandered into the fields in the daytime. The wild boars migrated to the distant reed-beds and the hills beyond the Terek. Mosquitoes and gnats swarmed in thick clouds over the lowlands and villages. A grey mist covered the snow peaks. There was not a breath of air and the atmosphere was fetid. Rumour declared that *abreks* had crossed the shoaling river, and were prowling on the Cossack side. Every night the sun set in a fiery red glow. It was the busiest time of the year. The entire village population swarmed in the melon fields and vineyards. The vineyards, thickly overgrown with twining tendrils of green, lay in cool, deep shade. Heavy clusters of ripe purple grapes hung behind the large translucent leaves. Creaking ox-carts laden with big black bunches of grapes moved slowly along the dusty road, strewn with grapes fallen and crushed by the wheels. Boys and girls in smocks stained with juice, grapes clutched in their hands and mouths crammed, tagged behind their mothers. Everywhere along the road one met Nogay labourers in tattered clothes carrying baskets of grapes on their splendid shoulders. Cossack girls, their kerchiefs pulled down to their eyes, drove bullocks harnessed to carts laden high with the fruit. Soldiers who passed on the road would ask for grapes, and the girls, clambering on to the carts without stopping them, would toss armfuls to the soldiers, who held out the skirts of their coats to receive them. Already, in some of the yards the wine-pressing had begun, and the smell of the juice filled the air. Blood-red troughs stood under every penthouse, and Nogay workmen with their trousers rolled up and their legs stained with juice were busy in every yard. Grunting pigs gorged themselves with the empty skins and wallowed in them. The flat roofs of the sheds and dairies were thickly spread with black and amber clusters. Crows and magpies flocked round the roofs, filching seeds and fluttering from one place to another.

The fruits of the year's labours were being gaily gathered in, and this year the harvest was unusually fine and plentiful.

Everywhere in the shady green vineyards, amid a sea of vines, there was laughter, song, merriment and women's voices, and glimpses of their bright-coloured clothes.

At noon Marianka was sitting in their vineyard in the shade of a peach-tree, getting out the family dinner from under an unharnessed cart. Opposite her, on a horse-cloth spread on the ground, sat the teacher (on leave of absence from the school), washing his hands by pouring water on them from a little jug.

Her small brother, who had just run up from the pond, stood wiping his face with his sleeve, breathing heavily and looking anxiously at his mother and sister, in expectation of dinner. The old mother, her sleeves rolled up over her strong, sunburnt arms, was arranging grapes, dried fish, clotted cream and bread on a little round low Tartar table. The teacher dried his hands, took off his cap, crossed himself and drew up to the table. The boy, seizing the jug, drank eagerly. Mother and daughter sat down by the table, folding their legs under them. It was unbearably hot, even in the shade. The air above the vineyard was rank and close: the fierce, burning wind which blew between the branches brought no coolness but only the monotonous sound of branches waving in the tops of the pear-, peach- and mulberry-trees growing among the vines. The teacher, crossing himself once more, took from behind him a pitcher of *chikhir* covered with a vine-leaf, drank from its mouth and passed it to his wife. His shirt was open at the neck, exposing his shaggy, muscular chest. There was a cheerful look on his thin, sly face, and neither his manner nor his speech revealed any trace of his usual wiliness: he was gay and natural.

'Well, d'you think we'll finish the bit behind the shed come nightfall?' he asked, wiping his wet beard.

'We'll manage it, if only the weather holds,' replied his wife. 'You know, the Demkins ain't even half through yet. Ustenka's all by herself, working herself to death.'

'What else could you expect?' said the old man loftily.

'Here, dearie, have a drink,' said the old woman, passing the jug to Marianka. 'Please God, we'll have enough to pay for the wedding feast.'

'Time enough to think of that later,' announced the teacher with a slight frown.

The girl hung her head.

'Whyfor not speak about it?' asked her mother. 'The matter all settled, and not all that time to go now.'

' 'Tis no use looking ahead,' said the teacher. 'We have to get the harvest in first.'

'Have you seed Luka's new horse?' inquired the old woman. 'That one the lodger gave him's gone – Luka got another for it.'

'Not yet I haven't. But I had speech with the servant today. He says his master's received a further thousand roubles.'

'Made of money, he is, no question,' asserted the old woman.

All the family felt content and happy. The work was making good progress. The grapes were more abundant and of better quality than they had expected.

After dinner Marianka threw some grass to the oxen, folded her *beshmet* for a pillow and lay down under the wagon on the juicy down-trodden grass. She had nothing on except a faded blue smock and a red kerchief over her head, but she was dreadfully hot. Her face was burning and she did not know what to do with her legs; and her eyes watered with exhaustion and the need of sleep; involuntarily her lips parted and she panted heavily.

The harvest had been going on for a fortnight now, and continuous heavy work filled Marianka's days. She sprang out of bed at dawn, rinsed her face in cold water and ran out barefoot to see to the cattle. Then she hurriedly put on her shoes and her *beshmet*, harnessed the oxen and drove away to the vineyards for the day, taking only some bread in a bundle. There she cut the grapes and carried the baskets, with a brief hour for rest at noon, and in the evening returned to the village, cheerful and unwearied, dragging the bullocks by a rope or driving them with a long switch. At dusk, after attending to the cattle, she would fill the wide sleeve of her smock with sunflower seeds and go to the corner of the street to laugh and chat with the other girls. As soon as it was dark she made her way home, had supper with her parents and her brother in the unlighted outhouse, then went indoors, carefree and glowing with health, climbed on to the stove and lay sleepily listening to Olenin's conversation. As soon as he left she would throw herself on her bed and sleep soundly till morning. The next day it began all over again. She had not seen Luka since their betrothal, and she waited without impatience for the day of the wedding. She had grown used to the lodger and enjoyed feeling his eyes fixed intently upon her.

30

ALTHOUGH there was no escaping the heat and the mosquitoes swarming and buzzing in the cool shadow of the wagon, and Marianka's little brother kept tossing about and knocking against her, Marianka, with her kerchief drawn over her face, was just falling asleep when their neighbour Ustenka suddenly came diving under the cart and stretched out by her side.

'Now for some sleep, girls, sleep,' said Ustenka, making herself comfortable under the wagon. 'No, wait!' she exclaimed, jumping to her feet again. 'This ain't no good.'

She broke off some green branches and stuck them in the wheels on both sides of the cart, and hung her *beshmet* over them.

'Get out of here,' she shouted to the little boy, as she crept back to her place. 'A Cossack has no call to be with girls. Get along with you!'

Alone under the wagon with her friend, Ustenka suddenly threw her arms round Marianka and hugging her tight began to kiss her cheeks and neck. 'Dearest! Darling!' she kept repeating, between shrill bursts of clear laughter.

'You've caught it from "Daddy",' said Marianka, struggling to free herself. 'Stop it now!'

And both broke into such loud peals that Marianka's mother shouted to them to be quiet.

'Ain't you jealous?' whispered Ustenka.

'Don't talk so silly! Let's go to sleep. What you come for, anyway?'

But Ustenka would not be silenced. 'Marianka, guess what I've got to tell you!'

Marianka raised herself on her elbow and straightened the kerchief which had slipped off.

'Oh, what?'

'I knows something about your lodger!'

'Ain't nothing to know,' replied Marianka.

'You ain't half a sly one, you ain't,' said Ustenka, nudging her with her elbow and laughing. 'Won't tell nothing. Do he come to see you?'

'If he does – what of it?' said Marianka, flushing all at once.

'Me, I'm a simple girl. Tells everybody everything. I ain't got nothing to hide,' said Ustenka; and her bright rosy face became thoughtful. 'I don't do no harm to no one, do I? I loves him, and that's all about it.'

' "Daddy", you mean?'

'Aye, of course.'

'But 'tis a sin.'

'Oh, Marianka, when is a girl to have a bit of fun if she don't whilst she's still free? When I gets wed I shall have children and cares. Look at you now – you wait till you're wed to Luka. You won't think of fun no more: nothing but children and work.'

'Well, other women's able to wed and be happy. It don't make no difference,' Marianka replied quietly.

'Do tell us just this once – how did it happen with you and Luka?'

'Wasn't nought happened. He offered for me. Father put it off for a year, but now 'tis settled and us'll wed come autumn.'

'But what did he say to you?'

Marianka smiled.

'What should he say? Told me he loved me. Kept on asking me to come to the vineyards with him.'

'The wicked brute! You didn't never go, did you? Still he ain't half a fine chap now – a regular dare-devil! They do say he enjoys hisself proper in the army too. Our Kirka was home t'other day, and he said we should just see Luka's new horse that he got for t'other horse. All the same he frets after you, I dare-say. Tell us what else he said?'

'Ain't there nothing you don't have to know?' said Marianka with a laugh. 'Well, one night he comes to my window, tipsy he were, and wanted me to let him in.'

'And did you?'

'I should say not! Once I says anything I sticks to it, firm as a rock,' answered Marianka in a serious tone.

'But he's such a great lad! No other girl could say no to him.'

'Well, let him go to them then,' proudly retorted Marianka.

'Doesn't you feel sorry for him?'

'Yes, I does. But I won't have no nonsense. It ain't right.'

Ustenka suddenly hid her face in her friend's bosom, threw her arms round her and shook with suppressed laughter. 'You're fair daft!' she exclaimed, gasping for breath. 'You doesn't want to be happy,' and she began tickling Marianka.

'Stop it, you're squashing Lazutka!' screamed Marianka through her laughter.

'Listen to them young devils still playing about! Can't they be quiet?' came the old woman's sleepy voice from the other side of the wagon.

'You doesn't want to be happy,' Ustenka repeated in a whisper, half sitting up. 'But, my word, you *is* lucky. All the lads are crazy with love. You're prickly as a hedgehog and yet they loves you. If only I was in your place now, I'd soon twist that lodger of yourn round my little finger! I watched him when you was at our place – fair eating you with his eyes, he were. You should see the things my "Daddy" give me! And your lodger's even richer – richest man in Russia, so I've heard tell. His orderly was telling us as he even has his own serfs.'

Marianka sat up and smiled thoughtfully.

'D'you know what he said to me once, our lodger?' she remarked, chewing a blade of grass. He said, "I wish I was Luka the Cossack, or your brother Lazutka." What d'you reckon he meant?'

'Oh, just saying anything that come into his head,' answered Ustenka. 'You ought to hear the things my "Daddy" says sometimes. You'd think he was cracked.'

Marianka dropped her head back on her folded *beshmet*, threw her arms over Ustenka's shoulder and shut her eyes.

'He wanted for to come and work in the vineyard today,' she said sleepily. 'Father asked him,' she added after a pause, and then fell asleep.

31

THE sun had now come out from behind the pear-tree shading the wagon, and its slanting rays, penetrating even the screen of branches devised by Ustenka, scorched the faces of the sleeping girls. Marianka woke and began arranging the kerchief on her head. Looking about her, she saw just beyond the pear-tree the lodger, with his gun on his shoulder, standing talking to her father. She nudged Ustenka, smiled and without speaking pointed to him.

'I was there yesterday but didn't come on a single one,' Olenin was saying as he glanced about anxiously and not seeing Marianka through the branches.

'Ah, but you should try over yonder, following the compass, so to speak, and in a disused vineyard there, commonly denominated as the Waste, hares are invariably to be found,' said the teacher, immediately changing the manner of his speech.

'Fancy running after hares and us so busy! You'd far better stay and lend the girls a hand,' the old woman said jokingly. 'Now then, girls, up with you!' she cried.

Marianka and Ustenka under the cart were whispering and trying hard not to laugh out loud.

Since it became known that Olenin had given Luka a horse worth fifty silver roubles his hosts had turned more amiable; and the teacher especially appeared pleased to see his daughter's growing friendship with Olenin.

'But I don't know the work,' said Olenin, averting his eyes from the screen of green branches under the wagon, where he had caught a glimpse of Marianka's blue smock and red kerchief.

'Come, I'll give you some peaches,' said the old woman.

'Do not take notice of the silly woman,' the teacher said quickly, as it were to correct his wife. 'She means to be hospitable in accordance with our ancient Cossack tradition. In Russia, I expect, it is not only peaches but pineapple jam and suchlike preserves you are accustomed to, which you could eat to your heart's content.'

'So you say there are hares to be found in the abandoned

vineyard?' inquired Olenin. 'I'll go there now,' and with a swift glance through the green branches he raised his cap and disappeared between the long straight rows of emerald vines.

The sun had sunk behind the fence and its broken rays glittered through the translucent leaves when Olenin returned to his hosts' vineyard. The wind was falling and a cool freshness was spreading over the vineyards. By some instinct Olenin recognized from afar Marianka's blue smock among the rows of vines and, picking off grapes as he went, he approached her. His excited dog also made a snatch every now and then with his slobbering mouth at a low-hanging cluster. Marianka, her face flushed, her sleeves rolled up, her kerchief down below her chin, was swiftly cutting the heavy bunches and laying them in a basket. Still holding the branch in her hand she stopped to smile pleasantly at him, and resumed her work. Olenin came up, and slung his gun behind his back to have both hands free. 'Where are your people? God bless you! Are you alone?' was what he wanted to say, but actually he said nothing and merely pushed back his cap in silence. He felt ill at ease alone with Marianka but, as though intentionally to torment himself, he came nearer.

'Mind you don't go shooting the women with your gun like that,' said Marianka.

'No, I won't shoot anybody.'

They were both silent. Then she said, 'You going to help me?'

He took out his knife and began silently cutting off the clusters. Drawing from low down under the leaves a heavy bunch weighing at least three pounds, with the grapes so close together that they flattened each other for lack of space, he showed it to Marianka.

'Do you cut them all, or is this one too green?'

'Give it here.'

Their hands touched. Olenin took hers and she looked at him with a smile.

'How soon are you going to be married?' he asked.

She looked at him gravely and turned away without answering.

'Do you love Luka?'

'What's that to do with you?'

'I envy him.'

'Most likely!'

'No, really I do. You are so beautiful.'

And suddenly he felt dreadfully ashamed at what he had said: the words sounded to him so vulgar and out of place. He blushed, lost his wits and took both her hands in his.

'Whatever I am, I ain't for you! Why d'you make fun of me?' replied Marianka, but her look showed how well she knew he was serious.

'Make fun! If you only knew how I . . .'

This sounded even more commonplace and out of harmony with what he felt; but he went on, 'I don't know what I wouldn't do for you . . .'

'Let go, you wicked man!'

But her face, her shining eyes, her swelling bosom and shapely limbs all told him something quite different. It seemed to Olenin that she understood how hackneyed and trivial were all the things he was saying but that she was above such considerations; he felt that she had long known all that he ached to tell her but wanted to hear how he would say it. 'And how can she help knowing,' he thought, 'since what I want is to tell her what she really is? But she will pretend not to understand, and will not answer.'

'Hey, there!' Ustenka's voice suddenly rang out from behind a nearby vine, followed by her shrill laugh. 'Come and help us, 'Mitri Andreich. I'm all on me own,' she called to Olenin, and thrust her round, naïve little face through the vines.

Olenin made no reply and did not stir.

Marianka went on cutting but kept looking up at Olenin. He was about to speak but broke off with a shrug. Then jerking his gun over his shoulder he strode rapidly out of the vineyard.

32

HE stopped once or twice to listen to the ringing laughter of Marianka and Ustenka as they joined forces and called across to each other. He spent the whole evening in the forest, and returned at dusk having shot nothing. As he crossed the yard he caught sight of a blue smock through the open door of the dairy. He shouted loudly to Vanyusha, so as to let them know he was back, and then settled down in his usual place on the porch. The teacher and his wife were already home from the vineyard: they came out of the dairy and went into their own hut, but did not ask him in. Marianka twice went to the gate. Once in the half-light it seemed to Olenin that she was looking at him. He watched her every movement with eager eyes but could not make up his mind to approach her. When she disappeared into the hut he left the porch and began pacing up and down the yard. But Marianka did not come out again. Olenin stayed out in the yard all night without sleep, listening to every sound in the teacher's cottage. He heard them talking earlier in the evening, heard them having supper, heard them pulling out their feather beds and lying down to sleep; he heard Marianka laughing at something, and then listened as all sound gradually died away. The teacher and his wife talked for a while in whispers, and he heard some one breathing. Olenin went back into his cottage. Vanyusha lay asleep in his clothes. Olenin envied him, and then fell to walking the yard again, as though in expectation of something; but no one came out, no one stirred, and all he could hear was the measured breathing of three people. He recognized Marianka's breathing, and listened to it and to the beating of his own heart. In the village everything was quiet. The waning moon rose late, and the cattle became more visible as they lay panting in the yard, struggled slowly to their feet, then lay down again. 'What is it I want?' Olenin asked himself irritably, but could not tear himself away from the enchantment of the night. Suddenly he distinctly heard the floor creak and footsteps in his hosts' hut. He rushed to the door but all was silent again, except for the regular whisper of breathing, and in the yard the buffalo-cow heaved a deep sigh, got to her knees, then on to all four feet, swished her tail, and there was a steady plop on the dry clayey ground before she lay down with another sigh in the silvery moonlight ... 'What shall I do?' Olenin asked himself, and made up his mind to go to bed; but again he heard a sound and in imagination saw the figure of Marianka coming out into the misty moonlit night, and again he rushed to her window and again heard the sound of steps. At last, just before dawn, he tapped softly on the shutter, ran to the door and this time really did hear Marianka's deep-drawn waking sigh and then her footsteps. He took hold of the latch and knocked. The floor creaked slightly under the cautious bare feet which approached the door. The latch clicked, the door grated, there was a faint fragrance of sweet marjoram and pumpkin, and Marianka's figure appeared on the threshold. He saw her only for an instant in the moonlight. She clapped the door to and, muttering something, ran lightly back. Olenin knocked softly several times but there was no response. He ran round to the window and listened. Suddenly he was startled by the sharp, shrill voice of a man.

'This is a fine thing!' exclaimed a short young Cossack in a white lambskin cap, coming across the yard and up to Olenin. 'I seen you. A fine thing!'

Olenin recognized Nazar and was silent, not knowing what to say or do.

'Nice! I'll go and tell the village elder, and I'll go to her father too. Smart girl, the teacher's daughter! One man ain't enough for her.'

'What do you want of me? What are you after?' Olenin managed to ask.

'Oh naught! I'll just tell 'em, that's all!'

Nazar spoke very loud, evidently intentionally. 'You're a wily cadet, aren't you?'

Olenin trembled and turned pale.

'Come in here – this way!' He seized Nazar forcibly by the arm and pulled him towards his own quarters. 'Nothing happened, you know, she wouldn't let me in, and I didn't mean any harm either ... She's an honest girl ...'

'We shall see about that ...' said Nazar.

'But I'll give you something all the same ... Here, wait a moment ...'

Nazar said nothing. Olenin ran indoors and came back with ten roubles, which he handed to the Cossack.

'Nothing whatever happened, you know that, but it was wrong of me just the same. So I'm giving you this. Only for God's sake don't let anyone know. Truly there was nothing ...'

'Very good!' said Nazar with a laugh, and was gone.

Nazar had come to the village that night on business for

Luka – to find a place for a stolen horse – and passing down the street on his way home had heard the sound of footsteps. Next morning when he returned to his company he bragged to his friend about his cleverness in getting hold of ten roubles. Olenin saw the family in the morning, and they knew nothing of what had happened. He did not speak to Marianka, and she merely gave a little laugh when she looked at him. He passed another sleepless night, vainly wandering about the yard. The following day he purposely spent shooting in the forest, and in the evening went to Beletsky's to escape from his own thoughts. He was afraid of himself and vowed not to visit the teacher's hut any more. That night he was roused by the sergeant-major. His company was starting on a raid at once. Olenin was glad of this, for he thought that he would not be coming back to the village.

The foray lasted four days. The commander sent for Olenin, who was a relative of his, and offered to keep him on his staff, but this Olenin declined. He found that he could not live away from the village, and asked to be allowed to return there. For the part he had taken in the raid he was presented with a soldier's cross – a thing he had formerly longed for but now felt quite indifferent about. And he was even more indifferent concerning his promotion, which had not yet come through. Accompanied by Vanyusha he rode back without incident to the cordon, and reached the village several hours in advance of the company. He spent the whole evening on the porch, watching Marianka, and paced the yard, without aim or thought, all night.

33

It was late when he woke the next day. The family was already away. He did not go shooting but wandered restlessly between his room and the porch, picking up a book or lying on his bed. Vanyusha thought he was ill. Towards evening he made a determined effort, got up, set himself to write, and wrote until far into the night. He wrote a letter but when it was finished he did not send it, for he felt that no one would have understood what he tried to say – nor did it matter whether anybody understood it besides himself. This is what he wrote:

'I keep receiving letters of commiseration from Russia. People there fear I am going to ruin, burying myself in these wilds. "He'll grow coarse and antiquated," they say. "He'll take to drink, and, who knows, he might even marry a Cossack girl!" They quote General Yermolov – "After ten years in the Caucasus an officer either drinks himself silly or marries a harlot." How terrible! Indeed, it won't do for me to go to ruin when I might have the great happiness of becoming Countess B—'s husband, or a Court chamberlain, or *maréchal de noblesse* of my district! Oh, how paltry and pitiable you all seem to me! You do not know what happiness is, you do not know what life is. One must taste life in all its natural beauty; must see and understand what I have every day before my eyes – the eternal, inaccessible snow on the mountain-peaks and a woman endowed with all the dignity and pristine beauty in which the first woman must have come from the hand of the Creator – and then it will be quite clear which of us, you or I, is ruining himself, which of us is living truly, which falsely. If only you knew how disgusting and pitiful you are in your delusions! When I look at my huts, my forests and my love, and then think of those society drawing-rooms of yours, the women with their pomaded curls padded with false hair, the unnaturally grimacing lips, the feeble limbs, hidden from view and distorted, the fashionable lisping which pretends to be conversation but has no right to the name – I feel unutterably revolted. I see those vacuous faces, those rich eligible girls whose expression seems to say: "It's all right, you may come up and talk to me, even though I am rich and eligible," all that brazen pairing off, the sitting down and changing places, and the interminable gossip and hypocrisy, the rules and regulations – with whom you must shake hands, to whom you only nod, with whom you may converse – and finally that everlasting *ennui* bred in the bone which passes from generation to generation (and the whole business conscious and deliberate, out of conviction that it is inevitable). Try to understand – accept – this one thing: once you have seen real truth and beauty, all you now say and think, all you wish in the way of happiness for me and for yourselves, will crumble into dust. Happiness is being with Nature, seeing Nature and discoursing with her. "What if – which God forbid! – he goes and marries a common Cossack girl! He will ruin himself socially," I can hear them saying of me with genuine sympathy. Yet all I desire is to be "ruined" in your sense of the word. I long to marry a common Cossack girl, and dare not, because it would be the height of happiness which I do not deserve.

'Three months have passed since I first saw the Cossack girl, Marianka. The conceptions and prejudices of the world which I had just left were still fresh in me. I did not believe then that it was in me to love her. I delighted in her beauty as I delighted in the beauty of the mountains and the sky, and I could not do otherwise, for she is as beautiful as they. Presently I felt that the sight of her beauty had become a necessity for me, and I began asking myself whether I did not love her. But I could find nothing within myself at all akin to love, as I imagined love to be. It did not spring from loneliness and a desire for wedlock, or some platonic affection, still less was it the sensual love such as I had experienced earlier in my life. I needed to see her, hear her, know that she was near; and if I was not exactly happy, I was at peace. After a party to which we both went and at which I touched her for the first time I felt that between me and this woman there existed an indissoluble though unacknowledged bond against which it was impossible to struggle. Yet I did struggle: I asked myself, "Can I really love a woman who will never understand my dearest interests? Can one love a woman solely for her beauty – love a female statue?" But I was already loving her, though I did not yet trust to my feelings.

'After the evening of the party, when I first spoke to her, our relations changed. Up till then she had been a strange but majestic object of the Nature all about me; after that evening she became a human being. I began to stop and talk to her, sometimes I went and worked in her father's vineyard, or spent whole evenings on end sitting with the family. And in this closer intercourse she still remained in my eyes as pure, inaccessible and right. Her behaviour was always and everywhere uniformly tranquil, haughty and cheerfully indifferent. At times she was friendly but for the most part every look, every word and gesture of hers expressed equanimity – not scornful but annihilating and bewitching. Day after day, with a simulated smile on my lips, I tried to play a part, and exchanged bantering remarks with her while passion and desire tore at my heart. She saw that I was dissembling but her eyes looked into mine, gay, direct and simple. This state of affairs became unbearable. I wanted to be honest with her, tell her all I thought and felt. Once, in the vineyard, I was particularly on edge, and began telling her of my love, in words that I am now ashamed to remember. I am ashamed because I ought not to have dared to speak so to her – she was immeasurably above such words and above the emotion I was trying to express. I said no more, but from that day my position has been intolerable. I did not want to degrade myself by keeping up my former bantering tone, and at the same time I felt that I was not yet fitted for a simple and straightforward relationship. "What am I to do?" I asked myself despairingly. In foolish day-dreaming I imagined her now as my mistress, now as my wife, and rejected both ideas with abhorrence. To make her a wanton woman would be dreadful: it would be death. To turn her into a fine lady, the wife of Dmitri Andreyevich Olenin, like a Cossack woman here who is married to one of our officers, would be still worse. Now if I could become a Cossack like Luka, and steal horses, get drunk on *chikhir*, sing rollicking songs, kill people, and when tipsy climb in through her window for the night, without a thought of who and what I am, it would be different. Then we might understand one another, and I might be happy. I tried throwing myself into that kind of life but became more conscious still of my own weakness, of my divided character. I cannot forget myself and my complex, inharmonious, distorted past. And my future appears even more hopeless. Every day I see before me the distant snowy mountains and this majestic, happy woman. But she, the only happiness I want, is not for me. The most terrible and at the same time the sweetest thing in my condition is the feeling that I understand her, but that she will never understand me; not because she is inferior – on the contrary, it would be out of the nature of things for her to understand me. She is happy; she is like Nature, stable, serene and sufficient unto herself. And I, a weak, deformed creature, expect her to understand my ugliness and my anguish! I spent sleepless, aimless nights under her window, unable to account to myself for what was happening. On the 18th our Company was sent on a foray into the mountains. For three days I was away from the village. My heart was heavy and I did not care about anything. The usual songs, cards and drinking-bouts, the usual chatter about promotions in the regiment, were more repulsive than ever. Yesterday I came home, I saw her, my hut, old Gaffer Yeroshka, I saw the snowy mountains from my porch, and I was seized with such a compelling unfamiliar joy that I understood everything. I love this woman with the first and only true love of my life. I know what has befallen me. I have no fear of being degraded by my feelings: I am not ashamed of my love, I am proud of it. It is not my fault that I love. It has come about against my will. I tried to escape from it by self-renunciation: I tried to persuade myself that I found happiness in the affection between her and Luka, but that merely inflamed my own love and jealousy. This is not the love which is all noble ideals which I knew before; nor is it that sort of infatuation under the influence of which you delight in your own love and feel that you yourself are the source of that love and you do everything yourself. I have known that too. Still less is it a seeking after enjoyment: it is something quite different. It may be that in Marianka I love Nature, the incarnation of all that is beautiful in Nature; but I have no will of my own: some elemental force loves through me. The whole of God's universe, the whole of Nature, impresses that love on my heart and says "Love her". I love her not with my intellect, not with my imagination, but with my entire being. In loving her I feel myself to be an integral part of all God's joyous world. I wrote before about the new convictions to which my solitary life had brought me; but no one knows with what labour they forged themselves within me, with what joy I recognized them and saw a new way of life opening out before me. Nothing could have been dearer to me than those convictions ... Well ... Love came along, and now they are no more and I do not even regret them! I even find it difficult to understand how I could ever have cherished anything so one-sided, cold and abstract. Beauty came and scattered to the winds all that painfully erected edifice, and I have no regrets for what has vanished. Self-sacrifice is all stuff and nonsense. That was all pride, a refuge from well-merited unhappiness, salvation from jealousy of other people's happiness. "To live for others, and do good!" Why? – when in my heart there is only love for myself, and the desire to love her and live her life. Not for others, not for Luka, do I now desire happiness. I do not love those others any more. Before, I should have told myself that this is wrong. I should have tortured myself with questions like "What will become of her, of me, of Luka?" Now it is of no consequence to me. I do not live of myself: there is something stronger than I am which directs me. I am suffering, but whereas before I was dead, now only am I alive. Today I will go to her and tell her everything.'

34

IT was late in the evening when Olenin finished writing and went across to the teacher's cottage. Marianka's mother was sitting on a bench behind the stove, spinning silk from silkworm cocoons. Marianka, with her head uncovered, sat sewing by the light of a candle. When she saw Olenin she jumped up, seized her kerchief and climbed on to the stove.

'What be the matter? Stay here with us, my dearie,' said her mother.

'I can't. I've got nothing on my head.' And she sprang up on the stove.

Olenin could only see a knee and a shapely leg hanging down from the stove. He offered the old woman some tea. She in return treated her guest to clotted cream, which she sent Marianka to fetch. But as soon as she had put the plate on the table Marianka climbed back on to the stove, and Olenin merely felt her eyes upon him. They chatted about household matters and farming. The old woman warmed up into an extravagance of hospitality. She brought Olenin preserved grapes and a grape tart, and some of her best *chikhir*, urging him to eat and drink with the rough but kindly, proud hospitality typical of country folk who produce their bread by the labour of their own hands. The old woman, who had at first so surprised Olenin by her rudeness, now often touched him by her simple tenderness towards her daughter.

'Aye, we mustn't grumble. We've got all we want, thank God: preserves and to spare, and wine pressed – we can sell three or four barrels and still plenty for drink. Don't be for leaving afore you need. We'll share a merry time at the wedding.'

'And when is the wedding to be?' asked Olenin, feeling the blood rushing to his face, while his heart beat unevenly and painfully.

There was a rustling on the stove and the sound of sunflower seeds being cracked.

'Well, might be next week,' replied the old woman, as simply and quietly as though Olenin did not exist. 'I've got all put by ready. We want to do right by our girl. There's only one thing that ain't very good: our Luka's been running rather wild of late. Drinking and running about too much, he is. He's up to mischief. T'other day a Cossack came in from his Company and said as Luka had been to the Nogay country.'

'He'd better be careful he doesn't get caught,' said Olenin.

'Aye, same as what I tell him. "Mind, Luka," I say, "don't you play the fool." To be sure, he's a young man and must be up to something. But there is a time for everything. "All right," I say to him, "you've had fights and you've stolen horses and killed an *abrek* – well and good. But you did ought to stop it, or else there'll be trouble." '

'Yes, I saw him once or twice with the division and he was drinking and larking all the time. He had just sold another horse,' said Olenin, and glanced towards the stove.

Two large black eyes flashed a stern, hostile look at him. He felt ashamed of what he had said.

'What of it?' said Marianka suddenly. 'He ain't doing nobody no harm. He pays for his fun with his own money, don't he?' and lowering her legs she jumped down from the stove and went out, banging the door.

Olenin followed her with his eyes until she was out of the hut, when he gazed at the door, waiting and hearing nothing of what Mother Ulitka was saying to him. A few minutes later some visitors arrived: an old Cossack, Marianka's uncle, with Gaffer Yeroshka, and behind them, Marianka came in with Ustenka.

'How is everybody today?' squeaked Ustenka. 'Still amusing yourself?' she added, turning to Olenin.

'Yes, still amusing myself,' he agreed, suddenly feeling awkward and uncomfortable.

He wanted to go away and could not. It seemed equally impossible to sit there and say nothing. The old man came to his rescue by asking for a drink, and they had a drink. Then Olenin drank with Yeroshka, then with the other Cossack, and after that with Yeroshka again. And the more he drank the heavier his heart became. But the old men got livelier and livelier. The two girls climbed on to the stove, where they talked in low voices and looked down at the men who went on drinking. Olenin was silent and drank more than anybody else. The old men began shouting. Marianka's mother drove them out and would not let them have any more *chikhir*. The girls laughed at Gaffer Yeroshka, and it was past ten when they all went out on to the porch. The old men invited themselves to go and make a night of it at Olenin's. Ustenka ran off home. Yeroshka took the old Cossack to find Vanyusha. Marianka's mother went out to tidy up in the dairy. Marianka was left alone in the cottage. Olenin suddenly felt fresh and wide awake. He noticed everything, and letting the old men go on ahead he turned back to the cottage where Marianka was preparing for bed. He went up to her and tried to say something but his voice failed him. She sat down on the bed, as far away as possible, curled her legs under her and silently looked at him with wild, frightened eyes. She was obviously afraid. Olenin realized this. He felt sorry and ashamed of himself, and at the same time was proud and pleased to have inspired even that emotion in her.

'Marianka,' he said, 'will you never have pity on me? I can't tell you how I love you.'

She shrank still farther away.

'That be just tipsy talk! You won't get nothing from me!'

'No, it isn't the wine. Don't marry Luka. I will marry you.' ('What am I saying?' he thought as he uttered the words.

'Should I say the same thing tomorrow?' – 'Yes, I'm sure I should, and I'll repeat them now.')

'Will you marry me?'

She looked at him earnestly, and her fear seemed to leave her.

'Marianka, I shall go out of my mind! I am beside myself. I will do whatever you bid me!' – and passionate incoherent words poured from his lips of their own accord.

'Don't talk so silly,' she interrupted, suddenly seizing the hand which he had stretched out towards her. She did not push his hand away but pressed it firmly between her strong, rough fingers. 'Whoever heard tell of gentlemen marrying Cossack girls? Go along with you!'

'Marianka, will you –? I will do all –'

He snatched away the hand she was holding and put his arms round her young body in a tight embrace, but she sprang away like a fawn and ran barefooted on to the porch. Olenin came to his senses, horrified at himself. Again he felt inexpressibly vile compared to her, but not for an instant did he regret what he had told her. He went home, and without glancing at the old men who were drinking in his room threw himself on his bed and slept more soundly than he had for many a night.

35

THE next day was a saint's day, and by evening all the villagers were in the street, their holiday attire making a brave show in the bright rays of the setting sun. That summer there had been more wine pressed than usual, and people were now free from their labours. In a month the men would be on the march, and many families were making preparations for weddings.

Most of the population had gathered on the square, in front of the Government Office and near the two shops, one selling candies and pumpkin seeds, the other kerchiefs and cotton prints. On the turf bank surrounding the office building old men sat, or stood about, in sober grey or black coats, without braid or trimming of any sort. In quiet, measured tones they discussed the harvest, the young folk, village affairs and old times, occasionally glancing at the younger generation with dignified indifference. The girls and women passing by them would pause and bow their heads. The young Cossacks respectfully slackened their pace and lifting their lambskin caps held them for a moment before their foreheads. The old men then stopped talking among themselves and looked at the passers-by, some sternly, others kindly, and in their turn slowly took off their caps and put them on again.

The girls had not yet started dancing. Collected in little groups, they sat on the ground or on the earth-banks about the cottages, out of the sunlight, wearing their gay *beshmets* and white kerchiefs pulled down to their eyes, laughing and chattering in ringing voices. Children ran about the square, squealing and shouting, and tossing their balls high into the clear sky. On another corner the rather older girls were dancing in a circle and singing timidly in thin, shrill voices. Young lads home for the holiday or not yet in the Service, in smart white or new red Circassian coats with gold trimmings, their faces festive and animated, strolled about arm in arm, in twos and threes, from one group of women or girls to another, laughing and joking with them. The Armenian shopkeeper, in a blue coat of fine cloth edged with braid, with the proud bearing of an Oriental merchant conscious of his own importance, was standing at the open door of his shop where piles of bright-coloured folded kerchiefs were displayed. A couple of red-bearded, barefooted Chechens who had come for the fête from the other side of the Terek squatted on their heels outside the house of a friend, lazily drawing at their little pipes, spitting on the ground and exchanging an occasional observation in their abrupt guttural speech as they watched the villagers. Now and again a soldier on duty, wearing his everyday greatcoat, hurried through the colourfully dressed crowd. Here and there a few Cossacks, already drunk, were breaking into song. All the cottages were shut up. The porches had been scrubbed clean the day before. Even the old women were out of doors. Pumpkin and watermelon husks littered the dry, dusty streets. The air was warm and still, the cloudless sky blue and transparent. Rising above the roofs the pure-white peaks, turning rosy in the evening sun, gave an illusion of being very near. Now and then, from the other side of the river, came the distant rumble of a cannon but in the village itself there was only a confused buzz of merry-making.

Olenin had spent the morning walking about the yard, hoping to see Marianka. But she had dressed in her best clothes and gone to church. After the service she sat with the other girls on the embankment, crunching seeds. She ran home once or twice, always accompanied by some of her companions, and each time threw a cheerful, friendly glance at the lodger. Olenin was afraid to speak to her playfully or in the presence of others. He wanted to finish what he had begun to say the night before, and to get a definite answer. He waited for another moment like that of the previous evening, but no such moment came, and he felt that to remain in this uncertainty was more than he could bear. She went out into the street again, and after waiting a little, without knowing where he was going he followed her. He passed the corner where she was sitting in her shiny blue satin tunic, and with an aching heart he heard behind him a peal of girlish laughter.

Beletsky's cottage looked out on to the square. As Olenin was passing he heard Beletsky's voice calling him to come in, which he did.

After a short talk they both sat down by the window, and were soon joined by Yeroshka in a new *beshmet*, who settled down on the floor beside them.

'There, that's the aristocratic party,' said Beletsky, pointing with his cigarette to a multi-coloured group at the corner. 'My girl is there too. Do you see her? In red. That's a new *beshmet*. Hey there, why don't you start your dancing?' he shouted, leaning out of the window. 'Let's wait till it gets dark,' he added, turning to Olenin. 'Then we'll go and join them, and invite them round to Ustenka's. We must arrange for a ball!'

'I'll come to Ustenka's, too,' said Olenin with determination. 'Will Marianka be there?'

'Yes. You must come,' said Beletsky, not in the least surprised. 'It's really a very pretty sight,' he went on, indicating the crowd of many-coloured dresses.

'Yes, very,' agreed Olenin, trying to appear indifferent. 'Holidays of this kind always make me wonder why everybody in a flash should become so contented and jolly. Today, for instance, just because it is the fifteenth of the month, all of a sudden everything takes on a festive air. Eyes and faces and voices and movements and clothes, the air and the sun – all proclaim a holiday. But *we* don't have saints' days like this any more.'

'Yes,' said Olenin, who was not fond of such deliberations. 'And you, why aren't you drinking, old fellow?' he asked Yeroshka.

Yeroshka winked at Olenin, as much as to say: 'He's a proud one, that chum o' yourn!'

Beletsky lifted his glass. '*Allah birdy!*' he said, emptying his glass. ('*Allah birdy*', meaning 'God has given it', is the usual toast of Caucasians when drinking together.)

'*Sau bul!*' ('Your health!') replied Yeroshka, smiling and draining his glass.

'You calls this a holiday!' he said to Olenin, standing up and looking out of the window. 'But this here ain't nothing of a holiday. You should've witnessed a holiday like this here in the old days. The women come out dressed in sarafans and galloon all over 'em, and a double row a gold coins hanging round their necks and gold-'broidered frontlets on their foreheads, and their petticoats a-rustling when they come by us. Every one of 'em like a princess. They'd come out, a whole herd of 'em, mebbe, and start singing songs till all the air be full o' the sound of it, and they'd keep it up all night long. The men'd be rolling out barrel arter barrel of *chikhir* into the yards, and sit drinking till morning. Else they'd go out holding hands, pouring down the streets same as lava, sweeping along with them everyone they sees, and stopping for a drink in first one house then another. Sometimes they'd carry on so three days on end. I remember father used to come home all red and swollen – lost his cap and everything else he had. In he'd come and lie down, and mother knew what for to do: she'd bring him some fresh caviar and a jug of *chikhir* to sober up on, and then she'd scour the village for his cap. After that he'd sleep the clock round for two whole days. What people they was in them days! And look at 'em now!'

'What about the girls in the sarafans – did they make merry all by themselves?' asked Beletsky.

'Aye, they did. Atimes the men would walk up, or come riding on horseback, and try to break up the dances, but the girls fought 'em with cudgels. Carnival Shrovetide specially, some young blade'd be sure to gallop up, and the girls'd fight and beat his horse, and beat him too. Then if the feller managed to break through he'd grab his sweetheart and carry her off. And then the love-making there'd be! Aye, the girls was reg'lar queens in them days!'

36

JUST then two men on horseback rode out into the square. One of them was Nazar, the other Luka. Luka sat slightly sideways on his fat bay Kabarda, which pranced lightly over the hard road, tossing its beautiful head with the fine glossy forelock. The carefully adjusted gun in its case, the pistol at his back and the felt cloak rolled up neatly behind the saddle showed that Luka had come from no peaceful place nearby. The swagger with which he sat a little sideways on his horse, the careless movement of his hand as he flicked the horse under the belly with his whip, and in particular his flashing black eyes, half closed and looking haughtily around him, all expressed the conscious strength and self-confidence of youth. 'Ever seen such a fine chap?' his eyes seemed to challenge, as they glanced from side to side. The splendid horse with its silver trappings, the glistening weapons and the handsome Cossack himself attracted the attention of everybody in the square. Nazar, thin and short, was not nearly so well turned out. As he rode past the old men Luka drew rein and raised his curly white sheepskin cap above his closely cropped black head.

'Well, how many Nogay horses have you stolen this time?' asked a withered little old man with a dark scowling face.

'Haven't you counted 'em, grandad, that you ask?' replied Luka, turning away.

'See as you don't drag my lad into it,' the old man muttered, looking blacker still.

'Oh, the old devil knows everything!' Luka growled to himself, and a worried expression appeared on his face; but noticing a number of girls at the corner of the square he spurred his horse towards them.

'Good evening, girls!' he shouted in a loud ringing voice, reining in his horse with a jerk. 'You're growing old without me, you witches!'

'Evening, Luka! Evening, laddie!' merry voices cried in reply. 'Have you got plenty of money with you? Buy the girls some sweets now! You come for long? 'Tis many days since us saw you.'

'Nazar and me, we're here on a flying visit to make a night of it,' replied Luka, brandishing his whip over the horse and riding straight at the girls.

''Tis been so long, Marianka here has forgotten you altogether,' piped Ustenka, nudging Marianka with her elbow and breaking into a shrill laugh.

Marianka stepped away from the horse and throwing her head back quietly looked up at the Cossack with large sparkling eyes.

'That's right, it's been ever so long. But what for are you trying to run over us with your horse?' she remarked dryly, and turned away.

Luka was visibly taken aback by Marianka's coldness. The gay, jaunty expression vanished from his face, and he frowned.

'Up in the stirrup with you, and away we'll go!' he suddenly cried as though to dispel his dark thoughts, and caracoled among the girls. He stooped down towards Marianka. 'I'll have me kiss, I'll have me kiss yet,' he said.

Their eyes met, and Marianka suddenly blushed. She stepped back.

'Look out or you'll crush me feet,' she said, bending her head and looking at her shapely legs in their tightly fitting pale blue stockings with clocks and her new red slippers trimmed with narrow silver braid.

Luka turned to Ustenka, and Marianka sat down beside a young woman with a baby in her arms. The baby stretched out its plump little hands and clutched Marianka's necklet of coins which hung down on to her blue *beshmet*. Marianka bent down to the child and glanced at Luka out of the corner of her eye. Luka was just at that moment getting from under his coat, out of the pocket of his black *beshmet*, a parcel of sweets and pumpkin seeds.

'There!' he said, handing the bundle to Ustenka and smiling at Marianka. 'That's for all of you.'

Again a look of perplexity came over Marianka's face. It was as though a mist gathered over her beautiful eyes. She drew her kerchief down from her lips, and abruptly leaning her head over the rosy-white face of the baby, who was still clutching her necklace, began wildly to kiss it. The baby pressed its little hands against the girl's high breasts and opening its toothless mouth screamed loudly.

'Stop it, you'll choke him,' said the mother, pulling the baby away from Marianka and unfastening her *beshmet* to give him the breast. 'You'd do better to make a fuss of your young man.'

'I'll just go and put up me horse, and then me and Nazar'll come back and make a night of it,' said Luka, touching the beast with his whip and riding away from the girls.

Turning into a side street, he and Nazar rode up to two cottages standing side by side.

'Here we are! Look sharp now!' cried Luka to his comrade. He dismounted in front of one of the cottages and carefully led his horse in at the gate of the wattle fence round his own yard. 'Hey, there, Stepka!' he said to his deaf and dumb sister, who, dressed in her best clothes like the others, came in from the street to take his horse. And he made signs to her to give the animal some hay but not to unsaddle it.

The deaf and dumb girl made a noise in her throat, smacked her lips, pointing to the horse, and kissed it on the nose. She meant to show that it was a fine horse and she loved it.

'How are you, mother? Why haven't you gone out yet?' shouted Luka, holding his gun in place as he went up the steps of the porch.

His mother opened the door to him.

'Well I never! I didn't expect you – I didn't think as you'd come,' said the old woman. 'Why, Kirka said as you wouldn't be here.'

'Go and bring some *chikhir*, mother. Nazar is coming, and we wants to make a proper go of it.'

'Straight away, Luka, straight away!' answered the old

woman. 'All the women are out enjoying theyselves. Looks as if our dumb one has gone too.'

And she picked up her keys and hurried across the yard.

As soon as he had put away his horse and taken off his gun Nazar came over to Luka's.

37

'YOUR health!' said Luka, taking from his mother's hands a cup filled to the brim with *chikhir* and carefully raising it to his mouth, craning his neck forward.

' 'Tis a bad business!' said Nazar. 'You heard what he said? – "How many horses have you stolen?" he said. So he knows.'

'A wizard!' said Luka curtly. 'But what of it?' he added, with a toss of his head. 'They're acrost the river by now. Let him go and look for 'em! They won't find nothing.'

'Still, it's awkward.'

'What is awkward? Go and take him some *chikhir* tomorrow. That'll be the way of it, and we shan't hear no more from him. Now let you and me enjoy ourself. Drink!' he shouted in the tone in which old Yeroshka would have cried the word. 'We'll have some fun with the girls out o' doors. Get some honey, will you? Or shall I send my dumb sister? We'll make a night of it.'

Nazar smiled.

'How long are we stopping here?' he asked.

'Till we've had our bit of fun. Run and fetch some vodka. Here's the money.'

Nazar ran off obediently to get vodka at Yamka's.

Old Yeroshka and Yergushov, like birds of prey, scenting where drink was to be had, tumbled into the cottage one after the other, both tipsy.

'Bring us another half-bucket,' Luka shouted to his mother by way of reply to their greeting.

'Now then, tell us where you stole 'em, you devil, you!' bellowed Yeroshka. 'You're a fine lad. You fill my old heart with affection, that you do.'

'Fill your heart with affection, is it?' retorted Luka with a laugh. 'Carrying sweets to girls from their lodgers, eh? You old codger!'

''Tis a lie, Marka, a right black lie!' And the old man burst out laughing. 'But you should have heard him begging me to! "Go on," he says, "arrange it for us." Offered me a gun, he did. But no! I'd have fixed it up, of course, but I feels for you. Now, come on – tell us where you've been,' said the old man, breaking into Tartar.

Luka answered him briskly.

Yergushov, who did not know much Tartar, now and again put in a Russian word or two.

'What I says is, you've driven off them horses and I knows it for a fact,' he insisted.

'Girey and me both went,' began Luka, dropping the 'Khan' deliberately to show off his familiarity with the famous Girey Khan. 'And soon as we was over the river he started bragging how well he knew the steppe, and how he would take us straight to the spot, but as we rode on – 'twas a right dark night – our Girey lost his way and we was just wandering round in circles, getting no place. He couldn't find the village, and we was stuck. We must have turned off to the right too early. I reckon we scratched about till nigh on midnight. Then, thank goodness, we heard dogs howling.'

'Ain't you fools?' said Yeroshka. 'Happened to us, too, times, to get lost in the steppe – 'tis a devil of a place to find yer way over. But I used to ride up a hillock and howl like a wolf – this fashion.' He cupped his hands to his mouth and howled on one note, like a pack of wolves. 'The dogs'd answer at once ... Well, go on – did you find what you was looking for?'

'Had halters on 'em in no time. Some old Nogay women come near catching Nazar.'

'How d'you mean!' Nazar, who had just returned, said in an injured tone.

'Well, we rode off, and again Girey lost his way and nearly fetched us among the sand-drifts. He kept telling us we was just getting to the Terek, but all the time we was riding away from it.'

'You should have gone by the stars,' said Yeroshka.

'That's what I says,' put in Yergushov.

' 'Course, but 'twas pitch dark, you see. I was beating about all over the place. At the finish I puts the bridle on one of the mares and lets me own horse go free, hoping he'd lead us out – and what d'you think? He gives a snort or two, puts his nose to the ground and gallops off straight to the village. And not too soon neither – 'twas very near light. We just had time to hide the horses in the wood. Nagim come across the river and took 'em.'

'Well done, I says!' cried Yergushov, nodding his head. 'Did you get much for 'em?'

' 'Tis all here, and ...' began Luka, slapping his pocket, but at that moment his mother came into the room and he broke off. 'Drink!' he shouted.

'I remember, Girchik an' me, once we rode out late ...' Yeroshka was beginning.

'Beg pardon now, haven't no time to listen to you,' said Luka. 'I'm off.' And swilling down the wine from his tumbler, he walked out into the street, tightening his belt.

38

It was dark when Luka went out into the street. The autumn night was fresh and still. The full, golden moon sailed out from behind the dark poplars that grew along one side of the square. Smoke from the dairy chimneys mingled with the evening vapours and made a grey pall over the village. In some of the windows lights were burning. The air was laden with the smell of *kizyak*, grape-pulp and mist. There was the same medley of voices and laughter, of songs and the crunching of sunflower seeds as in the day-time but now the sounds were more distinct. By the fences and the houses white kerchiefs and tall lambskin caps gleamed in the darkness.

In the square, in front of the shop which was still open and lit up, the moving figures of men and women silhouetted black against the light, or looked white beneath the moon, and there was the noise of loud singing, laughing and chatting. Joining hands, the girls made a ring and stepped gracefully in the dusty square. A skinny girl, the plainest of them all, began to sing:

'From a wood, a dark little wood,
Ai-da-luili!
From a garden, a green little garden,
Came out one day two handsome lads,
Two right handsome lads, two bachelors gay.
They walked and they talked and they stopped,
They stopped and quarrelled, and quarrelled they did,
Till up came a lovely maiden.
Along she came and to the lads she said:
"One of you two, now, soon I'll wed."
'Twas the fair-faced lad got the maiden fair,
Fair-faced lad with the golden hair.
Her right hand so white, in his own he took,
And leads her, leads her round the ring.
"Have you, comrades," he says, "in all your life
"Met a lass so sweet as my little wife?"'

The old women stood round, listening to the singing. The children ran about, chasing one another in the dark. The men stood close, catching at the girls as they whirled by, and sometimes breaking the ring and joining up with it. Olenin and Beletsky stood on the dark side of the doorway, wearing Circassian coats and lambskin caps like everybody else, but their speech was different from that of the Cossacks and though they spoke in low voices they felt they were attracting attention. The plump little Ustenka, in a red tunic, and the stately Marianka in her new smock and blue tunic were next to each other in the ring. Olenin and Beletsky were discussing how they might snatch the two girls away from the dancers. Beletsky thought Olenin only wanted to amuse himself, but Olenin was waiting for his fate to be decided. At all costs he must see Marianka alone, pour out his soul and ask her, could she – would she – be his wife. Although he had long been aware, inside himself, that the answer would be 'No', he hoped he would have the strength to tell her all he felt, and that she would understand him.

'Why didn't you let me know sooner?' said Beletsky. 'I could have got Ustenka to arrange things for you. You are a queer fellow!'

'Never mind. Some day, very soon, I'll tell you all about it.

But now, for heaven's sake, try to get her to come round to Ustenka's.'

'All right. That's easily done ... Well, Marianka, so it's the fair-faced lad gets the maiden fair, and not Luka, eh?' said Beletsky, speaking to Marianka first for propriety's sake; and then, without waiting for her answer, he approached Ustenka and began to urge her to bring Marianka home with her. Before he had finished what he was saying the leader started up another song and the girls moved on, pulling each other round in the ring by the hand.

They sang:

'Past the garden, the garden,
A young man came out to walk
Up and down the village street.
The first time past the garden
He did wave his strong right hand.
Second time past the garden
Waved his hat with silken band.
The third time past the garden
He did stop and cross the street
For his sweetheart there to meet.

' "I fear I fain must chide thee,
Why is it thou, my dear one,
Wilt not walk in the garden?
Dost thou scorn to talk with me?
But by and by, my fair one,
Thou'lt change thy mind and love me.
And I will send and woo thee.
Then when we shall married be
Thou shalt weep because of me!"

' "Though my answer I knew well,
Ne'er a word I dar'd reply.
In the park to walk went I,
In the park my man to meet.
I bowed me down in greeting.
As I bowed, so it befell,
To the ground my kerchief fell.
Up he picked it, where it lay."

'"In thy white hand take it, pray
Please accept it, dear, from me.
Say I am beloved by thee.
What to give, I cannot tell,
To the maiden I love well.
To my dear I think I will
Of a shawl a present make –
Kisses five for it I'll take!"'

Luka and Nazar broke into the ring and began to walk in and out among the girls. Luka joined in the chorus, singing seconds in his clear voice as he sauntered in the middle of the circle swinging his arms. 'Come on, one of you!' he cried. The other girls tried to push Marianka forward but she would not go. Shrill laughter, slaps, kisses and whispering made themselves heard above the singing.

As he went past Olenin, Luka gave him a friendly nod.

'Hey there, 'Mitri Andreich! Come to have a look?' he said.

'Yes,' answered Olenin with decided curtness.

Beletsky stopped and whispered something into Ustenka's ear, but before there was time to reply she was whirled away, and only on the second time round she said: 'All right, we'll be there.'

'Marianka too?'

Olenin bent towards Marianka. 'You will come, won't you? Please do, if only for a minute. I must speak to you.'

'If the other girls come, I will.'

'Will you answer the question I asked you?' he said, leaning nearer to her. 'You're light-hearted today.'

She had moved past him now. He went after her. 'Will you give me an answer?'

'An answer to what?'

'To the question I asked you the other day,' said Olenin, bending close to her ear. 'Will you marry me?'

Marianka thought for a moment.

'I'll tell you,' she said. 'I'll tell you this night.'

And in the darkness her eyes sparkled, kind and affectionate, on the young man.

Olenin still followed after her. He was happy to be leaning over her.

But suddenly Luka, without interrupting the singing, seized her forcibly by the hand and dragged her into the middle of the ring. Olenin was only able to repeat: 'Come to Ustenka's,' and stepped back to his companion. The song came to an end. Luka wiped his lips, Marianka did the same, and they kissed. 'No, no, "kisses five"!' cried Luka. Rhythmic movement and flowing song were succeeded by chatter, scuffling and laughter. Luka, who seemed to have drunk a great deal, began distributing sweets to the girls.

'It be my treat to everybody,' he kept saying proudly, with comical, pathetic self-admiration. 'But anyone who follows about after soldiers gets out of the ring!' he suddenly shouted with an angry glance at Olenin.

The girls grabbed his sweets from him and, laughing, struggled for them among themselves. Beletsky and Olenin stepped aside.

Luka, as if suddenly embarrassed by his own generosity, took off his cap and wiping his forehead with his sleeve went up to Marianka and Ustenka.

'Dost thou scorn to talk with me?' he said, quoting the words of the song they had just been singing, and turning to Marianka he repeated fiercely: *'Dost thou scorn me? Then when we shall married be, Thou shalt weep because of me!'* he went on, putting his arms round Ustenka and Marianka together.

Ustenka tore herself away, and swinging her arm gave him such a blow on the back that she hurt her own hand.

'Well, ain't you going to have another dance?' he asked.

'The others can do as they please,' answered Ustenka, 'but I'm going home and Marianka wanted to come along of me.'

With his arm still round Marianka, Luka led her away from the crowd to a dark corner behind a house.

'Don't go with her, Marianka,' he said. 'Let's have a last bit of fun together. Go home, and I'll come along there.'

'What'll I do at home? I wants to enjoy meself – 'tis what a carnival day is for. I'm going to Ustenka's,' replied Marianka.

'I'll wed you all the same, you know!'

'All right,' said Marianka, 'we'll see about that.'

'So you are really going?' Luka demanded, and pressing her close he kissed her cheek.

'Stop it! Why keep on so?' And Marianka wrenched herself free and left him.

'Ah, me girl! ... This won't lead to no good,' said Luka reproachfully, and he stood still, shaking his head. '*Thou shalt weep because of me!*' and turning his back on her he shouted to the other girls: 'Sing something, go on now!'

His last words had half frightened, half angered Marianka. She stopped abruptly. 'What won't lead to no good?'

'Why, that!'

'That what?'

'Carrying on with that soldier lodger of yourn, and not caring about me any more.'

'I'll do just what I likes about caring or not caring. You ain't me father, nor me mother. What are you after? I'll care for who I likes.'

'I see,' said Luka. 'But just you remember my words!' He moved towards the shop. 'Hey, girls!' he shouted, 'What are you standing about for? Give us another dance. Nazar, fetch some more *chikhir*.'

'Well, are they coming?' Olenin asked Beletsky.

'They'll be here directly,' replied Beletsky. 'Come on, we must get everything ready.'

39

IT was late at night when Olenin came out of Beletsky's hut after Marianka and Ustenka. Marianka's white kerchief gleamed in the darkness. The golden moon was sinking towards the steppe. A silvery mist hung over the village. All was quiet. There were no lights to be seen, and no sound save the receding footsteps of the two girls. Olenin's heart beat violently. The damp air cooled his burning face. He glanced up at the sky, then turned to look at the hut from which he had just come out: the candle was already snuffed. Then he peered through the darkness again at the two retreating shadows. The white kerchief disappeared in the mist. It was terrible to be left alone: he felt so happy. He jumped down from the porch and ran after the girls.

'Go away, someone might see!' said Ustenka.

'Never mind!'

Olenin ran up to Marianka and put his arms round her.

Marianka did not resist.

'Kissing again!' said Ustenka. 'Marry her first, kiss her after, but that's enough for now.'

'Good-night, Marianka,' said Olenin. 'Tomorrow I'll come and see your father, to tell him myself. Don't you breathe a word.'

'Whyfor should I say anything?' replied Marianka.

The girls started running. Olenin walked on by himself, going over in his mind all that had happened. He had spent the whole evening alone with her in a corner by the stove. Ustenka had not left the hut for a single moment but had romped about all the time with Beletsky and the other girls. Olenin and Marianka had talked in whispers.

'Will you marry me?' he asked.

'You be having me on, you wouldn't take me,' she answered him cheerfully and quietly.

'But do you love me? For God's sake, tell me!'

'Whyfor shouldn't I love you? You don't squint,' said Marianka, still laughing and squeezing his hand between her muscular fingers. 'What whi-ite, whi-ite soft hands you've got – like clotted cream!'

'Marianka, I mean it. Tell me, will you marry me?'

'Why not, if father says so.'

'Remember, I'll go mad if you deceive me. Tomorrow I'll talk to your mother and father. I'll come and ask for your hand in marriage.'

Marianka suddenly burst out laughing.

'What's the matter?'

'Nothing, 'tis so funny.'

'I'm in earnest. I'll buy a vineyard and a house, and I'll enrol with the Cossacks...'

'Mind you don't start running after other women! I wouldn't have it.'

Olenin repeated all this in his imagination, savouring every word with delight. The memory of them filled him now with pain, now made him catch his breath with happiness. The pain was because all the time they were talking Marianka had remained as calm and collected as she always was, and apparently not at all excited by this new state of affairs. It was as though she did not believe in him, and was not thinking in the future. It seemed to him she loved him only for the moment, in the present, and had no thought of their future life together. His happiness was in believing that she would keep her word and marry him. 'Yes,' he told himself, 'we shall only understand one another when she is all mine. There are no words for such love – it needs life, a whole lifetime. Tomorrow everything will be made clear. I can't go on like this any longer: tomorrow I will tell her father everything, I'll tell Beletsky, I'll tell the entire village . . .'

Luka, after two nights without sleep, had drunk so much at the fête that for the first time in his life his legs refused to carry him and he slept in Yamka's house.

40

IMMEDIATELY he awoke next morning, earlier than usual, Olenin thought of what the day was to hold for him, and in delight remembered her kisses, the pressure of her hard fingers, and how she had said to him: 'What white hands you have!' He jumped out of bed, meaning to go at once and ask her parents for their consent to his marriage with Marianka. The sun had not risen yet, and it struck Olenin that there was an unusual commotion in the street: people were moving about, on foot and on horseback, and talking together. He threw on his Circassian coat and hastened out on to the porch. The family was not yet up. Five Cossacks rode past, arguing loudly about something. At their head Luka was riding his broad-backed Kabarda horse. The Cossacks were all talking and shouting at the tops of their voices: it was impossible to make out what the trouble was.

'Strike for the Upper Post,' cried one.

'Saddle your horse and catch us up. Look sharp!' called another.

‘’Tis nearer by t’other gate.’

‘Never!’ shouted Luka. ‘We got to go through the middle gate . . .’

‘You’re right, that way’s quicker,’ said one of the Cossacks, all covered with dust and riding a sweating horse.

Luka’s face was red and swollen with drinking the day before; his lambskin cap was pushed to the back of his head. He was shouting orders as though he were an officer.

‘What’s the matter? Where are you going?’ asked Olenin, with difficulty attracting the Cossacks’ attention.

‘We’m off after *abreks*. Them’s out there in the sand-dunes. We should get going now, but there bain’t enough of us yet awhiles.’

And the Cossacks continued down the street, shouting and collecting others as they went. It occurred to Olenin that it would not look well for him to stay behind; besides, he thought he could be back soon. He dressed, loaded his gun with bullets, jumped on to his horse which Vanyusha had hardly had time to saddle, and caught up with the Cossacks at the village gates. They had dismounted, although they were in a hurry, and stood round in a circle, filling a wooden bowl with *chikhir* from a small cask which they had brought with them. Passing the bowl from hand to hand, they drank to the success of their expedition. Among their number was a smartly-dressed young cornet who happened to be in the village and who took command of the nine men composing the party. But though the Cossacks were all privates, and the young cornet put on all the airs of a leader, they only obeyed Luka. Of Olenin they took no notice whatever. And when they had mounted again and were started on their way, and Olenin rode up to the cornet and began inquiring what had happened, the cornet, who was usually quite friendly, treated him with marked condescension. It was with the greatest difficulty that Olenin managed to find out from him what it was all about. It appeared that a patrol which had been sent out to look for *abreks* had spotted a few of the hillsmen in the sand-dunes about six miles from the village. The *abreks*, who were sitting in ambush in a ditch, had opened fire, declaring that they would never surrender. The sergeant in charge of the two scouts had remained on guard with one of them, sending the other back to the village for help.

The sun was just rising. A couple of miles beyond the village the steppe spread out in every direction, and there was nothing to be seen save a dreary, monotonous waste of sand marked with the tracks of cattle, occasional tufts of withered grass, some low reeds in the hollows, and rare, scarcely traceable footpaths; and far, far away on the horizon the camps of the Nogay tribes. The total absence of shade and the austere aspect of the place were striking. The sun always rises and sets red in the steppe. When the wind blows it carries with it whole mountains of sand. When it is still, as it was that morning, the silence, uninterrupted by any movement or sound, is peculiarly impressive. That morning was dull and grey, although the sun had already risen: there was an especial feeling of emptiness and lassitude. Not a breath stirred the air: the only sounds were the soft trampling and the snorting of the horses, and even they had no resonance and quickly died away.

Most of the time the men rode in silence. The Cossack always carries his weapons so that they neither jingle nor rattle. For his arms to jingle is a terrible disgrace. Two Cossacks from the village caught the party up on the road and exchanged a few words. Luka's horse either stumbled or got its hoof entangled in some grass, and lurched forward. This is considered a bad omen among Cossacks. They looked round and then hastily turned away, trying not to notice the incident, which seemed particularly significant at such a time. Luka knit his brows sternly and clenched his teeth as he pulled at the reins and cracked the whip over his head. The horse, prancing from one hoof to another uncertain which to put forward, looked as though it were trying to fly into the air; but Luka slashed its well-fed flanks once, then again, and a third time, and the horse, showing its teeth and spreading its tail, snorted and reared, and staggered on its hind legs a few paces away from the others.

'Ah, a fine steed you've got there!' said the cornet.

That he said 'steed' instead of 'horse' was indicative of particular praise.

'A lion of a horse,' attested one of the other Cossacks.

The party rode on in silence, now at walking-pace, now at a

trot, and the change of pace alone broke for an instant the quiet, solemn rhythm of their movements.

Riding along, the only thing they met in a stretch of over six miles was one Nogay tent, placed on a tilted cart jogging slowly across the steppe half a mile away: it was a Nogay family moving from one camp to another. Farther on, near some swampy low-lying ground, they saw two ragged Nogay women with high cheek-bones, who with baskets on their backs were collecting dung left by the cattle that wandered over the steppe. The cornet tried to question them but could not speak their dialect well enough. They did not understand him and looked nervously at one another.

Luka rode up, reined in his horse and briskly gave them the usual greeting. Pleased and with a look of relief, the women loosed their tongues and talked happily to him, as to one of their own people.

'*Ai, ai, kop abrek!*' they said plaintively, pointing in the direction in which the Cossacks were going. Olenin understood that they were saying '*Many abreks*'.

Never having seen an action of this kind, and all his ideas about such expeditions being based entirely on Gaffer Yeroshka's tales, Olenin was anxious to stay with the party to the end, and see everything. He watched the Cossacks admiringly, kept his ears and eyes open, and made his own observations. Although he had his sword and a loaded musket with him, when he noticed that the Cossacks were avoiding him he decided to take no part in the coming fight, particularly as in his opinion his courage had already been sufficiently proved during the campaign with his detachment, and also – and this was the principal reason – he was now feeling very happy.

Suddenly a shot rang out in the distance.

The young cornet became excited and started making dispositions as to how they should divide up their forces and from which side they should approach. But the Cossacks did not appear to pay the slightest attention to these dispositions of his, and listened only to what Luka was saying, looking to him alone. Luka's face and whole bearing expressed composure and solemnity. He rode forward at such a pace that the others were unable to keep up, as he peered ahead with narrowed eyes.

'There's a man on horseback,' he said, reining in and falling into line with the others.

Olenin strained his eyes but could see nothing. The Cossacks soon made out two horsemen, and rode steadily towards them.

'Are they *abreks?*' asked Olenin.

The Cossacks did not answer: the question was quite devoid of sense – as if *abreks* would be such fools as to venture this side of the river on horseback!

'There's friend Rodka waving to us, I'm certain sure,' said Luka, pointing towards the two mounted men now plainly visible. 'See he's coming our way.'

Indeed, a few minutes later there was no doubt that the two horsemen were the Cossack scouts, and the sergeant rode up to Luka.

41

'How far are they?' was all Luka said.

Just then they heard the crack of a gun some thirty paces off. The sergeant gave a faint grin.

'That's our Gurka peppering 'em,' he said, nodding in the direction of the shot.

Riding a few paces farther, they caught sight of Gurka squatting behind a sand-hill and loading his musket. To while away the time he was exchanging shots with the *abreks*, who were behind another hillock. A bullet came whistling from their side.

The cornet turned pale and became flustered. Luka dismounted, threw the reins to one of the Cossacks, and went up to Gurka. Olenin dismounted too and, stooping down, followed Luka. They had hardly reached Gurka before two bullets screeched over their heads. Luka ducked, and looked round at Olenin with a laugh.

'Watch out else they'll get you, Andreich,' he said. 'You'd better go back anyways. This ain't no place for you.'

But Olenin had set his heart on seeing the *abreks*.

Behind a mound about seventy yards away he glimpsed caps and muskets. Suddenly there was a puff of smoke there, and another bullet whistled by. The *abreks* were concealed in marsh land at the foot of the hill. Olenin looked respectfully in the direction of the *abreks*. Actually, it was similar to the rest of the steppe but because *abreks* were there it made it distinct and different. In fact it appeared to Olenin exactly the sort of place *abreks* would choose. Luka went back to his horse, and Olenin followed him.

'We must get a hay-cart,' said Luka, 'else they'll pick us off one after t'other. There's a Nogay cart with a load of hay behind that sand-hill over yonder.'

The cornet and the sergeant agreed. The cart was fetched, and the Cossacks, sheltering behind it, pushed it in front of them. Olenin rode off to a hillock from the top of which he had a view of the whole scene. The hay-cart moved forward, with the Cossacks crowding behind it. The Cossacks advanced. The *abreks* – there were nine of them – sat in a row, knee to knee, and did not fire.

All was quiet. Suddenly the silence was broken by a strange, melancholy song, something like Gaffer Yeroshka's 'Ai-da-la-lai'. The *abreks* knew there was no escape for them, and to avoid any temptation to run they had strapped themselves together, knee to knee, had their guns ready, and were singing their death-song.

The Cossacks behind their hay-cart drew nearer and nearer, and Olenin expected firing at any moment; but the only sound was the *abreks'* mournful singing. Suddenly the song was cut short, there was a sharp report, a bullet struck the front of the cart, and Tartar curses and yells shattered the stillness. Shot followed shot, bullet after bullet smacked into the hay. The Cossacks held their fire and were now but five paces away.

An instant later, the Cossacks with a whoop leaped out on both sides from behind the cart, with Luka at their head. Olenin heard a shot or two, then shouting and moans. He thought he saw blood through the smoke. Abandoning his horse and quite beside himself, he rushed towards the Cossacks. Horror blinded his eyes. He could not make out anything but realized that all was over. Luka, pale as a sheet, was holding a wounded *abrek* by the arm and shouting 'Don't shoot, I'll take him alive!' It was the red-haired Chechen who had come to ransom his brother's body. Luka was twisting his arms. Suddenly the *abrek* wrenched himself free and fired his pistol. Luka fell. Blood spurted from his stomach. He jumped up but fell again, cursing in Russian and Tartar. More and more blood appeared on his clothes and on the ground under him. Some Cossacks went to him and began loosening his girdle. One of them, Nazar it was, before going to Luka's help fumbled for several moments with his sword, which he could not get into its sheath. The blade was dripping with blood.

The *abreks*, with their red hair and clipped moustaches, lay dead and hacked about. The only one alive among them, though badly wounded in many places, was the brave who had shot Luka. Like a wounded hawk, all covered with blood (blood was flowing from a wound under his right eye), pale and lowering, teeth clenched and enormous angry eyes glaring wildly round him, he crouched, dagger in hand, ready to defend himself to the last. The cornet went towards him, as though he merely intended to walk past, then with a quick movement shot him sideways in the ear. The *abrek* started up, but it was too late, and he fell.

The Cossacks, panting and out of breath, dragged the bodies aside and stripped them of their weapons. Each one of these red-haired *abreks* had been a man, and each had his own individual expression. Luka was carried to the cart, still swearing in Russian and Tartar.

'No, you don't! I'll strangle you with me own hands! You'll not get away! *Aha seni!*' he shouted, struggling. But he was soon too weak to make any sound.

Olenin rode home. In the evening he was told that Luka was at death's door but that a Tartar from across the river had agreed to try and save him by means of herbs.

The bodies were brought to the office of the village elder. The women and all the small boys flocked to look at them.

Olenin returned at dusk, and it was some while before he could get over all he had seen; but towards night memories of the evening before came flooding back in his mind. He looked out of the window; Marianka was crossing to and fro between the cottage and the byre, busy with her chores. Her mother had gone to the vineyard and her father was at the village elder's. Olenin could not wait until she had finished her work, and went out to her. She was in the cottage, standing with her back to the door. Olenin thought she was feeling shy.

'Marianka?' he said. 'I say, Marianka, may I come in?'

She turned round abruptly. There were traces of tears in her eyes, and her face was beautiful in its sadness. She looked at him in silent dignity.

'Marianka!' Olenin repeated. 'I have come –'

'Leave me alone!' she said. Her face did not change but the tears ran down her cheeks.

'What is it? What's the matter?'

'The matter?' she echoed in a rough, hard voice. 'Cossacks have been killed, that's all.'

'Luka?'

'Go away, I don't want you!'

'Marianka!' said Olenin, approaching her.

'You'll never have nothing from me.'

'Marianka, don't speak like that,' begged Olenin.

'Get out! I hate you!' shouted the girl, stamping her foot and moving threateningly towards him. And her face expressed such abhorrence, contempt and anger that Olenin suddenly realized there was no hope for him, and that his original impression that he could never be anything to this woman had been absolutely right.

And making no answer he rushed out of the cottage.

42

RETURNING to his room he lay down on his bed for two hours without moving. Then he went to his Company commander and obtained permission to join the Staff. Without bidding anyone good-bye, and sending Vanyusha to pay the landlord, he prepared to leave for the fort where his regiment was stationed. Old Yeroshka was the only one to see him off. They had a drink together, and then another and another. Again, as on the night of his departure from Moscow, a three-horsed post-chaise stood waiting at the door. But this time Olenin was not settling accounts with himself; nor was he saying to himself that all he had thought and done here was 'not it'. He did not promise himself a new life. He loved Marianka more than ever, and knew now that she could never love him.

'Well, good-bye, me lad!' said Gaffer Yeroshka. 'When you goes on an expedition don't go for to do nothing foolish, and remember what an old man tell you. I be an old wolf, you knows that, and have seen a thing or two in me time – so when you be on a raid or anything a that, and they starts shooting at you, don't stick together in a bunch, a whole crowd of you, same as you fellows always do: when you gets scared you all of you huddles together. You thinks 'tis more healthy to be with a lot of others, but that be where 'tis worse – they always aims at a crowd. Now I always kept away from people and went by meself, and as you sees, I've never had so much as a scratch. Yet what haven't I seen in me day!'

'But you've got a bullet stuck in your back,' remarked Vanyusha, who was in the room packing up.

'That were our own chaps, Cossacks, fooling about,' said Yeroshka.

'Cossacks? How was that?' asked Olenin.

'Very simple. We was drinking. Vanka Sitkin, one of our Cossacks, got merry and – bang! – his pistol went off and got me right here.'

'Did it hurt much?' inquired Olenin. 'Vanyusha, how soon will you be ready?' he added.

'Ah, where's the hurry? Lemme finish telling you . . . Well, so bang it went, but the bullet didn't break the bone but stuck in the fleshy part here. "You've gone and killed me, brother," says I. "Eh? What have you done to me? I won't let you off like that," I says. "You'll have to stand me a bucketful!" '

'Well, and did it hurt?' Olenin asked again, scarcely listening to the story.

'Wait, and I'll tell you. He brought a bucketful all right, and we drinks it to the last drop. But the blood kept squirting out of me. The whole room was a-swimming with blood. Then old Burlak, he says: " 'Tis all up with the lad, as you knows. Better stand us a bottle of sweet stuff, else we'll hand you over." Well, they fetched more wine, and we boozed and boozed . . .'

'Yes, but did it hurt you much?' asked Olenin for the third time.

'Hurt? What d'you mean? Don't keep interrupting, I doesn't like it. Lemme finish. We boozed and boozed till morning, and I falls asleep on the top of the stove, drunk. When I wakes in the morning I couldn't straighten out nohow.'

'Was it very painful?' repeated Olenin, thinking that now at last he would get an answer to his question.

'Have I said aught about it hurting? Nay, it didn't hurt but I couldn't straighten meself, I couldn't walk.'

'And then it healed up, did it?' said Olenin, feeling too wretched to laugh.

'It healed up all right but the bullet's still here. See, you can feel it.' And lifting his shirt, Yeroshka showed his brawny back where a bullet moved near the bone.

'Feel it moving?' he said, evidently taking pleasure in the bullet as though it were a plaything. 'There now, it's slipping down to me backside.'

'What about Luka? Will he recover?' asked Olenin.

'Only the good God knows. There ain't no dokh-tor. They're gone for one.'

'Where're they getting him from? Groznoe?' asked Olenin.

'Nay, me lad. If I was Tsar I'd have hung all them Russian dokh-tors long since. All they knows is how to chop you about. Look at our Cossack Baklashka: no good as a man now – they went and cut his leg off. That shows what fools they are. What's Baklashka fit for now? Nay, me lad, 'tis in the mountains as is the real dokh-tors. 'Twas just the same with me pal, Girchik. Girchik was on an expedition and got hisself wounded in the chest, and your dokh-tors give him up, but Saib come down from the mountains and put him on his feet. They knows about herbs, they does.'

'Come, come, don't talk rubbish,' said Olenin. 'I'd better send a surgeon from head-quarters.'

'"Rubbish!"' the old man mocked. 'You're a fool, that's what you are. "Rubbish!" says 'e. 'I'll send you a surgeon!" Don't you knows, if your fellows ever cured anybody, Cossacks and Tartars and all would come for healing, but 'tis your officers and colonels as send for dokh-tors from the mountains. 'Tis all fraud with you, fraud, all of it!'

Olenin did not bother to answer. He agreed only too well

that all was fraud in the world he had come from and to which he was now returning.

'But how is Luka? Have you seen him?' he asked.

'Lies there like a corpse. Don't eat, don't drink. A sip o' vodka's the only thing he can keep down. Well, so long as he can take vodka – 'tis not too bad. 'Tis a pity 'bout the lad. A fine lad he were, a brave like me. I come near dying like that once, you know. The old women was already beginning to wail over me. My head were a burning fever. They already had me laid out under the holy ikons. And so there was I a-laying, and up on the stove little drummers no bigger nor this beat a tattoo. I'd shout at 'em, and they'd drum all the harder.' (The old man chuckled.) 'The women brought the church elder to me, getting ready to bury me, they was. Said I'd lived worldly and gone with unbelievers. "Carried on with women," they said. "He were the ruin of people, he didn't never fast in Lent and played the balalaika. Repent now," they said. And so I begins to confess me sins. "I'm a sinner," I says. An' whatsoever the priest says I answers every time, "Aye, I'm a sinner." Then he come to the business 'bout the balalaika. "Aye, I sinned with that too," I says. "Where is the accursed thing?" he says. "Show it to me and smash it." – "I don't have it no more," says I. You see, I'd hidden it in a net in the outhouse: I knows as they wouldn't find it. And so they give over. But I went and recovered it. And – my word – how I strummed on that balalaika after that ... But, as I was just saying,' he continued, 'you do what I tells you, and keep right away from t'others, else you'll get killed like a fool. I got a fellow feeling for you, I have and all. You're a drinking man, I likes you. And you Russians always makes for rising ground. There was one lived here once, come from Russia like you, he always would ride up the mounds – bit funny, 'twas, he called 'em hummocks. Howsoever he'd spy a mound somewhere, off he'd gallop. He galloped off like that one day, very pleased with hisself, but a Tartar took a pot at him, and he were dead. Ah, they're clever at shooting from a gun-rest, them Tartars. Shoot better nor what I does, some of 'em. Nay, I doesn't like it when a fellow goes and gets hisself killed for nothing. When I looks at your men, a-times me mouth drops open. Fair daft they be! Marching along, the poor things, all in a clump – they even sews red collars to their coats, too. Fair asking for trouble. One gets shot, they drags the poor wretch away and another takes his place. Daft, I says!' the old man repeated, shaking his head. 'Whyfor not separate and keep to yerself? Then you can go right ahead. They won't pick you off that ways. Don't you go forgetting now.'

'Well, thank you! Good-bye, Gaffer. God willing, we may meet again,' said Olenin, getting up and moving towards the passage.

The old man continued where he was, sitting on the floor.

'Is that how you says good-bye? Oh, the foolishness in you!' he began. 'Bless me if I knows what's come over people these days. You and me have kept company – kept company well nigh a whole year, and now "Good-bye!" and off he goes! Don't you know I cares about you, feels sort of sorry about you? Kind of odd man out you is, always by yourself and alone. No one as loves you. Times when I lies awake I thinks about you and me heart aches. Same as the song says:

'Tis not easy, brother mine,
In a foreign land to live.

An' that's the way 'tis with you.'

'Well, good-bye,' said Olenin again.

The old man got up and held out his hand. Olenin pressed it and turned to go.

'Nay, give us yer mug – yer mug, now.'

And the old man took Olenin's head between his huge hands, kissed him three times with wet moustaches and lips, and began to cry.

'I loves you dearly, I does. Good-bye!'

Olenin got into the post-chaise.

'Well, be that how you're going? Leastways you might leave me something for to remember you by. Give me yer gun. What you want two for?' said the old man, genuine tears catching in his throat.

Olenin took his gun and handed it to him.

'Is there anything you haven't given him already?' muttered Vanyusha. 'He'll never have enough, the old beggar. Unconscionable people, the whole lot of them,' he remarked, wrapping himself in his coat and climbing up on the box.

'Hold yer tongue, pig!' called the old man with a grin. 'Proper stingy, you are!'

Marianka came out of the cowshed, glanced indifferently at the post-chaise, inclined her head and went into the hut.

'*La fille!*' said Vanyusha with a wink, and burst into a silly laugh.

'Get on!' cried Olenin angrily.

'Good-bye, lad! Good-bye! I won't forget you!' shouted Yeroshka.

When Olenin looked round the old man was chatting to Marianka, evidently about his own affairs, and neither he nor the girl had a glance for him.

[THE COSSACKS *was started in 1852, finished in 1862, and first appeared in print in 1863*]